75¢

3 1168 02229 2195

NORTH PORTLAND BRANCH LIBRARY
Fines: Adult $0.25/day, Juvenile $0.10/day, Videos $1.00/day

Books are due on the
latest date stamped
below. Fines are 10¢
per day for adult
materials; 5¢ per
day for juvenile
materials.

North
Po

PURCHASED FROM
MULTNOMAH COUNTY LIB
TITLE WAVE BOOKSTO

D1442632

10/93

ALSO BY BUD SHRAKE:

LIMO (with Dan Jenkins)

PETER ARBITER

STRANGE PEACHES

BLESSED MCGILL

BUT NOT FOR LOVE

BLOOD RECKONING

NIGHT NEVER FALLS

NIGHT NEVER FALLS

BUD SHRAKE

MULTNOMAH COUNTY LIBRARY
(Library Association of Portland, Ore.)

RANDOM HOUSE · NEW YORK

*Grateful acknowledgment is made to the following for
permission to reprint previously printed material:*
Warner Bros. Music: Excerpt from the lyrics to
"Anything Goes" by Cole Porter. Copyright 1934
by Warner Bros., Inc. (renewed) All rights reserved. Used by permission.

North Port

COPYRIGHT © 1987 BY EDWIN SHRAKE

All rights reserved under International and Pan-
American Copyright Conventions. Published in the
United States by Random House, Inc., New York,
and simultaneously in Canada by Random House of
Canada Limited, Toronto.

Library of Congress Cataloging-in-Publication Data
Shrake, Edwin.
Night never falls.

I. Title.
PS3569.H735N5   1987   813'.54   87–12712
ISBN 0–394–55872–3

Manufactured in the United States of America

BOOK DESIGN BY GUENET ABRAHAM

24689753

First Edition

For Dan and June Jenkins,
Richard Growald, Margaret
Cousins and Esther Newberg

DEC 3 1987

Mein Regiment, mein Heimatland,
Ich bin allein auf dieser Welt . . .
[My regiment, my homeland,
I am alone in this world . . .]

—SONG OF THE FOREIGN LEGION

We ought to have lived in the days of Russell
and the old *Times.* Dispatches by balloon.
One had time to do some fancy writing then.
Why, he'd even have made a column out of
this. The luxury hotel, the bombers, night
falling. Night never falls nowadays, does it,
at so many piastres a word?

—GRAHAM GREENE, *The Quiet American*

A C K N O W L E D G M E N T S

There was a writer on the old *Paris Herald* named Harry Sparrow, but all I have borrowed from him is his name. Though real people appear—Geneviève de Galard, the "Angel of Dien Bien Phu," for example—and major events of the story are faithful to fact, this is a novel, not a history.

Thanks to Sam Vaughan, Jeff Cohen, Jane Butterfield, Alan Themer, Joe Pollack and Jo Ellen Gent for their help. Also the works of David Halberstam, Jules Roy, Albert Camus, George Robert Elford, Michael Maclear, Bernard Fall, Nguyen Cao Ky, Alistair Horne, Jean-Pierre Dannaud, John Talbott, Heinz Hohne, Frantz Fanon, Jean-Jacques Servan-Schreiber and Marcel Bigeard.

NIGHT NEVER FALLS

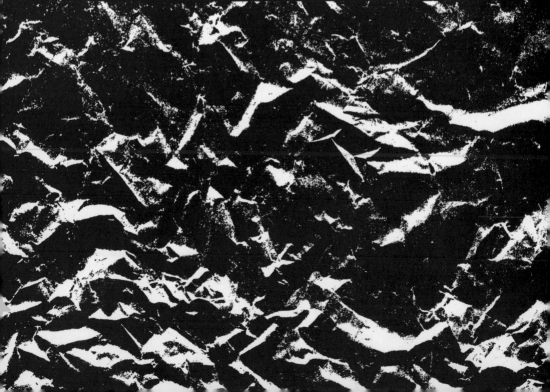

DIEN BIEN PHU 1954

1

He first saw them in the bar at the Hôtel Métropole in Hanoi. Louis, the manager, whose brother Meurice ran the George V in Paris, pointed the two out with a discreet lift of scar tissue in an eyebrow: the lanky, bearded wolfhound of a man in the bush jacket and emerald green beret, and the dark-haired, pretty girl in the uniform of a Red Cross air nurse. They sat with their elbows on a bamboo table beneath a ceiling fan that chirped like frogs on the shore of Little Lake. Each was leaning forward as if curious about the other's ideas. Harry was surprised to notice they were playing chess—the unmasterable game. Harry looked at the girl with aroused interest. The game of chess is beyond the scope of the human mind. Harry had never known a pretty girl who saw anything useful in chess.

"Louis, the deal I made is for me only. The nurse, sure. I can't complain about her. But not Rasputin. I don't want him on my plane," Harry said.

"He's a Legionnaire. Wounded at Dien Bien two or three months ago. He's going back to his unit, that's all," said Louis.

"Why doesn't he parachute in with the replacements? I gave you forty thousand piastres to arrange this plane for me, Louis. Loading my plane with fresh blood and morphine and coffin wood and carrying an air nurse, I accept all of that. But the guy who looks like a mad monk? No. Absolutely not. He doesn't ride on my plane."

"It's not *your* plane. It's a Red Cross plane. You're only a passenger. Do you think you could buy your own plane for a puny forty thousand piastres?"

Louis was a curly-haired ex-boxer with a broken nose who once hustled smuggled suede jackets to tourists on the sidewalk in Knightsbridge. He struggled to be charming, but couldn't hide his contempt for anyone who would do business with a man like himself.

"It's against the rules for a soldier to ride on a Red Cross plane unless he's dead or wounded and on his way out, not in," Harry said.

"Then *you* tell him," said Louis.

Harry glanced at the familiar faces in the bar. There was old Phibbs from the *London Daily Mail*, Brigitte Friang from *Indochine Sud-Est Asiatique*, Crichton of *The New York Times*, Wingo of the *Extrême-Orient*, Henshaw of *The Times* of London, the wire service reporters from United Press, The Associated Press, the International News Service and Reuters, several Scandinavians, a couple of Germans, the usual lineup of Japanese, maybe two dozen French. Fifty-odd journalists in all, reporting on the battle for some place called Dien Bien Phu, which was being fought 180 miles to the west, up in a valley in the highlands.

It was not, in most cases, any lack of courage that kept the journalists in the bar and out of the field. Tucking her cosmetics and a vial of Dior perfume inside her combat pack, Brigitte Friang had jumped into the valley in November with the first French Union Forces—FUF—paratroopers. They caught a Vietminh headquarters and a battalion of infantry having lunch. After a savage fight, the paratroopers chased out the Communists. French Union Forces began to rebuild an old Japanese airstrip and transform the broad, green valley, rich with rice and vegetables, into a land-air base for 17,000 soldiers.

All through January and February of 1954 there were junkets of journalists, politicians and military commanders into the valley. Reporters wrote that the valley, with its vast spreads of tents lined up in rows so thick they seemed all jumbled about, had taken on the look of a huge Boy Scout jamboree. Graham Greene had been escorted on a tour of the barbed wire, artillery and machine gun emplacements, and the novelist was told that they were guaranteed to withstand any Communist assault, that the Vietminh had no air power. Vice President Richard Nixon had rolled up his sleeves on the hot steel-mesh airstrip, unbuttoned his collar and exhorted the troops not to flinch at the gleam of Communist bayonets. Even old Phibbs had spent a few days in the valley of Dien Bien Phu after New Year's, and now, in the last week of March, the *London Daily Mail* still headlined all Phibbs's dispatches OUR MAN AT DIEN BIEN PHU—though Phibbs seldom left the Hôtel Métropole Bar, except for official briefings at the governor's palace across the street. After these he would rush back to his shabby room, dictate a story by phone to London, then set off on a solitary journey through the whorehouses near Little Lake, always winding up back at the bar for his grand-final nightcap, then his final grand-final nightcap, followed by the nightcap Phibbs called *el último.*

The Vietminh assault on Dien Bien Phu had taken on sudden fury two weeks ago. Official briefings had been optimistic, but rumors said the French were taking a beating. Two French journalists who hitched a ride into the valley on a Curtis Commando to report on the fighting were flown out again within six hours. One had been killed, and the other had lost a foot to the same mortar barrage. The French High Command ordered journalists to keep out, allowing only official army photographers on the scene. The latest *Ordre de circulation,* the official limits issued by the High Command to the press, placed Dien Bien Phu on the *Entrée interdite* list, along with Luang Prabang and Hue. Harry had paid the forty-thousand-piastre bribe to be smuggled into Dien Bien Phu aboard a plane. He was feeling very edgy about it, now the time had come—the feeling every journalist looks for, the sense that abrupt weirdness will occur.

"Greetings, Harry, old boy," Phibbs shouted from the far end of the bar. "Come knock back a few see-throughs with us. We'll play a game of matches if you dare."

"Later, Reggie. Got to get checked in first," Harry said.

Phibbs waved and drained another gin martini, which he called "see-throughs." He could drink twenty of them regularly during standup marathon match-game sessions at The Pig and Whistle pub on Fleet Street in London.

Picking up the *Daily Mail* in London and seeing PHIBBS: OUR MAN AT DIEN BIEN PHU had annoyed Harry Sparrow for weeks. Phibbs made the looming battle sound loaded with significance for the Western alliance. He bragged outrageously about being on the scene. "As I crouched in the battlements, peering at Commie positions a few hundred meters away . . ." Phibbs would dictate from the phone at the Métropole. Harry read each Phibbs piece with growing anger and threw them in the trash basket. One evening, sitting at the desk in his study at No. 5 Cheyne Place, looking out at the lanterns on the tugboats moving down the Thames, Harry had been groping for an inspiration. His job was doing feature pieces, columns and the occasional major news story for *The New York Dispatch*, its subsidiary, *The Paris Dispatch*, and 750 other newspapers around the world that subscribed to the *Dispatch* Syndicate. Harry considered himself a syndicated man. He was devoted to his work, to beating the opposition to the story and to staying ahead. During his eight years as a professional journalist Harry had never ceased to be thrilled at the sight of his byline on a front page under a black banner of type. His invisible worldwide readership held him like a lover he wanted to dazzle with prizes.

But that night Harry was especially anxious to find a story. Much better, it should be a series of stories. Harry needed to get out of London for a few weeks. He wanted to be far enough from Lady Cadbury that her temper couldn't reach him.

The willowy Lady Gwendoline Cadbury, tall and blond and rich, exuding languid sexual promises that brought aristocrats panting for her like dogs, had outraged her parents and stunned her social playmates when she began living with Harry. To her crowd she might as well have moved in with a tattoo artist as with a journalist. She loved Harry and stayed with him, despite harassment from family and friends, much longer than anyone expected. After she and Harry finally broke up, she punished him in ingenious ways. The previous Sunday she had ordered a load of sand dumped on the porch of his building—a reference to her cry that Harry would rather be blasting sand shots out of a bunker on the golf course at Royal Bowling Brook than doing "sips and dins" with her chums in Mayfair.

Harry ran a finger along the keys of his L. C. Smith typewriter. He stared at his burnished walnut humidor. His eye fell upon PHIBBS in the trash basket, and the inspiration he had been searching for struck him. The Pulitzer Prize is waiting in Indochina, he thought. It's right under the nose of *The New York Times,* but they won't get it because *The Times* doesn't understand the situation as well as Phibbs does. Harry wanted a Pulitzer; since high school he had wanted a Pulitzer. The words of Joseph Pulitzer, engraved in the lobby of the *St. Louis Post-Dispatch,* had inspired Harry toward a life of journalism. Harry's best chance this year to win the prize and the standing among his peers that goes with it was not in London, where not much was happening, but in Indochina. Phibbs was right. Dien Bien Phu *was* a big story.

Harry could imagine Phibbs's whiskey-red cheeks, the stringy hair that always tufted onto his collar leaving sprinkles of dandruff, the leer of satisfaction Phibbs always had when he was on to something important—and Harry wasn't in on it. Harry picked up the phone and called Gruber. The managing editor of *The Paris Dispatch* was far more likely to respond to Harry's requests than was Calvin Epps, chief of the foreign desk in New York. Gruber fished for salmon two weeks every summer on the Alta River in Norway. The rest of the year he was either at his desk or at the racetrack. He would listen. Gruber was a pro, not a politician.

"Harry, old man," Gruber said from his cubicle in the sooty second-floor newsroom at the *Dispatch* in Paris. "I hope you're not calling about the shooting stick? The one you put on your expense account? I had to turn it down. It was a good piece you did, romping through the forest with the dukes and earls. But the accounting department at the Syndicate said a shooting stick was an ineligible expense—actually, they said it was a swindle—so how can I argue that in front of the elegantini you couldn't have simply sat on your ass?"

"I want to go to Dien Bien Phu," Harry said. "I can leave for Hanoi in the morning."

"How would you get into the place? No one else can."

"You can arrange it, Elmore. Think."

"No use trying the government."

"You ran the United Press bureau in Hanoi after the war. Who do you know who could smuggle me in?"

"Smuggle . . . maybe. I know a hotel manager in Hanoi who used to be a smuggler. You know his brother Meurice? I did Meurice a favor. We buried a tourist hijacking story at the George Cinq—furs and jewelry—would have been bad mojo for Meurice. You haven't called Epps about this, I suppose?" Gruber said.

"Epps would say Dien Bien Where?"

"Why do you care about it, Harry? This is a wonderful idea, but you mightn't live to enjoy the plaudits and rewards you no doubt have in mind."

"This is a big one, Gruber. Let me have it. No plaudits; it's Pulitzer time."

Gruber was silent for a moment. "It's a long shot, but I'll call Meurice. Stay by your phone for an hour, Harry."

Harry hung up and started packing his canvas bag and changing the ribbon on his portable typewriter.

In the Métropole Bar, six days later, Harry was looking at Louis and saying, "The tall Legionnaire can't sneak into the battle on a Red Cross plane."

"He wouldn't be the first FUF officer to do it," Louis said. "Besides, Harry, this is romance. The captain met that hot French girl while he was on wounded leave in Paris. She volunteered as an air nurse and came to Hanoi with him. This is her first flight into

Dien Bien, so she asked her lover to accompany her. Doesn't that touch you, Harry? Have you no heart?"

Harry yelled to the bartender for two more drinks. The Métropole Bar didn't stock Harry's brand—The Famous Grouse—but he wanted whatever scotch whiskey they did have in a hurry—and he got it. Harry looked like a man who could cause trouble. Despite the London tailoring of his white linen suit and the flair of his Panama straw hat, there was something about Harry that gave him away as not exactly a gentleman. He had the air of one who squandered money even when he was broke, which came in part from living on the Syndicate expense account. Harry was medium height and strong-looking, built like the swimmer and platform diver he had been on teams at Catholic schools and at the University of Missouri. He had a powerful back and shoulders and a muscular neck. His face was pleasantly regular, with blue eyes, short brown hair and a quick, easy smile, but his expression became threatening and stubborn as he glanced impatiently at Louis.

"Listen, Harry, the only reason I have made this arrangement for you is as a favor to my brother," Louis said. Irritated and nervous, Louis lit a *Gauloise* and sucked ribbons of smoke up his nose. "I am not making a sou off this. The pilot made me change your piastres into American cash and give him the four thousand dollars this morning. Your newspaper is very powerful in Paris. You and Gruber can help my brother's business or you can hurt him—in Paris. But we're a long way from Paris now, Harry. Don't you be getting rude with me."

"Keep your voice down, Louis. This crowd can hear like bats. If they learn I'm going, half of them will try to climb on the plane with me, and the rest will run straight to Cogny's villa and turn me in."

"Why don't you stay here and cover the war from the bar like everybody else? Dien Bien isn't all that important that you should rush over there to drown in it. It's merely a blocking action. Navarre is going to start the real operation south in the Red River delta pretty soon. That's what you'll want to cover. I could tell you about Navarre's plans, make you a good story."

"I'll be in and out of Dien Bien Phu before Navarre gets *Opéra-*

tion Atlante going," Harry said. Louis pursed his lips in mild surprise. "Phibbs wrote about *Atlante* in the *Daily Mail* last month, but Dien Bien Phu has the classic elements—like *Beau Geste.* It can capture the world's imagination. As the only reporter there, I'll have it all to myself. I'll scoop the ass off Phibbs and his match-game pals."

"Well, you'd best get your outfit on." Louis sighed, glancing at the clock above the bar. "You're due at the airfield in about an hour."

"I'm ready now," Harry said.

The scars in Louis's eyebrows made a pair of arcs. He shook his head.

"Got my Smith-Corona in my canvas bag in the lobby," Harry said.

"But you're not going to Dien Bien dressed like that, are you? You look like a plantation owner."

"I don't want to disguise myself as a paratrooper, do I?"

"Your feet, Harry. For God's sake, your shoes."

Harry looked down at his cordovan loafers. The loafers were not stylish with the white suit, but they were good, solid shoes from Brooks Brothers. Harry knew that Dixie Reed, an American correspondent renowned for his reporting at Iwo Jima, had worn a double-breasted suit, a floral necktie and penny loafers on a two-day outing to Dien Bien Phu two months ago.

"Since when are you a fashion expert?" Harry said.

"The monsoon is about to start. You'll be hip deep in mud."

"Look, Louis, I told you I don't intend to stay at Dien Bien Phu for the rest of my life. I'm just going to slip in for a couple of days and then slip back out and file a bunch of exclusive pieces. So what if it rains? I've got a Burberry in my bag. Also two bottles of Five Star for Colonel de Castries, provided he doesn't have me arrested and sent back."

To Louis's relief, the concierge appeared in the doorway and waggled a finger.

"Your car is here," Louis said.

"Let me go out first, wait three minutes, then cue the nurse and the mad monk," Harry said. "Be clever about it, will you, Louis? Don't let on like anything's up."

Harry finished off two fast scotch-and-sodas.

"Thanks, Louis. Didn't mean to be rough with you just now. Guess I'm a little spooked. Better not shake hands. Phibbs will wonder why. See you in a few days."

"Good luck, Harry," Louis said.

"Where you off to, old sod? Got something hot?" called Phibbs as Harry walked toward the door. All the other journalists looked around.

"Yeah, my bathwater," Harry shouted back. He saw the air nurse look up at him from the chessboard and realized she was quite young, perhaps a university student. "Wait for me at the bar, Reggie. Don't move your wallet till I get back."

"I hope you brought lots of money from home." Phibbs laughed. "The price of the match game went up as soon as you arrived in Chinatown, Harry."

The Peugeot was parked at the curb down the block in front of the massive Bank of Indochina building. The pilot himself was at the wheel. Harry shouldered through people on the sidewalk, brushing aside vendors selling rancid-smelling sauce meant to drown the taste of ripe fish. The pilot hopped out and opened the trunk. He was an American civilian who introduced himself as Red. The French Air Force had more airplanes in Indochina than it had air crews. Many Americans flew missions to Dien Bien Phu, working as employees of the Civil Air Transport (CAT) Corporation, which Harry knew to be a CIA company helping the French fight the war in Indochina. Most of the CAT pilots were like Red, veterans of Korea or World War II or both, who flew under contract for two thousand dollars per month. Red said he thought he'd use the extra four thousand dollars he got from Harry to buy a new Cadillac.

"One of them big white Fleetwood four-door mothers, with white leather seats, an air conditioner, an FM radio with four speakers . . . Cruise that AIA down in Florida at Easter time, pile that Caddy to the roof with chicks in bikinis. Haw!"

"I hope this doesn't get you into trouble," Harry said.

Harry didn't give a damn, and they both knew it, but he was getting more jumpy.

"Trouble? Haw, that's good. I been to the Shit Pot and back three times in the last thirty-six hours. What kind of trouble do you suppose it would take to worry me?"

"Why do you call it that?" Harry asked. What he was doing might be very stupid, but he knew it was right. He could stand at the bar with Phibbs and the other reporters every night, drinking whiskey and playing the match game, and still thrill his readers with tales from Indochina—but not enough to win a Pulitzer. For that, he would need to be sensational. *Dispatch* readers in New York hardly cared about a French war on the other side of the Pacific Ocean. Now that the Korean War armistice had at last been signed, American newspaper readers wanted to forget that part of the world. Epps had told Harry that Americans were sick of reading about Asia. Dien Bien Phu might be hot stuff in Paris, but it was page seven in New York—Joe McCarthy's Communist hunt was page one.

But Epps had to agree that a dozen Harry Sparrow pieces with Dien Bien Phu datelines would be a very good thing for *The Paris Dispatch*, which sold all over Europe. It was a French war. Now that he was only an hour's flight from Dien Bien Phu at last, Harry found himself wishing he was back in the sports department of the *St. Louis Post-Dispatch*. At times like this, Harry often recalled covering the Cardinals for a year as the best job he ever had.

"Well, you know what a bedpan looks like," Red said.

"What?"

"You asked why we call Dien Bien the Shit Pot. The truth is, it looks more like a bedpan, but Shit Pot sounds better. Just picture a bedpan with ants crawling all over it. The ants on the rim are the Commies. The ants in the bottom of the pan are the FUF. That's where I'm taking you today—down to the bottom. I hate going down there. I hadn't planned on ever going down there again. It's tough enough just flying over and dumping parachute loads. Going to the bottom and out again would be impossible except for the red cross painted on the side of the ship, and I don't trust that red cross much. It's too good a target. But I'd do anything in the world for a white Cadillac. Haw!"

"How come you're letting a Legionnaire captain on board a plane with the red cross on the side?"

"Listen, mister, you're the illegal passenger on board."

"But I'm a noncombatant."

"As far as I'm concerned, you're a nonperson. You ain't on my plane. So is the Legionnaire a nonperson who ain't on my passenger manifest, except I owe the air control officer a favor to carry the guy. It's a love situation. The French love that baloney, even if the Legion captain ain't French. His name is Selchauhansen. Probably one of them Nazi SS that joined the Legion to keep from getting his neck stretched for a war criminal. No skin off my ass either way. I dream about a white Cadillac while them black roses blossom all around. Dreaming dreams keeps me lucky. Maybe I'll buy a convertible instead of a Fleetwood sedan."

"Is the flak pretty bad?" Harry asked.

"Getting worse by the hour," Red said. He gave Harry a Lucky Strike and lit it for him with a Zippo. "It's already as bad as anything I saw flying dive bombers in Korea. The old-timers tell me it ain't as thick yet as the flak over the Ruhr in 'Number Two,' but it's getting close. That Nazi and his girlfriend had better hustle, or we're leaving without them. I got a girl waiting in Hanoi to help spend your money. Haw, you bought a ticket to ride!"

"You'll come back and pick me up in two days?" Harry asked. "That's our deal—right?"

"Sure. Depending."

"Depending on nothing. I expect to see you day after tomorrow," Harry said.

"I said I would, didn't I? What else can I tell you?"

Harry saw them coming along the sidewalk, their heads bobbing above the crush. The green beret that designated a Foreign Legion paratrooper rode nearly two feet above the straw hats of the Vietnamese. The tall captain was wearing a field pack and hefting a duffel bag over his left shoulder. Four canteens hung from his web belt. He carried a French MAT 9 mm submachine gun. With the stock retracted, the weapon was eighteen inches long, and he handled it like a pistol. Half a dozen metal magazines full of bullets were stuffed into his web belt or inside his bush jacket. The air nurse had changed from the dress she had worn in the bar into the tiger-striped camouflage fatigues of the FUF paratroopers. But she had a Red Cross armband on each arm and a red cross on the American-style steel helmet she clutched against her chest. She was struggling to shut an Air France flight bag with her cosmetics kit stuck in the zipper.

"I'm sorry we're late," she said in English. Her voice had a husky French accent that Harry found appealing. Her gaze was direct and unapologetic, and her lipstick was smeared. The Legionnaire tossed his duffel bag into the trunk and held open the rear door of the Peugeot for the nurse. Who could blame them, Harry thought, if they had dashed upstairs for one last passionate rendezvous? Though he had no right, he couldn't help wishing she hadn't done it. A girl like her should have been with *him* this afternoon.

Red leaned on the horn as the Peugeot advanced through the taxicabs, bicycle cabs, brightly painted buses, olive drab jeeps, motorscooters, horses, pedestrians and two-and-a-half-ton trucks that jammed the streets of Hanoi. Bells jangled on trams. Girls in purple tunics weaved among Navy officers from Haiphong, artillery gunners with red tabs on their collars, Legionnaires in white *kepis*. A military band played in a plaza. The Peugeot passed the dragons of the Jade Pagoda and turned onto a long, straight avenue lined with trees and colonial villas. When they came to the towers of the red and gold stucco Roman Catholic cathedral, a rococo version of Notre-Dame in Paris, the air nurse leaned forward and asked Red if he would stop for a minute. "I promise I won't be long," she said.

Watching her enter the church, Harry had an impulse to follow. He had been born and raised in the Catholic faith and wrote *Catholic* on forms that required a religious preference, but he seldom went to mass and never to confession. Sometimes he felt the need to feed an inner hunger in a spiritual way, a need that was different from the need for challenge and risk that fed him as a syndicated man.

In the backseat, Selchauhansen's eyes were closed, his breathing deep and regular. He was either meditating like the insane monk he resembled, or he chose incredible places to catch a nap. Sweat rolled down his gaunt cheeks and long nose and glistened in his mustache and beard. Harry looked at the pilot and said, "Think I'll step inside for a bit, myself."

Inside the cathedral, bands of pink light from the stained-glass windows lay across the altar. Rows of candles flickered in the sanctuary. Two women—one French, the other Vietnamese— knelt on the red velvet before the altar, praying. Another lit a candle and bowed her head to a painting of a saint. A child clopped past in wooden shoes. But Harry couldn't see the nurse anywhere. She must have ducked into one of the confessionals. In the silence of the cathedral—an enormous contrast to the roars and shrieks out on the street—Harry soon felt a sense of peace, a sort of wholeness come over him. He felt a passion. He always felt that passion when he was quiet in a church. Instead of preaching and music, there came a surge of expectancy. Without consciously deciding to do so, Harry knelt and felt himself make the sign of the cross. The cathedral was filled, no doubt about it, no matter how few were there. Call it what you will, Harry felt the power of this peace, the presence of the "Old Man."

It had become the fashion of the time to pronounce the death of God, but to Harry all religious arguments were like puppies yapping in the dark. Whenever a moonlight philosopher with drink in hand pressed Harry to explain his position on religion, not wanting to argue Catholicism, Harry would reply that he agreed with Einstein. Albert Einstein, of all people, must know God was a ridiculous, outdated concept, but what Einstein had told Harry as they strolled together beside the duck pond in Green Park one summer afternoon was a different story. Harry had been doing a column on the scientist who had shown that the material world is matter in motion and that it was easy to extinguish human life by exploding the very building blocks of life itself, totally perverting the process of life into death. It was the formula for the end of the world, and Harry asked Einstein what that end would be. Einstein, taller than the popular conception of him, kept stopping to strike matches to light his briar pipe. "The most beautiful emotion and the most profound wisdom we can experience is the sensation of the mystical," Einstein said. "When I push my thoughts far as I can go, I reach a sublime state, and I see at the source of all is the Old Man."

"Who or what is the Old Man?" Harry asked.

"I'm afraid that is the Old Man's secret," Einstein said.

"So how does the world end?" Harry asked again.

"What you call the end of the world may be only the end of a civilization that wouldn't recognize the Old Man's plan. Not a bang or a whimper—but a wink. Our world is not what it appears to be. I don't understand the Old Man, but I know he's there," Einstein said.

Harry didn't put the Old Man in the column. He wasn't paid to be a deep thinker. *Dispatch* readers did not pick up a Harry Sparrow column to read metaphysics. They wanted action, drama and romance. But when Harry was alone and quiet in a church, he could feel the Old Man's presence. It was one thing Harry was not cynical about.

"Do you want to go to confession?"

The air nurse had come up quietly. Harry rose and brushed off the knees of his white linen trousers.

"No."

"My name is Claudette Frontenac," said the air nurse.

"Harry Sparrow."

"What a funny name."

The girl apparently didn't read *The Paris Dispatch*, but that was the only flaw Harry could see in her. That and the fact that she was having a love affair with a Legionnaire. It was not what he would expect of a pretty, fresh-faced girl who could play chess and spoke upper-class English. There must be a crack somewhere deep in her bell, Harry thought.

"Confession does me so much good," she said. "Are you sure you don't want to? The booth is just around that corner. We have time."

Harry answered her in French. " 'My words fly up, my thoughts remain below: Words without thoughts never to heaven go.' "

"Oh, you're French," she said. "I thought you were American. I'm sorry."

"My mother is French. I grew up speaking French."

"But you weren't born in France?"

"I was born in St. Louis, Missouri."

"You speak French beautifully," Claudette said, "even quoting from *Hamlet*—not an easy thing to do in my language." She turned her energy toward him for the first time.

Looking at her, Harry discovered an unsettling emotion. Something said, Look out, Harry, she might be the clever sort of girl you think you want to fall in love with.

"Six months ago my father died here," she said.

"In Indochina?"

"In Hanoi. A bomb in his car. Of course they shipped him back to Paris for the funeral. But I always wondered what this place was like. It's quite, well . . . oddly colored here, isn't it?"

She twisted the rosary beads in her fingers.

"We'll be all right." Harry wanted to put his arms around her and comfort her. "We've got the Red Cross on our side."

"Still, there's nothing like prayer to calm one. Don't you find it so?"

"Yeah," Harry said. What he had done on his knees just now was not the sort of praying he had done as a young Catholic boy. Today he had let his mind consider the Old Man, leaving it up to him as best he could. He didn't presume to ask the Old Man for anything. Though he had a fear of making a fool of himself, Harry did not have much fear of death. He was more afraid of being beaten on a big story by a brilliant sot like Phibbs, of not being in the first rank at what he liked and knew he was good at.

As they reached the Peugeot, Selchauhansen sat up and opened his eyes. He smiled at Claudette.

"The American speaks perfect French," she said.

Selchauhansen nodded.

"What are you, Harry, a spy?" she asked.

The Peugeot passed through an area of the city where buildings were on fire. Black smoke and red flames whooshed down the street with a smell of petroleum. Screaming people ran in front. With a Lucky Strike in his lips, Red whipped the car in and out of oxcarts and children and old women and fire trucks.

"He is a journalist," said Selchauhansen.

Harry turned and looked at the Legionnaire.

"I read your column in the English-language paper when I was in Paris. Quite a good column you wrote about Marcel Cerdan, the boxer," the captain said.

"Do you write about sports, Harry?" Claudette asked.

"I look for people who are making news," Harry said.

"You should stick to sports. You're good at that," said Selchau-hansen.

"I go where things are happening that I want others to see," Harry said. The girl's eyes made him think of deep water. Her eyes were oval and set a bit crookedly in her face. Their intense brown was made stunning by lush dark lashes. "I'm lucky. I pretty much get to pick where I want to go."

Red listened in disbelief. "You're a reporter? Hell, I thought you were a company man. You mean you're going into the Shit Pot when you could hang out at the Métropole Bar? You're a damn fool, fella."

Red waved an ID card at a Vietnamese MP blocking the gate to the airdrome. He parked the Peugeot in a white-lined quadrangle marked CAT beside the flight-control building. Their C-47 Dakota waited on the tarmac. Vietnamese workers were rolling crates of medical supplies up the ramp into the plane, which had red crosses on the fuselage, tail and wings. Red pointed to three parachutes stacked by the flight-control door and said to put them on. He went into the weather room as Captain Selchauhansen helped Claudette slip into her parachute. Harry picked up his chute and unbuckled the harness.

"Did you ever use one of these?" Selchauhansen asked.

"Yeah," Harry said. He had jumped twice at parachute school at Camp Gordon before his transfer to *Stars and Stripes* came through. It had been a disappointment to Harry's father, who had flown a fighter at Verdun, that his son became a mere newspaper writer.

"Then you know it's not as difficult as straightleggers think. A parachute is only a handy way of stepping out of an airplane in midair." The tall captain spoke softly, reassuring Claudette with his confidence. "Anyone who can hop off a tram can hop out of an airplane in a parachute and land on the ground like a veteran."

"They're bulletproof to sit on," Harry said. "Otherwise, para-chutes are dramatic but very dangerous. If we get into trouble, do what I do: Concentrate on pulling the ripcord."

"Why on earth are you going to Dien Bien Phu?" the girl asked Harry. "Your country is not at war."

"Newspaper guys are always at war," Harry said.

"You will not write about me riding in on an ambulance plane," Captain Selchauhansen said. It was a simple command, calmly uttered, but there was no mistaking the threat. Since he was a child, a threat had always made a freezing sensation start at the bottom of Harry's spine and grow into a hot ball in his chest. He could feel his ears turning red and his heart starting to pound. He turned toward the captain.

"It would be very bad for the populace in France to read such a story," the Legionnaire said. "Mail is dropped to the troops in the Dien Bien valley every day. Friends send newspaper clippings. I do not want to read that I flew back into Dien Bien on an ambulance plane.Do you understand?"

"Look Fritzie, no Kraut asshole tells me what to write," Harry said. "What the hell do I care how you get thrown back into the Shit Pot?"

"Other officers have ridden ambulance planes," Claudette said, looking at Harry.

"Don't tell him," said Selchauhansen.

"I'm telling him so he won't make a big thing of it," she said. "He should understand that it is done."

"He will make a scandal the Communists will use as propaganda."

"I'm not even going to write about how I, myself, got into Dien Bien Phu, much less how some SS Nazi got there," Harry said, "but I may get around to you later."

"I was never a Jew chaser," Selchauhansen said coldly.

Red came out of the operations room with a clipboard in one hand and a headset around his neck. He wore a parachute. He inspected his three passengers and checked the tightness of Claudette's straps.

"I didn't know Bob Hope was going with us," Red said. He pointed to the grip end of a golf club that stuck out of a canvas bag.

"It's my pitching wedge," Harry said.

"Beg pardon?"

"I'm taking my wedge." Harry intended to hit some practice shots around the airstrip. He kept a dozen Spalding Dots in a pocket of his canvas bag. Even the great Bobby Jones used to practice the short game in hotel rooms by placing a golf ball on the carpet three feet from the bed and trying to pitch the ball onto the bed and stop it there. There was something in the act of striking golf balls that cleared the brain. On a golf course, faced with the challenge of whacking a small white ball long distances onto a rug-sized patch of grass surrounded by sand and water and guarded by trees, one's best attention was required. There could be no wandering thoughts of deadlines to meet, bills to pay, dentist's appointments, phone calls from the office, explanations to make. Like his other favorite games—baseball and chess—golf was something you might get passably good at, but nobody could ever do perfectly, not even the world champion. Same with writing—you might do a pretty good piece on Wednesday, but it could have been better, and suddenly there's another deadline to think about. You had to take life a stroke at a time, Harry thought, keeping your goals in sight but always ready for the unexpected. That was why he carried his Haig Ultra pitching wedge and dozen Spalding Dots with him on his assignments. Even if Harry didn't get to hit balls at Dien Bien Phu, he could still have a game with Phibbs and the boys at the Club Indochine when he got back to Hanoi.

"I'm glad you're not a speedboat racer," Red said, slapping his clipboard against the leather grip of the wedge.

Claudette smiled at Harry. She was warming up to him, he could tell. If she lived through her experience as a volunteer air nurse, he would look her up later in Paris. He was thirty-four, about a dozen years her senior. But that was a comfortable difference—not so close that she would expect him to like rock and roll, nor so distant that she would be embarrassed to sleep with him.

"Well, come on, let's go," Red said. "The weather boys say there'll be a crack in the clouds over the Pot. That means the flak gunners will have their sights on us all the way to the ground. But at least they can't claim they didn't see the red crosses. Haw! 'Me doan see no led closses.' Haw, haw!"

2 Mountain peaks and crags rose out of the white fog that rolled over the jungle of the highlands. Looking out the co-pilot's window of the Dakota, Harry caught glimpses through the fog of the foliage below—mango trees, breadfruits, palms, orange and lemon trees, sisal plants. Here and there he saw the thatch roofs of villages with tiny black pigs running back and forth among chickens that scratched in red dirt. There were water buffalo tied between the huts. Cats, dogs, even small mountain ponies wandered into view in gaps in the fog. But there had been no sight of a human being down below in the hour since the heavily burdened ambulance plane had climbed off the runway at Hanoi.

Red invited Harry into the co-pilot's seat and tossed him a set of earphones. "Since I'm the captain and the crew on this flight, I'm giving you the seat with the view," Red said. "You paid for it." The engine noise made conversation impossible, so Harry put on the earphones and listened to the traffic, a dozen aircraft that circled the valley of Dien Bien Phu responding to Hanoi control and reporting targets to the garrison's artillery.

Looking back over his left shoulder, Harry saw Claudette and the Legionnaire captain mashed together among refrigerated containers of fresh blood, bound stacks of coffin planks, racks of stretchers and footlockers full of medical supplies. Harry saw the girl holding tightly to Selchauhansen's arm. She smiled when Harry caught her eye.

Over the earphones Harry heard a familiar voice saying, "I see you, Juno, big and clear. Do you see me?" He realized it was Red's voice. Red nudged him and Harry looked below to a spectacular vision: the valley of Dien Bien Phu, revealed as the fog drifted into patches.

Three Bearcat fighter planes, from the French aircraft carrier *Arromanches* cruising off Haiphong, were making strafing runs against the mountainside between blossoms of black ack-ack puffs. A flow of brilliant red and yellow burst among vividly different shades of green on another slope, and a Helldiver pulled up sharply through the billowing black smoke from the napalm tank it had hurled into the mountain. Flitting through the ack-ack and napalm smoke were a couple of tiny Cricket spotter planes from a French air base in Laos.

The blue mountains seventy-five miles to the north were the Chinese frontier. Twenty miles west, thunderhead clouds boiled into the sky above the border of Laos.

But what held Harry's attention was the layout of the valley below. He knew its dimensions: eleven miles long from north to south, three miles wide from east to west. He saw the narrow Nam Yum River turning and bending down the length of the valley. The limestone masses that formed the mountain peaks out on the rim soared two thousand feet above the valley floor. The view from the mountains dominated the new airstrip the way seats on the top row of an amphitheater command a view of the stage. Closer to the airstrip were smaller foothills of various shapes, some that resembled breasts, one that looked like an alligator, many of them jagged like fudge twists.

More than a hundred native villages perched in and around the valley, and ten thousand Indochinese of various tribal distinctions made a living there between wars, growing vegetables, poultry, pigs and rice in an area whose ancient tradition called it the "arena of the gods."

"I can hear you now, BY3408. We're moving twenty-eight wounded out to the strip for evacuation. Come on down."

"You better get this damn thing unloaded and loaded again before I come to a full stop, my little froggie buddy," Red said into his mike. "I ain't gonna cut my engines."

"You're in plain view now, BY3408. Come on down."

"Oh, Lord, I wish it was raining, I wish it was raining," Red said.

The valley floor was a quilt of sandbags, artillery pits, barbed wire, trenches, vehicles, bunkers, figures dashing about, wrecked airplanes and trucks and the steel-mesh airstrip. The French High Command had claimed this land-air base to be invulnerable. Visiting generals and politicians from France and the United States had not openly disagreed, but now Harry could see that the airstrip had been straddled with shell fire thousands of times, its aircraft smashed and burned in their shelters. Dozens of smokes drifted up as Red nosed the Dakota over in a steep dive. Harry's bile tasted bitter in his throat, his ears popped, his eyeballs strained at the pull of gravity. He heard the engines thundering and the wind screaming around the fuselage. He saw Red grinning crazily, sucking on a Lucky Strike and pushing forward on the wheel. Red must have been a very lucky bomber pilot to have lived through Korea and now this, Harry thought.

Harry saw the ground whirling up fast. In an instant of observation, he marveled at how barren the valley was: not a house or a tree or a bush that he could see. What looked like mounds of snow lying all over the valley were actually parachutes—thousands upon thousands of parachutes. Harry got a flash of thirty stretchers lined up at the edge of the steel mesh, dust blowing the rags off their bodies. The Dakota howled like an animal. The wheels hit the runway with a jolt that threw Harry hard against the seat harness. There was a moment of lightness as the Dakota bounced into the air again; then the plane struck the steel mesh once more, and the engines boomed into reverse. Red wrestled with the controls, trying to stop and begin his turn for takeoff in one motion.

Red reached over and jerked at Harry's harness as a signal for

Harry to unhook himself and scramble out. Looking back, Harry saw a hatch spring open. Thin little Asiatics in pajamas and undershirts swarmed on board. For a moment Harry thought they had been overrun by the Vietminh. Then he realized these must be PIMs—*prisonniers internés militaires*—the prisoners the French used as laborers.

Harry ripped off his earphones, jammed his Panama hat back on his head and ducked through the doorway of the pilot's compartment. Grabbing his canvas bag, he saw Red flicking his Zippo to light still another Lucky. Red gave him a thumbs-up signal. The PIMs jabbered and jostled as they heaved cargo onto the unloading ramp. Crates and footlockers tumbled off the plane. Europeans, stripped to the waist and shiny with sweat, clawed their way up the ramp carrying stretchers loaded with wounded. Harry saw a look of anger on Claudette's face as she was roughly shoved aside by men in desperate fear. Captain Selchauhansen crouched beside the cargo hatch, keeping out of sight of the gunners in the hills, his MAT 49 in his right hand, his canteens banging against his bony buttocks. Selchauhansen saw Harry and motioned with his left hand for Harry to jump over the stretchers and the PIMs and head for the hatch.

The first shell of the Vietminh salvo tore up earth, steel mat and bodies at the edge of the runway. The blast flung Harry into a pile of shouting PIMs. The second shell landed on the opposite side of the airplane. The Communist gunners in the hills had registered on the airstrip with precision. The third shell would come down right on top of the ambulance plane.

Harry saw Claudette lying against a bulkhead. She had been knocked down by concussion. Just as Selchauhansen turned back and saw the girl, Red tromped on the pedals and put the Dakota into a wheel-around in an attempt to escape the third shell. The violent movement caused Selchauhansen to disappear, thrown through the hatch onto the steel mesh below. Harry leaped to Claudette and clutched her wrist.

"Get off the plane! It's gonna blow!"

She stared at him with wide eyes, shook her head and yanked her arm away from Harry. "I'm assigned to this plane!" she shouted. "I'm not supposed to leave it!"

By now Red almost had the plane turned. Harry grabbed Claudette and pulled her toward the hatch, bashing aside PIMs with his canvas bag. At the hatchway, Claudette kicked him in the shin. Harry sprawled backward out of the hatch, his arms and legs outflung, and landed on a mat of bodies. Asians, Europeans, dead, wounded, living—who knew? Harry rolled over and began to crawl toward a drainage ditch, dragging his canvas bag—just as the awaited third shell whistled down at last and smashed a piece off the rudder of the C-47.

The explosion screamed shards of metal over Harry's head as he flattened against the steel mesh.

He saw Selchauhansen moving with incredible quickness. The long-legged figure vaulted back into the airplane. In an instant, the Legionnaire appeared again in the hatchway with an arm around the waist of Claudette, who was kicking and struggling. Selchauhansen heaved the girl off the plane and then jumped off behind her.

Harry could hear the *bum-bum-bum* of the French 105's in counter-battery fire, and he could see the Bearcats and Helldivers swooping toward the Communist guns, but it was too late. A fourth shell crashed through the cockpit windshield before it exploded. Harry saw Red blown through the side of the C-47. With a roar the fuel tanks burst into flame. Selchauhansen was prone on the steel mesh, facedown, probably dead. But Claudette was creeping on her hands and knees, dazed, blood on her face.

Driven by the sight of her, Harry turned and ran toward Claudette in a crouch. As if, he thought, ducking my head and bending my shoulders will make me less tempting to a sharpshooter or a hunk of hot shrapnel. Still, Harry was always amazed at how calm he felt in situations of violence. He was marvelously detached from his body, as if watching from somewhere outside but still making things happen. Claudette crept to the inert form of Selchauhansen.

"Justus," she said, "oh, my darling Justus."

"He's dead," Harry said. "Come on—run for it."

"No."

"You fool, that man is dead! Let's go!"

"No. He's alive!"

"Then I'll get him—but let's go!" Harry shouted.

Harry wrapped his fingers around the web straps of Selchauhansen's combat pack and began heaving the Legionnaire toward the drainage ditch. Claudette picked up Selchauhansen's machine gun and beret.

"Get my bag!" Harry yelled.

Jerking, yanking, straining against the dead weight of the tall man, Harry dragged the carcass a few yards and paused to wipe the sweat out of his eyes.

The heavy, white ground fog was pouring into the valley again, smelling of oily rain, muffling the explosions. The mountains faded in the fog. Dazzling bursts of lightning ripped through the mist.

With the *twang-twang* of snapping wires, sniper bullets spun off the steel mat at Harry's feet and whined into the sky. Harry gasped a deep lungful of dust and smoke, hooked his bleeding fingers into Selchauhansen's webbing again, and pulled the officer. A bullet struck Selchauhansen's backpack like a blow from a club. With one last, enormous effort, Harry heaved himself and his burden backward—and tumbled into the drainage ditch, Selchauhansen landing on top of him, breaking his fountain pen.

"We'll get him. Thanks, brother," said voices speaking German.

Two Legionnaires came sloshing along the ditch. They pulled Selchauhansen's body off of Harry. One of the Legionnaires wore a black cap with a silver skull and a silver badge of twin lightning flashes—the symbol of the SS. The lightning on the badge winked in the lightning that splintered the heavy fog. The captain's beard scraped Harry's cheek as he was lifted. The open, sightless eyes peered into Harry's face like the eyes of a statue.

As suddenly as they had come, the Communist shells stopped falling on the runway. The Dakota blazed into a skeleton, the tail gone, one wing broken. Red, the pilot, crumpled in mist among the broken crates he had delivered and the wounded—now dead—he had intended to retrieve.

Harry found himself dogtrotting along the drainage ditch, sloshing mud, Claudette by his side, the two Legionnaires carrying the long limbs of Selchauhansen in front. They continued past a platoon of Vietnamese paratroopers in FUF tiger-striped uniforms and thick-soled boots. The odor inside the trench made Harry retch: It was the smell of vomit, body rot, excrement and cordite. Harry was muttering, "Not since Verdun . . . not since Verdun . . ." composing a lead in his head as he trotted toward God-knows-where with his Smith-Corona and his pitching wedge and his Panama hat, his white linen suit already out at the knees.

If the airstrip and trenches had been horrible surprises, the hospital bunker brought the shock of encountering hell on earth.

The wretched were stacked in tiers of misery, one on top of the other. The wounded and dying in the hospital were forced to groan and shriek and babble from niches in the walls of dirt. There were only forty-odd beds in the hospital, all of them full. Harry guessed there were at least a hundred men and—to his amazement—a dozen women stuffed into those awful niches. The injured women appeared to be Vietnamese civilians. He saw a European woman, wearing the striped camouflage of an FUF paratrooper, working as a nurse. There were also several Vietnamese women in blood-smeared tunics helping with the wounded. Then Harry noticed women who looked like Arabs lifting bodies on and off the operating table, a process that never stopped, beneath the dangling electric light bulbs. The women were splashed with blood to the elbows.

But the worst thing was the smell.

Harry had a delicate stomach when it came to odors. Horribly gruesome sights, faces with chins blown away, amputated arms and legs still twitching beneath the operating table—such monstrous visions he could observe with a detached curiosity. He had reported on countless ugly messes for his newspaper readers, describing carnage with colorful energy.

But if it had a particularly overripe aroma, he couldn't change a baby's diaper without throwing up. This underground hospital smelled like soiled diapers, and the smell smashed against Harry's face.

The two Legionnaires carrying Selchauhansen bulled to the front of the line and dumped the captain on an operating table. The French surgeon wiped his spectacles on a bloody rag and tore open Selchauhansen's shirt. The surgeon wore only boots, khaki shorts and rubber gloves. His bare torso was gleaming with sweat, and his head was shaved bald. He laid an ear against Selchauhansen's chest, peered beneath the captain's eyelids and examined his pupils with

a penlight. The surgeon turned to look through rimless spectacles
at the anxious Legionnaires.

"He'll be all right," the doctor said. "He's just knocked out cold.
Lay him on a stretcher and let him sleep."

The Legionnaires grunted their thanks, picked up Selchauhansen, located a stretcher that had a dead man on it, tipped the
corpse onto the earthen floor and placed their captain on the
stretcher carefully.

"I'm glad you're here," the doctor said to Claudette. "Excuse me
if that's a horrible thing to say. I don't appreciate the difference anymore. For your sake, I am sorry you got stuck here. For the sake
of the hospital, I am happy to welcome you. My name is Dr.
Grauwin. The European woman is Geneviève de Galard, an air
nurse like yourself. Geneviève arrived here the same way you did—
the Communists destroyed her ambulance plane. Please go intro-
duce yourself to her and go right to work. You are most desperately
needed."

"I have to confess, I don't know much about nursing," said
Claudette, "but I'll do what I can."

"You will learn fast. The practice is continuous."

Dr. Grauwin looked at Harry.

"I am Harry Sparrow."

"I see. Where are you hurt?"

"I'm not. Just a few bruises."

"Are you quite sure? You look sick."

"I'm about to vomit."

"Then please go outside. We're very busy here, as you can see."

Harry nodded. He saw Claudette talking to the European nurse.
THE ANGELS OF DIEN BIEN PHU, he thought, seeing the headlines in
his mind's eye. Hell of a piece that would make. Let's see Epps try
to keep that headline off page one in New York. Gruber would
cover *The Paris Dispatch* with it. Harry would inquire about the
other nurses, too, the Vietnamese and the Arabs who were
swamped with gore in this cramped, airless, almost lightless, lower
depth of hell. But at the moment he could hold his breath no longer.
Sucking in a tiny hiss of air and pinching his nostrils, Harry ran
for the outside.

When Harry had finished throwing up, he saw a group of Vietnamese wearing steel helmets far too large for their heads, cleaning their rifles and submachine guns and politely not looking at him. The Legionnaires who had come out of the hospital bunker watched with interest as Harry's wrenching blasts splattered upon his cordovan loafers and his torn white linen pants.

"Hey, mister, do you speak German?" asked the Legionnaire who wore the black SS cap.

"Only a little. And only when I have to," Harry said.

"Well, we'll speak French then," said the Legionnaire. He had pockmarked skin and a thin, patchy beard. He was fat and greasy with heavy broken teeth. He reminded Harry of a Bavarian wild boar that might suddenly crash through the underbrush and crush a hunter's body like chicken bones. "My name is Corporal Pelwa. This ugly brute with me is Private First Class Ali Saadi. He used to be an anarchist. He's just a *raton*—an Arab bugger—but deadly as a snake."

"I am Algerian, you fat fucker," said Ali Saadi.

Pelwa clapped a tattooed hand—BORN TO DIE, printed in German across his knuckles—against the shoulder of the black-haired, athletic-looking boy of about twenty. The boy's face was streaked with mud that clung to thick black stubble of beard. He struck Harry as a young, slightly irregular Tyrone Power.

"You're a long way from home," Harry said.

"This *is* his home. We let him join the Legion because the French cops in the Casbah in Algiers are sadistic pricks," Pelwa said. "Don't think Ali Saadi is ungrateful. Anarchists don't believe in politeness, you know. Just in bombs and bullets and daggers."

"I learn how to kill from Pelwa," Ali Saadi said, grinning.

Ali Saadi was carrying Harry's canvas bag. Harry did not remember having dropped it. When he reached for the bag, Ali Saadi pulled back.

"I'll take my bag, please," Harry said.

"No." Ali Saadi still grinned. The boy has a smile that belongs in Hollywood, Harry thought.

"Ali Saadi likes fancy gentlemen. That's why he's being so chatty," Pelwa said. "He wants to carry your bag."

"Ask him to please give it back."

"No," said Pelwa.

"But it's got my typewriter in it."

"Your tommy gun?"

"My Smith-Corona Skywriter."

"Whatever you want to call it, that's your business," Pelwa shrugged.

"I want it back, damn it."

"Ho! What do you think, we are stealing it? Listen, my friend, we've got tommy guns out the ass. If we should need more, they fall from the sky. Or we go kill some little yellow apes and take theirs. We don't steal from a good friend of the Legion," Pelwa said.

"You mean me?"

"Sure. We watched you trying to save the chief. That was damn good of you. I thank you. Ali Saadi thanks you. We don't want to lose our chief. I have been with the chief in Poland, Russia, North Africa, the last six years in Indochina."

"Selchauhansen is your chief's Legion name," Harry said. "What did you call him back in Europe?"

Harry had read enough of the history of the Foreign Legion to recognize Justus Selchauhansen as the name of a Legionnaire hero of a Moroccan campaign around the turn of the century. He couldn't imagine an SS officer named Justus. The tall captain must have a sense of irony. It was common for a Legionnaire to adopt a *nom de guerre*. A prince of Denmark had served in the Legion under a pseudonym that was not discovered for fifty years.

"None of your business about names, mister. Take my advice. Don't ask rude questions of a Legionnaire. You might ask somebody who don't appreciate you like me and Ali Saadi do. And *schtuck!* they slice you a 'smile of Kabylia' just below your chin. Captain Selchauhansen is the chief of the Headhunters. That's all you need to know."

The Headhunters had been a Nazi battalion in Europe during the war. Security cops for the SS, Harry recalled. The Headhunters fought on both sides of the front in the east. Their foe was not the Russian Army, but the partisans—civilians in Russia and Poland who blew up bridges, derailed trains and ambushed truck convoys of SS troops. The Headhunters had been known and feared for their ruthless efficiency in finding and destroying partisan hideouts.

"Me and Ali are going to take good care of you, mister. You look to me like a high-class gentleman who belongs at the 'C.R.' with Colonel de Castries. Am I correct?"

"Maybe I'll just go with you and Ali," Harry said, sensing another story.

"Oh no! You'd get killed fast trying to follow us. You must stay alive until the chief can wake up and thank you himself. You follow us to the C.R. Ali Saadi will carry your bag. You want to get your tommy gun out of it first?"

"The tommy gun can wait."

"Okay. Come on then. Chop-chop."

Crouching behind Pelwa and Ali Saadi, Harry followed them through a warren of trenches, rounding bends in the streams of mud, hearing soldiers breathing and cursing through the fog.

"Lots of Vietnamese," Harry said.

"What? Where?" said Pelwa.

"I mean on your side. I thought the French Army and the Foreign Legion were doing all the fighting."

"Oh. Sure, lots of Viets on our side. Half the soldiers here are Vietnamese, I would guess," Pelwa said. "Brave little farts, too. They hate Communists. The tribespeople, they're monkeys that might fight or might run to the bush. But the Viets you see in uniform—especially the paras—they fight like the devil against the Communists. Wouldn't you fight to the death if the Communists were trying to take over Paris?"

"I'm American."

"Are you from Chicago?" asked Saadi.

"Pretty close," Harry said.

"I love gangsters. *Little Caesar* is the best. I see it five times. I want to go to Chicago," said Saadi.

"Well, Mister Chicago, if Communist gangs slipped into your town and hid in the sewers and started murdering your friends, you would fight to the death against them, wouldn't you?" said Pelwa.

"Yeah," Harry said.

Pelwa pointed to an area of the east bank of the Nam Yum that was dotted with caves and that fluttered with hanging laundry like the flags of a phantom army in the fog. It was a ghetto, isolated from the main encampment. "The rats of the Nam Yum." Pelwa grunted and spat with disgust. That was the first Harry knew of the thousands of FUF deserters and civilians who refused to fight in the battle but had no way to escape from the valley.

De Castries's headquarters bunker at the C.R.—the Center of Resistance—was piled high with sandbags and bristled with radio antennae. Ali Saadi gently put down Harry's canvas bag at the entrance. The Arab and Pelwa shook hands with Harry. Pelwa pointed to a low hill about a mile east of the airstrip. Harry could see the breastlike shape of it through a haze of smoke and red dust mixed with the fog.

"We call that hill Lola," Pelwa said. "That's where me and Ali Saadi run our show for the chief. Come see us, mister. The chief will want to thank you."

Pelwa and Ali Saadi loped away down the trench. A light machine gun began rattling. The husky corporal in his black SS cap and khaki shorts appeared to be shielding the slender Arab as they ran. Harry picked up his canvas bag and ducked into the bunker.

Colonel Christian Marie Ferdinand de la Croix de Castries wore the scarlet scarf of the 3rd Spahis and a red forage cap with five gold bands on it. He sat at his desk reading a novel and did not look up when Harry came in.

Typewriters clattered as clerks typed a constant flow of orders, reports, requests, requisitions, communiqués and correspondence. From dugout rooms that opened off the command bunker, Harry could hear the voices of radio operators keeping up communication with French Union strongpoints inside the valley, as well as with headquarters in Hanoi and aircraft overhead. The French High Command operated out of Hanoi. Eight hundred miles to the south, French troops in the relative peace of Saigon waited for the Red forces at Dien Bien Phu to be destroyed. Radios in the bunker crackled in French, German, Welsh, Spanish, Arabic and Vietnamese, mingled with the urgent dits and dahs of Morse code. The walls six feet underground were lined with sandbags and matting. Beams and rafters imported from Hanoi shored up the only corrugated iron roof in Dien Bien Phu.

Until three weeks ago, Colonel de Castries—aristocrat, cavalry officer, hero of World War II and holder of international equestrian records for the long jump and the high jump—had kept his private secretary with him at the command post. Before she was flown out of the valley, de Castries awarded her the *Croix de guerre* in front of a formation of troops. Harry had read a story by PHIBBS: OUR MAN AT DIEN BIEN PHU that made a scandal out of it, writing about the hazel-eyed woman smelling of perfume while her patron, de Castries, pinned the medal on her army blouse and the troops cursed aloud. Phibbs had heard about it in Hanoi and had possibly invented some of the details, but any story that involved de Castries with women or gambling sounded credible. He had a reputation as one of the greatest ladies' men in the history of France.

Behind the colonel was a large wall map covered with a clear plastic sheet, upon which an intelligence officer was marking new arrows and symbols as he studied aerial photographs that had been dropped from a Bearcat courier that morning. It was plain from the grease-pencil marks that the French position being drawn on the plastic was growing smaller. The new FUF lines no longer included two important positions called Gabrielle and Béatrice.

With a sigh, de Castries finished the last page of the novel, put the book down on his desk and lit a *Gauloise troupe*, the black tobacco issued to the troops. Coming to the C.R., Harry had seen acres of crates of toothpaste, razor blades and tobacco near the motor pool area where mechanics labored to repair tanks, trucks and jeeps fouled by shell fire and dirt. Generators hummed, driving the purifying machines that sucked filthy brown water out of the Nam Yum to produce drinking water for the soldiers. Thousands of soldiers were sick with malaria and dysentery. They had dug water wells, Pelwa said, but only oily mud came up. Without half a gallon of water a day, a soldier would die of dehydration in this heat.

"Have you read this yet?" de Castries asked, holding up the novel for Harry to see. It was *A Many Splendored Thing* by Han Suyin.

"No," Harry said.

"Quite touching, really. Total fantasy, of course, but romantic." De Castries stood up and stretched like a cat. He was a fine-boned man, thin and athletic, with a long jaw and a Roman nose, who ate cocktail glasses as a party trick. Using a cane, de Castries limped around the desk and stuck out his right hand. "Greetings, M. Sparrow. I'm something of a fan of yours. Been reading your column for . . . how long have you written for *The Paris Dispatch*?"

"Four years."

"I like your columns about racing. If you love horses you must not be a bad fellow."

"Never been happier than at the track."

"Nor I. Do you play bridge?"

"Yes."

"Chess?"

"Sure. I play the game," Harry said.

"A golfer, too, I notice."

"A nine handicap at Royal Bowling Brook," Harry said. He played to a twelve, but nine was what he intended to be next summer.

"Good." De Castries smiled, looking Harry up and down. "Well, I can see that you are quite a fashionable man. You look like good company. I'll fix you up with a uniform, something more suitable to wear here in the bloodiest shit heap in Asia."

"Thanks. I'd rather wear my own clothes," Harry said.

"As you wish. I like that touch, frankly."

Harry dug into his canvas bag and put the two bottles of cognac on the desk. With a nod, de Castries opened a bottle and poured a drink for each of them in crystal highball glasses.

Arriving at a military post was like entering a Jesuit monastery, where even an ordinary Catholic was a stranger—a secret society with its own rites, disciplines and professional codes that could never be truly shared with an outsider. Professional soldiers at a military post kept the same impenetrable distance from anyone not a brother-in-arms.

"I'm pleased by your hospitality," Harry said. "I expected you might be pissed at me."

"To the contrary. I'm delighted to have someone new to talk to. I want to hear how Paris is these days. Have they started cleaning the soot off the Opéra yet? What do they say about our little war here, eh?"

"You're not going to throw me out?"

De Castries stared at Harry, then barked a laugh. "Throw you out? My dear fellow, how on earth do you suppose I could throw you out, even if I wanted to?"

"You could arrest me and clap me in chains and stick me on the next flight to Hanoi."

De Castries found this even funnier. When he stopped laughing, he wiped tears from his eyes with his knuckles.

"What a droll sense of humor," de Castries said. "The next flight out, indeed. How amusing. Well, I suppose we had best make you as comfortable and safe as we can. You are an important journalist, you can use Major Piroth's bunker. It connects to the main C.R. here, so you can come and go without snipers potting at your straw hat."

"Won't Piroth object?"

"Hardly, dear fellow. He's dead."

"Piroth was killed?" Harry asked.

"Between you and me, Major Piroth was a suicide. He laid his honor on the line. He swore his artillery would destroy the Communists. All of us were wrong, *n'est-ce pas*? How could those fucking little coolies carry howitzers through the jungle and dig into the mountains on top of us without being destroyed by our air force? Why couldn't Piroth's gunners mop them up? But dear Piroth, his honor was vital to him. When he saw how tragically wrong he was, Piroth apologized to us all, went into his bunker, held a grenade under the stump of his left arm—he lost his arm fighting in Italy—pulled the pin with his right hand and placed the live grenade on his chest. He shouldn't have taken our failure as his fault alone, but he paid the debt. What are you doing, M. Sparrow?"

"Making notes," Harry said, wondering if de Castries was having a nervous breakdown.

"Oh, but you can't write about any of this."

"Listen, Colonel, nothing is just between you and me. I went to considerable trouble to get here, you know. I'm not a philosopher or a critic, I'm a reporter."

"I detest reporters," de Castries said. "I'd much rather you behave as a philosopher or a critic, even as an enemy. Reporters are such *belette* bastards. They'll eat the sandwich right off your plate while you're talking."

"I'll make a deal with you," Harry said. "Let me file the story on Piroth's suicide, and I'll forget about the Legion officer who came in on the Red Cross plane."

"The Communists knew Selchauhansen was on that plane," de Castries said. "I didn't know it, but I would wager big odds that the Reds knew it. They knew about you, too, I'm sure. You are another item that got past me until too late, but was no doubt on top of General Giap's daily briefing stack. Besides, there's no use your rushing to write about Major Piroth. General Cogny's headquarters announced his death to the press in Hanoi this afternoon. We didn't say suicide, but the gossips in the cafés will have picked it up by now."

Harry sat down. He was exhausted and disappointed now that he had been beaten by Phibbs on the Piroth story. His kneecaps were bleeding, and his shoulders ached from the blow he received when Claudette kicked him off the plane. Without his training as a diver, he could have broken his neck.

"Don't look so sad, M. Sparrow. Because I like your style, I have decided you can write a few stories, after all. But I have one requirement."

"What is it?" Harry said, looking up.

"Your two stories a week, or maybe three, no more, must be transmitted through this headquarters."

"So you can censor them?"

"M. Sparrow, there are at least fifteen hundred two-way radio sets in operation in this valley. All the various command groups have their own nets, naturally. There are channels at headquarters we use to communicate with Hanoi. I have a radio-telephone frequency on which I talk to General Cogny. Our intelligence boys from M-5 have secret frequencies they use in the jungle. We listen to music and news from Radio Hirondelle in Hanoi and to Red propaganda on the Voice of Vietnam from Truang Tan. There is so much communication here that you can practically see radio waves in the air. A resourceful person like yourself could find a way to relay your messages unless I actually locked you in chains, which

I won't do unless you force me. You had a proposition for me? I have an answer for you. Sergeant LeRuc!"

De Castries called the name again, and LeRuc appeared in a doorway. The sergeant's black mustache looked artificial in contrast to the pallor of his skin. Blue pockets of flesh hung beneath his eyes.

"Sergeant LeRuc is one of our best telegraphers," said de Castries. "He will send your stories for you."

"But sir," said Sergeant LeRuc, starting to protest.

"I appreciate that you are overworked, Sergeant, but this is an important journalist. He will put your name in the newspaper in Paris. He will write good stories of our bravery here."

"Very good, sir," Sergeant LeRuc said.

"Have you got a secret telegraph line into Laos?" Harry asked. "I don't want to use the radio. I want an untapped telegraph line."

LeRuc glanced at Colonel de Castries, who thought it over and nodded.

"You can read my stuff first, Colonel. But then I want it transmitted to Bangkok. If my stuff goes through Hanoi, those assholes will steal it."

Three officers in paratrooper berets and tiger-striped uniforms stomped into the bunker before de Castries could answer. Harry recognized the tall one as Lieutenant Colonel Langlais, commander of the paratroopers. The second, who had the face and build of a middleweight boxer, had to be the famous Major Marcel Bigeard. The third officer, Seguin-Pazzis, was chewing on the curved stem of a pipe. Harry could tell from the sterling silver band that the pipe was a Peterson, made in Dublin.

"Who the devil is this?" Langlais said. "Another fucking CIA man?"

"M. Sparrow of *The Paris Dispatch,*" said de Castries. "He's going to be using Piroth's bunker."

"Like hell he is," Bigeard said.

The officer with the Irish pipe stared stonily at Harry.

"Piroth's bunker was dug for a soldier. Not for a shit-eating leftist."

Harry said, "The worst thing I hate is a committee of bulletheads in brown suits telling me what to do. I'm no leftist. I'm an American."

"You're American?" said Bigeard. He looked at the others. "He must be CIA. Some kind of government son of a bitch, anyway."

Langlais glared at Harry. A tall Celt, given to heavy drinking and sudden rages, Langlais was a graduate of the military academy at Saint-Cyr-l'École. There was a strong anti-American feeling in the French Officer Corps. The antagonism rose in part from the U.S. Air Force having bombed Saint-Cyr to rubble toward the end of World War II. Though moved to Coëtquidan, the academy was still known as Saint-Cyr. The graduating classes had taken vows "to win back the good name of the French Army." The class of 1946 had chosen the name *Indochine.* Each year since then, enough Saint-Cyr officers had died in Indochina to empty a whole class.

"Who cares where the American sleeps? He'll get his fucking head blown off pretty quick. We've got more important things to worry about," Langlais said. He limped to the clear plastic map overlay, rubbed out a line with an elbow and used the grease pencil to mark the newest French position. The fortress had shrunk again.

Langlais had broken an ankle jumping into Dien Bien Phu. Harry thought of the coincidence that the three top French commanders of Dien Bien Phu walked with the aid of canes. De Castries had broken both legs during an ambush on Route 41. General Cogny, at headquarters in Hanoi, still limped from torture by the Gestapo.

"Now, here's what you tell Cogny," Langlais said, looking at de Castries. "Two thirds of the supplies dropped this morning landed in Communist hands. Of the 152 paras who jumped this morning, two platoons landed on top of the Reds and another in a minefield. Eighty fighting men reached our lines, and thirty of them are killed or wounded already. That means we've got fifty men today that we didn't have yesterday. But yesterday we lost three hundred. Does Cogny call that reinforcements? It's not even close to being replacements."

Langlais paused and looked at Harry, as if he had momentarily forgotten his presence. "You. American. Get your ass out of here. This is French security stuff," Langlais said. He turned abruptly back to de Castries. "We have a list of things that must be done at once. I expect you to turn your hand to them immediately." He looked at Harry again. "Well? What are you waiting for? Get the hell out of here. We have urgent business to conduct."

Harry followed Sergeant LeRuc along a clammy tunnel into Piroth's bunker.

"They've packed the major's personal things in that footlocker in the corner," LeRuc said. "We did the best we could cleaning up in here—scraped the walls and the ceiling, replaced the light bulb. The major's writing table was hardly damaged."

Harry put his battered Smith-Corona Skywriter in its gunmetal-gray case on the table. He dug into his canvas bag and found a carton of Chesterfield cigarettes, which he gave to Sergeant LeRuc. The sergeant grinned in appreciation, pulled a small brown bottle out of his shirt pocket, swallowed two pills from the bottle and offered it to Harry. The label identified the bottle as *Maxiton*— French benzedrine.

"Keep the bottle," LeRuc said. "I've got a whole case of this stuff when you need more. Be sure to say in your stories that I come from Toulouse. Never mind, I'll stick that in for you. I'm a writer, too, so I can be a big help. The colonel said I am one of the best telegraphers, but the truth is I am the very best, the epitome. I'll correct your sentence structure and grammar and spell the words right. I'm a perfectionist, you're lucky to know. Don't leave the Maxiton bottle sitting on the table, somebody will steal it. Everybody here swallows it like peanuts, but they deny it, because they don't want to share. Well? Where's your story? Why aren't you writing?"

Harry removed the cover from the Skywriter.

"Who's running the show here, Sergeant? I got the impression those paratroopers are giving orders to de Castries, instead of the other way around."

"Yes, the 'Band of Brothers.' That's what the paras call themselves—the Band of Brothers. You know, like in *Henry the Fifth*? But I call them the 'Parachute Mafia.' You're right, the paras have taken over. No outright mutiny, nothing like that, but they tell Colonel de Castries what to tell Hanoi. I should know. I send the messages. So how about your story? I'd better send it now before I get busy with the evening attack."

Harry was going over in his mind which story to write first: the true condition of the fortress, the paratroop coup, the poor devils who parachuted onto the Reds, the angels of Dien Bien Phu, the reason for Piroth's suicide, the SS battalion that held the vital Lola, the rats of the Nam Yum . . .

But would de Castries approve any of those stories?

At that moment something like an earthquake struck. The walls trembled, the timbers groaned, the light bulb danced, the floor shifted, the Skywriter bounced and rattled on the table, red dust drifted down from the ceiling and the sound of thunder upon thunder exploded overhead. Clutching the doorframe, a Chesterfield in his lips, Sergeant LeRuc regarded Harry with raccoonlike amusement as the journalist staggered and reached for support.

LeRuc looked at his wristwatch.

"It's 1730 on the dot," LeRuc said. "The Reds begin the bombardments at 1730 every day. Punctuality is a classic quality. I think a journalist especially would appreciate that fact."

A coffee cup fell off a shelf, and several books toppled to the floor as the thunderstorm grew louder.

"The Reds keep this up for hours," LeRuc said. "No use waiting for them to stop before you start your writing. When they stop the bombardment, the *bo-doi* come howling."

"*Bo-doi?*"

"Sappers, suicide squads, infantry—all *bo-doi.* Thousands and thousands of little yellow people. They swarm down the mountains and across the river. They come all night long. You may as well go to work."

Harry sat down and began typing.

3 Mrs. Gerta Primrose, housekeeper, climbed down off the red bus at the intersection of the King's Road and Flood Street. As she did each weekday morning, Mrs. Primrose entered the news agent's at the corner and bought the dozen different London newspapers and *The Paris Dispatch*, which competed for space on the racks. Coming out again, she said hello to the man in the wool suit and necktie who was sweeping the sidewalks and gutters with a broom. They talked of what a beautiful April it was turning out to be in London: warm sunshine, tender evening showers, a profusion of flowers in windowboxes and gardens. All of Chelsea was in bloom beneath the shade of tall oak trees.

Mrs. Primrose walked three blocks, toward the oily sea odor of the Thames. She came to the red-brick Chelsea Swimming Club and saw steam seeping from the windows. It made her think of her employer, Harry Sparrow. Two mornings a week Sparrow rushed to the club to swim laps and practice his diving. Keeping in condition, he told her, drowning The Grouse. Mrs. Primrose thought the miles he walked on the golf course should have been enough to keep a person in condition. Sparrow was a driven man in her view, restless, never satisfied to stay long in one place. He needed her.

At Bill Hull's bookmaking shop next to The Cooper's Arms pub—Sparrow always visited them after his swim—Mrs. Primrose turned left on Christchurch Street and walked on to the bell tower and leaded windows of Christ Church. Red chrysanthemums bloomed behind a black iron fence at the churchyard. Carved in a stone slab above the entrance to Christchurch School was THE FEAR OF THE LORD IS THE BEGINNING OF WISDOM. Mrs. Primrose found it reassuring. She walked across the cobbled street from the school and came to a grand red brick Georgian home that had been divided into flats. Oaks eight stories high spread their branches against the roof. At the corner on a black spike fence the sign said: CHEYNE PLACE, ROYAL BOROUGH OF KENSINGTON AND CHELSEA.

Mrs. Primrose walked up the eight marble steps to the front door, which was painted red with a brass knocker. She admitted herself with her key, crossed the foyer and rode a cage lift to the fourth story, where Harry Sparrow kept a two-bedroom flat. Mrs. Primrose, a widow, arrived at Harry's flat six days a week if Harry was in town, and seven days if he was not. Someone had to show up every day to feed Mr. Peepers, the Persian cat. If Mrs. Primrose happened to be ill or on her yearly holiday in Spain, she would send her nephew, Wilford, to take care of Mr. Peepers. Mrs. Primrose loved dogs and ordinarily did not like cats, but Mr. Peepers was different. He had a demanding personality, his eyes sometimes flashing with anger, at other times melting with love. The fourth-floor flat at No. 5 seemed to belong to Mr. Peepers and Mrs. Primrose as much as it did to Harry Sparrow.

Mr. Peepers awaited her in the kitchen with the gift of a partially devoured pigeon. At Harry's insistence, the cat had been allowed to keep his claws. The furniture showed rips and tatters as a result. Young Lady Gwendoline Cadbury, assuming she would be marrying Harry one day, had given him the blue-lynx Persian kitten as a reunion gift after a row over Harry's staying three weeks on assignment in Budapest and missing all the Christmas parties. The ensuing disagreement over whether Mr. Peepers should keep his claws had led to Lady Cadbury's throwing of a cold-cream jar, which smashed the bedroom window. The claws debate veered into sobbing accusations that Harry could not refute. She accused Harry of loving his work more than he loved her. Even though it was true, he would never admit it. Lady Cadbury presented him with two demands: The claws had to go and Harry had to quit being a journalist and take a proper position. There were loads of nice positions Daddy could arrange. She gave him two weeks to make up his mind. She moved her trunks out of No. 5 Cheyne Place and slammed the door on Harry's foot. The morning after she moved out, Harry fired the decorator she had hired to turn the guest bedroom into a nursery and called in a carpenter. The guest bedroom became a study, where Harry began to do much of his writing, even though he still loved the turmoil and clatter around his desk in the *Dispatch*'s London bureau at 21 Bramble Bush Hill near Fleet Street.

Not only did Mr. Peepers keep his claws, he was provided with a hinged cat-window so he could come and go as he pleased, prowling along the gutter-pipes and leaping into the branches of the trees in the old stable yard behind the house.

"Poor Mr. Pigeon, he's a dead boy now, he is, all right," said Mrs. Primrose. She swept up the feathers and deposited the carcass in the garbage. Mr. Peepers watched from a window ledge and flipped his tail back and forth with annoyance. He enjoyed conversation and company, but the reedy quality of Mrs. Primrose's voice could irritate him.

The cat followed Mrs. Primrose into Harry's study. She called it "the Library." She put all but one of that morning's newspapers on top of a stack. There were stacks of newspapers and magazines lining an entire wall. Mrs. Primrose kept the stacks neat and in order. She knew Mr. Sparrow would want to look through all of them when he got back. He was a compulsive reader of periodicals and daily newspapers, and he was constantly making cuttings that he would write a reference on—like *Kills for love*—and then toss into a cardboard box or place in a manila folder in one of his four filing cabinets. When his golf bag wasn't in his locker at Royal Bowling Brook, it leaned against a wall in the study beneath a St. Louis Cardinals pennant from the 1946 season.

Another wall held a floor-to-ceiling bookcase, crammed with books on every subject in a system that made sense only to Harry. Several new books a week entered the flat; very few ever left it. The closets in the hall hid more books.

Harry's desk was gleaming mahogany, the width of two windows. The windows looked across the Physic Garden and a large orchard to the gray water of the Thames, where a gambling ship floated at anchor, its rigging glowing with light bulbs at night. Beyond the far shore of the Thames, the amusement rides of Battersea Park could be barely made out through the trees in daylight, but at night they too lit up, red and yellow and green.

On a rosewood table beside the desk stood Harry's shiny black standard-model typewriter, smelling of machine oil. A ream of yellow paper lay nearby, along with a jar of pencils and pens. Two packs of Chesterfields and books of matches from the Pink Flamingo gambling club sat in a souvenir ashtray from the 1946 World Series. Harry's chair was leather and swiveled so that he could whirl in lazy circles while he pondered.

Mrs. Primrose sorted Harry's mail and put it into three cardboard boxes marked *Personal, Business* and *Other.* Tidying up the *Personal* box, Mrs. Primrose wagged her head and smacked her lips disapprovingly. "I don't know why he won't open that girl's letters from New York, Mr. Peepers," she said. "She seemed like such a charming lady and so in love with Mr. Sparrow. He liked her so much, too, for a few months—summer before last, was it? Well, who ever knows for sure, that's what I say. I think he's still stuck on your Lady Cadbury with her awful temper and her selfish ways. I believe he's naturally attracted to foul-tempered women with a mean streak. But who ever knows for sure, hey?"

There were two framed photographs on a shelf by the desk, along with a humidor and a rack of pipes. The handsome man in one photo looked like a screen lover with his thin mustache, furtive smile and hair parted in the center; this was Harry's father, Colonel Edward Sparrow, the aviator and hero of Verdun. He had returned to St. Louis with his French bride to found an airfreight service that paid his country club bills, even during the Great Depression of the 1930s. The lovely woman in the other photo, Harry's mother, challenged the camera with a forthright stare and a hint of sternness about her mouth. Born in Paris, Giselle Leguerre Sparrow had become the belle of St. Louis in the twenty years between the two world wars.

Hundreds of photographs of Harry with famous people were piled in a cardboard box marked *Photos Misc.* in red paint.

Mrs. Primrose inspected the bedroom to be certain Mr. Peepers had not left other surprises for her. The bedroom looked out the rear of the house into the stable yard. An enormous oak rose to the left of the windows. A white marble statue of a nineteenth-century real estate developer stood in the cobblestone court in front of the stable, which had been converted into a private home. The bedroom, bath and kitchen of Harry's flat surveyed the stable yard and the Chelsea rooftops. The living room—whose dominant furnishings were a large pine cabinet with a tiny television screen in it and a leather couch that bore patterns of cat's claws like buckshot—had the same river view as the Library, but there was a bay window that protruded far enough that one could see the Albert Bridge and farther on the green arms of the Battersea Bridge.

Carrying a steaming pot of tea and a plate of biscuits, Mrs. Primrose at last sat at the kitchen table and sighed with the contentment that comes from knowing one has done one's part. She broke off half a biscuit for Mr. Peepers and unfolded the morning *Paris Dispatch,* turning immediately to the op-ed page, where Harry's column appeared. But once again there was no Harry Sparrow column. More than a week now since he had flown off to the Orient, and still no column in the newspaper by Mr. Sparrow.

Mrs. Primrose was worried. "Do you suppose he has been fired? No, surely he'd have come home by now if they'd fired him, or if he has quit. I heard him shouting on the phone he would quit if they give him any more trouble with his writing. Dead? Maybe he is dead. In the Orient, you could be dead in a huddle of Chinamen, and who would care? Who would even know?"

With a disturbed click of her teeth, Mrs. Primrose folded the paper to take it to the stacks in the library. It was then she happened to glance at the front page and see the eight-column headline. It said:

ANGELS OF DIEN BIEN PHU

Beneath the headline were the magic words:

BY HARRY SPARROW
Dispatch Staff Correspondent

There was a half-column photo of Sparrow, wearing his brown Borsalino fedora. She thought the hat made him look older.

"My, my, Mr. Peepers," she said, starting to smile as she read, "it appears Mr. Sparrow is certainly on to something again, all right."

All over Europe that morning, every copy of *The Paris Dispatch* was being snapped up at sidewalk kiosks, Metro stands, hotel lobbies, airports and railway stations. The limited pressrun of *The Paris Dispatch* made each copy precious. Strangers requested others to pass the paper along. Hustlers dug them out of trash bins and sold them for the equivalent of a U.S. dollar. *The New York Dispatch* operated *The Paris Dispatch* as a gesture toward the American tourists who crowded into Europe in the fifties. *The Paris Dispatch* was indispensable for these tourists, who had nowhere else to get news of the world in English, including baseball scores, New York Stock Exchange prices, theater and book reviews and comic strips. But when the star feature writer and columnist, Harry Sparrow, got on to another major story, *The Paris Dispatch* would grow especially popular with politicians, international businessmen, the military elite, as well as fans of old-fashioned flamboyant journalism. Charles de Gaulle, it was said, read every word Sparrow wrote in *The Dispatch* while—to use the baseball parlance Harry favored—the general waited in the bull pen in Colombey-les-Deux-Églises for France to call on him to save the Republic in the ninth inning.

The New York Dispatch, which paid Harry's salary and his creative expense account, was a morning tabloid read by three million subway straphangers and commuter train paper-folders. Of the twelve daily newspapers in New York City, the *Dispatch* usually ranked first in circulation, just ahead of the *Daily News* and the

Herald-Tribune, but it was a struggle every hour to stay on top. The publisher, known to his staff as "the Immortal," saw himself in every way superior to Pulitzer and James Gordon Bennett and Hearst and hated to be anywhere but on top. The Immortal put correspondents in bureaus all over the world, used their work in his own newspapers and sold it in syndication to smaller papers. When the *Dispatch* Syndicate beat the wire services to a story, the Immortal fired telegrams of praise to his writers and editors.

To *New York Dispatch* readers, Harry Sparrow's name was as familiar as a foreign correspondent's could become, considering the emphasis on local news. Even when prominently displayed, Harry's pieces were trimmed to fit the space limitations of the tabloid format: "Hacked into senseless yelps!" is how he put it in his frequent complaints to Epps.

But *The Paris Dispatch,* a full-size newspaper with a small and grotesquely underpaid staff, used every column and feature of Harry Sparrow's at full length. The more the better, said Gruber, an old-time Chicago newspaperman who loved showmanship and rack sales. He liked Harry's pieces because Harry had a good eye and an ear for detail, his reporting attracted controversy and his copy always arrived on time. Dependableness was the virtue Gruber treasured above all. The result was that Harry Sparrow's views and opinions had taken on a fair importance in Europe, England, Scandinavia and North Africa, wherever *The Paris Dispatch* was sold.

Elmore Gruber had pulled out the 96-point Second Coming headline type for Harry's first story from inside the surrounded French fortress and had led the front page with it. ANGELS OF DIEN BIEN PHU was well played and very well read.

Gruber sat in a cloud of *Gauloise* smoke at his desk in his cubicle in the corner of the newsroom at the *Dispatch* building on the rue Scribe. He wore a polka-dot bow tie beneath his fullback's jaw. His wooden swivel chair creaked as he leaned back to peer over his half-spectacles, over the front page of the paper, at Calvin Epps, who was talking on the phone to New York. Teletype machines from United Press, The Associated Press, the International News Service, Reuters and the home office clattered steadily against the far wall, unreeling the world's stories on long rolls of yellow paper. Gruber's reporters were gathered at the horseshoe-shaped news desk, urgently typing local stories on deadline or editing copy that was inserted into pneumatic tubes to be whished away to the linotype shop. Gusts of soot issued from the heating ducts, but the editors no longer cared.

Gruber was proud of himself that morning. Calvin Epps had arrived furious from London, from one of his periodic tours of *Dispatch* Syndicate bureaus from Paris to Buenos Aires. In London Epps had discovered a $10,000 travel-expense-advance voucher for Harry Sparrow, approved by Gruber and paid out of the meager expense allowance of the Paris office. Every reporter on the Paris staff was angry at Gruber and at Sparrow. A trip to Hanoi with the hope of getting inside Dien Bien Phu was the kind of assignment good reporters would eagerly die for. When Harry had phoned Gruber in the middle of the night and asked to be sent to Indochina to win the Pulitzer Prize, Gruber thought it over and decided Harry was the man who might actually do it. A Pulitzer would be a good decoration for the front-page logo of *The Paris Dispatch*.

Calvin Epps hung up the telephone.

"It's a smash," he said to Gruber. "Page one at every client newspaper. Page three at the *Dispatch* in Gotham with a page-one teaser." Epps looked at the eight-column headline again and forgave himself a smile. "ANGELS OF DIEN BIEN PHU—pretty damned good. Harry'll never be able to top that. And you mark my words, Elmore, if Sparrow doesn't keep coming up with great news angles like this ANGELS beauty, his Indochina stuff will drop back to prop up the classifieds."

"I've been thinking about how to play Harry's copy from now on," Gruber said. "Harry obviously can't come up with an angle as good as this very often, but I've got an idea."

"Your readers over here eat up this French business, but American readers get bored with foreign crap real fast," said Epps.

Before taking over the foreign desk of *The New York Dispatch*, Epps had been the Washington political pundit for *The Brooklyn Eagle*. Epps tried to be polite sometimes, even downright nice on occasion, but it required an effort of will that exhausted him and made him still more grouchy.

"You think Americans don't want to read about Dien Bien Phu?" Gruber said, sharpening his copy pencil with the Boy Scout knife he kept in his desk drawer. Gruber had entered the newspaper business as a copyboy on the *Chicago Tribune* and had seen his first byline at the age of eighteen as a twelve dollar per week police reporter for the Chicago *Daily News*. He understood Epps well enough to know a lecture on world affairs was commencing.

"Americans don't want to *think* about Dien Bien Phu," Epps said. "I wrote an editorial about the billion bucks a year U.S. taxpayers are paying to finance this French war. We're paying eighty percent of the bill. The Froggies have already thrown away their— *our*—Marshall Plan money on this war. If they were as clever as the Germans they would have rebuilt their economy instead of fighting another war to put France right back where it was in 1939. FDR warned them about this. He said French greed would kill millions in Indochina, but de Gaulle insisted France had to be given back all its old colonies or he would screw up NATO. Ho Chi Minh begged us to be his friend—we told him to shit in his hat. Ipso facto, the Froggies go to war with the dinks using our money. They keep dragging us deeper into it by claiming anybody who's against their colonial empire must be in favor of the Communists—pure Froggie bullshit. But you know who believes this French hokum? John Foster Dulles, that potato with ears. Why Ike would make him secretary of state is beyond understanding. It must have happened at some Masonic Lodge meeting where they were all fucked up. The son of a bitch can't even pronounce Vietnam. Have you heard Dulles? Veet-num! *Veet-*num! It makes me sick!"

"So what happened to your editorial?"

"Huh?"

"I read *The New York Dispatch* every day. I didn't see any editorial denouncing John Foster Dulles for spending a billion dollars a year on the French colonial war in Indochina."

Epps shrugged. "The Immortal shot it down. He said the time is not right—meaning Joe McCarthy is who we've got to deal with first. The billion bucks is spent fighting Communists, so spend it."

"You want to hear my idea about how to use Harry's stuff?"

"Yeah."

"Harry fancies himself a great reporter, but he's more of a feature

writer than one-two-three with the news. So I think I'll run his
Dien Bien Phu stuff as columns and not try to disguise them as news
stories, like today. Instead of putting his column on the op-ed page,
where readers can lose it, I want to use it in a regular spot, top left
two columns on the front page, with a bold standing head on it.
One-column photo of Harry. Standing head: I, HARRY SPARROW.
That way, he won't need a hard news angle. Anything he writes
will work. The Dien Bien Phu dateline will see to that."

"Our Syndicate clients in Des Moines and Denver and Memphis
won't give a shit. They won't waste space on it. But the Latins
might go for it if it's gory."

"My only concern is *The Paris Dispatch*," Gruber said. "My paper
will print every syllable of it. My readers will eat it up. I want to
up the pressrun by ten thousand."

Epps nodded. "Harry could win us a Pulitzer if he does it right."

"I was in Hanoi, you know," said Gruber.

"I'd forgot. When was it?"

"I ran the UP bureau, 1945 to '47."

"Who was running the town then?" asked Epps.

"In forty-five? The Chinese nationalists. They had an army of
200,000 around Hanoi. Ho was afraid they'd stay another thousand
years like the last time they invaded his country. Ho made a deal
to let the French come back in for a short time in return for the
Americans' making the Chinese get out. When the Chinks left
Hanoi, they stole everything that could be carried—roofing tiles,
plumbing pipes, windowpanes, electric wire, you name it."

Gruber lit another *Gauloise* and looked at Epps, who appeared
to be listening attentively. Epps wiped his bifocals on his breast-
pocket handkerchief and studied the shine on his Johnston and
Murphys. It was not often that Epps would allow anyone to tell him
anything about contemporary events.

"I covered Ho's famous speech at Ba Dinh Square in Hanoi on
September second, 1945," Gruber said.

"What famous speech?" said Epps.

"His declaration of independence—when he proclaimed the
Democratic Republic of Vietnam an independent nation. The
bands played 'The Star-Spangled Banner,' 'God Save the Queen,'

the Chinese nationalist anthem and the 'Soviet Workers' March.' People were laughing and crying and hugging each other. You know what Ho said that day? How he opened his speech?"

"I don't recall," said Epps. "I did my war in Europe."

"He said, 'All Men are created equal . . . they are endowed by their Creator with certain unalienable Rights . . . among these are Life, Liberty, and the Pursuit of Happiness . . .' Sound familiar?"

"I don't believe it," said Epps.

"The words are engraved on the wall at the Museum of History in Hanoi."

"Bullshit, they are."

"The American Revolution and the French Revolution are the two events Ho said he admired more than any in the world," Gruber said. "He told me he loved Americans and American history and would never fight against Americans. He said all he wanted was for France to set him a date for independence, like we had done for the Philippines. We didn't tell Ho to shit in his hat. We didn't even answer the skinny little fellow. We walked away, wouldn't speak to him. When I left Hanoi in forty-seven to come to work for the *Dispatch*, Langlais and his French paratroopers were fighting house-to-house in Hanoi to chase Ho and his boys off into the jungle."

"Did the Reds put up much of a fight?" Epps asked.

"They littered the streets with forty thousand mutilated bodies of educated people, like civil servants, municipal judges, schoolteachers and newspaper reporters," said Gruber. "If you were wearing glasses or a nice suit, they killed you. It was madness, like what the Communists did in Spain—kill the smart ones first."

Epps swirled the last of his coffee in his mug and drank it, looking thoughtful and wary. "Ho is a Commie," Epps said. "I hate Communism. I mean that. I truly do. Regardless of how greedy the French are, and what a fool or villain Dulles is, and how dangerous it is for the American public to be obsessed with whether McCarthy can prove some Army dentist is a pinko—regardless of all that, I *would* rather be dead than Red. What the hell, Orientals don't understand politics in the Western sense. You couldn't let Ho Chi Minh run a country. He would be too dangerous."

A reporter came over from the news desk with pieces of copy paper covered with notes. Gruber smiled when he saw Epps notice the reporter's belt—rope, tied in a bow. Gruber's staff did such things to protest their wages.

"Excuse me, boss, but I've just been talking to the War Office and got a good sidebar for the Harry Sparrow shit," the reporter said.

"Can't you afford a belt?" Epps said.

"No sir, I can't," said the reporter. He looked back at Gruber. "The War Office—not officially, but according to my source there—says at every Army base in France soldiers are volunteering to go to Dien Bien Phu. I mean draftees—the kids the government promised could do their entire military service inside the borders of France. Thousands of draftee kids are asking to be parachuted into Dien Bien Phu—kids who have never jumped out of a plane before in their lives."

Epps took off his alligator belt and offered it to the reporter.

"I would not wear an endangered species on my body," the reporter said with contempt.

Epps nodded thoughtfully. "Well, fuck this creep," he reasoned aloud.

The reporter said, "Listen, Elmore, the craziest damn thing is, the recruiting stations are full today, too. Civilians are volunteering to go to Dien Bien Phu. According to my source, these civilians say they don't want to sign up for any three-year hitch or anything, they just want to be given a rifle and a parachute and pointed toward Dien Bien Phu."

"Give me eight or ten fast grafs for page one," Gruber said.

Epps buckled his belt back on as the reporter rushed to a typewriter.

"What's the time difference between here and Dien Bien Phu?" Epps asked.

"Seven hours." Gruber looked at the big clock on the wall above the coffee urn. "It's five-thirty this afternoon where Harry is. Assuming Harry is still somewhere."

"What do you mean?"

"Assuming Harry is not dead. All we've had from him so far is this one piece about the angels. Silence ever since. No answer to my cables."

"He wouldn't get killed at a time like this. I know Harry better than that. That vain, arrogant son of a bitch never answers a cable from us unless it suits him."

The bell on the teletype machine connected to the home office in New York began to ding. Gruber, Epps and others in the newsroom counted the dings. Eight dings meant you might want to hold the presses, something hot was coming. After six dings, Gruber and Epps raced to the crowd gathering around the machine. Two more dings.

The copy began printing:

BY HARRY SPARROW
Dispatch Staff Correspondent

DIEN BIEN PHU—(DS)—NIGHT AFTER NIGHT SUICIDE CHARGES OF BO-DOI COME HOWLING INTO THE BARBED WIRE, MINEFIELDS AND MACHINE GUNS OF THIS FRENCH UNION FORTRESS THAT COMMUNIST ARTILLERY BOMBARDMENT HAS MADE TO RESEMBLE 11 MILES OF THE MOON. THIS IS *Beau Geste* ON A GRAND SCALE.

"Good old Harry!" said Gruber.

"The lucky suckass," a reporter said. "I'd wear a rope belt around my neck to be in his spot."

4   The valley of Dien Bien Phu is the wettest place in all of northern Indochina. During the monsoon season—March through August—it is not unusual for eight feet of rain to fall. Five feet of rain is the average. A storm that pours six inches of rain in an hour is common. French Union Forces captured the valley in November, during the dry season. They flattened and trampled the rice and vegetables. There was no stone or gravel in the valley. The French could not build masonry fortifications. There was no timber in the valley, either. The French tore down the houses in the villages to use the wood for construction. After the first week of the actual battle, loads of coffin wood from Hanoi, such as had come in on the ambulance plane with Harry, also went into shoring up bunkers. The dead were buried in shell craters or trenches dug by engineers.

Dien Bien Phu is not the name of a town. The words mean "Seat of the Border Country Prefecture" or "administration center." The name of the now-destroyed village where the administration center was now located had been Muong Thang. It was a Tai village. The

Tais controlled the valley. The Xa tribe lived on the slopes. The Meos commanded the ridges and the highest mountains farther beyond. The yellow stucco building that had housed the French resident administrator was standing in perfect order when the paras of the FUF jumped in November. Now the yellow building on the hill known as Lola was flattened—only its wine cellar remained. A Chaffee tank was half-buried in the mud and rubble where the administrator's office had been.

In winter the temperature in the valley dropped to 30 degrees Fahrenheit at night, colder on the peaks. An exposed person could suffer and die from the wet chill. But with the monsoon rains came hot winds that blew seventy-mile-an-hour gales from Laos. When the battering of rain and wind paused, the heat and humidity in the valley became suffocating. FUF soldiers died from dehydration or exhaustion. Green flies, ticks and fleas flourished on the valley floor during monsoon. Within a short time after the Vietminh surrounded the valley and began their onslaught, another creature started to thrive: the maggot.

The Nam Yum flooded. Water poured into trenches. FUF troops at the southern strongpoint, called Isabelle, fought up to their knees in water and mud. Inside of every bunker the walls and floors oozed mud and the smell of sulphur and decay.

Harry emerged from the C.R. bunker on an early afternoon in the middle of April. In the three weeks he had been at Dien Bien Phu, Harry had changed in appearance. First to go had been the cordovan loafers—sucked off his feet and lost forever in a mudhole. Now he wore a pair of thick-soled paratroop boots Claudette Frontenac had given him. There were hundreds of empty boots around the hospital.

He had cut off his white linen trousers at midthigh and made them into walking shorts the color of a mechanic's apron. His suit coat and one good shirt were packed in a footlocker. A sniper's bullet had punched a hole through the crown of the Panama hat he still wore. Harry had heard a *theong!* and the hat had sailed six feet away. The sniper kept tracking him as Harry crawled after the hat. *Theong! Theong!* So close it seemed as if the sniper was letting Harry know he was being spared on purpose. Sick as he was with dysentery, Harry hardly cared about snipers and their bullets anymore. Harry had lost twenty pounds and had quit shaving. The thin, bearded face with bulging red eyes could have been that of a wino in a doorway in Soho.

Harry used his Haig Ultra pitching wedge to hold his Burberry up, like an umbrella above his head, as he stepped slowly into the slop. He also used the wedge for a cane, a scoop, a hoe, a hammer, a pointer, a scraper and a shovel. He even used it to stroke some ration cans and brass shell casings as he roamed the trenches. Harry could use the wedge as a bludgeon or a sword or, he figured, as a staff to tie a white flag on.

He lowered his wedge and Burberry and blinked. What was wrong? Harry smelled fried pork and diesel oil. Three weeks before, knowing the smell of fried pork meant burnt human flesh would have made him pause and reflect. Now he ignored the smells as he waded into the communications trench. He realized what seemed wrong: It wasn't raining. Heat rose from the mud carrying the odor of shit, but Harry had grown used to it now. Smoke and pungent cordite fumes made a haze below the clouds. The land around him was a steaming swamp. Nobody knew how many bodies lay under the mud.

By de Castries's accounting, the FUF could call on 3,000 fighting soldiers. Perhaps 6,000 deserters—most what de Castries called "Colonials," soldiers from Morocco, Algeria, Tunisia and Indochina—lived with trapped tribes in the caves. De Castries spoke of turning FUF artillery against the rats of the Nam Yum in their caves, but the ammunition was needed against Vietminh assaults. In the last twenty-four hours the FUF had fired 12,000 rounds of 105 artillery shells, half with the barrels cranked down to shoot directly into Communist troops swarming down the slopes. Incredibly, reinforcements kept parachuting in. A hundred volunteers—French and Vietnamese—jumped into Dien Bien Phu last night. Sixteen lived to see the dawn.

If Harry survived he knew he would never again underestimate the human capacity for courage, generosity, stupidity, or evil.

Harry was allowed to poke about the C.R. at will—unless Bigeard or Langlais was present. The paratroop officers were annoyed to have Harry there but could think of nothing to do with him. Besides, Harry was useful to them in a way. He played chess with de Castries and kept the colonel from bothering them for hours in a row. Playing chess with de Castries, Harry heard gossip and radio traffic in the command bunker. He couldn't write the information he learned in the bunker, but he would remember it for the future— if, indeed, there proved to be a future for him or for the world. The arms and munitions that were concentrated in this remote valley in Indochina were truly startling, even to Harry, who had seen the D-Day armada and the Patton armies.

Making notes of the lists of weapons used by both sides in the battle put Harry into a cynical mood, extreme even for a newspaperman trained to expect the worst from people. Reading his lists, Harry realized it was too simple to blame the arms merchants for this awful inventory of staggeringly expensive tools of doom. People must *want* to be armed to the eyeballs. The manufacture of weapons had become a very big business during World War II, but there was more to this lust for weapons than salesmanship. People loved weapons, they loved to fight and kill. The currency for weapons was human lives—but they kept crying for more.

Fifteen different types of U.S. aircraft flew at Dien Bien Phu. Harry listed F8F-1B Bearcats, SB-2C Helldivers, F6F Hellcats and F4U Corsairs. For bombers the French Union used B-26 Marauders and PB4Y2 Privateers made in the U.S.

Transport planes that flew daily were U.S. C-47 Dakotas and C-119 Packets, called Flying Boxcars. French-built Morane-500 Crickets shared the sky with U.S. RF8F Bearcats as reconnaissance aircraft. For liaison and evacuation—both now impossible—there were Sikorsky S-55 helicopters, DHC2 Beavers, L-19 Birddogs from the U.S., German Siebel NC-701 Martinets and French Morane-500's.

The French Union Forces could call on Bristol 170 Freighters for additional transport planes from England, S.U. Bretagnes from France and 307-B Boeing Stratoliners, C-46 Curtis Commandos and DC-4 Skymasters from the U.S.

As artillery at Dien Bien Phu, the French used 155 mm and 105 mm howitzers, Chaffee M-24 tanks with 75 mm turret guns, M-20

75 mm and 57 mm recoilless rifles from the U.S., and their own Hotchkiss-Brandt 120 mm mortars and 81 mm mortars and H-13 60 mm mortars.

The French Union troops were issued U.S. Browning .50-caliber and .30-caliber machine guns, model 1924/29 French Chatellerault 7.5 mm light machine guns, U.S. M-1 and M-2 carbines, French MAT 49 submachine guns, French MAS bolt action rifles of 7.5 mm and paratroop models of the same weapon with folding aluminum stocks.

Also MAS 49 rifles with grenade launchers attached, French F-1 Type A sniper rifles, U.S. M2A1 flamethrowers weighing seventy-two pounds with a forty-yard range; French M1937 offensive hand grenades, DM46 defensive hand grenades and MK59 anti-personnel mines; and U.S. M-20 3.5 rocket-launching bazookas.

From French intelligence reports in the bunker, Harry made a list of Vietminh weapons. A disturbing number had been manufactured in the United States. But now Russian-built weapons were showing up, and some from China.

The heavy anti-aircraft barrages thrown up from the mountains came from Russian M38-39 37 mm and 20 mm twin-barrel guns, and DShK 12.7 anti-aircraft machine guns with a two-mile range, and U.S. .50 caliber machine guns.

Russian Katyusha rockets of 122 mm with six tubes were rumored to be on the way to Dien Bien Phu, but the French High Command scoffed at the report. How could Katyusha rockets pass through the blockades? The Vietminh fired U.S. 105 mm howitzers, 75 mm pack howitzers, 75 mm and 57 mm recoilless rifles and Russian 120 mm and 82 mm mortars.

The Communist troops were barefoot and hungry, but they bristled with French MAT 49 submachine guns and MAS rifles; Russian Tokarev model 33 pistols; U.S. M1918-A2 Browning 30.06 rifles; Type 53 carbines from the People's Republic of China; Chinese 7.62 mm submachine guns; French Chatellerault 7.5 mm automatic rifles and 7.5 mm machine guns; anti-tank mines and five different types of hand grenades from the U.S., France and the U.S.S.R., and thousands of U.S. M-20 3.5 rocket-launching bazookas.

Reading the list of arms at Dien Bien Phu reminded Harry of his father's belief that the world would end in the year 2000. The atomic bombs at Hiroshima and Nagasaki had not dismayed Harry's father, nor would he join in the Civil Defense bomb-shelter panic that swept the United States. Colonel Edward Sparrow was not religious; he used New Testament prophecies only to help him make his point: The world would end in the year 2000. Harry's mother was the strong Catholic in the family. She was a spirited woman who went regularly to mass and confession; Harry's father played golf on Sundays. He could explain why he knew the world would end in the year 2000. He believed it was universal knowledge. It had something to do with being alive in the year 1900. Everyone who was alive in 1900 agreed, Colonel Sparrow said. The special knowledge was passed along in the genes in 1900. The end was one century away. Nothing to worry about until 2000.

But this was 1954, forty-six years till the aviator's doomsday, and Harry wondered if his father hadn't been optimistic.

Harry was amazingly clear-headed. He swallowed two more Maxiton pills. Sergeant LeRuc had stashed an entire crate of Maxitons. He had been prominently mentioned in two of Harry's dispatches.

That afternoon, in the relatively quiet time before the evening bombardment began, Harry was headed for the underground hospital to see Claudette. Folded in an oilcloth packet inside his shirt was a batch of clippings that had been dropped by a Bearcat courier that morning. Included was his first dispatch—the eight-column headline ANGELS OF DIEN BIEN PHU. Pieces written later—published with the I, HARRY SPAROW standing boxed head—had come to the valley earlier, and Harry had begun to wonder if the first transmission had gotten garbled on its journey around the world.

But it finally arrived, along with another cable from Gruber that said WORLDWIDE PLAYHOT EVEN EPPS PLEASED KEEP HEAD DOWN TYPE FASTER. And then an addendum that Gruber had known would irritate Harry: LONDON CLAIM PHIBBS IN THICK OF ACTION. HOW? PHIBBS COLORFUL INTERVIEW WITH LEGIONNAIRE SAYS 5,000 NAZI SS FIGHTING DIEN BIEN. PLS FOLLOW BEST GRUBER.

Harry figured Phibbs had gotten drunk with a French colonial soldier—could have been a Morroccan or Algerian or one of the African blacks—in Hanoi. The colonials hated the Legion. Harry knew there were at least two thousand Germans in the Legion at Dien Bien when Giap's assault began. Harry had heard Bigeard say, "If we had a division of those Nazi brutes, we would have taken up bayonets and won this fight by now." That was moments after Selchauhansen had led another successful counterattack from Lola. Radio reported to the C.R. that *bo-doi* bodies were piled six deep on barbed wire in the mud.

Harry heard harsh voices calling and looked up as a flock of crows flew across the valley. Every time the rain slackened, crows flew across the valley, their cries mocking the humans in the jungle and the mud below.

He found Claudette sitting on a pile of sandbags outside the hospital. Wounded and dead lay in the mud by the entrance. Engineers and PIMs dug trenches to dispose of the bodies, but it had become a hopeless task.

Claudette's skin and uniform were caked with blood and mud. She was smoking a cigarette. Her face looked ashen in the ghostly aura that hovered around the hospital.

"What do you suppose I just did, Harry?" she said, her voice full of wonder. "Sit down, please. I need to talk."

"What's the matter?"

"We had thirty wounded for abdominal surgery lined up in there. All of them hopeless. The doctor asked me to pick out ten who were suffering the most." She dropped her cigarette into a mud puddle and looked at Harry. Her eyes were sunken and saw past him. In her despair, she moved him. He wanted to be a part of her, to console her. "So I did it, and we killed them."

"What do you mean?"

"The ten I selected got an overdose of morphine. We didn't have enough morphine to kill all thirty. So we killed the ten I selected, and the other twenty are dying now."

Harry reached over and took her hand.

"I tried to choose the ones who were afraid of death, who were fighting it." Claudette began weeping. Harry put his arms around her. He felt her body shuddering. "But the ones who were ready to accept death—they could make the transition on their own. They were ready to leave their bodies. The ones with faith, their spiritual guides were here with them. Some had already welcomed the peace that comes with death." She pressed her face against his shoulder.

"Where do you get a spiritual guide?" Harry said.

"They are here for all of us, to guide us, to comfort us. All you have to do is ask and then listen to your inner self."

Harry thought, this little angel has been heavy into the Maxitons.

"I'm sorry," she said. "You don't need to hear all this." Claudette stepped back, wiping the muddy tears. "I better go to work."

"Let me show you something," Harry said.

Harry removed the angels story from the oilcloth packet.

"I didn't have time to interview you or Geneviève before I wrote this," he said. "Had to get something off to the *Dispatch*, and this was the best thing I could think of that would get de Castries's approval. Hope you don't mind."

He watched her as she read the story. She looked puzzled at first at seeing her name in print. Then she began reading with urgency.

"They have information on Galard and you in the files at the C.R. The intelligence boys sent it," he said.

"This is very flattering, Harry," she said, reading the story, "but I don't deserve it. Geneviève is the real angel. She stays on her feet for days and nights without sleep. She's amazing. What strength she's got. I must learn to be as strong as she is."

"You do what she does," Harry said.

"Why haven't you mentioned the other women? The Arabs? The Vietnamese? They do what we do, too."

"De Castries censored them. He says they're prostitutes."

"What a strange place to draw the line. A man who gives orders sending men to certain death and yet judges merciful women doing the work of God. If left to women, there would never be a war. And besides, in the Bible, Jesus didn't spurn prostitutes. What difference does it make what they are? If they are whores, they could go to the bordellos in the caves on the river. They're closer to being angels than I am, Harry. They didn't volunteer for this, but they're enduring it with responsibility," she said.

"I'll write about them after we get out of here."

"Get out of here?" she said.

"We got in. We can get out."

"Oh, Harry, don't treat me like a fool. I know what's happening."

She thrust the newspaper clipping back into his hands.

"You can keep it," he said. "For your scrapbook."

"I don't want the others in the hospital to see this story, Harry. It can only make things worse. Tear it up, please."

She turned and started toward the hospital bunker. There was something in the way her hips moved, her shoulders erect, that Harry found inexplicable and exciting.

"Are you in love with that Legionnaire?" Harry said.

Claudette glanced back at him.

"Have you heard news of him?"

"He's alive."

"Praise God," Claudette said. She crossed herself.

"How did you ever meet him? A girl like you shouldn't know a thug like him."

Claudette's face brightened at Harry's jealousy. She looked at him with her head at an angle, hair cropped too short to dangle, as if she were studying a chess move, Harry thought, pleased at the picture of her looking at him that way across a chessboard. She might be able to play him a fair game. The physical desire he felt for her, sick as he was and stuck in hell, pleased him.

"He came to my apartment in Paris."

"He looked you up?"

"He knew my father. He came to talk about my father, console me as a friend of my father. He was wounded. I cared for him."

"Are you in love with him? Is that why you're here?"

Claudette gave Harry an impenetrable female look. He had no idea what she might say or if he should believe it.

"What a stupid question," she said.

"But what's the answer?"

"I know now I didn't come here because of him—not for his love—and not to find some part of my father. Or for my country to control this land. I didn't come here for any of the reasons that I thought I did. I'm here to help those that I can. Maybe I'm here to learn how to love. I see love all around me in the hospital. Not being in love but loving."

Harry watched her walk back into the hospital bunker. He shoved the clipping into the oilcloth packet. He smelled the breath of a hog, and looked up to see Pelwa.

Pelwa's left arm hung in a sling; his left hand was wrapped in a bloody bandage. With his unmaimed hand, he pulled the black SS cap onto his large skull.

"What are you doing chatting up the chief's girl?" Pelwa said.

"How bad are you hurt?" Harry said.

"Nothing much."

"Your hand mangled is nothing much?"

"The chief wants to see you, mister. Where have you been hiding? You afraid to come to Lola with me?"

"Let's go," Harry said.

"No sense you getting hot for that girl. No girl ever leaves the chief unless he's through with her, and he likes this one. No insult intended, mister, but you ain't in the same world with the chief when it comes to women."

"How would you know?" said Harry.

"Don't lose your temper with me." Pelwa grunted. "I don't know, mister, maybe you're the top stud in Chicago, America, but I bet you can't make a woman leave the chief. Come on, now. Let's take the 'Metro' over to Lola."

The network of trenches that laced the valley floor and low hills inside the amphitheater had become so extensive that Europeans called it the Metro. The trouble with the Metro, from Harry's point of view, was that you never knew where to get off; you could round a turn in a trench and be face to face with *bo-doi* in green uniforms and bamboo helmets. FUF and Vietminh lines had come close enough together that soldiers shouted insults and taunts and jokes back and forth.

A loudspeaker from Communist lines was booming as Harry waded with Corporal Pelwa through the slush and blood of the Metro. The message today was aimed at the Foreign Legion.

"Why are you dying for French imperialism, you brave soldiers of the *Légion étrangère*?" said the loudspeaker in French. "Throw

down your arms and come over to us. We will send you home safely
to Europe."

Pelwa led Harry into Selchauhansen's command post. Beside the
entrance was a lone banyan tree. The command post was in the
wine cellar of what had been the French resident administrator's
house. The captain was giving firing coordinates on the radio when
they entered. He wore his green Legion paratroop beret and a faded
khaki jacket. Harry heard him asking for more flamethrower tanks.
Leaning against a firing slit, the handsome Arab Ali Saadi was
asleep standing up, stacks of brass bullet casings around his boots.
Attached to the wall with medical tape, Harry saw newspaper
clippings. Two of them were Harry's own stories from *The Paris
Dispatch,* but most prominently displayed was PHIBBS: OUR MAN AT
DIEN BIEN PHU. It was the Phibbs story about the 5,000 Nazi SS
fighting for the Legion at Dien Bien Phu.

Harry guessed the man who called himself Selchauhansen was
not much more than thirty years old. That meant he could have
been no older than twenty when he became an officer in the Headhunters. When Hitler's Panzers invaded Russia in 1941, Selchauhansen would have been a boy of sixteen. At age sixteen Harry's
dreams of the future involved playing shortstop for the St. Louis
Cardinals. He turned twenty-one in his junior year at the University of Missouri when the Japanese bombed Pearl Harbor. Until
December 7, 1941, playing the games of baseball and golf, starring
on the swimming and diving teams in high school and college,
dancing, drinking and the conquest of girls filled his life. He tried
to please his father by winning prizes and maintaining decent
grades in pre-law and his mother by going to mass with her at
Christmas, Easter and Good Friday. He didn't make the varsity
baseball team on the university level, though; he had good range at
shortstop and a fair throwing arm, but curve balls were his fatal flaw
at the plate. He won letters in high diving and freestyle swimming,
and he worked for the campus newspaper, rising from general
assignments to his own editorial column before Pearl Harbor. How
different life must have been for the German.

Selchauhansen's green beret brushed the damp concrete beam
above his head as he spoke into the American-made ANPRC-6

radio. Light from the petroleum-jelly lantern cast a dull gleam on the beret. Harry had expected to see an SS badge like the one on Pelwa's black cap. Coming into Strongpoint Lola, Harry noticed troopers wearing SS badges, caps and daggers mixed with their American-made World War II uniforms and steel helmets, and their French Legion khaki shorts and floppy campaign hats. But the badge Selchauhansen had pinned to his beret was the dragon and sword inside a circle: the universal mercenary symbol.

Looking at the man, Harry admitted it was reasonable Claudette could have fallen for him. There was a touch of the thoroughbred about him: long limbs, clean lines, intelligent eyes and a rich growth of reddish-blond beard. Harry's first impression of him as a mad monk was inadequate; the man looked like a modern Teutonic knight, glittering madness in his features. Imagine a black cross on his chest and a broadsword in his hands, and you understood why medieval Europe had feared the Teutons and popes had courted their favor. But Selchauhansen would at moments achieve a soft, feminine expression, a tenderness in the eyes and mouth that filled the onlooker with relief.

Selchauhansen handed the headpiece back to his radio operator and looked at Pelwa.

"How's your hand?"

"Good as new," said Pelwa.

"Three fingers blown off this morning, and now he's good as new," Selchauhansen said, shrugging at Harry. "Sit down, Sparrow. I've been hoping you'd come find the truth to write. The *London Daily Mail* claims to have been here already."

"It would be hard to count how many scoops have come entirely from the *Daily Mail*'s imagination."

"How is Claudette?"

"She's working at the hospital."

"I mean, how is she holding up?"

"She's okay."

"I want to thank you for helping me at the airstrip. I always repay a favor."

"Listen, whatever-your-name-is, I went through Poland in 1945.

I saw what the SS did. I wasn't trying to help you at the airstrip. If it hadn't been for Claudette, I would have left you for dead."

"Oh, I'm not fooled about your reasons. But I am in your debt."

Harry said, "Why did you bring Claudette here? You knew what this was all about. If you care for the girl, why would you bring her here?"

"This is her war."

"Because she's French? Or do you SS bastards routinely punish the people you love?"

"Hey, mister, you shut your mouth," growled Pelwa.

"It's all right, Pelwa. Find us some coffee, please. And some tobacco," said Selchauhansen.

"*Jawohl, Herr Kapitän!*" Pelwa gave an exaggerated salute.

Harry opened his last pack of Chesterfields, gave one to Selchauhansen and put the pack on the map case between them.

"You may as well put your feet up and listen. You can't find your way out of here by yourself. I know you want to hear about the girl. I'll tell you. But first you have to listen to me. I will tell you how my Headhunters came here. I'll tell you what this battle is about. You will have a chance to write the truth. The only thing you mean to me is you tried to save my life. But your newspaper is important."

Harry nodded. There was passion in the German's voice.

"You were military age during the war, Sparrow. I guess infantry, maybe parachutes. You have the look of an officer," said Selchauhansen.

"I was a corporal, like Pelwa," Harry said.

The captain snorted. "There is no other corporal like Pelwa. What was your branch then? Armor?"

"I covered the war in Europe for *Stars and Stripes,*" Harry said.

"You were a journalist even during the fighting?"

"I was where the fighting was, if that's what you mean," Harry said.

"Don't be offended, Sparrow," said the captain, "but no journalist can compare himself to a man like Pelwa. A journalist is an observer and a faker. Pelwa is right in the middle of the real stuff."

"Where do you think I am? Does this look like the Riviera?"

"Your press card is only a piece of paper; there are bullets flying here. But your press card wins you a dead officer's bunk in the C.R., doesn't it? I hear you play gin rummy and chess with the colonel. Is de Castries a good chess player?"

"Not bad. He's a quiet player."

"But forceful, they say. Let's see how good you are at chess."

Selchauhansen lifted a section of parachute silk that had been covering a mahogany chessboard and began to set up the ivory pieces.

Harry had learned to play chess from the third-base coach of the Cardinals in spring training in 1946. In the eight years since, Harry had followed the typical novice's road to the discovery that chess is unfathomable. At first he bought some books, learned fundamental rules and several openings. He learned chess language: *forks* and *splits*, *mates* and *checkmates*, *stalemates* and *draws*. He thought he could recognize patterns on the board. After two years he began to notice he was no longer improving. The good players kept killing him. And they weren't even good players compared to the bartender in The Cooper's Arms, who could beat any ten regulars simultaneously, blindfolded. And the bartender, good as he was, would have less chance against a grandmaster than Harry would have had in a golf match against Sam Snead. What hope did Harry have in chess? He lapsed into a style of play that used an established opening to a depth of six or seven moves, then he castled his king to the king side and tried to struggle into the middle game, hoping for errors by his opponent that were worse than his own. Harry had no prospect of chess brilliancy, not ever; he was discovering that chess was for few to be brilliant at. For players like Harry, chess was the conditioning of the logic circuits of the mind. Harry was impulsive; he wanted to be logical.

"I warn you, I am naturally gifted at this game," Selchauhansen said. "I am blessed. The first time I looked at a chessboard as a child, I could see all the squares and their importance. That's the secret to the game: Be aware of the entire board and understand the important squares. Do you want to play white or black?"

"White."

White made the first move. Playing white was like choosing to serve at tennis.

Harry made an opening of pawn to king four. The Legionnaire stroked his beard thoughtfully as his bloodshot eyes took in the board. Selchauhansen moved his black king's pawn two squares. Harry brought his king's knight out to bishop three. Selchauhansen replied with queen's knight to bishop three. Harry moved his king's bishop across to queen's knight five, attacking black's king four, a vital square. It was the Ruy Lopez, the opening Harry could play longest before the pieces started falling. Harry castled his king to the king's side on his fifth move. The moves went fast, the two men concentrating, not speaking. Selchauhansen's fifth move captured Harry's king's pawn with a knight.

"The Steinetz defense." Selchauhansen smiled. After that move, the captain relaxed. He had Harry sized up and the game won. "Do you mind if I continue my story? Can you think about your game with conversation going on?"

"I'm listening," Harry said.

"I was a farmer's son in Saxony in the thirties. I volunteered for the Elite Guard—the *Verfügungstruppe*. That's simply what one did, not a matter of choice. We were farm boys and boys who worked with their hands. When I joined the Elite Guard, one couldn't have a single filling in his teeth—that's how strict the standards were. You were proud if you got in. They changed the name of the Elite Guard to the Waffen SS and invited mobs of vicious hoodlums to join, but I was never one of them. I was always Elite Guard," Selchauhansen said. They accepted two canteen cups of muddy coffee from Pelwa. Coffee drippings made butterfly splotches on the sleeve of Selchauhansen's jacket, like the camouflage clothing the French parachutists wore. "The SS invented the camouflage uniform, you know. The French used to say we looked like tree frogs. Now they copy our style."

Harry scorched his lip on the rim of the metal cup.

"My father was a member of the Nazi party, of course. What big landowner wasn't? My family died in Dresden," continued Selchauhansen. "It's ironic. You Americans talk about war crimes and war criminals, but what you mean is you won the war and we lost it, so we are the criminals. What your bombers did at Dresden, dropping white phosphorous on top of a city that was already burning . . . Well, that's the story of human history, isn't it? Punish the vanquished? The winners stage a holy inquisition and hang the losers. The French made me an offer: Join the Foreign Legion or be hanged as a loser."

"But the SS is different from being an ordinary soldier."

"I was the Elite Guard of the SS. Not, as I said, a Jew chaser. I was not at Warsaw or the prison camps. We went to Stalingrad and back. I am a *Kopfjäger*. Do you know what that is?"

"A Headhunter," said Harry.

"We fought Marxist terrorists. The terrorists would blow up a hospital train and machine-gun wounded German soldiers. We would find the guilty terrorists and kill them."

"Or kill your hostages."

"Quite so. But we always announced our intention—who are the hostages, and what will happen and why. We set the terms loud and clear and showed no mercy whatsoever. But grabbing hostages and then killing them if you must is a moral thing, not a simple thing. It required examining the heart. It demanded careful consideration of the way one views the value of human lives in the course of history. I think I have learned the lesson my trials were teaching me. Check."

"Check?"

"Look at the board."

"Ah."

Harry moved his king out of immediate danger from a black bishop. How could that have happened, he wondered. Harry had concentrated on his brilliant moves—setting up Selchauhansen for a knockout that would dazzle the self-proclaimed chess master—but he hadn't noticed an open diagonal into the heart of his position.

"Lesson?" Harry asked.

"The world has changed forever. Terrorism is the war of the future," said Selchauhansen. "In future, men will fight the military machines with terror. A few dedicated terrorists can bring down an empire that has no will—or way—to defeat them."

"They say the hydrogen bomb is the war of the future," Harry said.

"Pardon?" Selchauhansen studied the chessboard and fingered a small scab on the bridge of his nose. "The what?"

"The hydrogen bomb."

"I am talking about war. The hydrogen bomb is not war. The hydrogen bomb is total extermination of human life. Hydrogen war can't be fought—it's meaningless, everybody dies. War in future will be fought by terrorism. Individual against individual, idea against idea, hand to hand. The battle we are fighting at Dien Bien Phu is the start of Armageddon, the final war between good and evil. If you don't think evil is real and struggling to take over the world, you are very naïve. The devil is real. I have seen him."

"Listening to a morality lecture from an officer in Hitler's Imperial Guard is too much for me. Let's stow the good-and-evil crap. Your move."

"Check and mate in two."

"What? Oh, yeah, the knight again. I see."

Harry knocked over his king, signifying defeat.

"Seventeen moves. You put up a crafty fight. Another game?" said the German.

Harry began setting up the pieces. They were oriental figures carved out of ivory from Siamese elephants. He felt the smooth, worn surface of the black knight that had invaded his second rank and caused his surrender.

"You say Phibbs overestimated the number of Nazis at Dien Bien?" Harry said.

"I'll tell you how many of us Headhunters there are," said Selchauhansen. "Seventy-eight. Six years ago, when we first joined the Legion, we were nine hundred. The Headhunters are only a few of the Germans in the Foreign Legion. But no other units were allowed to stick together the way we were. The French needed us together as a skilled anti-terrorist unit. See our Headhunter flag on the wall there? See what it says? *Deutschland, Russland, Nord Afrika, Indochina.* Well, there were three thousand of us in 1944, nine hundred in 1945 at the end of the war. Now there are seventy-eight Headhunters still alive here on the top of Lola."

It was the third move of the new game. Selchauhansen said, "Oh, no, Sparrow. Not the king's gambit, please. That opening hasn't been a winner since Napoleon."

"This is not the king's gambit. This is something else," Harry lied. He liked to try the king's gambit against a superior player because the games could become wild. Both sides could be in peril of sudden collapse—not his side alone.

"I am a Headhunter too," said Ali Saadi. His eyes were half-open, sultry, peering at the German officer. With his dimpled chin and straight nose, Ali Saadi again made Harry speculate that some Hollywood Casanova had visited the Arab's mother in the Casbah twenty years ago. He could probably look up which old movie produced Ali Saadi.

"A strange world it is, huh, Sparrow? Ali Saadi was an anarchist until he came to the jungle. Now he is our only real Nazi." Selchauhansen chuckled.

Harry heard a sound like crackling flames. The monsoon rain had begun again. The prickly-heat rash that covered his entire body, except for the sores from the flea and tick bites, made him want to scratch, but there was nowhere to start. He noticed the plaster cracking and peeling on the damp concrete walls of the cellar. Surely, he thought, it must have been a strange fellow who would build a wine cellar at Dien Bien Phu. Harry glanced at his watch: an hour yet before the evening bombardment.

"What about Claudette?" Harry asked.

"You came up here to Lola to get a story for your newspaper, didn't you?"

"Yeah."

"Stop looking at your watch, and I'll give you a good story, a story the newspapers haven't touched," Selchauhansen said. "My girlfriend Claudette is part of it."

"She won't be your girl for long," Harry said. "If we get out of here, I'm going to take her away from you."

Harry glanced up and saw Ali Saadi was grinning at him. Unaccustomed to hearing people speak up to the tall captain, the Arab enjoyed it.

An explosion spattered mud through Saadi's firing slit and shook the ground, but the cast concrete of the wine cellar held firm. Harry listened for more shells that would signal the evening barrage, but there was only the breathing of the men in the cellar, the rain rattling down and sporadic small-arms fire.

"That was a gunner clearing his tube," Selchauhansen said. "You still have time to listen, Sparrow. You'll never win that girl from me by being a coward."

"Nobody ever takes a girl from you, chief," said Pelwa.

The German's eyes drifted back to the chessboard.

"You want to quit?" he said.

"Start another game," said Harry.

5 The captain pinched the black queen between his thumb and forefinger. He tapped the chess piece against his teeth. In the first two games, he had moved quickly. Harry knew the Legionnaire wasn't thinking about chess.

"For us Headhunters, this war here in the jungle is the same war we were fighting in Russia. It's the same enemy: Marxism. We are sworn to fight Marxism to the death."

"Oh, come off it, whoever-you-are," said Harry. "This is an anti-colonialist war mingled with several civil wars. Ho wants a free and independent country."

"You are absolutely wrong. Ho wants a Marxist state. A Marxist state is totalitarian and directly bound to Moscow."

"The words *free* and *independent* probably don't mean the same to one of Hitler's samurai as they do to me," Harry said. "Ho believes in democracy. He says it in every speech he makes."

"Let me tell you how Ho's democracy works in fact. How we saw it in the jungle."

Looking at the chessboard, Harry saw that the game after twelve

moves was all but over. Once again, the black knight threatened
Harry's second rank, where it would fork the king and his rook.
Harry would be able to delay the end for a few more moves, but
winning was out of the question for him now.

He lit the butt of a brown cigarette. On the battalion radio net,
they heard voices speaking German.

"It is true that Ho did not want a war," the captain said, "but who
would not rather win without fighting? The French might have
ripped off Ho's head early, cleaned up their own garbage in Indochina and maybe put off this war a few years. But it was coming.
When the fighting started up again, it was Marxist-terrorist sadism
and brutality that made Indochina into a slaughterhouse. People
don't just fight battles here. They butcher each other. My Headhunters in the jungles, we saw it wasn't the French who started the
atrocities. The French didn't know how to fight a war that relied
more on murder as a weapon than on troops in uniform. They
called my Headhunters to the jungle to show them how to respond
to the Marxists in their own coin. You newspaper reporters are
wrong in accusing the French of beginning the brutality in Tonkin.
Terror and mass murder are Marxist specialties. Stalin invented
extermination camps. His state police tortured and killed their political opposition long before the Nazis thought up the Gestapo. Years
before the camps in Poland you spoke of, there were death camps
in Russia. Ho Chi Minh and Vo Nguyen Giap went to study the
methods of the Soviet Union. You must understand that they are
dedicated Marxists. They are your enemy—not me."

"Ho used to shovel snow for dimes in Harlem in New York,"
Harry said. "He was a dishwasher and a pastry chef and a waiter
in Paris. Giap was a history professor, a bush-league philosopher.
So what?"

Inflections crept into the tall German's voice that showed he was
straining to keep his emotions under control. Despite his impa-
tience, Harry felt himself drawn into the story.

"It is always the civilians who suffer the worst. No matter which
side they choose, they are wrong. In Indochina, if they don't choose
the Marxists, the terrorists chop off their heads with their own
garden tools. If they go Red, we Headhunters get them. If they try

to choose no side at all, they are trapped and crushed between. They cannot say, 'Leave me out of this, I am innocent, I prefer to ignore the situation.' That is not possible. You have to choose, you see. For all the people here there has been no choice but to fight for the Marxists or for you and me, Sparrow. Us. *C'est la guerre,* eh? The big one has begun, and we're on the same side now."

"The French need *you* here to lop off some Communist ears?" Harry said. "Why would they need the SS to do their dirty work?"

"The French tried to be European in their conduct of this war," Selchauhansen explained. "French troops died by the book by the tens of thousands. For Frenchmen and colonial troops to die because of the ignorance of the French government, that was no concern to us," he continued. "But the Headhunters refused to have their cocks sliced off and stuffed in their mouths by Marxist torturers in Indochina. Nor did they wish to be hanged by the neck in France. So the Headhunters fought Marxist terror the only way it could be fought—with terror. The Headhunters searched out terrorists and terrorized them."

"The judges at Nuremberg ruled you guys an army of outlaws and political fanatics," Harry said, tapping a hunk of mud off his heel with his pitching wedge.

"Let me tell you now—don't fidget and look at your watch," the German said. "It is important that you understand this. Marxism is deranged and evil. The worst of the Nazis could be Marxist commissars. There's one commissar we've hunted for years in Tonkin. His name is Chu-Lin. He learned his Marx from the lips of Mao Tse-tung. People who don't obey Chu-Lin, he straps them to the Yunnan Railway and runs over them with a locomotive for the pleasure of watching their bodies fly apart. You ought to write a story about Chu-Lin. Surely Chu-Lin is as interesting as Marcel Cerdan. Why don't you go show Chu-Lin your press card and ask him for an interview? Demand your rights as a journalist. Argue freedom of the press with Chu-Lin.

"Six years ago the Marxists were forcing the Stone Agers in the jungle to shoot French soldiers with arrows dipped in shit or cadaver poison. Now the Stone Agers are shooting with factory-made howitzers and mortars and machine guns."

Pelwa said, "You Americans are killing both sides. Your armies left so much weapons and ammunition in Korea that the Marxists never run dry."

"We're not the only country mass-producing weapons," Harry said. "How about the French and the British and the Germans and the Russians? War makes money. It costs a hell of a lot to kill people. You Nazis made America crank up our war machine, and now nobody can cut it off."

"You're a man of experience—not an ostrich," said the captain. "You know as well as I that the French can't win in Indochina. This war is being fought entirely wrong. If the French had tanks when they invaded Vietnam a hundred years ago, they'd still be stuck on the beaches. Our Viet allies are doomed because we make them do battle Western-style—marching in formation, loaded down with factory-made equipment. All a fighter in this war needs is a rifle, a pouch of cartridges, a knife and a bag of rice. Not a million parachutes tied to boxes of goods. No matter how many crates of toothpaste are dropped into this valley, we are lost. There's nothing ambiguous about this war—the Marxists are on one side, and the rest of us are on the other. But the tragedy is that the big shots in the West respect money above all. As you say, money is all that really matters to them. Do you know about the Oriental Mafias with private armies of thugs in uniform right here in Tonkin? Their chiefs are laughing and drinking in Hanoi and Saigon nightclubs with French politicians and whores, while Communists are murdering French soldiers at their posts in the suburbs. Do you know how Giap's coolies managed to haul supplies here for fifty thousand *bo-doi* all the way from China through mountain passes? By pushing the supplies on the Peugeot bicycles the French still sell them!"

Harry said, "I'm not a political philosopher, but I would bet on greed to overcome any ideology. The lure of the buck will come out on top eventually. It's a lot more comfortable to blame a system than to blame human nature. Greed is what motivates most people. Communism can never work for long."

"You could be an important figure at Armageddon, Sparrow. You have a forum that is seen in the capitals of the West. You could tell the people the truth."

"I tell the truth as near as I can make it out," Harry said.

"You journalists depict the Marxist terrorists as heroes who are fighting for independence and human rights. You don't protest against Marxist outrages. When the Marxists killed three thousand government officials, policemen, priests, teachers, students in Hue a few months ago, there was nothing about it in the press. The Reds tied their prisoners' hands and bashed their skulls and buried them alive. French intelligence has proof of thirty thousand civilians murdered in cold blood by the Marxists in Tonkin. But when my Headhunters kill one terrorist with the blood of a hundred people on his hands, it makes headlines in Europe and America as another French war crime. When my Headhunters rough up a terrorist butcher, there are demonstrations and protests in Paris. The *Daily Mail* writes that five thousand Nazi beasts are fighting the poor agrarian reformers at Dien Bien Phu, and people in London think it is the truth."

"Phibbs is not a good example," Harry said.

"Is he a Marxist?"

"Phibbs? Good God, no. He's a Tory."

"How many people read these stories Phibbs writes?" asked the German."

"The *Daily Mail* has a circulation of four million."

"Four million!" The Legionnaire looked aghast. "Four million people read that shit every day?"

"His paper sells four million a day. They claim six million actually look at it," Harry said.

"How could he write total lies? Doesn't he have any morals? Can't he see what harm he does? People like him make me sick to the pit of my stomach." The German bent a copper .30 caliber shell casing like a fishhook in his hands. He stared at Harry, as if wondering whether he was wasting his breath. Then he grunted and continued.

"A few months ago, there was a photograph on the front page of *France Soir:* six terrorist heads impaled on stakes. More barbarism from the Legion, is what *France Soir* said. The paper failed to mention that the Communists had lined Route Nineteen with bloody heads on stakes—ten per kilometer for forty kilometers.

Press attention focused on the six impaled heads of Communists. But those six terrorists had been top officers in one of Giap's battalions. They had surrounded a French garrison in a stockade defended by a company of Legionnaires and a young Saint-Cyr lieutenant.

"The Reds lined up forty French prisoners two hundred yards from the palisade in plain sight of the fort, then sent a message that they were going to kill a prisoner every five minutes until the French lieutenant surrendered the garrison. The Reds began their executions. They would spread-eagle a prisoner and chop off first his right arm, then his left arm. Then they broke both his legs with an iron bar. Finally they would shoot him in the head. This happened to each prisoner at five-minute intervals. After the first dozen prisoners died, the terrorist commander gave the Saint-Cyr boy one hour to think it over inside the fort.

"The Headhunters were three miles away, in the jungle, hearing the calls for help from the fort on the radio. By the time we could chop a new path to them—using the existing trails would have been suicide—it was too late. The young lieutenant had made a gentleman's agreement with the Reds. He surrendered the fort. When we arrived, we found swollen, naked corpses of Legionnaires. Their flesh had been beaten into a purple pulp and mutilated beyond what even we veterans could summon words to describe. Corpses sprawled in blood over acres of smouldering ground. The stockade was burning, the Buddhist temple was destroyed, the villagers who had begged for French protection against the terrorists were murdered—every man, woman and child. Pelwa found the young French lieutenant with his penis and balls cut off, disemboweled, his eyes gouged out. His eyeballs were placed side by side on a rock. The last thing the Marxists did before they left the village was shit in the water well."

"If the Vietminh are so unpopular, how come we are surrounded?" Harry said.

"The Marxist appeal is simple: Kill the landowners and seize their land. This is popular with the scum of any country. The intellectuals are caught with the bait of independence and change. Intellectuals are too vain to understand what Marx and Lenin mean by revolution. Marxists kill rich people and government officials in the first two waves, intellectuals in the third. All the Asians in Indochina agree on one thing: Get rid of French rule. But the Marxists have moved in to take over from the French. This is no Social-Democratic-Reform party—this is Marxist dictatorship."

"This is also their country," Harry said.

"This is not an Indochinese phenomenon. It is an international struggle for survival. This is *not* a local affair."

"Kill all the politicians," said Pelwa. "Anybody who makes a franc or a dollar from politics—left, right or center—I would machine-gun all of them, without exception, without mercy."

"All the politicians must die," Ali Saadi said.

Harry pushed away the chessboard. He hadn't made a move while the German was talking. He could see no useful move to make. The chess term for it is *Zugswang*—several available moves, but each of them a loser. Roughly, it means you are riding on the pig train. At the very best, Harry was going to lose his last bishop on the next move, and he knew it was senseless to play on against a master of the German's strength. "I don't get paid to argue ideology. Seventy-eight Headhunters still alive is a good story. I'll go back to the C.R. now, if you will excuse me from the classroom, please."

"I'm getting ready to tell you about Claudette."

"Later," said Harry.

"You don't care anymore? I thought you were attracted to her."

"Sure, I care. I just don't want to get stuck up here. You can tell me later."

"Are you afraid?"

"It's your duty to fight to the death—*sans esprit de recul,* what's-your-name. It is my duty to write about it."

"And say what?"

"I won't know until I sit down at my typewriter," Harry said, heading for the door. The empty bins that had once stored bottles of fine wine now were packed with military debris: ration cans, ammunition boxes, shell casings, bandages. The cellar smelled of sulphur.

"There's no wine left, or I would bribe you to stay," said the German. "Isn't wine the weakness of journalists?"

"Second weakness," Harry said. "Curiosity is first."

Harry lifted the cover at the door with his pitching wedge. The canvas was heavy under the weight of falling rain. Thick muddy brown water sloshed over his boots.

"This wine cellar was engineered with monsoons and earthquakes in mind. It is strong and has a superb drainage system," the German said. "Claudette's father designed this wine cellar, himself."

Harry felt the rain drumming against the canvas through the grip of his Haig Ultra.

"Claudette?" he said.

"That's right."

"Her father was a civil engineer?"

"No."

"An architect?"

"Claudette's father ordered this house to be built for the French resident administrator. Her father was an M-5 operator. He controlled the bureaucrat who ran the resident administration office here at Dien Bien Phu," the German said. "Her father designed this house and wine cellar."

"She told me he was in the Ministry of Finance," Harry said.

"He did have an official office in the Bank of Indochina building in Hanoi, but that was a cover. The fact is—her father was an important man in the opium trade."

"A smuggler?" Harry said.

Sitting down again, Harry shook a Chesterfield out of the pack and looked the Captain in the eyes but saw no joking there.

"What do you think is the crop they grow in the mountains around Dien Bien that makes this place so valuable?" said the German. "Do you think farmers raising rice and pigs and chickens are worth the blood that has soaked this valley for centuries? It's true this valley is a roadway to the Mekong, to Laos, to China. But the reason men fight over this place is not the access of transportation. The reason is opium."

"You're telling me the French High Command decided to chal-

lenge Giap to a battle here because of opium? I don't believe it,"
Harry said.

"Who controls this valley controls the opium traffic in Tonkin
and Laos. Opium caravans were gathering here long before the
French ever heard of the place. After you and I are dead, opium
caravans will still be gathering here. Ho wants control of the opium
trade as bad as the French do. Ho sells the opium to buy guns and
bullets."

"But what do the French use the opium money for?"

"You must ask that question in Paris," the German said. "The
sale of opium in Indochina is a French monopoly. To move opium
out of here, you had to have a license from the resident administrator. The Oriental Mafia made their arrangements with Claudette's
father."

"How did you know him?"

"The first time the Headhunters came into this valley, six years
ago, the old resident administrator's quarters had been burned by
terrorists, and a new house was being built," the German said. "The
wine cellar was being dug by coolies. Henri Frontenac, Claudette's
father, was supervising the construction. There was a junior civilian
present, a young bureaucrat wearing a seersucker suit. But it was
clear that Henri Frontenac was running the show. The valley of
Dien Bien Phu was a remote place, a Shangri-la to outsiders. The
Meos grew opium poppies on the heights. The Xas on the slopes
did the work of hauling the raw material. In the valley the Tais
processed the opium. The Tais wore turbans and colored tunics,
and their women jangled with jewelry. The air was filled with the
sweet smell of opium cooking in cauldrons. Frontenac had a detach-
ment of *Garde indochinoise*, local recruits, assigned to protect him
when he visited the 'Seat of the Border County Prefecture,' and he
had protectors among the Oriental Mafia who also guarded him in
Hanoi. But it was regular drill for the Foreign Legion and the
colonial paras to keep an eye on the resident administrator's well-
being.

"A hundred years ago it was the Chinese lording over the opium
of this valley, then the French, then the Japanese, then the Chinese

followed again by the French, and later by the Marxists. Who knows whose opium it will be next year?"

"Who killed Claudette's father?"

"The French say the Reds blew him up, but it could have been an opium quarrel," the German said. "He had sticky fingers."

"But what else? What was Henri Frontenac like?"

"He was a big, jovial fellow," said Selchauhansen. "Always with jokes and laughter and plenty of wine for us when we came to check on him. He kept his hand on his heart and the flag on the flagpole. Frontenac was a grandmaster chess player, as keen as I am. By the way, Sparrow, you had better not run off your mouth about chess to Claudette. That girl could beat you at chess with her eyes shut. She was a teaching assistant in mathematics before she volunteered for the Red Cross."

"Why did you look her up in Paris?"

"She told you?"

"You sent her roses and a calling card."

"I became friendly with her father. He was the type who urges his friendship on you if it's in his best interests to have you like him. Not repulsive with it, just persistently good-humored. When my Headhunters came to this valley, Frontenac was always eager, attentive, pleasant. Couldn't do enough for us. I hate opium. The use of opium is a subhuman activity, but my approval wasn't required, of course. Frontenac used to talk about his daughter. He was very proud of her, showed me new pictures of her every time. Used to say Claudette had her mother's beauty and brains. Her mother was killed by British bombers. The girl was raised by an aunt in Switzerland. She's got an apartment on Île Saint-Louis in Paris. Posh little place—not the student hovel you would expect of a teaching assistant in mathematics. Paid for by a trust fund provided by her father from his profits in opium. Very tough-minded girl, Claudette. Not the political type at all. More the spiritual bent, mystical, Catholic, faith can move mountains, all that nonsense.

"I went to Paris while I was recovering from stepping on a shit-tipped spike that had pierced through the sole of my boot and came out the top of my instep. Because of Henri Frontenac, I was curious about Claudette. Frontenac was a cynical and corrupt man, but the joy of his life was his daughter. He used to brag about her spirituality, her faith in the church, as if she could be redemption for the dirty game he was into up to his neck. A year before I had been in the resident administrator's house drinking wine and talking about the French citizens' having no real will to fight the war in Indochina. A colonial para officer who was at Dien Bien Phu on patrol got drunk and kept asking Frontenac, 'What is our goal? Give me a moral reason for being here—if only something I can tell my men!' Frontenac was drunk, too, and he kept laughing and answering, *'La Cage dorée, La Cage dorée.'* The golden cage, the governor's palace in Hanoi—that was the only answer Frontenac would give. The para officer was frustrated and wept."

Harry said, "A thing like that, it could drive a patriot crazy."

"I'm a Legionnaire, a mercenary. I weep for my comrades when they fall. That's all in the world I weep for anymore."

"But you love Claudette?"

"Oh, yes, I do very much."

"And still you brought her here."

"It was her idea. She thought that by coming here as a nurse, she could do good work for her country—like she thought her father had been doing. She was proud that her father had been in the Ministry of Finance. Don't forget, Sparrow, that girl is French through and through. To her, Indochina is French. Get her on the subject, she sounds like de Gaulle. There's a strong bond between being a Catholic and a colonialist. The Church and the government arrived in Asia hand in hand. Once Claudette got the idea to come here, I couldn't have stopped her. She has a powerful will of her own. I wouldn't have stopped her if I could have. This is, as I said, her war."

The wine cellar suddenly jolted as if a railroad car had fallen on it from a great height. Tinned goods rattled out of the shelves, and the room filled with muddy, smoky mist. As his shoulders slammed against the concrete wall, Harry cursed himself for having stayed too long on Lola. His eyes bounced in their sockets from the shock wave.

"It's a bangalore!" shouted the captain. "Pelwa, cover the door!"

Crashing through the canvas in a gust of rain, a thin little man staggered at them with a bamboo pole stuffed with explosives, a tool for blowing gaps in barbed wire. His eyes made Harry think of cockroaches when you turn on the kitchen light. With a leap, Pelwa was on top of the man. Pelwa's belt knife flashed into the *bo-doi*'s liver with a thump.

Another *bo-doi* stuck his head up from the rain and mud in the doorway, as if he had swum in the trench, and there was a Thompson in his hands, bucking and blasting and shattering glass and spinning tins. Selchauhansen shot him dead with a stutter from his submachine gun.

The radios were a babble of tongues. Harry's ears popped from the noise. Smoke and the raw odor of black powder floated in the cellar.

"They're hitting everywhere," the radio operator said. "First platoon is overrun in the trenches, fighting hand to hand. They want a counterattack."

Now the wine cellar began to shake, and Harry heard the whumping and felt the quakes of a heavy artillery barrage.

"Tell GAP-2 to lift their fire until I call for it," the Captain said.

"It's not GAP-2, sir. It's the Reds. They're throwing everything at us."

From overhead Harry heard the crack of the Chaffee tank firing its main gun and then the coughing of the quad-50's. He heard the C.R. on the radio asking what the situation was—it was LeRuc's voice, sounding quite calm—and Harry wondered how anyone could be expected to answer such a question.

But the captain said into the mike: "The full 98th Infantry regiment is coming to get us. I don't know if we can kill them fast enough. Fire on our forward slopes, please, all the big stuff you've got."

Ali Saadi helped Pelwa lift the flamethrower tank onto his back and adjust the straps.

"Two companies of the 1st BEP are on the way to help, sir," the radio operator said.

The German captain looked at Harry and smiled wearily. "A hundred paratroopers coming to our rescue. That means it's probably not more than forty to one against us out there." He tossed

Harry a MAT 49. "Here's your new press card. Pray for the rain to stop. You do pray, don't you?"

"On occasions like this."

Now there was a new sound: the engines of B-26 bombers. Harry realized the rain had slackened.

"All right, it's time to clean off this hill," the captain said. "Come on. Let's have a look."

Harry followed the German officer out of the wine cellar and stopped beside the banyan tree. They beheld an incredible vista:

Parachute flares were bursting in the sky and drifting, spreading green light in the rain on the slopes of Lola. Peering over the top of the trench, Harry saw endless heaps of bodies in the mud, and thousands of figures moving, swarming from the mountain slopes toward Lola. Bodies had been covered with mud and sandbags to use as revetments, destroyed by shells, covered and used again and again.

Bombs began exploding on the *bo-doi* in the saddle between Lola and the mountains. Searchlights from the mountains crisscrossed the sky, searching for the B-26 bombers, showing the night full of ack-ack. The American-made Lazy Dog bombs—designed especially to slaughter masses of people caught in open ground—skewered millions of steel slivers into the flesh of the *bo-doi*.

Harry saw that the captain had organized the French Union troops. Headhunters, regular Legionnaires and Vietnamese paratroopers attached their bayonets and began to move forward at the tall captain's command.

To Harry's amazement, he heard the Legionnaires and the music. First it was the Germans singing in their own language:

Give us your hand, my friend,
The good soldier remains true to himself
Whether he comes from Berlin or Belgrade.
You die without recrimination,
Alone and unsung, in place of
A Frenchman who did not have to die . . .

Then he heard French voices singing:

When the regiment marches out early,
With the drummer beating his drum,
I would not change places with any duchess.
Her life is no happier than mine.
I want no officer
Because he promises his girl a lot,
It can only be a Legionnaire
To whom I will give my heart.

And then the oddest sound of all: As Harry crouched in the trench, the Vietnamese paratroopers of the French Union arose from the mud of Lola and marched forward with the Legionnaires. The one song that every Vietnamese schoolboy knew was the "Marseillaise," the French national anthem. Written during the French Revolution, the "Marseillaise," was a battle hymn. The little Vietnamese paratroopers in the American steel helmets sang it that way, as they formed a line with the Legionnaires and marched with bayonets pointed straight into the hordes of Vietminh milling on the lower slopes of Lola.

Allons, enfants de la patrie!
Le jour de gloire est arrivé!
Contre nous de la tyrannie . . .

"Screw you, Phibbs! Top this one, Phibbs!" Harry heard himself screaming.

He began sliding and sloshing and clawing down the Metro on the slope away from the FUF counterattack. The uppermost thing in his mind was to get back to the C.R. and write a story about the bayonet charge under the parachute flares, the voices singing in German and French and the mountains illuminated by explosions. Harry fell headlong in the mud and lost the MAT 49. But he kept his golf club in his right hand, and his Burberry rolled up beneath his left arm, as he frantically scrambled down the trench in the general direction of the C.R.

Rounding the corner of the trench in the murky glow of flares and exploding shells and bombs, a creature barred Harry's path. Harry jabbed the parachute-covered figure with his golf club.

"Hands up!" Harry shouted.

The parachute nylon fell away, revealing a Vietnamese boy about twelve years old. The boy wore a harness of dynamite. Harry had stumbled across a suicide sapper. He drew back the pitching wedge to clout the kid.

"Please, don't hit me," the boy pleaded in schoolboy French. "Please, I give up, don't hit me."

"Take off those explosives," Harry said.

"Yes sir, please sir," said the boy, unhooking his harness and lowering the canvas pouches into the muck. "Please, I am not your enemy, I love the French. The Communists made me come here. You're killing all of us. It's a butchery, please, all I want is to go home, please."

"Run for it," Harry said.

"Sir?"

"I said run for it! Get out of my way!"

The boy sobbed with relief.

"Thank you, thank you," he said. The boy started away, then stopped and lobbed something back at Harry. "Oh, this is for you."

Harry's instinct was to reach out and catch what the boy tossed him. With a muffled blast and a shower of mud, the grenade exploded under two feet of water, flinging Harry sideways out of the trench.

Which saved his life. For in the next instant, the boy's abandoned harness of dynamite exploded.

6 "This is the day the Lord has made; let us rejoice and be glad."

Chaplain Tringuard said Easter mass early Sunday morning in the chapel bunker near the hospital. Harry and Claudette knelt in mud among Legionnaires, paratroopers, engineers, PIMs, clerks, wounded, lame, blind. White ground fog, called *crachin,* seeped through the canvas and sandbags at the entrance. Clods of earth fell onto the altar from the roof, which was timbered with coffin wood. Red artillery had kept pounding all night. The Reds would fire thirty shells per minute into a two-acre area and would then move to a different two acres. This had continued for eleven hours.

"Give thanks to the Lord, for He is good, for His mercy endures forever."

Harry heard Claudette moan softly beside him. Out of the corner of his eye, he saw that her mouth was hanging open. He squeezed her shoulder to make her look at him. He felt how thin she had become inside her greasy paratrooper fatigues. She had the vacant expression of the shell-shocked.

"Be intent on things above rather than on things of earth. After all, you have died. Your life is hidden now with Christ in God."

It was three days since Harry had written the story that made Selchauhansen famous in all the papers that subscribed to the *Dispatch* Syndicate. The Reds had switched their tactics at Dien Bien Phu. Only a few in the valley knew that the stand at Lola had become a front-page story, but they could tell that the Communist approach had changed. The swarms of *bo-doi* had stopped; instead, Red artillery smashed the French night and day.

"When Christ in our life appears, then you shall appear with Him in glory. We who are raised in Baptism must live the risen life of grace."

The stand at Lola should have gotten good play in New York, Harry was thinking. The singing would have put it across. The Foreign Legion was famous for its singing during their distinctive slow-step marches, but to sing during a bayonet charge was the touch that made the Legion legendary. Harry had received quick approval for the Lola counterattack story from de Castries. It was good news, at a time when the French needed good news in the worst way. The paratroop officers read the Lola story and told Harry he had done a fine job; they removed his references to Nazis and gave the credit where it belonged—to the Foreign Legion.

After the Lola story was tapped out by LeRuc on the secret telegraph line into Laos, a bulletin arrived that de Castries had been promoted to brigadier general. Langlais and Lalande were now full colonels, Bigeard was a lieutenant colonel and many captains had become majors. In the custom of the service, de Castries would pass his old insignia to Langlais. But de Castries's five stripes were on a red cavalry background. Langlais sat up all night coloring the background black with India ink to make it look like infantry.

Major General Cogny in Hanoi had kept his old brigadier's stars for eleven months. He ordered the stars to be parachuted to de Castries with a personal letter of congratulations and a bottle of Dom Perignon. The package landed on a mountainside in a cave occupied by an enemy Vietnamese anti-aircraft platoon.

The senior officers at Dien Bien Phu had to deal not only with the enemy but hundreds of other matters. They were faced with administration, supply, logistics, weather reports, aerial photography, morale and dinner. The sudden promotions and the success at Lola brought an air of cheer into the command bunker. The most massive human wave attack of the war had been beaten back with such awesome loss of Vietminh life that M-5 reported that General Giap had overruled his Chinese advisers and given up the plan of a *coup de main*. Giap could not afford to throw his troops at the French every day.

Instead, coolies and engineers began to dig toward the French trenches. In places on the valley floor the two armies were thirty meters apart. Harry had tried longer putts than that at Royal Bowling Brook. Giap sent for coal miners. They dug with engineers and coolies. The weather turned freakishly fair. Thousands more tons of goods were parachuted into the valley. More equipment than ever was falling from the sky, but the drop zone at Dien Bien Phu was shrinking into a small target. Like Cogny's brigadier's stars and champagne, most of the parachutes landed in Communist lines.

"This is the day the Lord has made; let us rejoice and be glad. Alleluia! Alleluia! Alleluia!"

At the end of the mass Harry helped Claudette to her feet.

"Why don't you come to the command bunker and sleep?" Harry said. "Get a long rest in an iron bunk with six feet of dirt over your head. I'm worried about you. I want to be sure you're here to spend some time with me after this is over."

"When I was a little girl my father came to see me at school one holiday in Paris. He brought me a picture of a guardian angel watching two little children crossing a dangerous footbridge. He said a guardian angel was watching out for me. I always kept that hanging by my bed. I know that angel is here with me, too. Besides, how would it look, me in the command bunker?" she said.

"Who cares? The bunker used to be full of women."

"Let them bring us all in there then. All the women from the hospital. Let them take our places while we rest."

In corners of the chapel bunker, Chaplain Tringuard and Father

Guidon had fashioned confessionals out of parachute shrouds and storm lanterns. Harry saw a Vietnamese paratrooper emerge from one of the confessionals.

"I'm going to confession now," Claudette said.

"I'll wait for you."

"Don't bother. I'll go straight back to the hospital."

She ducked out of sight beneath the parachute silk. He wondered what she found to confess. Drenched continuously in blood and excrement, what could be her sins? Forgive me, Father, for as I witness souls leaving their human bodies, my thoughts drift to squirming on a feather mattress with a samurai? Who could guess what sins haunted a Catholic girl? Harry put on his Panama hat with the bullet hole in it, picked up his pitching wedge and ventured into the Metro. Being syndicated meant you had to knock out the words, no matter what. Self-trust was the first secret for success for a syndicated man: Get the story.

Harry ducked and twisted and turned from the chapel bunker to the C.R. along the Metro like a veteran tunnel rat. Sergeant LeRuc was taking a break. He was lying on Harry's bunk smoking a cigarette.

"Where's the general?" Harry said.

"Visiting the wounded. Christ, does he ever dread it. Well, I wouldn't like it, either, looking at the results of his work."

Harry rolled a piece of paper into the Skywriter. He thought for a moment, got up and went along the tunnel to the iron coffee urn in the main office, came back and sat down with a steaming canteen cup. Harry lit a *Gauloise troupe;* he had forgotten the taste of Chesterfields by now.

"What's going on at headquarters?" Harry said.

"The general keeps asking Hanoi why they don't send us periscopes and flak jackets for the trenches. Nobody will give him an answer. Hanoi demands a list from us of everything we need to keep from drowning in the monsoon flood: pontoon boats, life jackets, oars. Pretty quiet, otherwise. Why don't you call it 'a mood of cautious optimism'?"

"Stop it, LeRuc. I've got to think."

"How much do you get paid? Much more than I do, I am sure.

It's not fair, the cards life deals. I can write better than you. When I punch your words on the telegraph key I think, it's not hard to do what this man does in return for living like a big shot. How do you get a job like you've got?" said LeRuc.

"Give me an angle, LeRuc. What can I get past them today?"

"The general left a request for you. He wants you to write glorious things about Strongpoint Isabelle. The North Africans down there need a lift in morale. Well, that's an understatement. France needs to know the North Africans haven't mutinied."

The Foreign Legion demi-brigade six miles south at Strongpoint Isabelle was cut off from the main base by Vietminh troops who had laid railroad ties across the road. The North African Legionnaires lived and died up to their hips in water, nakedly exposed to direct fire and shrapnel. It took less than a second for a high-flying cargo plane to cross the Isabelle drop zone. Their resupply hopes did not exist.

"I mean it," said LeRuc. "Colonel Lalande asked General de Castries to mention the Algerians at Isabelle in official dispatches to headquarters, and the general thinks you should praise them in your newspaper, too."

"For what should I praise them?"

"Courage."

"It's not courage that planted those poor bastards in that swamp. Now shut up for a minute. I'm beginning to feel very weird all the sudden. I think the coffee has been poisoned."

The yellow paper in the Skywriter whirled before Harry's eyes. He heard veins pounding in his brain. The air was unusually foul. He felt about to launch a violent sneeze. He realized he had never been so hot in his life. His tongue burned the roof of his mouth. He fell from the chair in a swoon. LeRuc's face went out like a picture on a movie screen when the film breaks.

For more than a week of burning and delirium, Harry thrashed in his bunk. LeRuc diagnosed the illness as "jungle fever." The sergeant scrounged a bottle of one thousand tablets of a sulfa drug that was being tested before sale to the civilian market. LeRuc stuffed the pills down Harry's throat, brought him water and kept him as dry as was possible in the gloomy purgatory of the bunker beneath the monsoon's steady downpour.

Three days into his illness, Harry received a cable from the packet: HUGE PLAY WORLDWIDE SINGING CHARGERS CONGRATS FRONT PAGE NYALLPAPERS EVEN QUOTE ALL TV NETWORKS WORLDWIDE IS BASEBALL STILL MORE FUN BEST GRUBER.

Having learned the obligations of deadlines from Harry, LeRuc decided to fill in for the sick man. Journalism seemed an easy enough game. LeRuc knew he was better at it than Harry. The keys on the Skywriter kept jamming on LeRuc's fingers. Typing was too slow, anyway, for LeRuc's mind. He took six Maxitons and wrote Harry's story in black ink on the back of a map.

General de Castries squinted at the scrawl LeRuc presented at his desk.

"Sparrow wrote this?" said de Castries, glancing up at LeRuc.

"Sir."

"God, the poor man must have lost his mind. Listen to this, will you, LeRuc? 'The multitudinous seas incarnadine.' He must mean the monsoon. 'Bid amaranthus all his beauty shed.' What the devil do you suppose that's about?"

"Sir."

"Well, I'm not actually a critic, LeRuc, but Sparrow must be sicker than I thought. He's delirious. Let's be kind to the poor devil." The general ripped the map in half and threw it in the garbage can. "By the way, tell Sparrow that I didn't put that fellow Selchauhansen in for the Military Cross, after all. Too much Nazi stench. Closets we don't want to open, eh?"

An inquiry came from the gilded halls of the quai d'Orsay in Paris as to Harry's whereabouts and condition. De Castries told Hanoi to inform Harry's bosses that their man had tropical influenza. The announcement of Harry's illness was picked up by all the wire services and appeared in more than five thousand newspapers. Gruber ran a three-column picture on page one in Paris of Harry cheering at Longchamps racetrack in the Bois de Boulogne with a caption that said SPARROW GRAVELY WOUNDED. (It was corrected to "on death's bed with mysterious Oriental pox" in a follow-up story written by Gruber himself the next day.) *Time* magazine used a photo of Harry wearing a fedora and trench coat.

Harry woke in a delirium, drenched with urine-smelling leakage from the roof and walls. A brown dog was sitting on the foot of his bed. The dog studied him. Bewildered but comforted at the sight of someone's pet, Harry sat up and reached out to stroke the dog. The dog's black eyes glittered; a wheezing screech tore from its throat.

Harry leaped out of bed. This was no dog—it was a rat! Harry hurled a boot at the rat. The rat snarled but refused to move. Harry limped screaming into the radio room. "A monster rat!" he yelled. "He's gonna eat me if I go to sleep!" Sergeant LeRuc grabbed Harry and tried to calm him.

"Was it a black rat or a brown rat?" LeRuc asked.

"Brown."

"Oh, there's not much danger from the brown ones. It's the black ones that eat your face," LeRuc said, putting Harry back to bed. The rat had moved, but they could hear it snarling inside the wall.

After a week of fever, Harry slipped into profound slumber with the bottle of sulfa pills in an inch of muddy water on the floor beside his bunk. LeRuc guessed Harry had taken three hundred of the pills. Having given up on a journalism career, LeRuc was relieved to see Harry's suffering lessen and the jungle fever fade away. LeRuc left Harry to sleep in peace, arousing him occasionally with a can of Campbell's soup. Harry would eat a chunk of soup cold with a spoon, drink all the water LeRuc could find him and sink back to sleep.

Harry was prodded awake on the morning of April 30. He smelled wild-boar breath and felt a left hand with the three fingers missing. He sat up, trying to remember where he was. He saw the BORN TO DIE tattoo shaking his shoulder.

"The chief has got to see you right now. Come on, hurry up, you can't be late," Pelwa said, lifting Harry out of the iron bunk. Pelwa laced the paratroop boots onto Harry's feet. "Mister Chicago, it stinks in here. You need to get some air. Whew! Come on, now, that's the good boy. Now you're on your feet. Let's get going. Out the door, Chicago."

Corporal Pelwa led Harry out of the C.R. bunker and into the Metro. Though the mud sloshed over their boot tops, the sky was clear and bright blue. Harry looked up, amazed, at a sky full of parachutes, thousands and thousands of parachutes. It was the biggest cargo drop of any day of the battle. Above the parachutes was another layer of sky dotted with ack-ack blossoms. Way above the ack-ack, nearly two miles high, were the tiny specks of a hundred C-47 and C-119 cargo planes. The pilots refused to fly lower. They heaved their goods out the doors from high above the anti-aircraft fire.

Parachutes were raining down all over the mountains and the valley.

Then Harry heard the loudspeaker:

"The French Army was besieging Puebla. The Legion had been ordered to protect traffic and ensure the security of convoys over seventy-five kilometers of road . . ."

It was a voice broadcasting in French, to the entire fortress and the encroaching *bo-doi*, the opening lines of *The Official Account of Camerone.* This must be the *Fête de Camerone,* the holiest of Foreign Legion holy days. Harry had put it down in his notebook to remember to do a Camerone Day story, but he had lost the notebook and forgotten Camerone until the loudspeaker jarred his memory.

". . . On reaching Camerone Inn, a vast building including a courtyard surrounded by a nine-foot-high wall, he decided to dig in there . . ."

Camerone Day—Harry tried to clear his head as he followed Pelwa through the Metro. A bulldozer tore loose from its parachute and crashed into the side of a jagged mountain. Nuts and bolts flew like shrapnel. Harry could see a a score of tiny figures dangling from parachutes—more volunteers, plunging into certain death. Even worse, Harry thought, they would die in obscurity. Who would remember their names or why they did it? What was the perverse streak in human nature that would force these people to fly halfway around the world to die painfully and uselessly?

". . . He swore to defend himself to the death and required his men to swear the same oath. It was now ten A.M. Until six P.M., these sixty men,

*who had neither eaten nor drunk since the previous day, and despite
extreme heat, hunger and thirst, defended themselves against two thousand Mexicans—eight hundred cavalry, twelve hundred infantry . . ."*

Harry remembered now what Camerone Day was about. Ninety-
one years ago—in 1863—a company of the Foreign Legion had
stood to the death against Mexican battalions from Veracruz, Córdoba and Jalapa. The Mexicans were regular troops. The Veracruz
and Córdoba battalions wore sombreros, but the Jalapa battalion
sported kepis with neckcloths, like the Europeans. From a distance,
Jalapa soldiers could have passed for Legionnaires. Peasants joined
the regular Mexican battalions as barefoot militia.

Thousands of Mexicans would not gather on the Puebla road
northeast of Mexico City merely to pick a fight with sixty Foreign
Legionnaires. The Veracruz, Córdoba and Jalapa battalions had
come to ambush a convoy that was en route to the French Army
besieging the city of Puebla in the service of Louis-Napoleon and
the Second Empire.

The French convoy was headed by siege guns pulled by mules.
But most important, one hundred and fifty mules pulled the sixty
wagons that carried three million gold francs bound for the French
general outside Puebla. It was the entire French treasury contribu-
tion to the expenses of the Mexican campaign. If the money were
lost, Louis-Napoleon would have to give up his conquest of Mexico.

Harry saw the lone banyan tree that marked the entrance to the
wine cellar on Lola. Hearing the loudspeaker booming on and on
about Camerone, Harry ducked under the canvas into the headquarters of the Headhunters.

*". . . The Mexicans were taken by surprise. They realized that, hence-
forth, they would have to reckon with the Legion . . ."*

A Foreign Legion colonel, wearing an immaculate full-dress uniform with braid, medals and polished shoes, was in the wine cellar
reading *The Official Account of Camerone* into a microphone. Harry
recognized him as Lieutenant Colonel Lemeunier, the senior Legionnaire at Dien Bien Phu.

Harry saw Selchauhansen towering at attention in clean khaki shorts and shirt with shoulder boards. Among those assembled at attention, listening to Lemeunier reading on the public address inside the wine cellar, Harry saw Brigadier General de Castries, Colonel Langlais, Colonel Lalande, Lieutenant Colonel Bigeard and Geneviève de Galard.

Pelwa guided Harry into rank beside Selchauhansen.

". . . Inscribed as a battle honor on the colors of the Foreign Legion, and the names . . . engraved in letters of gold on the walls of Les Invalides in Paris . . ."

The Legionnaire colonel read out of a book with a black leather cover.

". . . In 1892 a memorial was built on the scene of the fighting. Ever since, when Mexican troops pass the memorial at Camerone, they present arms."

Yeah, sure, Harry could picture that scene. Mexican soldiers saluting in honor of the foreigners who gave their lives to save Louis-Napoleon's money.

Lieutenant Colonel Lemeunier closed the leather book and unfolded a document that had a gold seal and a blue ribbon. His eyes searched the faces in the wine cellar.

"We begin with you, Private First Class Taurog," the colonel said.

Taurog, sharply turned out in full-dress uniform, stepped forward. Harry had seen Taurog in the C.R. He was the batman for a Legionnaire major. His head was bandaged.

"As godfather, I nominate for a Legion rank Mlle. Geneviève de Galard, sir," Taurog said. Geneviève de Galard had been the original angel of Dien Bien Phu before Claudette arrived.

"Step forward, Mlle. de Galard," the colonel said. "The serial number of Taurog, your Legion godfather, will from now on be your own Legion serial number. You are permitted to wear the Foreign Legion rank of private, first class. Congratulations. Step back, please."

Harry stood and watched as Bigeard was named an honorary Pfc.

Two more Legion godfathers stepped out and called the names of de Castries and Langlais without their French Army ranks. Lieutenant Colonel Lemeunier appointed de Castries and Langlais honorary corporals in the Foreign Legion.

Then the tall German captain answered his call and took a precise stride forward.

"I nominate M. Sparrow. I swear to be his godfather and to honor him with my Legion serial number, sir."

Pelwa nudged Harry in the small of the back. Harry looked up in surprise at Selchauhansen, then turned to the solemn gaze of Lieutenant Colonel Lemeunier.

"Sparrow, you are permitted to wear the honorary Foreign Legion rank of private. Congratulations. Step back, please."

The public address screeched as Lemeunier tapped on the microphone.

"In conclusion, I quote from Colonel de Corta, one of the great figures of the Legion in Africa:

Legionnaires are masons, navvies, electricians, plumbers, carpenters, artificers or mechanics—anything you like. They know how to paint, sew, bind, rough-cast a wall, decorate a room, put up a roof or build a road as well as they can attack or listen to Schumann or Strauss when the band is playing by the sea in the evening. We are not dealing with schoolboys here. Our soldiers are men who know about life and whom one cannot lead up the garden path. They have all worked, struggled and traveled. Their professions are as different as their nationalities. That is why, with the Legion, one can do anything . . .

And I might add, with the Legion one can *be* anything one has the guts for. Thank you, my friends and comrades."

Lieutenant Colonel Lemeunier saluted the assembly in the wine cellar. Everyone saluted back. Harry found himself saluting. An electrician switched off the public address.

"Tradition calls for a bite of blood sausage and a toast to be drunk to this occasion with red wine," the colonel said for the benefit of those in the cellar. "If you will wait for just a few minutes, please. There is no blood sausage, but the wine is on the way. Unfortunately, it was parachuted into enemy country, but we have gone to get it. It shouldn't be too long, if you will bear with us, please."

It had been like this in the Cardinals' locker room after they had swept a series from the Dodgers or the Giants, Harry thought, the same air of pride and mystery and fellowship, with excitement and handshaking all around. He heard Geneviève de Galard tell Taurog, "If we get out of this alive, I'm going to buy you a bottle of champagne."

"What did you do this for?" Harry asked Selchauhansen.

"I owed you. Aren't you honored?"

"Well, yeah."

"You better look like you're honored, then. Don't look like you're taking this lightly," said the German. "The rest of them don't take it lightly, I assure you."

The canvas curtain was flung aside by the muzzle of a MAT 49. Major Coutant of the 1/13 Foreign Legion stepped into the cellar. His face was black with powder burns and mud, his eyes bulging, his yellow teeth bared in a grin. He saluted Lieutenant Colonel Lemeunier.

"The wine is here, sir," he said.

Into the cellar strode four Legion Sappers—legendary giants, the Sappers, all well over six feet tall, full-bearded and long-haired, wearing leather aprons and carrying long-handled axes.

The Sappers placed four crates on the floor, from which dangled severed parachute cords. With blows of their axes, the Sappers opened the crates.

Inside the crates was not wine but *vinogel*—the bitter jelly of dehydrated wine. Mixed with water, *vinogel* made the lips purse like the taste of persimmon juice. But there was not enough pure water in the cellar to prepare the *vinogel*. The Sappers broke open the tins of *vinogel* and passed them around. Like the others, Harry dipped a forefinger in and came out with what looked like a glob of Vaseline.

"*Legio patria nostra,*" said Lieutenant Colonel Lemeunier.

"*Legio patria nostra,*" was repeated around the room.

"To our friends who are in the sands," said Lemeunier, lifting his *vinogel*-covered finger and proclaiming the traditional Camerone Day toast.

"To our friends who are in the sands."

Copying the rest, Harry licked the *vinogel* off his finger. Lemeunier slapped his hand hard against his thigh. If there had been real wine, the wineglasses would have been banged on a table. Shaking the sand out of the glass, they called it. Harry slapped his hand against his thigh.

There was more handshaking all around. Brigadier General de Castries, now an honorary corporal in the *Légion étrangère*, paused and congratulated Major Coutant.

"Where did you have to go for the wine?" asked de Castries.

"Far enough that we blew up three Red blockhouses with *plastique* and killed at least twenty *bo-doi*, sir," said the major.

"Good show, damned good show," de Castries said. He looked at Harry. "Coming with us, Sparrow?"

Harry noticed Pelwa and Ali Saadi kneel down on their hands and knees toward the rear of the cellar and press their ears to the ground.

"I'll be right behind you, General," Harry said.

De Castries, Langlais, Bigeard, de Galard and the others left the wine cellar with an escort from the 1/13. Harry was still looking at Pelwa and the Arab. The captain handed Harry an empty coffee can.

"Go and listen," he said.

Harry knelt and placed the coffee can against the damp earth and put his ear against the can. Listening through the can, the sounds were loud and distinctive. He heard chinking and clunking of picks and shovels.

"In a few more days, the Reds will be directly beneath us," the captain said.

7 The day following Camerone Day was May Day, the holiday of the international Communist revolution. Thirty thousand red flags fluttered on jungle slopes or waved from bayonets poked above the trenches. The "Chant des partisans" ("Companions, freedom is listening to us in the night . . .") and oriental flutes and gongs played from loudspeakers in the Communist dugouts. The mountains writhed with Vietminh infantry. Communist heavy guns were hauled within plain sight of the headquarters bunker.

Listening to radio traffic in the bunker, Harry heard masses of Communist reinforcements, entire new divisions, arriving in the mountains. As the M-5 report droned on the radio, the voice might have been reading lists of shipping notices from the *Financial Times*. Harry had started a chess game with de Castries. As a player, de Castries spoke of Nimzo-Indian defenses, Gruenfeld defenses, English openings. The bartender at The Cooper's Arms could beat him, but Harry did well to get into the middle game. The general had grown somber since the gaiety of the Camerone Day ceremony. The climax was upon them. Something must happen soon. They felt pregnant. Colonel Langlais stomped back and forth in front of the acetate map and cursed the High Command in Hanoi.

"We must have full battalions dropped in here—not mere dribbles of men," Langlais shouted. "The Communists are closing in for the final showdown. This is no secret to anyone. Personnel says we have just over two thousand men able to fight. Supply says we have three days of food."

"How much 105?" asked de Castries.

"Fourteen thousand rounds. We've shot more than that in a single night. What are those fools in Hanoi thinking? They can see the attack coming. Must we fight with our hands?"

De Castries studied the chessboard and looked at Harry with weary amusement.

"The way you play chess, it's like shaking up the pieces and scattering them on the board like dice. Don't you ever have a plan?"

Langlais radioed to Hanoi: "We will win the battle without you and in spite of you. This message, a copy of which I shall transmit to all airborne battalion commanders here, will be the last I shall address to you."

"They'll be calling you a sorehead, Langlais," said the general. "You'll get a reputation as a troublemaker."

"The Geneva Conference begins in seven days. I'm sure Giap intends to cook our asses by then," said Seguin-Pazzis, the chief of de Castries's twenty-three-man personal staff. A cavalryman before he became a paratrooper, Seguin-Pazzis sat on an ammo box, wearing a pair of shorts, barefoot with mud up to his knees. He was burning off leeches and sorting through messages received from Hanoi in the past hour. "Here's a good one: DEFENDERS OF DIEN BIEN PHU HAVE UP TO NOW COVERED THEMSELVES WITH GLORY AND ARE AN OBJECT OF ADMIRATION FOR THE FREE WORLD."

"What do they mean 'up to now'? Do they think we're about to show the white flag?" Langlais said with disgust.

"Dr. Grauwin says there's something odd going on at the hospital," said Seguin-Pazzis. "Wounded men are struggling to their feet and demanding to join their units. There's the feeling going around, he says, that this is the fight-to-end-it-all in this valley. Nobody wants to die underground."

"What does your girlfriend say about it, Sparrow?" De Castries smiled.

"You mean Claudette Frontenac?" Harry said. "I've got nothing going with her."

"I'd like to make love to her," said de Castries. "When this is over, I think I will take a fuck on that girl."

"You always have sex on the brain," Langlais said.

Harry saw an advantage and moved his knight to the seventh rank, forking the general's rook and bishop. It was unlike de Castries to leave such an opening.

"Listen to that rain," said de Castries. "I believe this is the hardest it's rained yet. Well, if it rains on us, it rains on the Reds," the general said.

"Giap can pull his *bo-doi* back into the caves to rest them and dry them out. Our poor bastards have to just sit in the mud and take it," said Langlais.

"You, being an American, you must have always had a secret dream of wondering what it was like at the Alamo," de Castries said, smiling at Harry.

"You can have an Alamo with two hundred defenders. But with seventeen thousand?" said Harry.

"Whatever our fate—you are doomed to share it," said Seguin-Pazzis. "Unusually bad luck for a journalist, isn't it?"

"You ever hear of Little Big Horn?" Harry said.

"Custer's Last Stand? Of course," said de Castries.

"A newspaper reporter was killed at Little Big Horn thirty steps from Custer," Harry said. "Little Big Horn is what this reminds me of, not the Alamo."

"We've set every hand to digging drainage ditches," Seguin-Pazzis said. "A man would rather die from shell fire than drown like a rat in his trench."

"It's tragic, tragic. The wounded piled on top of each other in holes filled with mud. The dugouts collapsing. Men digging their own tombs." De Castries's expression became dull with sorrow.

"That sounds like rain out of biblical times. Just listen to it," said Seguin-Pazzis. "This is what Noah must have heard."

Then they knew it wasn't only rain they were hearing. Over the thunder and rain was the sound of tens of thousands of mortars and howitzers and machine guns firing.

"The final confrontation has begun," said de Castries. The general tipped over his king on the chessboard. "I resign, Sparrow. You're actually improving. What a shame your chess game will be snuffed out with everything else."

For the next six days, Harry could not go outside the C.R. bunker because of the shelling and the rain. The FUF fortress drew in upon itself under the beating of the monsoon and the continual exploding of the shells. Harry listened to the radios. He heard the pilots of C-47's and C-119's refusing to come lower to unload their drops of supplies and volunteer paratroopers who amazingly still arrived each night. Harry was listening when the famous American pilot code-named Earthquake McGoon discovered that the tail had been shot off his C-119. Earthquake wrestled the controls and managed to crash his six tons of explosives into Communist soldiers on a ridge. The last thing Harry heard Captain James P. McGovern say was, "Looks like this is it, son."

The *bo-doi* kept digging closer. Rather than the human wave attacks of the first weeks of the battle, now anywhere from a dozen to a few hundred *bo-doi* would suddenly pop up in their flat helmets, throwing grenades and firing submachine guns. The radios in the C.R. chattered cries and shouts and fire-mission requests around the clock, as the FUF grew smaller hour upon hour.

It was dawn by the clock—in the rain and explosions there was no sense of the time—when Harry picked up a microphone that LeRuc had dropped from exhaustion. While LeRuc went looking for Maxitons, Harry flicked the band to the Lola frequency.

"Hello, Selchauhansen? What's-your-name, are you there? This is Harry Sparrow, over."

"Hello, Sparrow. Glad you're still with us."

"Who is this?" interrupted a voice. "Get off this net. Observe radio etiquette."

"Tell the girl hello for me, Sparrow. Is she holding on?"

"Get off this net, damn it! I'll crush your balls for you!"

"Here, what is this? Put down the microphone!" said LeRuc.

"The girl is okay. I got to go now. Over and out."

LeRuc pushed him roughly aside.

"You're not a radioman," LeRuc said. "Get up and get out of the way."

"What's the matter with you, LeRuc?"

"This is my job. You're a journalist. Go and write a newspaper story."

Messages from Gruber were stacked in a C-ration crate in Harry's room in the bunker. The Bearcat courier had dropped a packet of *Paris Dispatch* front pages that carried the I, HARRY SPARROW two-column boxed head, with the smudgy photo of Harry in the brown Borsalino fedora, and the boldface italic story by Gruber explaining that Harry was gravely ill in his bunker at Dien Bien Phu. A *Daily Mail* piece by PHIBBS: OUR MAN AT DIEN BIEN PHU claimed word had reached the fortress that formations of American B-29's were about to take off from air bases on Guam and in the Philippines to demolish the Red ring around Dien Bien Phu with high explosives. Phibbs reported that Dulles and the American joint chiefs had offered to lay eight or ten atomic bombs on the heads of the Communists in the mountains. Phibbs said the French High Command was considering the American plan, but President Eisenhower was wary of using nuclear weapons on Giap's army.

Two years earlier, Eisenhower and Truman had refused General MacArthur's demand to atomize the Communist Chinese Army approaching the Yalu in Korea, and they had survived the political pressure. Now Eisenhower's decision against atomic bombs at Dien Bien Phu was being appealed to Winston Churchill. Phibbs was probably right about all that, Harry thought. It was the sort of thing Phibbs was often right about, due to his golfing pals in Whitehall. But how the hell would anybody in Dien Bien know? Christ, Harry thought, if they decide to light up the mountains with hydrogen bombs, we'd be the last people they'd want to tell. In the mountains, the Reds could hide in caves. In the valley, the dirt floor had turned first to sand too fine to dig in, and then into marsh. There would be no place to hide from nuclear explosions in the valley.

Harry rolled a piece of yellow paper into the Skywriter. They were all about to die—what was the point of writing a column? The point, he remembered, is I am a syndicated man. They are counting on me. You don't let down the Syndicate.

LeRuc stuck his head in Harry's doorway.

"Get your ass out of here. I'm working," Harry said. "Don't try to apologize."

"You've got a visitor," said LeRuc.

At first Harry didn't recognize the gaunt muddy figure that stood before him.

"Please, Harry. Please. I'm so sick," said the familiar husky voice.

Into Harry's bunker staggered Claudette Frontenac.

LeRuc helped Harry lift her into the iron bunk. She felt like ninety pounds at most. Raw sores covered her face and arms. Her skin was hot but clammy. The large, deep eyes that Harry had admired were sunken into puffy slits. She reached up to Harry as if handing him a flower.

"This is rosemary for remembrance," she said. She plucked another imaginary flower for LeRuc. "This is a daisy for thought."

"She's nuts," said LeRuc. "Got the jungle fever like you had."

"Where's those pills?"

LeRuc dug the bottle of sulfa drugs out of the footlocker under the bunk. They pried Claudette's mouth open with a spoon, but they couldn't make her swallow. LeRuc brought a canteen cup of coffee. Harry dumped thirty of the pills into the hot coffee and stirred it with the butt of his wedge to make the pills dissolve.

"Sergeant LeRuc, damn it, you're supposed to be on duty!" said the voice of General de Castries from the tunnel. De Castries looked inside Harry's room and saw Claudette in the bunk.

"What's the matter? Is she dying?" the general said.

Claudette groaned, and a gush of torrid, excrescent breath hit Harry's nostrils.

"I don't know," Harry said.

"Sorry, old man," de Castries said. "She came to you a little too late. Come on, LeRuc, get to work out here. The radios are all going at once, and half you operators are unconscious. How do you expect to win a war like this?"

"Shit on it," LeRuc said. He shoved the bottle of sulfa drugs into

Harry's arms and followed the general back into the tunnels toward the command bunker.

"Can you understand me?" Harry said to Claudette.

Harry raised the back of her head with his left hand and forced her to drink the canteen cup of coffee laced with sulfa drugs.

"Thank you. That's wonderful," she said.

Harry lowered her head. She was unconscious. Well, he thought, wet clothes couldn't possibly be good for her. He found a knife and cut the laces off her boots. Her bare feet seemed very small and white. He unbuttoned her fatigue trousers and pulled them off. Her legs were white and thin as bone. Harry pulled off Claudette's panties and slung them underneath the bunk. He undid the buttons on her camouflage shirt and slid her out of it. Lying back again, deeply asleep and totally naked, she would have looked like a skinny child except for the mound of public hair. Sprawled on her back, she had the breasts of a boy.

Harry wadded up Claudette's clothes and tossed them in a corner. He opened his footlocker and took out the white linen coat and the cotton shirt he had worn on the flight into the valley in the ambulance plane. Both garments had been washed and ironed and carefully packed away for him by one of de Castries's batmen. The trousers of the suit still hung from Harry's pinched waist as tattered, oily shorts.

He dressed Claudette in the cotton shirt. It fit her like a brief nightgown. He draped the linen jacket over the foot of the bunk. She breathed in deep gasps. There was nothing more he could do for her, but he was pleased that she had come to him for help.

Sitting down at Piroth's old table, Harry lit a *Gauloise troupe* and pulled the Skywriter over closer. Now he felt like writing a column. But what to write? He looked at his watch: 6:30. But was that 0630 or 1830? The ceaseless din of rain and thunder overhead made him lose any clue to day or night. Like most of them in the C.R., Harry was gulping Maxitons by the handful. Nobody had slept in days.

He sat and smoked one brown cigarette after another. He got up a few times to choke more sulfa pills down Claudette's throat, wipe her face and mouth and stroke her hands. He wanted to care for her, make her well, no matter that it appeared impossible.

Harry's door canvas opened. De Castries stood there with a peculiar look on his face, an expression of embarrassment, curiosity and anger. Standing beside de Castries was an Oriental, less than five feet tall, wearing a bamboo helmet with a red star on it.

"They've come to get you, old man," the general said.

The tiny Oriental spoke in French.

"I am Comrade Chou. We have come under the white flag to take you out of here, M. Sparrow."

Harry looked at de Castries.

"It's true," the general said. "There's four more of them out here with a stretcher. They believe you're sick."

"Take me out of here? I don't get it."

"Orders from Chairman Ho," said Comrade Chou.

"They say today is the day they will trample us into the mud once and for all," said de Castries. "Apparently, you've got some readers on the Communist side who want you to come through this alive. Do you actually know Chairman Ho?"

"I knew him a little in Paris. He used to wait on my table at the Brasserie Lipp. I was a hell of a tipper."

"I'll be damned," de Castries said, shaking his head. "Well, you'd better take this little fellow up on his offer, if you ask me. No point in you dying here. You're not a soldier."

The tiny Oriental nodded vigorously, in a hurry to leave the bunker. Harry hesitated. A ticket out of the valley had dropped into his hands.

But he couldn't leave Claudette here. She had come to him for salvation, and he was going to answer her prayers.

"Bring your stretcher in here and pick up the girl," Harry said.

"My orders say only take M. Sparrow," said Comrade Chou.

"I'm not leaving without this girl," Harry said.

"No," said Comrade Chou. "No girl."

"Don't be stupid. Get out while you can," de Castries said.

"Go back and tell them Harry Sparrow sends his personal regards to his friend Chairman Ho, but he wants to share the fate of the French woman," Harry said. "Take us both, or leave us both."

"You are crazy," said de Castries.

"I'm not crazy. The rest of you bastards are crazy."

"You must come with us," said Comrade Chou.

"Not without the girl," Harry said.

Comrade Chou was growing increasingly agitated.

"You come, you come, you come," he screeched.

"Bring the stretcher in here and pick up this girl," Harry demanded. "When Chairman Ho learns you refused me, he'll nail you to a telephone pole."

Comrade Chou unloosed a string of shrill commands in his own language. Harry wondered if Chou might be saying, "Fuck you, Tay pig dog shitheel," but four little men—looking like teenagers in clean green uniforms and bamboo helmets with red stars—trotted into Harry's bunker, unrolled their stretcher and hefted Claudette Frontenac onto it.

When de Castries saw Claudette was wearing only Harry's shirt, he took Harry's linen jacket off the bunk and gallantly tucked it around the unconscious girl. Harry stuck the bottle of sulfa pills on the stretcher under the jacket. He covered Claudette with his Burberry.

"Well, I guess we'll be going," Harry said.

He put the metal cover on his Skywriter, clapped the Panama hat with the bullet hole in it onto his head and picked up his Haig Ultra pitching wedge.

"Right thing to do. Good luck to both of you," said de Castries.

"Good luck to you, General." Harry shook hands with him. "Someday when this is all over, I'll beat you at chess. We'll call that last game a draw."

"Never. You'll never beat me," de Castries said and laughed.

The Oriental stretcher team lifted Claudette out the door. Harry stopped and shook hands with LeRuc.

"Thanks, LeRuc. You saved my life. I wish I could do the same for you."

"That's the breaks," LeRuc said. "Listen, Sparrow, one thing. Will you put in whatever story you write about the finish of this matter that I, LeRuc, truly love my wife and child in Toulouse, and I don't hold anything against my father anymore."

"You can also say LeRuc has won the Military Cross," said de Castries.

"Nice work, LeRuc," Harry said.

With a last look at the iron coffeepot and the plastic-covered wall map, Harry waved to the staffers who gathered in the main office of the C.R. Then he ducked outside, into the rain. He realized the artillery had stopped.

Comrade Chou and the stretcher-bearers hurried out of French Union lines. Harry trotted to keep up with them in the Metro, splashing mud, using the Haig Ultra as a cane to pry himself loose from suckholes, clutching the Skywriter under an armpit.

Abruptly, the faces in the trenches changed. Now they were the brown and yellow skins of the *bo-doi*.

The date was May 7. It was the eve of Buddha's birthday.

8 They plunged into a tunnel shored up by timbers high enough for Harry to walk without stooping. Beside them, Vietnamese coal miners wheeled out carloads of dirt on railway tracks. Heading toward them, from deeper in the tunnel, came coolies pushing Peugeot bicycles with cases of explosives lashed to the handlebars. From the direction the tunnel turned, Harry guessed the explosives were going toward Lola.

Emerging into the jungle, Harry followed Comrade Chou and the stretcher-bearers up a slippery slope. Harry slid and fell and scrambled up again. He hooked his wedge into the crotch of a mango tree to pull himself up the path worn slick by the feet of the *bo-doi.*

The climb made Harry wheeze for breath. His legs trembled. They came to a clearing on a knob of rock. The clearing and the entrance to a cave were hidden from the air by camouflage netting that threw speckles of light on the grass. The stretcher-bearers, Comrade Chou and Harry all climbed over the rock ledge into the clearing at the same time.

Three Communist officers squatted beside a small fire, drinking tea and eating rice. They looked up as Harry clattered over the ledge. A European trotted out of the cave with a Speed Graphic camera. He was a free-lancer Harry had seen hanging around the Press Club in Rome. Harry thought he remembered Miles Kinnick of the Chicago *Daily News* beating this photographer at Ping-Pong and the photographer getting drunk and trying to seduce Miles's wife. Changing plates quickly like a good news photographer, the European snapped half a dozen photos of Harry surmounting the ledge as the stretcher-bearers hoisted the unconscious Claudette into view.

"Hey, Harry, I'm Roman Lazanevich Karmen," the photographer said, extending a hand. "We met in Rome. Congratulations on getting out of the Shit Pot. Nobody else will make it."

"Who are you working for?" Harry asked. The European shot more pictures of Claudette draped in Harry's Burberry on the stretcher.

"I'm free-lancing. Trying my hand at motion pictures," Karmen said. He indicated a 16-millimeter movie camera atop two large black boxes stacked beside the mouth of the cave. "I came to film the end of Dien Bien Phu. But when I saw you struggling up the path with a girl, I thought, brother, what a shot! So I grabbed a few. I think I'll hustle 'em to Black Star. Got a better idea?"

"You know I do—the *Dispatch* Syndicate."

"Bad pay."

"They'll go tops for these."

"Slow pay, too."

"Not this time."

"Okay. I'll hit the *Dispatch* Syndicate first, then."

One of the Communist officers arose from the small cooking fire and came forward with a cup of tea that he offered Harry. As he accepted the tea, Harry realized the officer, whose hair was brushed neatly over his left temple and who smiled at him in a wise and pleasing manner, was General Giap himself.

"Ah, one of the angels of Dien Bien Phu," Giap said, nodding toward Claudette. "You didn't really have to bring her with you,

M. Sparrow. We have no intention of harming the hospital people, especially not the famous angels you wrote about so movingly."

"She's very ill," Harry said.

Giap spoke softly. The stretcher-bearers carried Claudette into the cave. The other two officers followed them in. One had a medical bag.

"We will give her the best of care," Giap said.

Giap was in his early forties, slow and clumsy of movement for such a small man, five feet two. He wore badly cut trousers and a closed-collar tunic with no insignia of rank.

"Where's Chairman Ho?"

"He sends you his best regards," said Giap.

"Then it really was his idea to get me out of Dien Bien Phu?"

"Oh, yes. It was his idea. Chairman Ho says you used to compliment him very highly when he was working as a waiter in Paris. Your compliments bucked him up at a time when his spirits were low. He is grateful to you. He never fails to read your stories in the newspapers. He thinks you are top rate, he says to tell you. He very much looks forward to reading your story on the fall of Dien Bien Phu. I strongly agree. We want you to see the end of the battle from up here, in the front row of the balcony with a perfect view of the show."

"I don't do propaganda," Harry said.

"Simply tell the world what you see, that's all we ask."

Giap beckoned to Harry. The little professor led the newspaperman over to a porch beside the cave entrance. Harry's boots clumped on the timbers of the porch, and there were wooden steps leading down a height of five or six stories into a ravine. With a gentle touch, Giap stopped Harry from starting down the steps.

"Just look." Giap smiled.

At the bottom, Harry now saw, the ravine became a two-lane highway. Lined up bumper to bumper on the highway were Russian-built Molotova two-and-a-half-ton trucks. There were hundreds of trucks. Utterly invisible from the air beneath three canopies of jungle roof, filled in heavily with camouflage netting, this highway, Harry realized, must be the rumored secret highway—the hidden thoroughfare French intelligence had reported was being clawed out of the earth by twenty thousand coolies for the past three months. It ran parallel to the old Provincial Road 41 that led down from the Chinese frontier. The French High Command had dismissed the rumors of such a secret highway. It was impossible, they said, for the Reds to build a road through the mountains and jungle in a short time with a primitive work force. It had, after all, taken the Americans a year and a half to build the Burma Road with all the earth-moving equipment a modern industrial nation could provide. And the Americans hadn't been forced to keep their road hidden from bombers. It was impossible to build a secret highway from Mu Nam Quau all the way south to Dien Bien Phu.

But there it was, the highway, beneath Harry's eyes, with eight hundred Russian trucks on it: the Ho Chi Minh Trail.

"Don't you wonder what surprises those trucks have brought us? Come over here and have a look. You'll see in a few minutes, what is in the trucks," Giap said.

They returned to the limestone ledge. A canvas-covered stool had been brought out for Harry, and a card table set up with his Skywriter on it. A pair of 24-power binoculars lay on a table beside a stack of typing paper and a carton of *Gauloise* cigarettes. A radio operator, wearing earphones, was turning knobs to put a big American short-wave radio set into operation, adjusting the dials while a boy in a green uniform rigged the antenna into the trees.

"Just look at it down there. Isn't it amazing? The real nature of violence," said Giap. "This has been a horribly violent conflict, M. Sparrow. It is frightening what men are capable of."

From high on the ledge of limestone, Harry looked down at the valley where he had spent the last six weeks. He was surprised at how large the valley looked from up here. Even now the main FUF position was still one mile square. Parachutes were falling into the valley as Harry picked up the binoculars. He saw the muddy green Nam Yum swollen with rain, and the rats' caves with the laundry. Using the binoculars, it was easy to find the main C.R. bunker under heaps of sandbags and a thicket of antennae.

Harry sharpened the focus and looked at Lola. He saw the concrete rim of the wine cellar on the hill where the French resident administrator's yellow stucco house had stood. The hull of the Chaffee tank was all that showed above the mud. Somewhere in there, Harry thought, Selchauhansen was probably giving fire commands on the radio. Pelwa and handsome Ali Saadi were strapping on their flamethrower tanks for the last fight.

"The whole world has read at least two of your stories from down there," Giap said.

"Yeah?" Harry said. "Really?" He lowered the glasses and looked down at the little man who smiled with an amiable glow. "Which two?"

" 'The Angels of Dien Bien Phu,' first. That one got the French very stirred up. Frankly, M. Sparrow, it is ghastly for me to think you would encourage such a foul, filthy, corrupt, brutal regime as the French have had in Indochina."

"Which was the other one?" Harry asked.

"Why didn't you put in the story that Captain Selchauhansen was on your ambulance plane?"

"It wouldn't have got through the censors."

"You write that we blew up an ambulance plane, but you don't mention it had a Nazi murderer on it. Can you call that objective reporting?"

"Which was the other story everybody read?" Harry insisted.

"The singing bayonet charge."

"Ah." Harry nodded.

"We have been chasing that Nazi criminal Selchauhansen for years. He's a cold-blooded killer. Your story about the bayonet charge made him sound heroic. He's a madman."

Through the binoculars, Harry could see the concrete burned black around the firing slits of the wine cellar.

A man in green twill popped out of the jungle. He whispered with Giap for a moment. The general smiled and shook the man's hand. Giap turned to Harry.

"I'm telling them to fire the petards," he said.

The radio operator relayed the command. Harry wondered what it meant.

Then Lola disappeared.

Harry lowered the binoculars and looked again. The entire hill had vanished in black smoke. As the smoke lifted he could see the hill was gone. It had collapsed.

Giap's words had set off tons of explosives heaped in the tunnel the coal miners had dug underneath Lola. Harry saw the flash and heard a distant rumble, like thunder underground. A plume of black smoke rose. There was no sign of Lola remaining—no tank hull, no wine cellar, no banyan tree. It was all gone, and there was nothing left of Lola but a crater of mud and water.

"It is time for the surprise from the trucks," Giap said.

The little professor's smile seemed without rancor as he spoke in Vietnamese to the radio operator. This was a day of revenge for Giap, who had spent two years in French prisons in Indochina. The French had shot Giap's sister against a prison wall for political agitation. His wife had died in prison in Hanoi.

Yeee! Yeee! Yeee! Yeee!

Howling sounds, like the cries of wounded cats, filled the air. Trailing smoke, thousands of Katyusha rockets soared through the sky.

The sudden devastation on top of the main C.R. down below took Harry's breath away. The entire FUF center appeared to bounce and light up like a Bastille Day fireworks display.

Yeee! Yeee! Yeee! Yeee!

Thousands more Katyusha rockets crashed into the main C.R. What Giap had called "the surprise from the trucks" was the mobile launching pads of six-tube field rockets called Stalin Organs.

Depots in the C.R. exploded and burned. Uncollected ammunition packages blew up where parachutes had landed them. It was a hurricane of pyrotechnics. Bunkers and trenches were smashed and buried. Not even the deepest dugouts could have withstood the storm of Katyusha rockets that rained on Dien Bien Phu.

Giap twisted a knob on the radio.

To Harry's astonishment, he heard the voice of General de Castries, coming from the C.R. bunker.

"The following strongpoints have fallen: E2, E4, E10. The 6th BPC, the 2/1 RCP, and what was left of the Algerian Rifles," de Castries said over the radio.

"*Oui.*"

"Anyhow, might as well write them off."

"*Oui.*"

Harry realized the person saying *oui* was General Cogny in Hanoi. Though it seemed impossible that de Castries could have survived the Katyusha rockets, the general was not only alive, he was making a report to Hanoi in his calm, aristocratic voice.

"*N'est-ce pas?* There remains at present, in very weak shape of course, because we have pulled out everything we could on the western flank to shore up the east . . ."

"*Oui?*"

". . . three companies of the Moroccan Rifles, but which aren't worth anything, *n'est-ce pas?* They weren't worth anything. They have collapsed," said de Castries.

"*Oui.*"

"Two companies of the 8th Parachute Assault . . ."

"*Oui.*"

"Three companies of BT2, but that's only normal because, as always, it is the Moroccan Rifles and the BT2 which have the most men left because they don't fight."

"Sure."

"*N'est-ce pas?* And there are about two companies left at the 1/2—at the 1/2 Foreign Legion. And there are just about two companies at the 1/3 Half-Brigade. It's . . . they are companies of seventy or eighty men . . ."

"*Oui.* I understand."

Through his binoculars, Harry could see swarms of *Bo-doi*. The valley floor was full of them now. Incredibly, there was the smoke of gunshots fired in defense from the FUF lines. The *Bo-doi* were spreading over the valley like the flood.

And still, General de Castries in the bunker carried on his dialogue with General Cogny in Hanoi.

"Well . . . well, we're holding on claw, tooth and nail," said de Castries.

"*Oui?*"

"We're holding on claw, tooth and nail and I hope, I hope, that by using our means to the maximum, we should be able to stop the enemy on the Nam Yum."

Harry could see *bo-doi* pouring across the Nam Yum on Bailey bridges.

"Hello, hello," shouted Cogny.

"Hello. Can you hear me, General?"

"That by stretching your means to the utmost . . .?"

". . . Would be able to stop the enemy at the Nam Yum."

"*Oui.*"

"*N'est-ce pas?* Even so, we have to hold on to the eastern river-bank or we would be without water."

"*Oui.* Of course."

"*N'est-ce pas?* We're submerged. The three strongpoints east of the Nam Yum have just fallen. I don't know anymore where my wounded are and my unit commanders are trooping around me asking me what to do next. My men are simply automatons falling apart for lack of sleep."

"Tell me, old boy, this has to be finished now, of course," said Cogny, "but not in the form of a capitulation. That is forbidden to us. There can be no hoisting of the white flag. The fire has to die of its own. Do not capitulate. That would mess up all that you have done that is magnificent until now."

"All right, General. I only want to preserve the wounded."

"I haven't got the right to authorize you to capitulate. Well, you'll do as best you can. But this must not end by a white flag. What you have done is too fine for that. You understand, old boy?"

"Well, then, *mon Dieu,* I'll keep here, well, those units that don't want any part of breaking out," said de Castries.

"That's it, yes."

"Then . . . well, how shall I put it? There are the wounded, of course, but many of the wounded are already in the hands of the enemy. There are the service troops. There are the rats of the Nam Yum."

"Of course, yes."

"*N'est-ce pas?* And then, I'll keep all that under my command."

"*Oui,* old boy," said Cogny.

"That's it, then."

"*Au revoir*, old boy."

A new voice spoke on the radio. Harry recognized Sergeant

LeRuc: "In two minutes everything will be blowing up here. The Viets are on the roof. Greetings to everybody."

De Castries took the microphone back. "This is the end," he said.

"Come, come—*au revoir*, de Castries, old boy."

"*Au revoir*, General."

"They're here, they're here," said LeRuc.

"*Au revoir*, old boy."

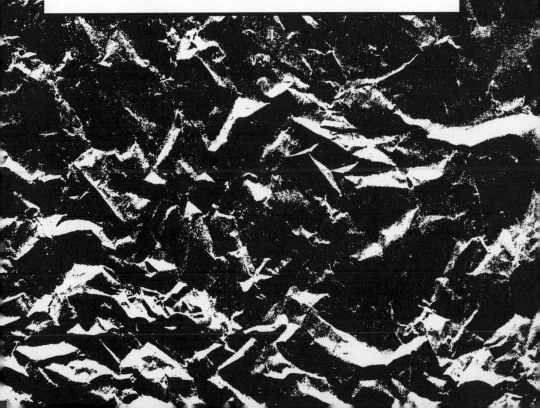

PART TWO

BANGKOK LONDON PARIS

Harry leaned an elbow over the railing and dropped a poppy-seed roll into the *klong*. Red shiner minnows tugged the bread back and forth. One yellow glass-eyed carp rose and swallowed it with a gulp that sent bubbles fleeing across the brown water. A dugout canoe glided along the *klong*, poled by a woman and steered by a man with a paddle. Two naked children giggled and played among buckets of melons and squash headed for markets.

Harry looked across the breakfast table at his host, Jimmy Roma, chief of the Bangkok bureau of the *Dispatch* Syndicate. Roma lived in a floating house on the canal that entered the Chao Phraya River. He wore a white cotton short-sleeved shirt with epaulets and brushed his long white hair back in ducktails. Roma had been born in Kazakhstan, before the Bolshevik revolution. The son of a shah, he spoke twelve languages.

Though he was bureau chief, Jimmy Roma didn't report or write or answer the telephone. Those jobs fell to his assistant, Domi Prittiwongi, a Siamese boy who studied French and English at

Chulalongkorn University. Jimmy Roma's value to the *Dispatch* Syndicate was at a higher level. He was a fixer: He could fix hotel rooms, airplane tickets, visas, trips to temples buried in the jungle, anything the *Dispatch* wanted. With high cheekbones, an Asian squint, skin the color of a Palm Springs tennis pro, white shirts starched and ironed, a gold Rolex watch on his hairless wrist and his smile always ready, Jimmy Roma embodied his favorite American expression: Don't sweat it, baby.

It was to Jimmy's Bangkok bureau that Harry had directed his telegraph copy from Dien Bien Phu—Harry trusted Jimmy Roma to get the stuff on to Paris and New York. And it was to Bangkok and the care of Jimmy Roma that Harry had brought Claudette and himself.

After Harry had written his story on the fall of Dien Bien Phu, and it had been transmitted over Giap's radio from the limestone ledge, the Communist general offered to deliver Harry and Claudette to Hanoi. But certain trouble was awaiting Harry from the disappointed French government and his jealous colleagues. Giap had edited out the details of how Harry came to view the Red victory from the same vantage point as the Communist commanding general. The general had cut out mention of Claudette's escape. But he liked the story and agreed when Harry asked to be sent to Bangkok.

Harry and Claudette were driven in an ambulance up the Ho Chi Minh Trail to the Chinese frontier, loaded into an unmarked Curtis Commando and flown to an airstrip in the jungle near Chiang Mai in northern Thailand. Harry was near collapse from exhaustion. He barely remembered Jimmy Roma picking them up with a Royal Thai Army helicopter ambulance crew and speeding them three hundred miles south to Bangkok.

Harry slept under sedation in a corner room at the Phra Mongkat Army Hospital. Jimmy Roma registered him as "Eddie Snow, tourist." Harry was fed intravenously. Two orderlies stood at his bed-netting to whisk flies and mosquitos and to fan the hot, heavy air that curled around his sleeping figure. When Harry was allowed to wake up, beside his bed stood the smiling Jimmy Roma with a basket of fresh plums, a carton of Chesterfields, a bottle of The

Famous Grouse, and the chief tailor of the best shop on the Charoen Krung Road.

In a cotton robe and rubber sandals, Harry shuffled down the hall to see Claudette. Bottles hung with tubes that ran into each of her thin arms. A nurse in a white uniform sat on a stool beside her pillow. Orderlies fanned Claudette and wiped sweat from her face. She saw Harry and smiled weakly at him. Her lips formed his name. Harry felt excited that she would be coming around and that she depended on him. He had never before liked feeling that a woman depended on him. The Syndicate depended on him: That was his way of life.

Jimmy Roma took Harry for a walk in the hospital gardens. Gardenias and orchids grew among shrines and fountains. A brown elephant grazed in the bougainvillea. It made Harry think of old Siam. Jimmy said the hospital had been the Phraya Thai Palace until the revolution twenty years ago had thrown out the absolute monarchy. Thailand had not been handed over to Europeans after World War II because it had never been a colony. Thailand had been a buffer between the French in Indochina and the British in Burma and Malaya. The Thai government was a coalition of the military, the police, the king, the Buddhist priests and the spirits.

Jimmy said there were rumors in Paris. Harry's stories were fake, Harry was dead, Harry was a Communist, Harry had never been in Vietnam but was shacked up at the Hotel Carlyle in Manhattan with a woman photographer from *Life* magazine.

But the *Dispatch* Syndicate distributed a Roman Lazanevich Karmen photograph of Harry climbing over the limestone ledge with his pitching wedge and Skywriter, wearing his hat with the bullet hole. The figure being lifted onto the ledge in the stretcher at first was called "an unidentified European." In later editions, the United Press bureau in Hanoi identified her as Claudette Frontenac, one of the angels of Dien Bien Phu.

Once it was known that Claudette had escaped the valley, the press searched for her. Everybody wanted Claudette's story, but she was tucked away at Phra Mongkat Army Hospital, registered as "Mrs. Harriet Snow, tourist."

Tailors on Charoen Krung Road sewed Harry two new suits,

one linen and one silk, and four cotton shirts. Jimmy Roma moved Harry out of the hospital into a suite at the ramshackle Oriental Hotel under the name Eddie Snow.

Harry phoned *The Paris Dispatch*.

"Harry, old friend," said Gruber. "Good work. Your Dien Bien Phu stories are the hottest stuff we've ever had. This whole country is cursing you or praising you, but we sold out every edition you were in."

"What does Epps say?"

"Fuck Epps. The Immortal himself sends you 'thunderous con-gratulations.' The brass in New York are putting together a Pulitzer entry for you, dolling your stuff in leather scrapbooks. You're getting the first-class push on this one. The Immortal descended from his tower and ordered Epps to give you a ten-thousand-dollar bonus. We stuck the money in your London account already. Now, Harry old boy, when can I expect your next piece?"

"I need a few days off, Elmore."

"Fine. Take the whole weekend."

"I want thirty days off."

"Impossible. We're counting on you for four columns next week and every week thereafter."

"Elmore, I've never let you down before and I never will again. I'll see you in thirty days. Goodbye."

Harry put the phone in its cradle and smiled. It was good news about the Pulitzer push and the bonus. Gruber had almost made him feel guilty about letting down the *Dispatch*, but Harry knew he had earned the time off—he hadn't had a vacation in three years—and he wanted to get to know this strange French girl he had brought out of Dien Bien Phu.

Bangkok was a down-at-the-heels country town that sprawled across steaming swamps and canals and thickets of jungle. Vegeta-ble gardens grew in patches of red dirt amid tropical flowers. Much of the movement around the city was by boat in the canals. The major avenues were asphalt tracks, bordered on either side by the more populous waterways. The European community was in the neighborhood of Charoen Krung Road, near the wide, brown Chao Phraya River. On the other side of the river was the town of Dhonburi, which had once been the capital of Thailand. The Americans and the British built their embassies far out in the suburbs of Bangkok. They had erected the new Erawan Hotel to service them. Out on Wireless Road, the Americans and the British were cut off from the inner life of the town along the river.

Harry sat on the deck of Jimmy Roma's floating house and watched boats pass with loads of fruit and vegetables. The boats were brightly painted with good-luck symbols. Umbrellas of yellow and green and red shaded handsome people, arms and chests tattooed with lucky signs and sayings, wrists and necks adorned with lucky amulets. Like all people who live close to nature, they believed that all things are inhabited by spirits and that most spirits are malicious.

Elephant's-ear fronds shaded the sun off Jimmy Roma's deck as he and Harry ate croissants, plum jelly, fresh butter, bananas, grapes, pineapples, barbecued sausages and drank coffee with hot milk. The air on the *klong* smelled of fish and water and the barnyard.

Harry could have lobbed the sugar bowl across the canal into a shop where three women and two small girls were weaving silk. The canal was wide enough for four dugouts laden with onions and beans and chili peppers, or for two larger boats with umbrellas covering loads of melons and mangos and pumpkins and strawberries. Never had Harry seen so much food. With every step he took in town, he had to look down so as not to fall over some person squatting at a charcoal brazier, whipping up fried bananas and pancakes. It was no wonder the Thais put such stock in luck.

Jimmy Roma was smoking a Turkish cigarette and reading *Le Monde*. The French newspaper said that the conference at the United Nations Palace on the shore of Lake Geneva had become a tragic failure for France. French Foreign Minister Georges Bidault had been forced to sue for peace in Vietnam and to promise a swift withdrawal by France from the entire country. Molotov of Russia, Chou En-lai of China, Pham Van Dong of Vietnam, Anthony Eden of Great Britain and dozens of other diplomats and their staffs sat in witness to Bidault's embarrassment and anger. John Foster Dulles, U.S. secretary of state, stalked out of the conference and refused to speak to the Vietnamese delegation or discuss the future of their country. The date of France's capitulation in Indochina was the ninth anniversary of the date World War II had ended in Europe. In those nine years of peace, the French Expeditionary Corps had lost 92,000 dead, suffered 114,000 wounded and had 30,000 taken prisoner. The French held a final military parade of the Expeditionary Corps in Hanoi to celebrate the ninth anniversary of V-E Day. Most of the officers and enlisted men in the parade limped. The crowd jeered at them and threw bottles. The French soldiers and the Foreign Legion marched onto boats and sailed off to Europe and North Africa, leaving their Vietnamese allies to face their enemies, the Reds.

On the evening of Bidault's speech in Geneva, French radio and television canceled regular programming and played Hector Berlioz's *Requiem* instead. The Paris Opéra lowered the curtain on the visiting Moscow Opera Ballet Company. Philosopher Jean-Paul Sartre, brain humming from his usual dose of amphetamine, announced it was the end of France as a world power, the worst colonial defeat for France since the defeat of Field Marshal Montcalm at Quebec. The nation was in shock. In the streets of Paris, politicians were greeted by citizens with shouts of "To the firing squad!"

"Well, well, it says here that one of your American senators has his piss hot over Vietnam," said Jimmy Roma.

Harry continued to peer across the *klong* at the women weaving silk. He was pleased at the play his stuff from Dien Bien Phu received in U.S. newspapers. His "Fall of Dien Bien Phu" story was page one in *The New York Dispatch*. *The New York Times* had stuck their man Crichton's story of the French defeat on page six.

"Don't tell me Joe McCarthy is mooching in on Indochina, too," Harry said.

"This is a speech by a senator from Texas named Johnson," said Jimmy Roma. "Listen to what he says about Vietnam: 'Never in all of history has our foreign policy suffered such a stunning reversal. We have been caught bluffing by our enemies, our friends and our allies. They must never, never catch us bluffing again.'"

Jimmy Roma put down *Le Monde* and flicked his cigarette into the canal.

"This Lyndon Johnson, he sounds like the senator from Paris, not Texas. What the hell is he talking about?"

"He's carrying the ball for the oil and construction companies and the military contractors. Our government's not going to give up Vietnam now. We've got billions invested in Indochina and billions more to spend," Harry said. "Listen, Jimmy, how do I get across this canal? I want to buy a piece of silk."

"Not over there, Harry. I'll take you to the right place. You stick with me. Don't sweat it, baby."

Walking through Jimmy Roma's house was a trip through the quarters of an aristocrat of old Siam. It was exquisite, full of jade and ivory, smelling of the oil of polished mahogany and teak, the scent of burning joss sticks. Sculptures of human and animal forms and amulets hung above each door and guarded each corner. Jimmy believed in the spirits. Outside his front door on a painted pole stood a gaily decorated spirit house the size of a birdhouse. It was for the spirits to use so they would not move into Jimmy's house. Spirit bells jingled in a mahogany tree. Beyond was a cluster of tamarind trees that were in turn swallowed by the green foliage of banana plants.

Stepping into the life of Bangkok exploded the senses; everything was brighter and closer and more aromatic than one had expected. Smells of dung, ginger, pepper and sweat assaulted the nose. Voices kept up a clamor. Boats and people sloshed in the canals. Naked children dived off porches and swam to the boats. Women bathed beside their houses, brown breasts bare. Naked young boys and girls chased each other through the grass. The sensation of sexual desire was inflamed by the heat and the growth. It was 110 degrees in the shade. The damp heat pressed against Harry's skin like steam. May was the hottest month of the year in a town where it never got cool. In June the rainy season would start. But Harry intended to be back at No. 5 Cheyne Place before then.

Harry's leather sandals raised puffs of red dust as he and Jimmy walked along crowded Sipraya Road. It was hard to imagine any foodstuffs that could not be bought on the roads or canals of Bangkok. There were glass jars of monkey brains, bamboo cages of grasshoppers ready for the frying pan, bags of snakes touted for boiling in peanut oil. Harry and Jimmy went past the storefronts of Chinese businessmen. "The Jews of Southeast Asia," Jimmy Roma called them, explaining that the Chinese kept their own culture and refused to mix socially with locals. The Chinese worked harder than any people in the world and owned pawnshops, retail stores and restaurants in every Asian city.

"Every couple of years," Jimmy continued, "the natives of Bangkok or Kuala Lumpur or Djakarta decide that the Chinese are the root of their problems. Thais or Malays storm Chinese districts and the Chinese families rush out of their restaurants and shops to defend themselves with cleavers against the daggers and clubs of the attackers."

They turned in to Suriwong Road and stopped at the *Dispatch* Syndicate bureau. The bureau was in a small wooden house on a canal. Domi Prittiwongi met them in the doorway with a proper *wai*, a Thai greeting—hands pressed together in a gesture similar to the Western attitude of prayer. As the lower of the three in social status, Domi Prittiwongi made his *wai* first, lifting his hands higher than his superiors.

Four teletype machines clattered in the bureau, pouring out copy from the *Dispatch* Syndicate, the United Press, The Associated Press and Reuters. To have four machines in a small bureau like Bangkok was a lavish expenditure for the *Dispatch*, but the Immortal believed an era of heavy news from Southeast Asia was near at hand. Keeping four teletype machines and five telephone lines cost the bureau twice as much as the salaries of Jimmy Roma and Domi Prittiwongi combined. Domi was paid 120 *bhat* per day, about five American dollars. Jimmy Roma drew a flat three hundred dollars per month. Even in a town as cheap as Bangkok, three hundred dollars per month would nowhere near maintain Jimmy's life in his floating house full of art treasures. He earned large sums dealing in artifacts from temples and tombs in the jungle. Harry believed Jimmy worked for the CIA, which had placed many reporters in the wire services. A man with Jimmy Roma's contacts was a natural for the CIA—or the Russians. But the important thing to Harry was that Jimmy Roma got the copy through.

"This one is urgent," said Jimmy, holding up a message. He reached for the phone. "Pour Harry a cup of tea."

The young Siamese poured for Harry and asked his opinion of Shakespeare. Domi's English literature class at Chulalongkorn University was studying *Hamlet* and *King Lear*, Harry's favorite plays. With a supply of The Famous Grouse at his elbow, Harry could talk about the melancholy prince who had a problem with his mother, or the old king whose daughters drove him to blind howling on the heath. Domi said that the ghost that came at midnight in *Hamlet* should have been obeyed at once. He believed in ghosts and understood their power, but he could see Shakespeare's predicament: If the ghost had been obeyed straightaway, *Hamlet* would have been a very short play.

Harry said:

Why should a dog, a horse, a rat have life,
And thou no breath at all? Thou'lt come no more,
Never, never, never, never, never.
Pray you, undo this button. . . .

Harry did that speech from *King Lear* frequently at The Pig and Whistle. Domi studied him with Buddhist placidity; to a Buddhist this speech was nonsense.

Jimmy Roma hung up the phone. "That was a friend who deals objects from Tonkin. This week he sat on a mountain in the jungle where he's digging out a temple. He watched the French prisoners stagger past on the trail below."

"Prisoners from Dien Bien?"

"My friend hears there were ten thousand prisoners captured at Dien Bien Phu. The French won't like it that there were so many, but they're dying fast on the road. Men with amputated legs dragging themselves along, blind men, men with chest wounds. He saw a Moroccan who'd wrapped his turban around his stomach to hold his guts in. It's a death march."

"Like the Japanese did to the U.S. prisoners at Bataan," Harry said. Like the Reds forced their American prisoners in Korea to make a death march into Manchuria, he thought, automatically turning the information into a column idea.

"The Japanese marched the Americans only seventy miles," said Jimmy. "My friend says the Reds are marching their prisoners three hundred and sixty miles to a camp on the Chinese frontier. The Reds are whipping and kicking the Vietnamese prisoners on the trail, killing them; the French, they die if they fall. The lucky Frenchman gets a little water and tea and half an ounce of rice per day, but the Vietnamese prisoners get nothing to eat or drink. My friend says no Vietnamese prisoners will survive to the prison camp."

"Did he see any officers?"

"My friend saw officers in a truck with their hands tied behind their backs with telephone wire. He thinks he saw de Castries in a red beret and red scarf with blood oozing from his wrists."

"Hey, Domi," Harry said.

"Yis sah?"

"Pull up a typewriter. This is your story."

"Oh, but, sah, I am not the great writer."

"You ever had a byline?"

"No sah!"

"Type your byline at the top of the page." Harry looked at Jimmy Roma. "Okay with you, Jimmy? It's your bureau."

"Don't sweat it, baby," Jimmy Roma said.

"Good. Now, Domi, type in a dateline. Put Chiang Mai on it."

"Why?"

"The foreign desk in New York doesn't know where Chiang Mai is. It gives your story a ring of authority."

"I see." Domi typed a moment. "Now what?"

"You heard what Jimmy told us. Write ten paragraphs about it, put it on the wire to New York, and hit six bells. Come on, Jimmy, let's go buy some silk."

"But sah! How do I begin the paragraphs?"

"Well, use 'Communists' and 'death march' in the first sentence to wake them up in New York. After that, follow the formula: who, what, when, where, why and how. Answer those questions in ten paragraphs, and you're a great writer. See you later, Domi. Good luck."

They left Domi hunched over his typewriter, chewing on a pencil. The first word he had written was *The.*

"I put Domi's byline on many stories he writes," Jimmy said as he and Harry walked into Suriwong Road. "New York takes Domi's name off. Either they put my name on, or they don't use a byline. Or they throw away the whole story, for all I know. Why didn't you write this story yourself? It seems in your line."

"I don't want to get cast as the Indochina expert. I don't want to be the guy the Syndicate decides it needs in Vietnam, Jimmy."

An American named Thompson owned a silk shop on Suriwong Road. Thompson's weaving was done by a family of Muslim weavers living at the edge of the Bangkrua canal. Thompson persuaded them to weave fabric in commercial lengths for him. He bought aniline dyes from Switzerland to replace their vegetable dyes, which faded. The finished silk Thompson showed Harry was gleaming and iridescent, with a rough texture. Harry stroked it with his fingers. He tried to imagine how it would feel on Claudette's body.

Claudette was sitting up in bed when Harry arrived at the hospital with a package tied in ribbon. She wore a gardenia in her hair and cherry-red lipstick. He realized again how young she was. The bottles and tubes were gone from around her bed. She had gained weight. He saw her breasts through the white cotton of her hospital gown. The neck-string was undone.

"Oh, Harry, I'm so glad to see you," she said. "Give me a kiss, please."

She put her arms around his neck, and he leaned forward, intending to kiss her lightly. Surprised, he felt her mouth open when their lips met. Her hands pulled his head farther forward, their teeth clicked together, their tongues touched. Her tongue explored his mouth. He took her into his arms, smelling her Nivea cream and the gardenia in her hair. Her breasts moved against him, one of them almost out of the gown. He clutched it in his fingers, feeling the nipple. The package fell to the floor. Her sudden passion startled him. He heard the inward hiss of her breath, and then she gently lifted his head and looked into his eyes.

"You stole my breath."

"I swallowed it," Harry said.

She saw the package on the floor.

"Is it for me?" she asked. "What is it, Harry? For me? Let me see it."

She tore open the wrapper and saw the silk. She held the silk against her face and began to cry. It was as if the tears she had been holding back all burst out at the sight of the silk. The sound of her sobbing alarmed a nurse, who called Dr. Sataphong, the chief of staff.

"Here, here, what's going on?" said Dr. Sataphong, rushing into the room. He was a small, cheerful man who had been an obstetrician in Baltimore after graduating from Johns Hopkins. "Hello, Mr. Snow. Oh, she's crying over her gift. A very good sign. She needs to cry. Tears bring her release. You have done well."

Harry sat beside her on the bed. She blew her nose on Harry's handkerchief. He wiped tears from her cheeks with his fingertips. Her eyes were swollen from crying, but they were no longer the dazed, sunken eyes of the girl he had gone to Easter mass with, or the red squints of the apparition who staggered into his bunker. Now they were the eyes that had attracted him in Hanoi.

"I'm sorry," she said, blinking away tears, turning the depth of her gaze full onto Harry. "It's just that it's so beautiful I can't help it. Oh, Harry, to see such a beautiful piece of silk . . . everything was so ugly, so hopeless . . . oh, Harry, this silk, it's the most beautiful thing I've ever seen in my life. Thank you, Harry, thank you."

"Let's go out to dinner," Harry said.

"Tonight?"

"Well, we don't have to wait until tonight. We could go out to dinner this afternoon."

"Give me four hours, Harry. Come back and get me in four hours."

She put her arms around him and kissed him again. This time he was ready for her devouring mouth. The intensity of her kiss scared him a little. He returned the kiss, probing her mouth, sucking her lips. Her body felt electric to him, charged with desire. He wanted to roll her over and make love to her on the hospital bed. "Stop," she whispered. "Please. Come back in four hours. Take me out to dinner, Harry. Please."

Harry spent the four hours drinking The Famous Grouse at the Bamboo Bar in the Oriental Hotel. He sweated at a table under a thatch and looked out at sampans and junks on the brown river. He could see the spires of Dhonburi across the water. Harry tried to remember if he had ever wanted any woman as badly as he wanted Claudette right now. He must have wanted Lady Cadbury in the beginning, but surely not as much as he wanted Claudette. Most of the time with the languishing Lady Cadbury, they had been so drunk they could hardly remember if they had made love. The actress from New York he'd had the affair with last year had excited him, but not with the mystery of physical discovery he felt with Claudette. The actress was a good sport and was ready for Harry, but Claudette thrilled him.

Few women had occupied a serious romantic position in Harry's life. In the sixth grade he had been in love with a poultry-and-egg dealer's daughter, with whom he had exchanged marriage vows behind a henhouse. They traded underwear to prove their love. In junior high school a girl with the face of a baby doll, the breasts of an Australian beach bunny and the moral outlook of Pope Pius had captured his heart. She loved to watch him dive off the fifty-foot board at Forest Park, but she wouldn't go beyond a tight-lipped kiss. In high school he fell in love with a cheerleader who bounced his senior ring on a chain between her breasts and draped his letter jacket over her shoulders. The freshman-class sweetheart at the University of Missouri won his love when he heard her sing "Embraceable You." Harry courted her with all his guile. They were engaged when he joined the army, but while he was in Europe she married the quarterback. Harry fell in love with the wife of a ballplayer when he was covering the Cardinals. It almost got him murdered.

He and Lady Cadbury had lived together on and off for nearly two years before the row over Mr. Peepers's claws led them to reveal how they felt about each other.

"You know the trouble with you?" Lady Cadbury had screamed. "You're a selfish bastard! You don't love anything but your work!"

Harry denied it. He said he loved other things besides his work. He loved golf, for example. He loved baseball, chess, The Famous Grouse, the racetrack, the match game, hotel rooms, airplanes, deadlines, competition, the radio, the theater . . .

"But that's not a life—that's all part of your work," she said.

"What is life then?" Harry asked.

"Life is . . . well, I suppose some work must be involved in it sometimes, but mostly life is having a home to take care of, buy things for, and give wonderful small dinner parties with witty people. I suppose you could play golf in life, a lot of men do it, but you should talk about golf only in locker rooms, shouldn't you? Life is having babies and loving them and bringing them up to make you proud of them. They mustn't have only a mother and a nanny, but a father too, Harry. Life is driving to the country for weekends at grand houses. Life is opera and ballet and late dinners in little cafés in the Strand. Life is cocktails in front of the fireplace. You don't know what life is, Harry. All you do is work."

But in Bangkok he was involved with a side of life neither he nor Lady Cadbury had mentioned. She might have placed that activity in the category of work, too. For he loved the idea of making love.

10 Four nurses, gathered outside Claudette's room, were making excited gestures. Dr. Sataphong hurried to join them. Harry felt a bolt of apprehension. His sandal heels flapped on the tile floor as he trotted, waving the orchid corsage like a relay baton.

"What's wrong?" he yelled. "What are you doing? Get out of my way!"

Scattering the nurses and Dr. Sataphong, Harry threw open the door.

There stood the girl he had been looking for all his life. She wore Harry's iridescent silk around her body like a sari. Her wide shoulders were bare and erect. A crucifix on a gold necklace rode the swell of her breasts. Her hair glistened. Opal earrings trapped the light in tiny flashes of color. Claudette had touched her cheeks with rouge to offset their paleness. She fluttered a bamboo fan to drive the sweat from her face. Her large eyes searched his with curiosity and doubt.

"Do you like it?" she said.

Harry realized he had been gaping at her. He heard the nurses giggling in the doorway.

"The dress, I mean, Harry. All we had time to do with the silk was make it into a sari. Later I'll make it into a real dress."

The way she appeared at this moment, she was some form of genius that was beyond explanation. Harry was stunned, speechless. She looked wonderful and strange, young but wise, heaven's gift to him. Harry's mind tended to fly from hope to hope; now it flew to a glorious future with this girl.

Her eyes devoured him.

"Your wife looks beautiful, does she not, Mr. Snow?" said a smiling Dr. Sataphong. "She is a strong woman. You are lucky to have such a wife. She will give you many healthy children. They will take care of you in your old age."

"Why did you tell them we were married?" she whispered. "Who is Harriet Snow?"

"Jimmy did it."

"Well. Do you hate this sari, or what? Don't keep me in agony. I feel like a bug on a pin, Harry. How do I look?"

"You look . . . uh . . ."

"Oh, damn," she said dejectedly. "I know—I look like a starved refugee dressed in somebody's party outfit. I was afraid I would. I hoped the mirror was lying. I'm so thin."

"You hold that wrapper together better than I could have dreamed, and believe me I've been dreaming."

"You like the sari, then?" she said with a frown of inquiry.

"You are the most beautiful woman I've ever seen."

"Is my hair too short for you? It grows fast. Would you like it down to my shoulders?"

"Your hair smells like orchids."

"The orchid you smell is in your hand." She laughed. "Here, let me have it." She pinned the corsage on the sari above her left breast. Harry wanted to pin the corsage on her, but his hands were trembling and he felt clumsy. He had decided after Lady Cadbury that he had poor taste in women and should not trust himself to choose one. Claudette changed his opinion of his judgment.

"If you're not ashamed of me, let's go to dinner," she said. "I'm always hungry now. I warn you, I eat like a horse."

Jimmy Roma had booked them a table at the Café Paradise on the outskirts of Bangkok. Harry had requested a restaurant that was scenic and romantic, with a minimal insect problem. A black Bentley limousine with Royal Thai flags on the fenders drove them out Rama IV Road into the flowering jungle. The driver wore a white military uniform. The sign above the carved mahogany doorway of the Café Paradise was in the Arabic-looking writing of the Thai language.

The driver stopped the limousine beneath a spirit house in front of the Café. Harry saw water sparkling like crystal through the tropical foliage. Frogs croaked in the dusk. The heat fell on them like heavy mist, suffocating in its intensity. Harry thought he saw figures in the shimmery vibrations of the jungle. The mahogany door slid silently open. The owner of the Paradise greeted them with a *wai,* touching his hands prayerfully, and gave each of them a palm fan. A short brown man with plump arms and round face, he guided Harry and Claudette to their table. A basket of wild plum blossoms awaited them with a card from Jimmy Roma. The window beside the table was covered with mosquito netting. Joss sticks burned in saucers on the table to drive away flies and gnats. To the music of flutes and gongs, two graceful Siamese dancers performed their ancient art barefoot on a small hardwood floor. Customers watched from three sides. A painting of Angkor Wat covered the rear wall.

The tables were occupied by middle-aged Asians and their female escorts. The men wore white short-sleeved shirts, but some had shoulder boards that meant they were military officers. The women wore expensive dresses in Western style. They were not wives. The shadowy figures Harry saw outside were bodyguards. This was a place where military heavyweights could bring their girlfriends. The men looked at Claudette with admiration. But once she and Harry were seated, the men returned their attention to the dancers and to their own affairs, as if they had been told the two *farangs* were protected.

"I respectfully ask the privilege of selecting the meal for you, Mr. and Mrs. Snow, on the instructions of Mr. Jimmy Roma, please."

"Very good. We are honored," Harry said.

The chubby owner bowed and turned to motion to the waiter.

"Why does this man think we're married, too, Harry?"

"We're using a pseudonym."

"Why?"

"We're hiding."

"What for?"

"I didn't know what else to do with you. When you were sick, you wouldn't give me anybody's name to get in touch with."

"There's not anybody, really."

"That's what you kept saying. Well, now you have me."

The owner of the Café Paradise presented them with pride a bottle of Château Lafite-Rothschild 1937. Harry grinned and nodded, "Splendid."

"A nurse showed me a newspaper picture of me on a stretcher, and you standing over me like a 'white hunter' with some trophy he had bagged. Where do people think I am now, Harry?"

"Who knows?"

"Are you trying to keep me all to yourself?"

"Yeah."

Harry smacked his lips at the tang of the red wine and smiled at the owner in appreciation. The owner poured both glasses full of wine.

Claudette glanced around the café. "This room has the feeling of power to me," she said. "I like it. I admire your style, Harry. From the minute you walked into that hotel bar in Hanoi, you impressed me."

"I didn't know you'd noticed."

"You're a good-looking man, Harry. You were wearing the only Panama hat in the Métropole Bar. My father used to wear a Panama hat like yours. He could roll it into a cone, pass it through a napkin ring, and put it back on his head. Tell me, do you live like this all the time?"

"Only when I'm working."

"You must lead a very glamorous, exciting life, Harry."

The owner directed waiters wearing pajamas to set two sizzling charcoal braziers in front of them. *"Tom yam gum,"* the owner said, "hot soup." Harry poked into the soup. His spoon found a fat prawn that had lemon and seaweed clinging to its claws.

"If you thought I was so interesting back at the Métropole, how come you didn't let me know?"

"Harry, I was desperately praying that I would live through each day and do the things that were expected of me. It didn't seem the right time for flirting."

"*Gang pet.*" The owner grinned as the waiter put another dish on the table. "Hot curry chicken."

"I thought you were too madly in love with that German to see me. What was his real name?"

"He wouldn't tell me. He said his family name perished in the war, and his only home was the Foreign Legion. You might not think it to look at him, but Justus had a streak of the romantic dreamer in him. He was trapped by circumstances."

"I can look it up at the archives in Bonn," Harry said.

"Could you? Do they have such a place?"

"Yeah. The Germans keep records of everything. It shouldn't be difficult to figure out which SS Headhunter captain is the man we knew."

"Harry, is it honestly true that you could find out his real name?"

"I could. But why not let him rest in peace?"

"I read your story of the fall of Dien Bien Phu in a *Bangkok Daily Times* at the hospital. You made the blowing up of Lola sound like the eruption of Vesuvius," she said.

"I won't pretend I'm sorry he's gone. A girl like you had no business falling in love with a professional killer. You couldn't have loved him. It was a schoolgirl crush. A mysterious warrior who suddenly appears and excites your curiosity and then dies in battle. It was a fantasy."

"I'm not a schoolgirl. I'm twenty-three."

"You look younger."

"I'm old enough to know. I was so much in love with him, he seemed like my first lover. But now he is dead, so please shut up about him," she said.

"Okay."

"Maybe it was only the physical attraction between Justus and me," she said, shrugging. "I don't think so, but maybe it was the sex."

"Let's shut up about him," Harry said.

"Well, don't look shocked. He was an enormously sexy man." Claudette finished her third glass of wine, and the waiter beat Harry to the bottle to pour her another. "I haven't done well with men. I always was attracted to boys who were difficult. You know— unattainable, moody, unpredictable. Boys who couldn't love or be unselfish. I have been awfully stupid about falling in love."

"Am I going about this wrong?"

"You're doing everything exactly right, Harry." Her eyes sparkled in the glow from the braziers. "I adore being wooed and wanted."

Claudette lightly rubbed her palm across her breasts, caressing herself and the silk.

"This silk, really it's the most wonderful fabric I've ever touched," she said. "You know what this makes me think of? My mother wore a silk dress that felt like this when she went dancing. I remember her coming into my room to tell me good night wearing a dress of silk that I touched with my fingers like this. I was very small."

"Dancing with daddy?"

"Yes. With Daddy. Why would you ask a question like that?"

"Well, there was a war," Harry said.

The owner poured from a second bottle of Château Lafite. "*Haw mok*—hot," he said, indicating a salad of dry chilies, onions, greens and shredded coconut. "*Gai yang*—hot." *Gai yang* was barbecued chicken stuffed with peppers, bacon and coconut.

"It was before the war. She wore the silk dress when I was six or seven years old. Daddy worked for the government before the Germans came."

"And after the Germans came? What did he do?"

"We had a farm south of Paris as well as our house on the Avenue Foch. Mother took me to the farm to be safe from the German bombers, but the British bombed our farm. They said they thought our house was a Panzer command post. Daddy smuggled me out of France and put me in school in Switzerland. He went to London with de Gaulle. He was on de Gaulle's staff. He went back to France and worked for the Free French underground. After the war, Daddy was rewarded with an important job in the Ministry of Finance. Indochina was his department. He went to Hanoi in 1946."

"But you stayed in close touch with him?"

"I saw my father every Christmas. When I got my degree at the Sorbonne, he came to the ceremony and wept. The last time I saw him was at a celebration when I started teaching at Holy Cross School."

"The German said your father bragged about you and showed pictures of you to the soldiers."

"Harry, let's make a bargain. Let's don't talk about Dien Bien Phu tonight. Have you considered that you and I went through what we did for a reason? Maybe we belong together. Maybe we are star-crossed."

"*Kao pat.*" The owner smiled as waiters placed on the table platters of fried rice covered with lumps of crab, chicken, pork, onion, egg and saffron. Beside the rice were dishes of green onions, sliced cucumbers and chopped chilies.

"Hot?" Harry said.

"Hot," said the owner.

"Harry, it's been so long since I've drunk this much wine, I'm feeling a little intoxicated," Claudette whispered. "Will it hurt the man's feelings if we leave?" She smothered a small sound behind a napkin. "How can you drink so much wine without it showing?"

"Newspaper guys are obliged to drink a lot," Harry said. He didn't mention The Famous Grouse he had put away in the Bamboo Bar while he waited for her. "It's the custom of the news profession to stand at the bar and knock back whiskey with the boys all night and then write a thousand words of fast-but-pearly prose at dawn."

Claudette rubbed a fingertip around the edge of her wineglass and looked up at Harry with a troubled drawing together of her brows. He thought perhaps she was about to be sick.

"I'll get you out of here," Harry said. "Don't worry about a thing."

She shook her head.

"There's something I must tell you," she said. "I suppose the wine is loosening my lips, but it wouldn't be fair not to tell you."

He waited.

"In the hospital they tested me for everything, Harry. Blood sugar, adrenaline levels, heartbeat patterns, brain waves. My physiology has no secrets from Dr. Sataphong."

"You don't look as if you've contracted a tropical disease," Harry said. "You look very fit."

"I'm pregnant," Claudette said.

Harry slowly poured himself another glass of wine and lit a Chesterfield.

"What's the old joke—'I'm just a little bit pregnant?' Well, I am. Only a few weeks. Dr. Sataphong is excited about it. He wanted me to tell you tonight, Mr. Snow. Your wife, Harriet, is pregnant.

"The German?" Harry said carefully. "Is he the father?"

"I said I'm only a few weeks pregnant. What do you think I am? Do you think I take lovers right and left? Do you think I wouldn't know who the father is? Of course it was the German."

"Calm down. I didn't mean anything."

"I suppose you don't want me anymore," she said.

"No. I want you," he said.

After a dozen tumblers of The Grouse and five glasses of wine, Harry received the news of her pregnancy through a filter that strained out annoying thoughts of consequences.

"It's strange, but I think I know when it happened," she said. "I've heard women say they knew the moment they conceived, some deep down feeling that it had happened. It's true. I felt it when it happened. It was in Hanoi. The day we flew to Dien Bien Phu."

"What are you going to do about it?" Harry said.

"Go back to Paris and have the baby," Claudette.

"How will you explain it to your friends?"

"I don't have to explain it to anyone but my priest," she said. "That's one thing about being a Catholic, isn't it Harry? Confessions are for the confessional, not for the curious. A man like you, Harry, you must have found your Catholicism handy many times."

"What do you mean by that?" Harry said.

"Don't be foul with me tonight, Harry. Let's try to put everything else out of mind for a few days and enjoy each other while we can," she said. "We'll have to face reality soon enough."

Claudette searched in her purse and handed Harry a small box wrapped in tissue.

"For you," she said. "Open it."

Harry tore off the tissue. He lifted out of the velvet-lined box a small jade amulet in the shape of a cat with large eyes and a heart-shaped face. Harry turned the cat over and over in his fingers, examining it, his smile of pleasure growing wider.

"How'd you know I like cats?" he said.

"Do you? Oh, I was hoping. That's called a *Korat*. It's the lucky cat of Thailand. Your friend Jimmy Roma found it for me, but I told him what to look for. As long as you wear the *Korat*, nothing bad can happen to you."

"Let's go back to my hotel," Harry said.

Harry motioned to the owner and asked for the bill.

"Friends of Jimmy Roma no pay here, please." The owner smiled, making a *wai*. "You have good time, yis?"

In the backseat of the Bentley, driving through the inky, wet night, Harry kissed Claudette hungrily, touching together with sweat and perfume, hearing the tires humming on the dirt road. Birds and prowling beasts screamed in the jungle. The safety pin that held the orchid corsage to Claudette's breast came open and pierced Harry's forefinger. Seeing the blood, she lifted Harry's hand and placed her lips over the finger and sucked it.

Harry's suite opened onto a lawn beneath coconut palms and banana fronds that creaked in the breeze off the Chao Phraya River. He dug through his pockets, searching for the room key. He discovered the key in his fist with a large wad of purple and red *bhat* notes and copper coins. Inside the suite were a sitting room and bedroom with ceiling fans that hummed in the scented air. Claudette opened a screen door and stepped onto a patio set apart from the hedges and bougainvillea by a low wall of white stone. She looked off at the lanterns of the sampans moving downriver toward the Gulf of Siam forty miles away. Harry came out with a glass of wine for her and a scotch for himself.

His eye was caught by Claudette's pale, broad brow and delicate nose. She was thin and looked fragile, but in the last six weeks she had lived through a bloody holocaust that had killed tens of thousands of mean, brawling sons of bitches trained and armed for the confrontation Claudette had survived. Not only had she lived through it, she was carrying another life inside her belly.

Her eyes flicked toward his as she took the wineglass. He stroked her short, silky hair, the nape of her neck. He bent down to kiss her bare shoulder and inhaled the essence of Claudette, a musk of spice and female sweat.

She smiled quickly and nervously and said, "No more wine for me, please, Harry. Could I have some mineral water?"

Back inside the suite, Harry turned on a lamp beside the sofa. Through a door they could see a double bed with a white iron headboard and a coverlet of bright striped cotton. Mosquito netting hung from bamboo poles at each corner of the bed. Harry opened a bottle of Evian water and poured a glass for Claudette.

As he watched her drink, he realized his neck felt tense and his breathing was rough. What was he scared of? The worst he could do was make a fool of himself. He took the *Korat* out of his shirt pocket.

"You say wearing this cat is going to bring me luck, huh?" he said. He put the amulet chain around his neck.

Claudette kicked off her shoes and sat on the arm of the sofa.

"I want to make you happy, Harry. If it weren't for you, I wouldn't be alive now."

"You'd have made it through. You're tough," Harry said.

"No. The *Korat* will always remind you of the depth of my gratitude and my love."

Harry stared at the form of her body beneath the sari. He could feel his heart thumping like a piston.

"Claudette, I'll wear this *Korat* forever."

She stood up and dreamily pulled Harry forward. As his arms closed around her, he heard her gasp. Her mouth opened when his lips brushed hers. He felt her pelvis move against him, pressing close, arousing him. He knew she could feel the sudden surge of strength of his desire for her.

Claudette looked into Harry's eyes.

"You're exciting, Harry. I love being with you." She traced the outline of his mouth with one finger. Then she reached down between her breasts into the sari and brought out one end of the bolt of silk. She placed the silk in his hand as an invitation. In the dim light of the table lamp, Harry took the piece of silk between his thumb and forefinger and began to pull it gently. The sari began to unwrap. Her breasts were revealed as the silk fell away. They looked perfect to him, not heavy but somehow swollen now, her brownish-pink nipples erect. Her skin glowed, luminous as a sea-shell, her abdomen smooth and flat, her hipbones flared, the muscles in her slim thighs curved down to narrow, elegant feet. The silk slipped to the floor. She was naked.

He picked her up and carried her to the bed. Moisture ran down her long neck and gathered in the hollow of her throat. Harry kissed her throat, tasted the salty sweat, smelled her spicy flesh.

They came into each other's arms, murmuring, then beginning to moan, their slick bodies sliding against each other on the linen sheet.

Hours afterward, Claudette said something too softly.

"What?" he asked.

"Mr. and Mrs. Eddie and Harriet Snow, tourists." Claudette said. "Doesn't it sound authentic, though?"

Much later Harry remembered that was when the idea of marriage had begun to grow in his mind.

The floor of the suite was strewn with Claudette's clothes. Dresses, blouses, skirts, underwear lay in neat piles where removed from shopping bags, in heaps where flung from her body. She discarded clothing as she crossed a room like a scout leaving a trail. Her lack of tidiness surprised Harry. No other girl he had known with solid Catholic schooling had been careless or frivolous in placing a doily or an ashtray, much less her own new clothes. When a garment was on Claudette's person, she would preen and inspect herself and ask for reassurance. Like most beautiful women, she was unsure around mirrors and a bit guilty that she looked so striking. Hard-minded as she was and a tigerish chess player, mirrors still made her stop and take another look. If the mirror told her that she had chosen the wrong garment, the garment was tossed aside like yesterday's newspapers.

Harry lay back in bed and breathed the sweet scent of the bougainvillea and the wet, lush grass outside the bedroom windows. He rolled over in a glow of contentment and rubbed a knee along the warm indentation Claudette's body had left in the feather mattress.

"You want to go to the races again today, don't you, Harry?" she called from the bathroom.

Harry hadn't heard her come back to the suite. Early on their first morning together, Claudette had gone searching for a Catholic church. For the last eight or ten mornings—Harry wasn't counting, being unexpectedly happy—Claudette had risen at first light from the bed that had occupied them passionately for more hours than Harry could have believed himself capable of. She had dressed while Harry slept. She would stand and look at him, his face relaxed into a smile of satiation as he snored softly, the lucky jade *Korat* on the gold chain around his neck lying in a fluff of brown hair in the center of his deep chest. Claudette liked the curve of Harry's powerful shoulders, the look of strength in his hairy forearms and his rather delicate hands. She would pull back the mosquito netting, kiss him tenderly and then go off to mass every morning.

She told Harry what she was doing and left it open for him to come with her or not. He said he would start going to mass with her pretty soon, but he stayed in bed and slept instead.

"Well? What about the races?" she called. "Harry! Do you hear me?"

How could he be so lucky? She loved horses. On top of being beautiful, having her own trust fund and being the sexiest person he had ever known, she enjoyed going to the racetrack and betting on the horses. She had grown up riding and grooming horses on the farm south of Paris and at boarding school. She was a good judge of the little Malay ponies that raced at the Royal Turf Club. She'd picked three winners at the track yesterday. Harry reached out of the mosquito net and found a pack of Chesterfields on the bedside table amid a mound of crumpled *bhats*. Claudette had won close to seven hundred dollars yesterday. Not only was she a winner, she was generous about it. The usual practice when Harry took a woman to a racetrack was he gave her money to bet with, she called it "our money" and then, if she won, it became *her* money. But Claudette had turned up with her own money that first week, as soon as Jimmy Roma could put the Royal Thai Bank in contact with her bank in Geneva. At the track with Harry, she called her money "our money," and after she won, it was still "our money."

"Do you love me?" she called from the bathroom.

Harry grinned. "You know I adore you."

"I don't! I'm not clairvoyant. You have to tell me."

Harry looked up from lighting a Chesterfield and saw Claudette come out of the bathroom. She wore a short housecoat and a pair of sandals.

"Tell me you love me," she said.

"Come closer."

"You do love me, don't you?"

She crawled beneath the mosquito netting and knelt on the bed looking down at him.

"Why is it difficult for you to say you love me, Harry? I know what you're thinking. 'Well, I told her last night that I love her, so why do I have to tell her today?' You were drunk last night, Harry. You might say anything when you're drunk."

"Claudette, I worship you."

"Not adore. Not worship. I want you to say you love me."

"I love you, Claudette."

"I've never felt like this before. I do love you, Harry."

The Buddha in the garden wore a garland of flowers around his neck. Flower petals floated in the reflecting pool at his feet. There were always people praying and burning incense at the shrine outside the hotel. Harry liked the little Buddhist shrines around the town. He gave offerings to Einstein's Old Man at the little shrines, but the big temples didn't move Harry. He saw them as garish, dirty lodge halls, always infernally hot, occupied by bald-headed monks peddling jars of pickled monkeys and "Sneeks! Sneeks!" When he wandered to the foot of the Reclining Buddha at Wat Po and discovered that the figure was made of plaster of Paris and chicken wire, Harry quit going to temples. What a Buddha was made of didn't matter to Buddhists, but a chicken-wire saint annoyed his Catholic sensibility.

He was feeling especially good this afternoon. Leaving Claudette napping in the suite, Harry spent two hours in the barbershop at the Oriental Hotel. He had a haircut, shampoo, shave, manicure, his ears cleaned and his head, neck and shoulders massaged. All barber-shops in Bangkok kept private rooms where girls waited to mastur-bate the customers, but Harry tilted back in the barber chair and shut his eyes while the barber's fingers dug into his scalp. Half-asleep in the barber chair, knowing Claudette was waiting for him to go to the races, Harry had never felt so fortunate.

Harry lit joss sticks in a bowl at the shrine, tossed a daisy into the pool and stuffed fifty-five *bhats* into the slot in the little box beneath the Buddha's smiling face. He crossed himself and then made a *wai* to the Buddha, touching base with the Old Man.

Claudette came out of the hotel, looking eager, in a white cotton dress and a white straw hat. It was late afternoon, but the sun was still fierce. Harry took Claudette's hand and helped her into the pedicab. The elderly fellow gripping the handlebars wore a coolie hat. His toenails protruded past the bicycle pedals four inches. The man was proud of his toenails and painted them black—the same color as his teeth. Every afternoon he picked up Harry and Clau-dette and pedaled them out to the Royal Turf Club on Sri Ayudhya Road. The old party liked Harry, who was a big tipper, and he liked the sound of Claudette's merry laughter.

Ringing the bell on his handlebars in exasperation, as the pedicab stalled behind a water buffalo laden with wicker crates of chickens, the pedicab man looked around at Harry and Claudette.

"I am sorry we cannot go faster," the old man said in French. "Pretty soon, they are going to pave the *klongs*. Then we will have many speedings."

"What do you mean, pave the canals?" Harry said.

"That is what I hear," the man said, ringing his bell.

Harry said, "Would we be stupid enough to pave the canals? My God, without the canals this town would be a stinking, suffocating parking lot."

"Many bombers coming to big new air base here, is what they say. We need much pavements for many, many trucks and automo-biles for the bombers and the soldiers that are coming."

"Coming from the U.S.?"

"The United States of America," the man said. "I carry two

United States generals in my cab last night to the Erawan Hotel. I listen to them talking."

"Since when do you speak English?" Harry said.

"I am studying English with my son and daughter-in-law. We will know good English by the time the Americans arrive. We will make very much money indeed."

The old man was Vietnamese. He said he had fled with his family when the Vietminh became rulers of their region. A schoolteacher, he had feared he would be arrested by the Communists and beheaded.

The narrow road in front of the Hua Lompong Railway Station was jammed with humans and animals and machines trying to move in different directions in the crushing heat. Amid the incredible clamor, Harry heard flutes and drums from the windows of a new concrete building that was already cracking and had sunk several inches into the muck of Bangkok. The building had a sign that advertised palm reading. There was a musical ceremony taking place inside. Harry could see golden spires, cupolas and pyramids rising above the boat traffic in the canals. He smelled the stagnant water, fish and human excrement that perfumed the center of the town.

Rajadamnern Avenue was designed by former Siamese King Rama V to compete with the mighty avenues of Paris and Berlin. Its mahogany and tamarind trees offered shade to the broiling traffic. Cackling with delight at finding space to move, the driver pedaled briskly to the intersection at Sri Ayudhya Road and turned right toward the Royal Turf Club. The pedicab halted to allow a procession of monks in saffron robes to cross. The monks carried silver bowls and chanted as they shuffled along. They were escorting a new monk into residence at the Wat Bemchamabophit, the temple across from the Royal Turf Club. That particular wat featured a gold-leaf spirit house, a spinning fortune wheel that could foretell race results, and a huge lingam—a Hindu phallic symbol that could be stroked for luck.

Jimmy Roma greeted Harry and Claudette at the iron-gate entrance to the club.

"You have ten minutes to get your bets down for the third race," he said, escorting them past police in white full-dress uniforms. The old Vietnamese driver climbed into the passenger seat of his pedicab to wait. Harry and Claudette were the only white faces in the crowd. Settling into Jimmy Roma's box on the veranda at the finish line, with a full view of the grass track, they could see shaggy little ponies jostling into rough order for the start, their tiny jockeys in bright colored silks. Jimmy translated the names of the horses from the signboard at the eastern bend of the track:

"Pearl of the Mountains, Love Potion, Desire Me, Devil Racer, Opium Dream, Silom Rose, Lovely Lady, Roughneck . . ."

Bookmakers gathered around the box competing for Claudette's business. Harry saw one bookmaker hanging back, his eyes downcast. Claudette had busted him yesterday.

"What do you think, Harry?" she asked.

"I sort of fancy Opium Dream."

"Very well, then. Suppose we bet Opium Dream on the nose to win for five hundred and put five hundred on Silom Rose across the board?"

Thinking about it later, Harry wondered why he had happened to pick Opium Dream. He had no idea of the pony's record, or even what color horse it was. The name was beguiling, he decided, but somehow it must have been connected with Claudette and her father and the small ponies like these that carried opium in the highlands.

Opium Dream, at 20 to 1, won the race handily. Silom Rose, 12 to 1, ran second. The rest of the day and night became euphoric, like an opium dream, when he thought back on it. As shadows covered the infield grass and the sun descended into the Chao Phraya River in a vivid orange ball, Claudette and Harry continued winning. A waiter dressed in white kept bringing Harry glasses of The Famous Grouse, cold rum and coconut drinks for Claudette and cold tea for Jimmy Roma.

Jimmy's box was on the same shaded veranda as the boxes of the heads of the army, the navy, the air force and the police, and the royal box as well. The Thai officials—attired like Jimmy Roma in white short-sleeved shirts, white cotton trousers, leather sandals and sunglasses—and their wives, decked out in jewels and Western

clothing, began to laugh at the bookmakers and applaud for Claudette and Harry.

After the seventh race, a messenger came from King Bhumibol's
box asking Claudette for the winner in the eighth and final race of
the day. She gave King Bhumibol the name of Plum Lady. The
odds fell from 8 to 1 down to even money and then Plum Lady was
announced as a 2 to 5 favorite.

But King Bhumibol and powerful people in the military and
police boxes informed the bookmakers that Plum Lady would run
at 8 to 1.

When Plum Lady won by a head, the king and members from
the royal and official boxes stood and applauded.

The bookmakers cheered and whistled as Claudette and Harry
left the track.

"They're yelling for you to take your business to the Bangkok
Sports Club." Jimmy Roma laughed as he escorted the two *farangs*
to the pedicab.

"Come on to dinner with us, Jimmy," Harry said. "Let's celebrate."

"Let's take that poor boy Domi with us. He looks like he could
use a good meal," Claudette said.

"Good food is wasted on Domi," said Jimmy Roma. "He's a
vegetarian. Besides, Domi leaves the bureau only to go to class at
the university."

"He sleeps at the bureau?" said Claudette.

"Sure. In the news game, you never know what hour something
is liable to pop," Jimmy said.

They were traveling along Rajadamnern Avenue beside the National Assembly building, heading north past the Dusit Zoo to a
restaurant called the Villa Flora. Harry was riding a rush of eupho-
ria. He wanted to keep on living like this forever. He saw a government office with a sign that said DEPARTMENT OF DOMESTIC
INCIDENT. On an impulse, Harry grabbed Claudette's hand.

"Why don't we get married?"

Laughing at something Jimmy Roma had said, Claudette turned
and looked at Harry.

"What?"

"Why don't we get married?"

"Did you say 'get married'?" she asked.

"Yeah. Why not? All we have to do in Bangkok is sign the register, and we're man and wife."

"Aren't you forgetting something?" Claudette said. "I'm going to have another man's child, you remember?"

It was true that Harry had pushed the irksome reality of her pregnancy out of his thoughts. But now that he considered it again, it didn't seem an impossible obstacle. This was not Lady Cadbury. This was the woman he loved. Let her have her baby. It might not be bad. She had the money to handle nannies and dancing lessons and private schools. It seemed reasonable that Claudette, resourceful and tough as she had proved to be, could have a baby without disrupting Harry's life. At the moment he could see no reason why a child seven months yet to be born should prevent him from marrying the girl he loved.

"Will you marry me?" Harry said.

"You don't need to make an honest woman of me, Harry. Don't ask me for that reason."

"I'm not sure of all the reasons. I want to marry you."

"The office looks closed," she said.

"Would you do it?"

"It doesn't matter if I'd do it, the office is closed."

"Well, Jimmy?" said Harry.

"Don't sweat it, baby."

"I'd be honored to marry you, Harry," she said.

Within twenty minutes, Harry and Claudette signed the official marriage register with a junior clerk and a senior minister of the Department of Domestic Incident looking on. A proudly beaming Jimmy Roma and a sentimentally weeping old pedicab driver with black toenails and black teeth were witnesses.

"You are now married," said the minister.

"That's it? That's all done?" Harry said.

"Congratulations," said Jimmy Roma.

Harry took Claudette into his arms to kiss her.

"Not yet," she said.

"But we're married," Harry said.

"No, we aren't. Not yet. Come on with me."

Claudette led Harry and Jimmy Roma and the old man back to the pedicab.

"Take us to the cathedral," Claudette said. She smiled at Harry. "He knows the way. He's been taking me to mass every morning."

Harry and Claudette knelt in front of a young French priest in the Roman Catholic church on Jetupon Road near the river and the hotel. Jimmy Roma and the old man sat on a polished mahogany pew in the front row. Two French nuns stood in candlelight on either side of the priest, looking down at Claudette with what struck Harry as pitying smiles.

They took the vows. Despite The Grouse, Harry knew what he was doing. He understood what it meant to take a vow in the church.

When the priest finished the ceremony, Claudette's eyes were proud and happy.

"Now we're married," she said. "Thank you, Harry. You've made me full of joy."

He kissed the tears on her cheeks. The nuns hugged and kissed Claudette and appeared to be consoling her. Harry beckoned Jimmy Roma off to one side.

"Do me another favor, please, Jimmy."

"Sure, Harry. What is it?"

"Make certain there is no news story filed about this wedding— not a word. I want our honeymoon to be private. Journalists are not welcome."

"Can I fix the honeymoon?" said Jimmy Roma.

"Who do you know in Singapore?"

"The Raffles Hotel? Don't sweat it, baby."

They were at the entrance to the church. The old driver had gone to the pedicab and was singing happily to the crowds passing in the street. The night air was hot and soupy with mosquitoes. Inside the church, Claudette said goodbye to the sad-eyed nuns.

Months later, after she was gone, he remembered his vow to love and protect her, and the look of happiness on her face when she spoke to the nuns.

12 The morning they arrived at Heathrow Airport in London, the news vendors were selling the *Daily Mail* fresh off the press. The front-page headline said:

NUDE ANGEL OF DIEN BIEN PHU
WEDS NEWSPAPER COLUMNIST

Another of Karmen's photographs showed Claudette on the stretcher with the Burberry pulled back to reveal her legs.

Harry grabbed a paper and began reading, his face reddening with anger.

BY REGINALD PHIBBS
Daily Mail Correspondent

————

Claudette Frontenac, 23, one of the so-called Angels of Dien Bien Phu, was secretly wed to the man who saved her life, columnist Harry Sparrow, 34, in a Catholic service in Bangkok, Thailand, three weeks ago, the Daily Mail has learned.

I uncovered this exclusive story in interviews with highly placed church officials in Paris, where the marriage documents have been forwarded from Bangkok.

The new Mrs. Sparrow and her husband were in Paris the past few days staying at her apartment on Île Saint-Louis. There was no answer when I knocked repeatedly at their door and rang their phone.

Neighbors told me the happily wedded couple were returning to London, where Harry Sparrow keeps a flat in Chelsea. Sparrow is little known in London, but his newspaper stories are widely read in The Paris Dispatch, The New York Dispatch and other papers around the world that subscribe to the Dispatch Syndicate.

Sparrow is thought to be the leading candidate to win the Pulitzer Prize—a trophy unknown here but regarded as an honor in the U.S.—for his reporting from inside the doomed French fortress of Dien Bien Phu.

When Dien Bien Phu fell to the Reds on May 8, Sparrow and his girlfriend somehow escaped the fate of the wretched French soldiers and watched the final battle from a mountaintop beside Communist General Giap.

French officials are extremely critical of Sparrow's behavior in running out on his beleaguered comrades and reporting their demise from what Foreign Minister Bideault has called "obviously a Red-tainted point of view."

No political criticism has been leveled at young Claudette Frontenac, daughter of a Finance Ministry official murdered by a car bomb in Hanoi last year. It is known to correspondents near Dien Bien Phu during the fighting—where your Daily Mail reporter was covering the carnage long before Sparrow luckily arrived on the scene—that Mlle. Frontenac worked gallantly in the French hospital beside Mlle. Geneviève de Galard, the first "Angel of Dien Bien Phu." According to the European photographer who shot the accompanying picture, Frontenac was unconscious and nude except for a raincoat when carried on a stretcher into the Communist position.

The news of the wedding came as a shock to Sparrow's former fiancée, Lady Gwendoline Cadbury. "I feel sorry for the poor girl who married that two-legged rat," she told me. Lady Cadbury considered herself engaged to Sparrow when he went to Indochina and jilted her. "But I am happy to have him out of my life. He was often an embarrassment to me," she said. Sparrow's housekeeper, Mrs. Gerta Primrose, refused to say when he is expected to return home or to express an opinion of his marriage to a French heroine. "Who ever knows for sure?" is all she would reply to my questions.

Mrs. Frontenac-Sparrow is a graduate of the Sorbonne with a degree in mathematics. She taught at Holy Cross, a Catho-

lic girls' school in Paris, before volunteering as an air nurse for the French Union
Forces. Speculation is that she asked to be
sent to Indochina to take some measure of
revenge against the Communists who
murdered her father, a former hero of the
Free French underground in World War
II.

If I may insert a personal word here to
my colleague, with whom I peered across
many a battlement during the thick of the
fighting in France, Belgium and Germany, as well as Indochina, let me say,
"Congratulations, Harry, and welcome
home. Sorry I had to scoop you on your
own wedding, old chum."

Harry heard a cry at his shoulder. Claudette had seen the headline.
She jerked the paper out of his hands and stared at the photograph.
Her face in the picture was indistinct but her legs were exposed
almost to the crotch.

"How can they do this?" she said.

"You're news," he said grimly. "We can't stop it."

"I don't want to be in the newspaper, Harry."

"They'll be all over you the next few days. The best thing we can
do is call a press conference and tell our story."

"But I don't want to tell our story."

"If we tell them now, you'll be in the news for a few days. Then
something else will take your place, and the reporters will forget
you. If we try to hide, they'll chase you for the rest of your life."

"But, Harry, you're a reporter. If marrying me is news, why
didn't you write it?"

"That's what my bosses will want to know."

"Tell me first."

"I didn't want reporters in bed with us during our honeymoon."

"I'm grateful for that at least."

"We don't tell them the whole story. We don't mention the

German. He's a personal thing between you and me. He's nobody else's business."

"Our marriage is nobody else's business," she said.

"One more thing about the press conference."

"What?"

"The photographers will ask you to lift your skirt and show your legs."

"But that's insane. They wouldn't dare. What do my legs have to do with anything?"

"We'll wrap your legs in bandages. Call it 'contagious tropical phlebitis.' Look ugly, discourage them."

"I don't like the newspaper business, Harry."

"Once this press conference is over, it'll be fun, I promise. We'll go to France for the races, we'll stalk the salmon in Scotland. I'll show off my high diving at Cap Ferrat. You didn't know I'm a great diver, did you? It'll be a wonderful life, Claudette. In the winter we'll go to Chamonix to ski. I'll bet you're a first-class skier."

"In the winter you can ski down my belly. I'll be very pregnant."

13 "Must be the devil for a sod to be newly wed to a wealthy, young, lovely French heroine. Oh yes, you have been the celebrity couple of the summer, no doubt about it, Harry. Don't it frost your balls?"

A stranger in The Pig and Whistle might have thought the eight men were standing at parade rest. Each had both hands crossed in the small of his back as he faced the bar. This left untended the cigarettes, cigars and pipes puffing furiously in their mouths.

They were playing the match game.

"I am speaking to you only as the game requires, Phibbs," replied Harry. "Ask me no questions about my private life. Leave my wife alone. Of all the assholes in Fleet Street, you're the only one who still pesters her. I have *told* you to leave the girl alone. I will punch you in the nose if you try to invade our privacy again."

"Aha! Mark this day on your calendars, my friends," Phibbs said. "This is the day Harry admits he can dish it out but he can't take it. This man has trampled on more private lives than Scotland Yard."

Thoughtfully, Harry placed his left fist on the bar.

In a moment, seven more left fists landed on the bar. Eight right hands reached for drinks and smokes. Harry had the maximum three matches hidden in his fist. If his colleagues were holding likewise, the correct guess would be twenty-four. Pound notes were stacked beneath an ashtray. In the nine years since Phibbs had taught him the match game in the bar at the Ritz Hotel in Paris, Harry believed he was several thousand pounds ahead of Phibbs in the betting.

"After all, Harry, that Russian film chap who took your picture told me your bride was nude under the trenchcoat. I didn't make it up. The photograph proves it."

"She was wearing clothes. Karmen is a liar. He faked his movie of the final attack on the command bunker. He was with me when the bunker fell. He went down later and staged the attack again for his camera. He lied to you about Claudette. But what am I talking to you for? You're on my shit list forever."

"Are you chaps going to play matches or not?" said Jocko Conlan. He was an ex–Spitfire pilot who covered golf and boxing for the *Evening Star*. His gray wool trousers concealed a wooden leg.

"But you're syndicated, Harry. You're an established person, a self-made man. You go where you want and do what you please. I'm only a drudge who depends on the kindness of editors," Phibbs said.

"All right, then, fifteen. I say fifteen, damn it all," said Jocko.

"A word of advice on marriage," said Phibbs. "Don't be a typical American and treat her reverently. Women don't like being on a pedestal. They can't live up to lofty standards of conduct and virtue. A steady, consistent husband makes a wife yearn for more interesting company. Be yourself, Harry."

"Listen to Phibbs, Harry. He knows all about women. He should—with five ex-wives of his own roaming around out there," said Burleigh Crenshaw, who covered Whitehall for the *Sunday Standard*. He was a tall man with stooped shoulders, his body bent like the pipe he smoked.

"Yes, listen to me, indeed," Phibbs said. "Your wife fell in love with you for the way you wore your hat, Harry. Women adore stupid touches like that. As long as you parade about in snappy clothes and handle headwaiters and make a decent fourth at bridge, a woman will put up with you until you run screaming."

"Perhaps if you changed tailors, you might find yourself a sixth wife, Phibbs," said Nigel Meredith, city editor of the *News-Chronicle*. A Savile Row man, Meredith sneered at Phibbs in his rumpled blazer and slacks that stopped at the ankles, revealing white socks and brown brogans.

"I don't want another wife," Phibbs said. "I'll tell you chums a fact that's sad but true. I loved every lady I married, loved them with all my soul. It's sad but true that a woman will never leave you—unless you love her."

It wasn't that Harry preferred the company of Phibbs and the boys at The Pig and Whistle to spending another entire evening with Claudette—though that was certainly part of it—but after a few rounds of the match game and sloshes of The Grouse, it became difficult to make himself want to leave.

"I knew you drank a lot, but I didn't realize how much. Why *do* you drink so much?" she said that morning as he sat at the kitchen table with his hands squeezing his skull, his stomach knotting at the sight of two fried eggs sunny-side up and runny.

Mrs. Primrose faithfully scrounged London to keep him supplied with eggs for breakfast. Though German bombs had not fallen on London in nine years, many areas of the city remained in ruin, and items such as eggs were still scarce. What happened to eggs when Claudette fried them was a disaster. Harry had thought every Frenchwoman was a good cook, but Claudette had no hand for the kitchen. As a dutiful bride she insisted on making his breakfast, and he tried to eat it.

Claudette sat at the other end of the table that morning, stroking the loudly purring Mr. Peepers in her lap and looking at Harry as if he were some merchant sailor who had awakened in her bed.

"I'm sure you thought you were clever last night," Claudette had said. "Sneaking out of the theater to slop down whiskey and leaving me to see the third act alone. Well, I don't blame you so much for

that. These new British playwrights are awfully boring and dirty.
But I hated the drunken laughter and the wisecracks when I tried
to tell you what I thought of the play. Then you topped off the
evening by raping me."

Harry peered between his fingers at his wife.

"We made love," he said.

"You didn't take off your socks or your wristwatch," she said in
a rising temper. "You didn't lead up to it with any affection. You
didn't care if I wanted to or not. You wrestled me down on the bed.
Wouldn't you call that rape?"

Mrs. Primrose stuck her head into the kitchen. "I'll be trundling
the stacks of newspapers off to the wastebin now," she said dubi-
ously, glancing at Harry.

"I'm not finished with them," he said.

"But they keep piling up," said Claudette. "We've been here six
weeks, and you haven't thrown out a single newspaper or magazine
from those old stacks."

"I get ideas out of those stacks. Ideas make my living. I live by
my wits. I need all the help I can get. Leave the stacks, please, Mrs.
Primrose."

Mrs. Primrose nodded and ducked out again after a glare at Mr.
Peepers, snuggling in the interloper's lap.

"It doesn't help things for you to overrule me in front of Mrs.
Primrose," Claudette said. "I'm not a child, Harry. What do you
expect from me?"

"Don't lay the French temper on me this morning."

"You're making me very angry, Harry. I am going to get dressed
and go for a long walk. If you come home late and drunk tonight,
please sleep on the sofa."

Playing matches again that evening, Harry kept being nagged by
the conversation at the breakfast table. If he wanted to maintain a
happy home, he would have to spend less time at The Pig and
Whistle.

"Come on, Harry. For Christ's sake, will you spit out a fucking
number of some kind?" said Jocko.

Harry realized they were waiting on him. He downed his whiskey, stuck his matches into his pocket and said, "Sorry, boys, but count me out. Phibbs stalled so long he's made me late for dinner."

"You can't walk out during a match game. It's unheard of," said Phibbs.

"I shouldn't play matches with you again, Phibbs. You are a strain on my sense of humor," Harry said.

"How many do you have, Harry? How many matches?" asked Jocko.

"Two," Harry lied.

"That would have made twelve—my number," said Burleigh Crenshaw. "Damn the roof, why has dinner become suddenly more important than the noble match game? Because one gets married is no reason to lose all sense of proportion, Harry."

As Harry went out, he heard Phibbs ordering another see-through. Phibbs said, "Life's a bitch, and then you marry one."

The cage lift at No. 5 Cheyne Place hummed and clanked and lurched to a stop at the fourth floor. Harry paused in front of the door to his flat. He could hear loud rock-and-roll music. Harry pressed an ear against the door and listened.

He turned the knob and quietly opened the door. The noise of the rock and roll put his teeth on edge. Claudette didn't see him enter. She was in the middle of the living room, facing toward the river, a glass of white wine in one hand, the other arm flung toward the ceiling. She was dancing by herself. Though in her third month of pregnancy, Claudette had not begun to show it, other than adding a few pleasing pounds. Harry went over to the bar and poured whiskey into a tumbler. There was still enough light in the long summer evening that he could see strollers feeding gulls on the Chelsea Embankment.

Claudette noticed him. Not embarrassed that he had seen her dancing, she punched the reject switch on the new phonograph.

"Sorry," she said. "I know you hate this kind of music, but I went past a shop in the King's Road today and couldn't resist buying this

American record player. It's the newest 'hi-fi.' Then I had to have records. Music I like, I mean."

Harry took a sip of scotch and recited:

Good authors too who once knew better words
Now only use four-letter words
Writing prose,
Anything goes.

Claudette laughed. At least she was in a good humor. It cheered him up to hear her laughing after her mood of the morning. He wondered if she was drunk. He noticed the wine bottle was three-quarters empty.

"I like that poem," she said. "What is it?"

"A piece of lyric from *Anything Goes,* musical by Cole Porter, Guy Bolton and P. G. Wodehouse, written 1934," Harry said. "They don't write lyrics like that anymore."

"Harry, don't be an old grouch. You loved *The King and I* the other night. You cried and held my hand. You told me nobody has ever written better songs than Rodgers and Hammerstein. You sang to me and kissed me. You were wonderful."

"What I mean is, this rock and roll."

"You don't understand rock and roll. It's not your generation."

"Going to trot that one out again, are we?"

"Trot what out?" she asked, pouring the last of the *blanc de blanc* into her glass.

"The age difference," he said.

"I have never mentioned our age difference to you."

Mr. Peepers wandered in from the bedroom and stretched luxuriously.

"I think Mr. Peepers enjoys watching us fight," Claudette said. "So let's disappoint him and not fight this evening."

"Mr. Peepers is happy the rock-and-roll attack is turned off. Mr. Peepers prefers Brahms—or anything classical. Chamber music is more his style. Mr. Peepers despises a lyric about a long-ah neck-ah goose-ah."

"But Harry, you aren't supposed to listen to rock and roll for the lyrics. You listen for the beat, that's all. The only thing I pay attention to in rock and roll is the drummer. You go with the beat, give in to it."

"Don't be so damned condescending," Harry said. "I was jitter-bugging to rock and roll when it first started after the war. You never even heard of Joe Turner and Big Mama Thornton. 'Honey Hush'? We called them 'shouters' around St. Louis and Kansas City. Some called it race music, or rhythm and blues—upright sex is what it is."

Harry noticed the novel Claudette had been reading. *The Robe* by Lloyd C. Douglas lay on an arm of the couch with a bookmark about halfway. It struck him that Claudette was more bored than he had realized. She drank half her glass of wine and turned on the BBC on the radio. The program was *Top of the Pops.* They heard Rosemary Clooney singing "Hey, There."

"Come on, Harry. I know you like this one." Claudette said, putting her glass down on top of the radio.

She moved into his arms. Her body felt light and graceful as they danced. Holding her, feeling her ribs, her hair against his cheek, Harry knew he was in love with her. He remembered why he had proposed marriage to her.

"I've been in a bad humor lately," Claudette whispered into his ear. "I'm sorry. I don't like being this way. I don't know what's the matter. Maybe it's the baby wanting attention. Are you sure you love me, Harry?"

"Yeah. I love you. Do you love me?"

"I adore you, Harry."

"No. No. Do you *love* me? Adore later."

"I love you, Harry."

Now the BBC was playing "Little Things Mean a Lot," sung by Kitty Kallen. Harry slipped out of his Brooks Brothers loafers. He sailed his hat onto the couch. Harry had been the best dancer at Holymount High. The two of them whirled around the living room. They danced through "Young at Heart" sung by Sinatra and "Three Coins in the Fountain" by the Four Aces, danced on through the living room and into the bedroom, where they tumbled onto the bed and began to make love, slowly at first, then in a mutual, mad scramble.

Later they climbed into a hot bubble bath in the gigantic old tub with its claw feet. The bathroom window was open to the summer breeze. Facing Claudette, feeling her on the insides of his legs, Harry rested the back of his neck against the cool porcelain and tried to keep his Chesterfield out of the bubbles. He was relaxed now, their arguments were history. This, he thought, was paradise.

Harry stood at the bedroom window in his striped cotton pajamas and smoked a cigarette. In the stable yard, the oak trees and the statue of the real estate developer cast shadows in the moonlight. Somewhere out there in the night, Mr. Peepers was prowling.

"Claudette, I want to ask you something," he said.

She was propped up with several pillows on her side of the bed, the side with the reading lamp. She wore a light blue nightgown. Sticking a finger into *The Robe* to keep her place, Claudette looked up at Harry and smiled.

"What is it, darling?" she said.

"Do you think I'm going to change the way I live?"

"What do you mean?"

"I mean, just because I'm married, do you think—"

"Just because you're married!" she interrupted. Harry knew he had phrased his question poorly.

"Don't you think I'm married, too? I certainly have changed the way I live—just because I'm married! Yes, I expect you to be different now than when you were single."

"I don't mean running around with women. You're more woman than I could ever want," he said.

"What does that mean, Harry? Are you tired of living with me?"

"No, no. I really do like having you around."

"Well, thanks a hell of a lot," she said, slamming down the book.

Harry bit his tongue. He had screwed up.

"And while we are speaking of such things, it's silly to put this off any longer, Harry. We're going to have to start looking for a bigger place."

Harry knew it had been coming, but he had hoped it would be later.

"Obviously there's not room in this flat for your stacks of newspapers and magazines, much less room for raising a baby," Claudette said.

"What do you have in mind?" he said.

"A house in the country," said Claudette. "Why don't we take a few days and drive through Kent and look for a house? Sandwich is a pretty little town. I hear they have golf courses there, and it's not all that far from London. Or there's Sussex or Cornwall. We need space, Harry. We need grass and trees and flowers around us. I don't want to bring up a child in the middle of Chelsea."

"I can't live in the country. I need to be close to the bureau. Stories don't happen in the country."

"Well, there's Wimbledon or Maida Vale or all sorts of other places inside of London where we can find a large house with grounds," she said. "But we have to start looking now, Harry. The baby will be here in six months."

"Maybe we can get another flat in this building and knock out some walls or something," Harry said.

Claudette stared angrily at him. "No," she said. "We need a house—a large house. We need to start looking for one tomorrow."

"I don't see why we couldn't compromise," Harry said. "There's plenty of parks around here where you can take the kid. You could cross the bridge to Battersea and roll in the grass and flowers all you please. There's Hyde Park, Green Park, St. James's Park, loads of football and cricket grounds, the zoo, the gulls to feed on the river, the pigeons in the windows, Mr. Peepers to play with. Mr. Peepers would like a kid. Maybe."

Claudette got out of bed and went to her closet and pulled out her suitcase.

"What are you doing?" he said.

"I'm going to Paris. I'll do what I was going to do before you stupidly asked me to marry you and I stupidly agreed. I'll have my baby—the kid, you call it—in Paris as I had intended to, and later I'll find a house in the country outside of Paris and the kid and I will roll in the damned grass all day long."

"Put that suitcase back," Harry said.

"I hate London," she said. "It's a dirty city. It will be nice to go back to Paris where I don't always have soot on my hands and face and clothes."

"Claudette, please, put the suitcase back," he said. A soot contest between London and Paris would be a nasty tie—both cities burned coal.

"The Thames is boring, too," she said, opening a dresser drawer and throwing lingerie into the suitcase. "The Thames is not even picturesque. I want to go back to my own apartment and look out at the beautiful Seine. The Seine is what I call a river. The Thames is a sewer."

Harry heard her voice catch, as if she was covering a sob. She jerked away when he tried to embrace her.

"Leave me alone, you prick," she said. "Yes, you're a selfish prick, Harry. You want me to shut up about your habits, to sit in this miserable damn little flat all day and half the night while you're carousing with your chums . . ."

"I'm not out there carousing. I'm working."

"It would be work for me to have to get drunk with those rummies at The Pig and Whistle, but it's not work for you. You actually like it!"

"You think I don't have to work to write four columns a week for the Syndicate? You have no idea how hard it is to think up the topic and do the legwork and then actually write the damned thing. And then comes the scariest part of all—what do I write about tomorrow? It might look like I'm carousing, but all the time I'm wondering what to write about tomorrow."

"What did you write about today?"

"The British Open."

"What is the British Open?"

"A golf tournament that starts next week at Royal Birkdale."

"Why is it worth writing about?"

"Why is the British Open worth writing about?" The question stopped Harry. He had never considered that the British Open might *not* be worth writing about. He searched for an answer that would satisfy her. "Well, Ben Hogan is coming back to defend the title he won last year at Carnoustie."

"I see. Who is Ben Hogan?"

"The greatest golf player in history is all."

"Does this mean you intend to go to a golf tournament next week?"

"I want you to come with me."

"Why would I want to go to a golf tournament?"

"Not just a golf tournament. I'm talking about *the British Open*. I'll do a couple of columns around the Open, and we'll stay at The Prince of Wales Hotel in Southport. You'll like The Prince of Wales. It's on the Irish Sea. They have a ballroom, an orchestra, a classy restaurant. Afterwards, we'll go to Scotland for a week."

"I've always wanted to see Scotland," she said with renewed hope.

"I'm writing a series of columns called 'You'll Not Do That Here, Laddy—Golfing in Scotland.' I need to play Troon, Turnberry and Prestwick to finish the series."

"More golf?"

"But we'll stay at the Turnberry Hotel for a week. You'll love the Turnberry. It overlooks the Firth of Clyde and the Ailsa Craig—a granite bird sanctuary that sticks out of the water halfway to the Irish coast. You'll see the mountains of Arran and the Mull of Kintyre. You'll see the sheep on the green hills, the brooks full of trout, the shaggy cattle. You'll love Scotland."

"Will your drunken chums be there?"

"They'll be in the press tent. We might see them around the hotel, but I've warned them to keep away from us. Most of them are decent enough. They don't care about Dien Bien Phu now that it's not news. Wars don't impress them. Jocko Conlan shot down eleven Messerschmidts. He wouldn't bother you."

"What about the one who smells like gin and has piss spots on his pants?"

"I told Phibbs I'd beat him up if he comes close."

"The hotel overlooks the Firth of Clyde? Is it moors and crags and hills covered with sheep?"

"Will you go?"

"I'd love to give it a try, Harry."

He kissed her and shoved aside her suitcase with his foot. He raised her nightgown and cupped her buttocks with his hands. She reached for him inside his pajamas.

After they made love, Claudette spoke to him in the night.

"I want to be a good wife to you, Harry, but we're going to need a house with grass and trees around it. You're going to have to face it: Being married and being a father will change the way you live."

14 They caught the Royal Highlander passenger train out of Waterloo Station at 8 A.M. on Tuesday. Harry booked a compartment with windows on the west for the view. He read *The Stranger* by Camus as the train went north out of London, past brick row houses into green fields and hedges surrounding tidy farms and Elizabethan villages, into Brontë country with moors and mists.

The town of Southport is an hour's ride north of Liverpool on the Lancashire coast of the Irish Sea. Before World War I, the red brick Victorian buildings along the wide, stony gray beach housed one of England's most elegant spas. The Prince of Wales lent his name to the town's grand hotel and his title to the golf links. Royal Birkdale is one of the few golfing layouts in the world to feature back-to-back par fives for its finishing holes. Four of the last six holes at Royal Birkdale are more than five hundred yards long—a ferocious test of the will, even on calm days. But the wind was whipping in off the Irish Sea and stinging the town with cold salt spray.

It was British Open weather that was brewing as they took a taxi to The Prince of Wales. The flags in front of the hotel popped like rifle shots, in wind-blown rain that hurled umbrellas and furniture rolling on the lawn. The taxi driver turned to Harry and said, "If it's nae wind, it's nae gowf!" Having played in gale and blizzard, Harry had sympathy for the concept. If you lived in the north latitudes and loved golf, you had to embrace wind and rain as part of the game.

Though the weather did not, The Prince of Wales Hotel excited Claudette as Harry had hoped. Porters moved in silence on the maroon carpet. Their room was second floor on the front. Claudette opened the window and wind and sea mist blew the curtains into her face. They had dinner beneath the chandeliers in the dining room. The trout and vegetables were fresh; the wine was cold.

Harry tried to explain why he liked baseball as well as golf. He told her of the day in 1946 when Red Miller of the Giants came to bat with a live frog stuffed in his jockstrap. The frog's first frantic lunge for freedom made plate umpire Murdock swallow his tobacco. When a croak betrayed the frog, Murdock called another strike on a curve ball in the dirt. The Cardinal pitcher, a left-hander, thought they were making fun of him. He cut loose a fastball aimed at Miller's ear. Miller flung himself onto his back as Murdock's arm shot up for strike three and the frog kept hopping inside the jockstrap. Miller later told Harry he'd had an orgasm. He didn't know if it was the fastball or the frog that did it.

She laughed and asked about growing up in St. Louis. He told her how his father, the aviator, met his mother in Paris during the First World War, married her and took her to Missouri. Claudette had already heard the story but pretended she hadn't. The romance of it moved her and made her love Harry all the more. She said Harry must be like his father. Harry didn't know his father well enough to answer. He could say he loved his mother and had learned his love of games from her, but his father was running the airfreight business or playing golf or entertaining at social affairs with his mother while Harry was growing up. Harry left home at eighteen for Missouri and had been back to the large white house on Peach Street for brief and infrequent visits. Claudette understood the way life put distance between parents and children. She had learned from her father. But her father's death had taught her that life should not be allowed to put up distances. It would never happen between Claudette and her child.

Harry and Claudette danced in the ballroom. They went to their room at midnight and made quiet, sweet love. Harry relaxed as she drowsed with her head on his shoulder. The noise of wind and rain against the windows made them feel secure and warm. They slept in each other's arms.

Harry was up at seven. He left Claudette sleeping and had breakfast in the grill. Turning up the collar of his Burberry and jamming his old Borsalino tight on his head, he plunged into the rain. The doorman struggled to keep an umbrella over Harry as a taxi pulled up, but the wind ripped the umbrella inside out with a loud crack.

"Good day for gowf, Mr. Sparrow."

The clubhouse at Royal Birkdale loomed through the rain and fog. The place made Harry think of an eerie white railroad station for haunted trains that ran between the sea and the moors on the edge of Brontë country.

He found Corky Braeburn blowing smoke breath in the locker room. Corky, the pro at Harry's home club, Royal Bowling Brook, would be going to the first tee to begin his annual pursuit of the British Open championship. He wanted a British Open title worse than Harry wanted a Pulitzer Prize. Corky was nervous, but more than anything he was disappointed that Ben Hogan had decided not to return to the British Open. Corky's dream was to win the Open by beating Hogan one shot man-to-man by curling an eight-footer sidehill into the cup at the eighteenth for a birdie in front of twenty thousand fans.

"Bloody fookin' Wee Ice Mon," Corky said, twisting his shoulders from side to side. "Loosening up the grease," he said. He wore a tweed cap of the Hogan style and a slicker over a Harris Tweed jacket. Corky had convinced himself this was the year he would finally win this tournament. He had been looking forward to playing the last thirty-six holes on Friday in the same threesome with Hogan, his idol.

"Beat his bloody fookin' brains out, thas what I wudda doon, Harry."

"I'd love to have seen it, Corky. Too bad."

Harry had written a column scolding Hogan and praising the dedication of men like Corky Braeburn to a noble championship.

"Say, Harry, I almost forgot. The board met about yer pitchin' iron. They say there's nae need for another pitchin' iron fer the Trophy Room. They say havin Auld Bawlky is all the pitchin' iron the cloob will ever need. Sorry, Harry."

Auld Bawlky was the niblick Young Thom Scott used while winning the Royal Bowling Brook championship eleven straight years up to 1913. There was no club tournament from 1914 through 1918. The good players had marched off to die in the trenches in France and Belgium.

"Between you and me, Harry, it's fookin' politics. Most members don't like havin' a bloody journalist in the cloob. I don't know what string you pulled to get in, Harry, but it tightened around some ancient danglin' ballocks, that's a fact. Lord Dunston said if he wanted bloody war souvenirs in the Trophy Room, he would gladly donate the family sword used at Balaklava. The board are oopset with you, Harry."

Harry nodded. He had suspected the board would vote against him. There were only seven members at Royal Bowling Brook that Harry would play golf with. The string he had pulled to get in was paying the four-hundred-pound induction fee and twelve pounds a month in dues. Corky thought every member of Royal Bowling Brook was rich, powerful and devious.

"The hell with them," Harry said. "Don't worry about the board, Corky. Who are you matched with today?"

"Peter Thomson, the Aussie. And Bannister from Wales. Bannister can't play. I'll beat their bloody fookin' asses. Aussies don't know gowf."

"Good luck to you, Corky," Harry said.

"Aye," said Corky. His gray eyes squinted fiercely out at the rain, like a fisherman contemplating putting his boat to sea to fight the elements for life or death.

The ropes that pegged the press tent to earth hummed in the wind, and canvas billowed and boomed. Inside were a hundred tables with typewriters and chairs. A man wearing the blazer of the Royal and Ancient Society of Golfers stood on a ladder marking hole-by-hole numbers on the scoreboard as information reached him by messenger. Harry found Admiral Sir James Bentley-Harrison, chairman of the R and A, huddled with his assistant, Rodney Litton-Smythe, around a filing cabinet. They were searching for credentials for a photographer from *Time* magazine.

"You don't appear to be accredited. What is the name of your publication again?" said the admiral. In the press tent they called him "Big Silly." Litton-Smythe, face red as the juniper berries that went into the "cozy gin thing" he drank, was known as "Little Silly." Both wore brown shoes with white socks and their gray wool slacks struck them at the anklebone. Their arms were inches too long for their blazers. Their R-and-A neckties showed soup and dessert. Harry thought Phibbs tried to dress like Big Silly and Little Silly in hope he might someday be admitted to the select company of gentlemen that form the Royal and Ancient.

"Ya beddah fin' th' fuckin' ahmband, ya asshole," the photographer from New York said.

Harry saw Big Silly glance at Little Silly and knew the armband would not be found.

"Not going out to watch the golf, are you?" said Phibbs. He was typing at his table in the back row. "No reason to go out in this weather, unless, of course, it shapes up historic."

Harry was toying with a column topic. He could make a case that the best thing the British Empire had given the world was golf. Golf was a philosophy, a discipline, with rules that must be obeyed without regard to punishment or reward. A golf card had a space for the score made on the hole but no place to write excuses or remarks. P. G. Wodehouse wrote that many considered golf to be a microcosm of life, but that life was actually a microcosm of golf. The British spread golf through the Empire. Golf courses like the Royal Selangor in Malaya were islands of order in an ocean of chaos. While people shouted, "You die!" outside the hedges, on the greens people said, "You're away." The Australian pro, Peter Thomson, had played golf throughout Asia. Harry decided to follow Thomson and Corky Braeburn. He would talk to Thomson later for the column.

"I think I'll go to the room and take a nap," Harry said to Phibbs.

"And a tickle with the bride?"

"Keep away from her, Phibbs."

"I gave you my word, didn't I?"

Royal Birkdale is laid in valleys between towering sandhills. The greens are outlined by the dunes as definite targets, unlike most seaside courses that hide their greens behind mounds of gorse and fields of whin. But to miss a green by inches at Birkdale means your ball disappears into willow-scrub rough. Harry compared famous links such as Troon to playing across Nebraska, through the wheat and across the roads, finding a footpath that became a fairway, a hidden bowl of slick hard grass that was a green. He was always playing toward a gray horizon at Troon. The only time Harry knew the distance to a hole at Troon was when he would look at a tee box sign that said: 440 YARDS, PAR 4. Harry had little patience with searching for golf balls in gorse and whin. The fairways at Royal Birkdale are mowed, but they are only thirty paces wide. A ball out of the fairway at Birkdale is as gone as a ball in the wheat at Troon.

The wind was howling off the sea when Harry caught up with Thomson, Braeburn and Bannister at the sixth tee. Thomson's game was steadiness and accuracy; he was even par. Corky was a long hitter; off the tee he liked to give it a "proper right oopercoot." Corky was four over par. Rain poured from his cap. The caddie he had brought from Royal Bowling Brook, Old Blind Ned, chewed a stem of grass. "You'll want the true value of the driving club here," said Old Blind Ned.

The sixth is 468 yards, par 4. The fairway runs along a deserted RAF airstrip and bends toward the Irish Sea. Harry held his hat with both hands. He guessed the wind at forty miles an hour and rising.

Thomson hit a smooth driver low into the wind and landed his ball short of a ridge of sandhills that crossed the fairway 230 yards out.

Bannister was five feet four and stocky, with the face of a cherub. One over par, he played safe, if the word may be applied to a shot struck in wind that was by now in the fifties. Corky took his address, peering at the ball, he said, "like a Scotsman looking for a penny." Corky believed in starting the swing by throwing the left shoulder toward the ball, then at the top of the backswing hurling the left shoulder violently upward. Harry had stopped taking lessons from Corky.

Corky knocked a hole in the wind with his tee ball. The drive carried the ridge of sandhills. "Nice shot," said Thomson. Corky growled. He was on his game again. He and Old Blind Ned trudged rapidly up the fairway and were lost in the rain.

Thomson and Bannister hit spoons over the sandhills to the neck that led to the green, which could be dimly seen through the spray. Corky's ball was on the edge of a rabbit hole two hundred yards from the front of the deep green. Old Blind Ned licked rain off his lips and said, "The 2-iron. True value of the club."

"Give me my brassie."

"The 2-iron. Best we lay a wee below."

"I'm shootin for the flagstick," Corky said.

Hunched over the sidehill lie, at the rabbit hole, Corky hit the brassie shot of his life. The ball sprang from the club face and drilled through the wind 227 yards. It came down on the back of the green, three feet beyond the flag, bounced once and vanished into the willow scrub.

The wind rose as they stomped in the scrub, searching for Corky's ball. Waves crashed across the beach, across the highway and onto the golf course.

Old Blind Ned was poking the scrub with Corky's driver, when a blast of wind carried him off the rim of the green and tossed him down into the prickly heather. He kicked and flailed his thin limbs. The wind screamed. Corky bent over and picked up his driver. The shaft was broken in half. Harry felt sympathy for the pain, humiliation and frustration he saw in Corky's freckled face.

Corky said, "Yesterday I knew how to play the game of golf. But today I have stone-forgot it all. Nae recall e'en how to grip a cloob. There's nothin left fer me now but to hang meself."

With the wind at his back, Corky drove the ball four hundred yards off the eighteenth tee using his 3-wood. He could birdie the hole for an 87. Harry carried Corky's golf bag. Blind Ned hobbled with an umbrella for a crutch. He was bareheaded and furious.

Corky hit a wedge into a greenside bunker for his second, then blasted out and took four putts for his double-bogey 7. Bannister shot 75. Thomson holed out for 68 and was leading the tournament.

"Sixty-bloody-fookin'-eight. Aussie's too doom to know there's a gale struck us. I hate a fookin' Aussie, the bloody convicts," Corky said. "Fookin' Wee Ice Mon wudda showed up I wud nae been roond with no sheep-fookin' Aussie."

"Screw you," said Thomson.

Harry stepped between them. Corky had been middleweight boxing champion of the Black Watch. He was dangerous when he lost his head. Blocking off Corky with his body, Harry walked toward the clubhouse with Thomson. Harry discussed his idea about the British establishing islands of golfing-order in the chaos of Asia. Thomson told him anecdotes he could use for the column. In Kuala Lumpur a golf tournament had continued through an attempted coup. The tournament chairman, an Asian, was assassinated with the players' prize checks in his pocket. Thomson's winning check of three thousand dollars was smeared with blood.

Harry had his column now, except for the writing of it. The wind had become gale force. Gusts near eighty miles an hour blew rain horizontally, and it stung like gravel. From the changing room, Harry phoned Claudette at the hotel. She didn't answer in their room or when paged in the restaurant.

Phibbs was leaning against the wood bar in the Grill Room at the clubhouse, blowing cigar-smoke rings and studying the olive in his see-through. Claudette clutched a wet newspaper and was shouting at Phibbs when Harry entered. Wind had smashed a pane of glass onto the hardwood floor. A maid swept up shards while two carpenters nailed boards over the window.

"Why do you write something like this, you pig?" Claudette yelled. "You're supposed to be Harry's friend!"

"I am your husband's colleague and rival. It's deeper than friendship," Phibbs said.

Claudette stood in pools of water, wet hair clinging to her skull,

drops flying from her raincoat as she brandished the *Daily Mail.*
They saw Harry.

"Hullo, Harry. Appears I've offended the little lady," Phibbs
said.

"Look what he wrote," Claudette said.

PHIBBS: OUR MAN AT THE OPEN was on this day a series of sketches
about people who gathered at Royal Birkdale. The second sketch
said:

> Appearing at the Open with his bride, the
> once-famous angel of Dien Bien Phu, syn-
> dicated columnist Harry Sparrow felt the
> shame of rejection today when he learned
> the pitching wedge he had carried into
> battle in Indochina had been turned down
> for a spot in the Trophy Room at Royal
> Bowling Brook. Such is vanity. Golf is a
> humbling game in more ways than putting
> club face against ball. Sparrow was made to
> look foolish by this episode, but he should
> have known he is a Johnny-come-lately
> indeed at a club founded in 1865. Dreams
> of winning the Pulitzer Prize have made
> Harry's hat too tight. Tell you what,
> Harry. I'll put your wedge on the Memora-
> bilia Wall at The Pig and Whistle beside
> Winston Churchill's cigar butt . . .

"Why did you do it?" Harry said to Phibbs.

"It's my job. Don't underestimate your notoriety, old sod. You're
a celebrity. You're married to a celebrity. You live in the cross hairs
of the public's telescopic sight. Suffer fame with joy. Before you
know it, nobody will remember you."

"This isn't news. People don't care about this. You wrote it to
humiliate Harry," Claudette said.

"Ask Harry if he would write a humiliating item about me."

Claudette looked at Harry. "Well, Harry?"

"At the next opportunity," he said.

Phibbs drained his see-through.

"I have a deadline to meet. Much as I adore marital discord, I must toddle," Phibbs said.

"Are you going to let him walk away?" Claudette said.

Phibbs was moving faster. The broad back of his blazer went through the door.

"What do you expect me to do?" Harry said.

"Punch him in the nose. You said you would."

"Not for this, Claudette. If he'd insulted you, I would."

"Then I'll punch him in the nose for you," she said.

Claudette ran after Phibbs. He saw her coming and quickened his pace. Harry pursued them through the rain, splashing across the field between the clubhouse and the press tent. The tent heaved, the ropes sang in the wind.

Phibbs darted inside the tent, but the uniformed guard stopped Claudette.

"You have no press credential, madam."

"This is my wife," Harry said. "Let her in."

"Not without a credential."

Big Silly appeared in the tent flap. The wind blew off his glasses. He caught them with a leap that would have brought cheers on a cricket field.

"Give my wife a press credential!" Harry shouted above the wind.

"Women are not allowed in the press tent," shouted Big Silly.

Claudette broke between Big Silly and the guard. She jumped around the grasp of Little Silly. Harry and the guard ran after her. Phibbs sat down at his table and rolled paper into his typewriter. Inside the tent the wind sounded like the engines of a bomber straining to take off.

"This is what I think of you and your profession," Claudette screamed.

She lifted Phibbs's typewriter and dashed it to the floor. Screws popped out and the carriage broke off. Phibbs stared at the typewriter as if he had seen his mother struck by a bus.

"Old Trusty! The bitch killed Old Trusty!" Phibbs cried.

Claudette whirled on Harry.

"You don't need a wife, Harry. You need a psychiatrist!" she shouted. "I hate your job, I hate your life, I hate the company you keep! I refuse to be third in your affections behind a blank piece of paper and a noisy pub full of gin-soaked old fools who act like little boys! You're a syndicated man, you keep saying. You send yourself out in a thousand pieces every day, distributing yourself in little pieces that leave nothing of your life to share with your wife—and certainly nothing for a child. I'm going to Paris, Harry. Don't try to stop me."

Halfway to the door Claudette looked back and shouted, "And I hate golf!"

As if her words were the cue, the mighty engines that had been straining at the press tent began to triumph. The far side by the scoreboard went first, pegs popping from the earth, ropes slashing, canvas crumpling. Rapidly the western portion of the tent collapsed on the writers at their typing tables. The center pole bent, but still held up the canvas behind Big Silly's registration desk.

Claudette ran to catch a taxi that had pulled into shelter at the clubhouse. Harry watched her dress blowing halfway up her thighs. The *Daily Mail* was torn out of her hands and spiraled away in the gale. The doorman struggled to help shut the taxi door. Red tail-lights flashed as the taxi drove out of the Royal Birkdale grounds.

A chair went flying by. Police searched the fallen canvas for buried sportswriters. Voices screamed for telephone lines, for short-wave radios. Then Harry remembered he had a column to write. His deadline was an hour and a half away.

Jocko Conlan had been pulling his typewriter from the splintered scoreboard. He tucked the portable under his arm and patted Harry on the shoulder.

"Don't let her get you down, Harry," said Jocko. "Remember, Sunday morning we're playing Prestwick."

15 DOZENS KILLED IN ALGERIA REBEL ATTACKS ON POLICE POSTS said the headline in *Le Monde*. It was a two-column story at the bottom of page one. Harry read the French newspapers on a cold November morning on the channel ferry crossing to Ostend, Belgium. He was taking the boat-train to Paris to persuade Claudette to return to London with him. He was willing to compromise. A two-story house off the first fairway at Royal Bowling Brook had come up for lease, and Harry had taken an option on the property.

It was nearly four months since Claudette drove away from the wreckage of the press tent at Royal Birkdale. They had argued on the phone for the first few weeks and had exchanged letters of accusations and demands.

"Dear Harry," she wrote.

That you would rather chase a ball through a rainstorm and side with the very persons who threaten our existence as a family clearly states to me that you never intended to change your life for me at all. I must create a nurturing atmosphere for my child. I shall be nesting in Paris if you have any legal papers for me to sign. Please understand, Harry, in the last year my father has left my life, Justus has died and left me pregnant—and now you expect me to stay home and wait till you get through at the bar with your games and your friends. Every time you go away, I think you might never come back. You would eventually abandon me, too. So now I have left you. Please leave me alone. I need my strength to raise my child. I love you, but I see it is not enough . . .

Claudette

Like Lady Cadbury, she thought he could cover the world from a house in the country. He wanted Claudette to understand why he loved writing his column and to be proud of him for it. He missed her. The past three days no one had answered when he phoned her apartment. Harry was feeling suspicious.

Paris was gray and cold. Rain dripped from the plane trees along the Boulevard Saint-Germain as Harry got out of a taxi in front of the Hôtel Forchet. He had wired for his regular room, and Maman Forchet met him at the door. A plump woman who wore a red wig and theatrical makeup, Maman had been given the Hôtel Forchet as a love-gift thirty years ago from one of the Rothschilds. Harry kept a wardrobe in a cedar closet in the attic of the hotel. When he arrived in Paris, Maman Forchet would have his clothing hung in the room, a stack of yellow paper and an L. C. Smith on the desk by the window and an oil painting of the road hole at St. Andrews on the wall.

"How wonderful to see you, Harry," she said as Harry hugged her and kissed her on both cheeks, tasting the pancake and talcum powder. She reeked of Chanel. "What a touching piece you wrote about my dear friend Colette. You've got a warm heart, Harry, regardless of what people say. You're a real—how do they say?— softie-down-deep, I know. It's a tough profession you're in, with no alibis, and you have learned to take care of yourself. But you be careful, Harry. You have many enemies in Paris. They'll never forgive you for your story on the disgrace at Dien Bien Phu. There

are some who would 'kill the messenger.' You understand, don't
you?"

Elmore Gruber met him for dinner in a Sikh bistro named Garanja
in the Marais district. "Yeah sure, a lot of people hate your guts.
What do you expect? France gets humiliated at Dien Bien Phu: The
flower of the Expeditionary Corps is crushed under Michelin Rubber sandals worn by little yellow people who in French eyes are still
in the Stone Age. And who tells the world all the embarrassing,
bloody details? Not only that, but the Red monster Ho Chi Minh
himself saves your ass. That makes you a Communist *and* a traitor
to millions of well-meaning Frenchmen. The survivors of Dien
Bien Phu have a grudge: You ran out on them and reported their
defeat. They go on a death march through the jungle, spend three
months in prison camps starving and having the shit kicked out of
them and—worst of all—listening to Communist indocrination lec-
tures. And when the three thousand survivors finally come back to
France, what do they hear from the populace? Do they receive a
hero's welcome? No, they get spat on. Longshoremen won't unload
their ship, railway porters won't carry their luggage. Let's face it,
it must be very hard to go fight a mean, dirty war, to have close
friends maimed and killed, to do your best to do your duty, and then
come home and be insulted by crowds of your countrymen. Plenty
of the survivors put the blame on you, Harry."

"Who do they think we are—*Pravda*?" Harry said. "Why not
blame the government for sending them to Indochina in the first
place?"

"It's easier to blame *you* than to blame the big boys who mucked
it. The Communists won the war, but you came through with the
bad news. Even the people who agree with what you said are angry
at you for the way you phrased it.

"De Castries, Langlais and Bigeard are among the survivors,"
Gruber said. "My sources say those three soldiers—and most of the
other Dien Bien Phu veterans—will be sent to Algeria soon.

"It's starting up again, Harry—another colonial war. The rabble
is arising in Algeria. The army intends to show it can do a proper

job this time; make France forget they lost Indochina. Nine million Arab Muslims against one million French settlers protected by the 'Parachute Mafia'—that label you stuck on them made them very angry, I hear. They like being called the 'Band of Brothers.' "

Gruber said that two weeks ago on All Saints' Day, a few dozen rebels calling themselves the *Comité révolutionnaire d'unité et d'action* had raided colonial police posts in Algeria. They had ambushed a passenger bus and shot two French schoolteachers in cold blood, on the roadside near Biskra in the Aures Mountains east of Algiers. Gruber's sources told him the leaders of the *CRUA* had met in Bern, Switzerland, in July to plan the raids. They had fooled the *Deuxième bureau* by traveling to Bern to attend the Germany-Hungary World Cup game. After All Saints' Day, the rebel attacks had become sporadic but persistent. The reaction of the French government was to send paratroopers to Algiers. The Armistice Day parade in Algiers the previous week had starred a battalion of paratroopers in red berets and tiger-striped battle dress marching down the boulevards. By now the paras had climbed into the mountains in pursuit of the growing army of rebels.

"It's becoming very brutal in Algeria, Harry. The army intends to win this one. One of my Deputy friends told me they will shoot every 'nigger' and *raton* in Algeria, if that's what it takes to stamp out this new Communist threat to France. Torture is being used by both sides."

"Forget it, Elmore. I'm not going to Algeria," Harry said.

"Did I ask you to? I wouldn't ask you to, Harry. It would be very dangerous." Gruber had tied a large checkered napkin beneath his chin. He filled their glasses with cold beer and dug into his curry. "How do you like doing the column as a regular thing by now?"

"I like it," Harry said. "Front-page play on *The Paris Dispatch* four times a week is a dream. Thanks, Elmore. I appreciate what you're doing for me."

"I hear you're writing a book about Dien Bien Phu."

"I turned it down."

"Good. I was afraid that's why you're doing so many think pieces these days. Think pieces are not where your strength lies, Harry. You know that. I mean, you've done some good stuff lately, some nice essays, but how long can you last with so many think pieces?

You're basically not a thinker. You need to go out in the field to do some old-fashioned legwork."

"I'm not going to Algeria," Harry said.

"The army believes the way to handle the press is the way they did it at Verdun. Do you remember, Harry? Seven hundred and fifty thousand French and Germans killed and wounded in a battle not a hundred miles from where we sit tonight? Not a word about it in the Paris newspapers while it was happening? Some papers used white space with the word *Verdun* at the top. I would hate to think any government would be able to get away with something like that again. We can call ourselves a free society only if we guard our freedom. You're a natural-born watchdog, Harry."

"I haven't lost anything in Algeria, Elmore. I'm not going to Algeria. I like staying home and writing think pieces."

"I'm telling you this as a friend," Gruber said. "You're at your best when you're out among the action. Your readers want thrills and adventure. What have you been giving them lately? A column on flying saucers, columns on the deaths of Colette and Matisse that were well done but not front-page stuff, Harry. You've been writing about the dockers' strike in Britain, the rearmament of West Germany—Haile Selassie, for God's sake. You did a nice column on your fistfight with Hemingway, but the news was nine years old. If you don't get off your butt and give me the real Harry Sparrow, I'm moving your column back to the editorial pages—by popular demand."

Gruber called for the check.

"Your Syndicate readership is falling off. Phibbs says the Immortal is worried that you're loafing on him. I know you're going through a tough patch in your personal life. But your readers don't know it. Should I put an italics insert in your column that says: *Forgive the dullness, Harry is having a fight with his wife?*"

"The column I did on de Gaulle waiting in the bull pen got more newspaper play and more mail than anything since Dien Bien Phu," Harry said.

"Yes, congratulations. But the column you did on Jean-Paul Sartre, nobody printed but me. I hate to put it to you this way, old man, but I don't want to read a column about golf more than six times a year, certainly not twice a week like you did last week.

You'd better get on to something juicy, Harry. Our competition never fights with its wife."

Harry declined Gruber's invitation to accompany him to the rue Scribe. He thought it prudent to stay away from the paper at night when the staff would be drunk and hostile. There was nothing so caustic as the tongue of a frustrated journalist. It was taken for granted by the staff that Harry would win the Pulitzer for the Dien Bien Phu stories. Every good reporter at the *Dispatch* thought he or she could have done a better job at Dien Bien Phu than Harry. They all thought they could write a better column than Harry. They all wanted Harry's job.

Even more than London, Paris was a city for walking. Enough rain was falling to shine the narrow sidewalks of the Marais and make halos around the streetlamps. His cordovans clicked on the pavement of the place de la Bastille. A prostitute called to him from the memorial column. He turned into the medieval rue Charlemagne, crossed the moat on Pont-Marie and was on the Île Saint-Louis. He stood in front of Claudette's building.

It was a five-story whitewashed house with wooden shutters and wrought-iron balconies. A Mercedes, a Citroën and a Saab were parked around an octagonal curb that made an island for six bare chestnut trees and an iron lamppost with six white globes. He looked up at Claudette's third-story windows and saw that her lights were on. He sat down on a bench beneath the chestnut trees and smoked a Chesterfield. He thought about what Gruber had said. Harry had no defense against Gruber's accusation. How could he explain the cold necessities of his life to her?

The longer he waited, the more nervous he became, the more difficult it was to ring Claudette's bell. He saw the rain drizzling against the lights from her windows. It looked warm and cozy inside the apartment. Harry watched for a figure to cross in front of a window. He realized his hands were shaking, but not from the cold. He flipped a cigarette butt into the gutter and walked along the rue Budé to the quai d'Orléans. He took the iron footbridge across the channel between the Île Saint-Louis and the Île de la Cité. The towers and spires of the rear of Notre-Dame were lit up with floodlights through the wet chill. Harry felt lonely.

He crossed onto the Left Bank and walked through the maze of the Latin Quarter until he came to the Boulevard Saint-Germain. He went past the Hôtel Forchet, down the boulevard to the block where the Café Flore and Les Deux Magots sat side by side across from the Brasserie Lipp. Harry looked through the steamy windows at the noisy drunks. He saw journalists of his acquaintance drinking beer in the Lipp. Watching them gesturing with their steins and jabbing with their cigarettes made Harry feel wary of their company. The Flore and Les Deux Magots were crowded with intellectuals, writers, painters and tourists. Through a window at the Flore Harry saw the handsome Albert Camus at a rear table, writing in a spiral notebook with an attitude of total concentration, as debates raged around him.

Harry liked the narrator's description of Paris in *The Stranger:* "A dingy sort of town, to my mind. Masses of pigeons and dark courtyards. And the people have washed-out, white faces." But Harry found it a disturbing book. The narrator lazes his days in Algiers, drinking and sleeping and making love without love, interested in nothing, absorbed in the present moment and the immediate future, unable to reflect or regret. But when he is convicted of murdering an Arab and sentenced to be decapitated, he looks for loopholes. "What I felt was not despair, but fear," he says. Harry had no sympathy for the narrator, who stumbles stupidly into a fate that could have been too easily avoided. Harry understood *The Stranger* to be Camus's vision of what France was doing in Algeria. Literary critics praised the novel for its existential philosophy, but Harry read it as a prophecy.

Camus had recently written a piece called *A Letter to an Algerian Militant.* In it he wrote, "It is as if two insane people, crazed with wrath, forced to live together and incapable of uniting, decide at least to die together."

Harry wanted to go into the Flore and talk to Camus about Algeria, but he remembered he was not going to Algeria. He was going to live where the first fairway doglegs toward the green, at Royal Bowling Brook.

Through the window of Les Deux Magots, Harry saw Sartre at his regular table. The philosopher's eyes bulged lopsidedly. Wrapped in a dirty trench coat, waving a cigarette, Sartre talked steadily, people bending forward to listen as if it were confidential.

In his column Harry had written, "In the major league of intellectuals, Einstein is a fastball pitcher who wins twenty games for a contender. Sartre is a bum in the bleachers."

Harry found a café on the rue Jacob that stocked the proper scotch. Drinking at the bar, he thought about Gruber's warning. Gruber meant it for Harry's own good. As a columnist, Harry had to produce four pieces every week: two hundred and eight pieces every year. Who could have that many opinions that would excite the public? In baseball if you got one hit every three tries, you were hall-of-fame material. To write two unappreciated columns out of every four was batting .500, but it was not good enough to stay in the big league with the Syndicate in New York.

A fight broke out on the sidewalk. A student with a FREE ALGERIA sign was hurled against the wall of an Art Deco *pissoir.* Harry put his back to the street and his elbows on the bar and looked into the mirror. He saw the Borsalino, the cigarette dangling from his lips, the black knit tie jerked down from the shirt collar, the rain-spattered trenchcoat. Time to decide: Would it be Algeria or a home on the first fairway at Royal Bowling Brook?

Harry went out and pushed through the crowds on the sidewalks. Rain had started popping in the puddles in the gutters. Harry detoured around a rally where a tough-looking man under an umbrella was shouting about the need to organize hundreds of thousands of Algerian Arabs who were working as cheap labor in Paris and other cities in France. A dozen trade unionists shouted the organizer down. No "nigger dog-eaters" in their unions, they cried. The crowd was taking sides. Rain glinted on the riot batons of police trotting toward the speaker. The *yee-yaw* of an ambulance was heard. Harry pushed ahead of a student and his girlfriend and grabbed a taxi as the driver slowed in an attempt to swerve away from what was becoming a riot.

"Stinking Communists. France needs de Gaulle," the driver said. He honked his horn three long and two short—*Al-gé-rie fran-çaise.* "The general would straighten this bunch out."

Harry gave the driver the address of Claudette's building. He listened to the windshield wipers and wondered what he would say to her. In the glow of the scotch, everything seemed possible. Perhaps she would fall into his arms.

When he pushed the buzzer beside her mail slot in the vestibule, her voice sounded sleepy over the intercom.

"Who is it?"

"Harry."

"Harry?"

"Your husband," he said.

"Oh, Harry!" Her voice brightened. Then sobered. "Come on up."

He heard the hum and the click of the door lock. Harry climbed the stairs to Claudette's apartment. She was standing in the open doorway, waiting for him, smiling. She wore a blue housecoat. Harry was struck in the chest at the sight of her. She had poise and an attraction that always perturbed him, made him want to hug her.

But he was astounded at her size. When she fought with Harry at Royal Birkdale, she was slender and girlish. Now her stomach was swollen and heavy and pregnant.

"Could I have a drink?" Harry said.

She left him standing with his wet hat and trench coat, but she brought him a small glass of whiskey. He sipped—The Famous Grouse.

"May I hang up my duds?" Harry said.

"What do you want?"

"Couldn't I at least sit down?"

Harry draped his coat over his knees and sat on the arm of the couch.

"I've thought about our situation," Claudette said. "Divorce is out of the question, of course, but we could ask for an annulment. We could use the grounds that we were crazy. You could say you didn't know I was pregnant; it's all right with me."

"I want you to come back to England with me. I found us a house surrounded by grass and trees. You'll love the place. You and the kid will have plenty of space out there. As for me staying home more, I'm going to try. It will be difficult, but I'll try."

"I thought you wanted an annulment."

"An annulment? We took vows, dear. Who said anything about an annulment?"

"You did, the last time we talked. You called me from The Pig and Whistle. Don't you remember?

"I didn't mean it. I want you to come to London with me tomorrow."

"Sit down on the couch, Harry. You don't need to squat. Finish that, and I'll make you a real drink."

Harry watched her amazing bulk as she filled a highball glass with The Grouse, soda and two ice cubes. Claudette gave him the drink and stood by the window, looking at the river.

"I have found the house of your dreams, Claudette. Big oak trees, a fence, quiet surroundings, and I can be at the Syndicate office in half an hour. How does it sound?"

Claudette looked around, but not with the smile Harry anticipated.

"It's not the same anymore, Harry. My feelings have changed."

"Sure, they've changed for the better. I'm offering you a dream house in the forest and me to go with it. You feel happy."

Claudette looked at him with pity and remorse.

"You don't understand. I want to have my baby in France. My baby will be French. We will live in France. If you want an annulment, my lawyers will file the appeal with the Church. There should be no problem, but my lawyers say we will appeal to the College of Cardinals if necessary."

"Do *you* want an annulment?" Harry asked.

"No. I also took a vow, dear."

"Then what's going on? What's happened? You look at me like you barely know me."

"I can't help how I look."

"What are you not telling me?"

Claudette rested her hands on her belly a moment, then lifted her fingers to massage her eyes. She opened her eyes and Harry saw tears.

"I don't know what it is," she said. "I love you, but I'm confused. I'm not doing the right thing if I try to live with you. I owe my child the life my father would have given me if he could. I owe a debt to my child's father. I am carrying Max von Eschel's baby."

"You went to Bonn and looked up his real name? What did you do that for?" Harry was angry. "The German is dead. We agreed to forget him. Why did you bring him back now?"

"A child should know its own father's name," Claudette said firmly. "Max won two Iron Crosses in Russia. His child has a right to know. Max owned a farm near Dresden. It's in East Germany now, but his child has a right to know about the family land and his ancestors who were killed at Dresden. Max is listed as missing in action. His child should know these things."

Harry stood up and put on his trench coat.

"I'm not going to compete with a dead man," he said.

"You always speak of competing. This is not a competition between you and Max. I don't know what I'm feeling right now, Harry. You must remember you're talking to a pregnant woman. You're talking to me and the 'kid.' "

Harry put on his hat. "The kid would have liked growing up on a golf course."

"The house you found is on a golf course? Oh, Harry, you're not going to change. If you want me to come home with you, why did you get drunk and wait till midnight to ask me?"

"I brought the kid a gift."

He handed Claudette a package wrapped in brown paper that was spattered with rain.

"It would protect him from the golf balls."

He slammed the door when he went out. He paused on the landing and smoked a Chesterfield, giving her time to call him back. Inside the package was a picture of a guardian angel watching two little children cross a dangerous bridge. He had found it in a shop near the Sorbonne and was sure it was the same picture her father had bought for her many years ago. Finally, Harry took the steps two at a time going down. Outside he stood in the rain under the bare chestnut trees. Claudette's shadow was in the window. He waited for her to beckon him back up to her apartment. But she simply stood there, bulky, looking down at him. Harry turned and walked away.

He woke up at the Hôtel Forchet with a hangover, an unpleasant feeling about himself and their conversation and took the morning train out of Gare Saint-Lazare back to London.

16 It was a nasty winter. Bus conductors walked beside their vehicles like elephant handlers in the fog. Ten million Londoners sought heat by burning compressed coal dust called "nutty slack." Black smoke mixed with fog formed a vile cloud that added the hacking and coughing of pedestrians to the din of traffic.

Harry sat at his desk in his study and looked at the fog that hid the Physic Garden and the river. Trying to think of a column, he gazed around the room and saw the 1946 St. Louis Cardinals pennant. Mrs. Primrose brought a pot of tea and a saucer of biscuits into the study. Mr. Peepers sprawled in front of the electric heater. Harry smiled at Mrs. Primrose and the cat. He lit another Chesterfield and studied the Cardinals pennant.

Remembering that 1946 season made Harry nod with pleasure. It was the greatest season in the history of baseball. The Cardinals beat the Brooklyn Dodgers for the National League pennant on the final day. The World Series matched the Cardinals against Harry's second favorite team, the Boston Red Sox, and the great Ted Williams. The series lasted the full seven games. Left-hander Harry "the Cat" Brecheen beat the Sox 3–1 in the seventh game for his third win of the series. St. Louis went crazy, and everybody in town read Harry's stories in the *St. Louis Post-Dispatch* during the season. Harry was a celebrity. Saloon owners never let him see a tab. Never again would he feel as famous as he did in St. Louis, even after he became more widely known.

Suddenly, in London, Harry could smell the cigar smoke of the third-floor city room of the *Post-Dispatch*. The three St. Louis newspapers—the *Star-Times*, the *Globe-Democrat* and the *Post-Dispatch*—all stood on Olive Street near the Jefferson Hotel, where Harry drank and gambled with his army mustering-out pay. He hadn't always been a local hero.

Harry had visited each newspaper on 12th Street with a folder of clippings from *Stars and Stripes* and *Yank* and applied for a job as foreign correspondent. They laughed at him. All three St. Louis newspapers already had their own foreign correspondents. It was the toughest job to get on any paper. But Joseph Pulitzer's words were burned into his mind. The great man's words were carved on a brass plaque above the elevators in the lobby of the *Post-Dispatch:*

> . . . ALWAYS FIGHT FOR PROGRESS AND RE-
> FORM. NEVER TOLERATE INJUSTICE OR COR-
> RUPTION, ALWAYS FIGHT DEMAGOGUES OF
> ALL PARTIES, NEVER BELONG TO ANY PARTY,
> ALWAYS OPPOSE PRIVILEGED CLASSES AND
> PUBLIC PLUNDERERS. NEVER LACK SYMPA-
> THY WITH THE POOR, ALWAYS REMAIN DE-
> VOTED TO THE PUBLIC WELFARE, NEVER BE
> SATISFIED WITH MERELY PRINTING NEWS,
> ALWAYS BE DRASTICALLY INDEPENDENT,
> NEVER BE AFRAID TO ATTACK WRONG,
> WHETHER BY PREDATORY PLUTOCRACY OR
> PREDATORY POVERTY.
>
> JOSEPH PULITZER
> APRIL 10, 1907

After his third rejection as a would-be foreign correspondent, Harry had wandered into the Bismarck Bar and Grill. There, two Greeks named Steve had served turtle soup and whiskey to newspaper people for decades. When Harry entered, the baseball writer who covered the Cardinals for the *Post-Dispatch* was demonstrating the art of the hook slide. The sportswriter crashed into a spitoon and broke his hip against a barstool. Harry ran to apply for a job in the sports department of the *Post-Dispatch*.

The sports editor had been in the air force in Europe and had read Harry's stuff. Harry was hired for thirty-five dollars a week and packed on a train bound for Florida. He was sent as a replacement to cover the Cardinals in spring training. If he did a good job, he'd have a job. If he did an outstanding job, he had a chance to beat out the regular writer and stick for the season. As a boy, Harry had sat in the bleachers and cheered for the "Gashouse Gang." Now suddenly he was on a first-name basis with Marty Marion, Stan Musial and Country Slaughter. Harry's understanding with the players was that he would write what they did on the fields, not what occurred in saloons or bedrooms—unless the police were called. The players liked him and began to feed him stories. Soon Harry was an edition ahead of the other two papers on every front-office move. By opening day, Harry had won the job.

The previous year's Cardinals writer went to the copy desk. Harry was accepted at Fahey's Bar as a valuable person. Fat Fahey was obsessed with hearing gossip from the Cardinals' locker room. Fat kept three bookmakers busy. Harry taught the match game to Fat and the boys. With the money Harry made playing matches, betting on baseball and gambling at golf with bad players, he bought a Buick convertible, which he drove until the Immortal, a Red Sox fan but an admirer of Harry's writing nevertheless, called him to be a feature writer on the big paper in New York. On a salary of seventy-five dollars a week in St. Louis, plus what society had a way of dropping on a celebrated sportswriter, Harry had lived as if he had come into a great inheritance. Before long he missed the old days in St. Louis, but what he had learned about newspapering in St. Louis worked in New York even better. The Immortal was watching him. . . .

The phone call from Claudette interrupted his reverie.

"Harry, it's time," she said. "The pains have started. I'm scared, Harry. Please pray for me."

Harry flew from Heathrow to Orly and took a taxi to the Hospital of Notre-Dame. The mother superior, in a white nursing habit, met him in the lobby. She looked at him with a frown of disapproval, but led him upstairs. He could hear Claudette moaning in pain as they walked down the tile hallway.

Claudette had scraped the flesh off her elbows in agony. Her lips were chewed and cracked, and a nurse was wiping white spittle from her mouth. Claudette's wide, wild eyes took in Harry with bare recognition. He clutched her hand as they wheeled her out of the room on a rolling bed. Her skin felt dry and hot. The sound of her cries made Harry jerk with pain.

During the twelve hours she was in labor, Harry paced and smoked in the waiting room, like a husband was supposed to do, he thought, but he had never imagined himself doing it. The mother superior entered the waiting room at last and beckoned to him.

"It's a boy," the mother superior said.

"Is my wife all right?" said Harry.

"She's fine. They're cleaning her and the baby up a bit right now. You can see them in a few minutes."

The baby was snuggled in Claudette's arms when Harry came into her room with the armload of roses he had bought at the flower shop in the lobby.

"Well? What do you think of him?" Claudette asked.

Claudette looked tired, but she was glowing with a happiness Harry had never seen in her before.

"He's very red," Harry said.

"He's new, Harry. He doesn't know what to make of the world." She kissed the baby's lumpy, fuzzy head and hugged the child gently.

"I'm going to name him Henri, after my father. Henri Frontenac. Do you like it? Henri, Harry, they sound alike," she said.

"What will you put on the birth certificate where it says father?"

"His father is deceased. That's all I'll put on the birth certificate," she said. "I'll explain it when he's old enough."

The baby was making little popping noises with his mouth. Claudette opened her gown and held the child to her breast. Harry watched, silently, and found the sight unexpectedly moving. He wondered what it would be like to raise a child. Perhaps it would be the deepening, fulfilling experience they wrote about in the women's magazines.

"My option on the house runs out in three months," Harry said. "The offer stands."

"Poor Harry," said Claudette. "You don't need to look miserable. Little Henri and I aren't going to ruin your life. You mustn't worry about us."

"I want you and the kid to come back to England," he said.

"Do you really?"

"Sure. We'll work it out, Claudette."

"No," she said. "I'm not coming back to England. My son is going to grow up in France. You don't owe us anything, Harry. I owe you my life, and I'll always be grateful."

"The kid needs a father."

"But you're not cut out to be a father. No, you've done plenty for us already."

"You must leave now, M. Sparrow," said the mother superior from the doorway. "She must rest."

"I'll be back later," Harry said.

"You don't need to come back, Harry. I know how busy you are with your work. You have to get the story. This birth was just the biggest story of the day. Thank you for coming when I called and for being with me. But you live a different life from the life Henri and I will live. Goodbye, Harry."

Harry caught a taxi at the hotel and went to the rue Scribe. He rode the cage to the second-floor newsroom. It was early and most of the writers and editors had not yet reported for work. But Gruber swiveled in the wooden chair in his cubicle, his green eyeshade pulled down to cut the lamp's glare on his glasses. He cradled a phone at his shoulder, lighting a cigar and editing copy as he spoke. Harry approached the cubicle to ask Gruber for another three months of think pieces. In Harry's mind the deadline was the day the option ran out on the house at Royal Bowling Brook. If Claudette didn't come home in three months, he would consider an annulment, and he would go to Algeria.

"Harry, old boy," Gruber said, regarding his Havana cigar that had a glowing ash an inch long. He puffed gently and watched the ash grow another quarter inch. He was still listening to the phone. "Yes. Well, it's not fair. We were screwed. Maybe the rescue spoiled it for the judges. Dead, he would have been a cinch. No, you tell him. Here he is."

Gruber gave the phone to Harry.

"Sparrow?"

Harry recognized the prep-school tones of Calvin Epps.

"Where are you, Calvin?" Harry said.

"In the old war room at the foreign desk as always. Bad news about the prize. Didn't hit it right with the judges for some reason. I think you should have won."

"The Pulitzer?" Harry said, feeling chill.

"The committee just announced the winner for distinguished excellence in reporting for 1954 is Jim Lucas. The Scripps-Howard Newspaper Alliance wins the statue to put on their mantle."

"For what?"

"Jim Lucas did a hell of a job on the Korean War armistice. Not as obscure as your subject. Much more widely read. Hit home with Americans. But you did win an honorable mention. Congratulations. By the way, Harry, Elmore says you're cooking up a hot idea for another series that will sell the front page. What is it?"

"Let me tighten the bolts before I tell you."

"Okay, Harry. But don't take too long, hear? We need more readers." Epps hung up.

"Sorry, old man. I'm as disappointed as you are," Gruber said.

Harry tried to absorb the blow. He wanted the Pulitzer. He deserved it. The loss made him feel bad enough, but losing was also an indication that Harry's position as a star would be in jeopardy.

"I'll win it this year, Elmore. They won't screw me two years in a row."

The ash fell from Gruber's cigar. He brushed off his knees with his fingers.

"How do you plan to do this, old friend?"

"I don't know. Give me a few weeks."

"That's a long time to stay on the front page with think pieces. You will not win the Pulitzer with columns on golf in Scotland."

"Did you give me my front-page column because you thought I'd win the Pulitzer? I thought you liked what I wrote."

Gruber sighed.

"If I were the only judge, you could stay on the front page and write think pieces until you start writing in-my-day-we-did-it-differently columns. But I am not the only person you must please. The man who dispenses newspapers at the kiosk must be happy with the end result of what you write."

Back in London, Harry took off the jade *Korat* and put it in the drawer with his socks.

He passed up going to the study at No. 5 Cheyne Place and began going every morning to the Chelsea Swim Club for a workout before taking a taxi to his office at the Syndicate. The Syndicate was on the third floor of a dirty brown brick building that looked like a piece of pecan pie. Across the street rose the six-story London *Daily Mail.* He had to walk around rolls of newsprint on the sidewalk and *Daily Mail* trucks with PHIBBS: OUR MAN EVERYWHERE on posters. Harry worked hard at his column trying to keep it on the front page of *The Paris Dispatch.* It occurred to him that he might do a series on the opium traffic at Dien Bien Phu with interviews in Hanoi and Paris.

"Boring. Nobody cares," Gruber said. "I'm quoting Epps, but I agree. More corruption exposed in Indochina? Is that interesting?" Harry was glad the idea was turned down. Doing the opium story in Indochina would have made tracks around Claudette's father.

Harry kept searching for an angle. Weeks passed as he discarded, or Gruber and Epps rejected, one idea after another. His column fell off the front page of *The Paris Dispatch* and appeared again on the op-ed page—I, HARRY SPARROW reduced to a one-column format instead of two columns wide. His picture was cut down to a half-column mug shot.

In his cubicle on Bramble Bush Hill, Harry could see over half-panes of glazed glass and watch action around the horseshoe-shaped copy desk in the bull pen. He loved the sound of teletype machines. Their hammering stimulated him. Their music carried the message that something was happening that Harry needed to know about. Teletype machines were one reason Harry loved the newspaper business.

The copyboy, Thorpe, was filling paste pots at the empty news desk when the United Press machine began to ding. Harry looked up, counting the dings, as Thorpe strolled to the machine. It was too early for the staff to be at the bureau, but Thorpe was a tough kid from the East End who wanted Harry's job. Thorpe came in early and stayed late every day. Harry suspected Thorpe slept at Harry's desk.

"Six dingers, Mr. Sparrow!" cried Thorpe.

Harry swung his feet down off a stack of magazines.

"Eight dingers!"

Harry walked over beside Thorpe as the story began to unreel on the teletype:

> ALGIERS, ALGERIA, MARCH 17 (U.P.)—CLAU-
> DETTE FRONTENAC, 24, ONE OF THE "ANGELS
> OF DIEN BIEN PHU," AND HER INFANT SON
> HAVE BEEN KIDNAPPED BY THE REBEL FLN, A
> POLICE SPOKESMAN SAID HERE TODAY.
>
> MISS FRONTENAC—IN PRIVATE LIFE THE
> WIFE OF SYNDICATED COLUMNIST HARRY
> SPARROW—WAS DISCOVERED MISSING BY PO-
> LICE OFFICERS MAKING A SECURITY CHECK
> OF THE LUXURIOUS HOTEL SAINT-GEORGES.
>
> POLICE SAY MISS FRONTENAC AND HER
> CHILD WERE GRABBED OFF HER BICYCLE
> ALONG THE SEAWALL BY THREE ARABS IN A
> TAXICAB.

The machine clicked and throbbed and gathered itself for the next burst of news. The phone from the Paris office rang on the news desk.

"Hello, Elmore," Harry said into the phone. "I'm looking at the story now."

"What's she doing in Algiers?"

"I don't know."

"Oh, come on, Harry, spare me any bullshit. Al Lewis is doing rewrite on the horn to our guy in Algiers. We must know what your wife is doing down there. We know the two of you are separated, but is she on vacation, or what?"

"I haven't talked to her lately."

"What's this about a baby, Harry? You never told me about a baby."

"No, I didn't."

"One of the angels of Dien Bien Phu having a baby should have been a story in *The Paris Dispatch*," Gruber said. "As the father, you should have been proud to write it."

"Your local boys should have caught it."

"I'm sorry your personal life is so bad, huh? Terribly sorry," Gruber said. "But you've got to help us. Our guy in Algiers has a terrific angle. Guess who turned your wife and the baby in to the police as missing? It was that singing bayoneter you wrote about at Dien Bien Phu."

"What?" Harry could not believe what he was hearing.

"That fellow Selchauhansen. Don't I remember you killed him off in the fourth paragraph?"

"He's dead, Elmore. I saw him die."

"This may be a ghost, but it's a confirmed ghost, Harry. Sabatini, in Algiers, is trying to find out how Selchauhansen got out of Dien Bien Phu despite the fact we reported him dead. What is his connection to your wife? Did he know her? The Nazi won't talk to our stringer."

"I won't be filing my column for a while, Elmore."

"I rather hoped you would cover this story with first-person pieces. Tracking the kidnapped angel of Dien Bien Phu."

"You'll get your stories, but my wife comes first," said Harry.

"Right, Harry. When you find out what this is all about, let us be the first to know, eh? Happy landings in Algiers. It could win you the Pulitzer, Harry."

PART THREE

ALGIERS
1955

17 From a window in the Air France DC-6, Harry saw the city of Algiers laid out on the Mediterranean coastline, a jumble of red tile roofs and whitewashed terraces that reflected the bright winter sun. High on a green hill, among pine trees and palms, stood the Catholic shrine of Notre-Dame d'Afrique. It looked like Sacré-Coeur in Montmartre. On another hill with a view of the turquoise bay, he saw the Hôtel Saint-Georges, a colonial plantation surrounded by gardens. The Saint-Georges had been Eisenhower's headquarters in 1942 during the North African campaign. Below the hotel's flowering lawn was the roof of the governor-general's mansion. The Saint-Georges was a sanctuary for French businessmen, local government officials, police informers, army officers and deputies visiting the new war. Harry knew Phibbs would be arriving at the Saint-Georges today with reporters from London and Paris. Claudette was again front-page news in Europe. With a glance at the snow peaks of the Djurdjura mountains as the airplane dropped toward its landing, Harry let his fingers creep inside his shirt to touch the jade *Korat* that was again on the chain around his neck.

The city of Algiers was the same size as San Francisco, which it resembled, arranged on a deep-water bay with mountains on the horizon. Algeria was the tenth largest country on earth, four times bigger than France. European engineers had transformed swamps and marshes along the central plain between the mountains and the sea into grape country for wine. The coast was heavy with fruit orchards. South of the high plateau and the peaks of the Atlas Mountains began the Sahara, an ocean of stones and sand interrupted by surprisingly green wooded canyons, rock ridges and crags that rolled deep into Africa.

Rodolpho Sabatini, the *Dispatch* Syndicate's man in Algiers, picked Harry up at the airport terminal. A customs agent conferred with two scowling paratrooper officers before slapping the passport hard on the counter and waving Harry through. Harry heard the paratroopers muttering *"Journaliste."* They tapped their holsters.

It was a crisp, lemon-colored morning. The air was bracing and smelled of flowers and fruit. Harry carried his Burberry slung over one shoulder, his Borsalino pushed back on his head, a Chesterfield stuck in the corner of his mouth. His canvas bag with the Skywriter preceded him out of the airport in the pudgy right hand of Sabatini, who was known, naturally, as "Curly" because of his brilliant bald head with a semicircle of wiry black hair. Curly Sabatini tossed Harry's bag into the backseat of a 1947 Dodge four-door and heaved his belly behind the wheel.

"Sorry about your situation, Sparrow. These filthy pigs, these swine, these donkeys, these rats. The veneer of civilization is very thin here, let me tell you *that*. Scratch it with your thumbnail and what appears? Savage violence, like jungle animals. I despise the filthy, lice-ridden 'sand-niggers' from out in the *bled*. They cut a throat with as much care as I use screwing in a light bulb. They're the ones who've got your wife. Hey, Sparrow, don't look at me like that. It's the truth I speak, that's all."

Sabatini was a *pied noir*, a black foot, the slang name for a European born in Algeria. His father was Italian, his wife's father was Spanish, but he and his wife and son, Curly said, were Algerian. "All my life, growing up here in the Bab-el-Oued section, I've lived elbow-to-asshole with Muslims in their tarbooshes and red slippers, and we got along fine. But now the sand-niggers in the *bled*, they bring hatreds even into my neighborhood. It's a crazy world when my own kitchen boy turns on me with a butcher knife and screams Arab curses. Me! A true Algerian, a friend of Muslims. I don't sleep good, Sparrow. But I'm selling a lot of stories."

Harry looked out the car window and wondered how long it would take Max von Eschel to find him. They went along the French boulevards of rue Michelet and rue de l'Isly, with expensive shops and sidewalk cafés that could have been on the Champs Élysées. In front of military headquarters on the rue de l'Isly, paratroopers in tiger stripes and red berets stood among sandbags and barbed wire. They carried MAT 49 submachine guns. The cafés were crowded except for one on the rue Michelet that had an iron grill shut and locked over a smashed window.

"Some dirty *raton* threw a homemade bomb in there last night. Black powder and sodium chlorate packed inside an Esso tin. Wounded two European students and killed an Arab. That's their tactics, the cowardly scum. They use terror on innocent people. They're scared to fool with us *pieds noirs* much so far, but they don't hesitate to kill other Arabs. You see a Muslim being friendly with a white man, working in a white man's shop or vineyard, holding some minor government post, and you know that good Muslim is doomed. He gets a reputation as a *Beni Oui-Oui*. Pretty soon they blow him up or shoot him or cut his throat. They slaughter his wife and children. The Arabs in the *bled*, they claim the only government representatives they've ever seen are the tax collectors. Well, they should have been happy to get off so lightly, I say. Now the tax collectors go with escorts of Lizard Men. The Arabs are being blasted to pieces by the paratroopers, according to headquarters."

Around the harbor, where Barbary pirates had once auctioned slaves, Harry smelled diesel oil, salt and fish and saw the obligatory statues—the monuments to the dead that the French placed throughout their empire. French banks and mercantile companies operated on the waterfront in arcaded buildings. Curly Sabatini had checked Harry in at the Hôtel Aletti to avoid Phibbs and the rest of the journalists assembling in the bar at the Saint-Georges. The Aletti was on the water near the *Echo d'Alger* newspaper, where the

Dispatch Syndicate rented an office for its one-man bureau. *The Paris Dispatch* was not widely distributed in Algeria—there weren't many English-speaking tourists buying the paper at kiosks in Bône or Constantine or Sétif—but copies were flown into Algiers nightly by Air France and sold at the airport and at hotels like the Saint-Georges. The Immortal in the tower in New York believed in operating bureaus in every important city in the world. The Syndicate demanded a steady outpouring of words to stay ahead of the competition.

"Well, no, that German giraffe didn't actually go to the cops and turn your wife in as missing," Curly said, puffing a black Algerian cigar and thumbing through a stack of messages on his desk at the bureau. Besides the *Dispatch* Syndicate, Curly also strung for several European and American radio networks and magazines. All of his clients were wiring requests for stories on the bombs and the shootings in Algeria and now the kidnapping of one of the angels of Dien Bien Phu. Curly had never made so much money in his life. "As a matter of fact, the German is a cop himself. He's one of the special operators, the top-secret boys. The police were making a routine patrol of the halls at the Saint-Georges and they passed an open doorway and saw that tall shithead. He was in your wife's room, reading the note her kidnappers left on her pillow. The police surprised him and pointed their guns at him. I wouldn't doubt the army would have hushed up the kidnapping—they hate the press, you know—but suddenly it was in the hands of the police."

"On her pillow?" Harry said. "I thought she was snatched on the waterfront."

"Witnesses later told police that the FLN got her while she was riding a bicycle with the baby in the basket on the handlebars."

"How and why did the kidnappers leave a note on her pillow?"

"Nobody in this town will explain anything. Nothing makes sense. The kidnappers are Arabs. It's hard to understand what an Arab means by what he says."

"Stupid for the police to point guns at a Foreign Legion paratrooper unless they intended to kill him."

"Oh, but this big, lanky prick doesn't wear a uniform. I told you he's a special cop. He wears a white cotton burnoose like an Arab. He had on a blue tarboosh with a pink tassel and sunglasses like aviators wear. This is a very weird son of a bitch, Sparrow. They say he caught a bad case of the *mal de jeune* in Indochina. The asshole gives me a cold chill, I don't mind admitting. He's got a look in his eyes like an old Berber chief I used to know who was a monster for cruelty. They call the German *le Chinois.*"

Raoul Salan, a former French military commander-in-chief of Vietnam, had been nicknamed "The Chinaman" because he adopted oriental clothing, consulted horoscopes and collected white ivory elephants. For a moment Harry wondered if Salan had been transferred from NATO to Algeria and Curly had gotten his stories confused.

Curly looked up through a fog of cigar smoke. "Those boys who went to Indochina, they came back with a sickness. They are a different breed of human. That German looks at me like I'm a piece of shit on the heel of his slipper. I saw his *nom de guerre* on the kidnap report at police headquarters and recognized it from your Dien Bien Phu stories. I went to question him at the DOP . . ."

"At the what?"

"*Détachement d'opération et de protection.* The Indochina boys organized a special intelligence group to catch the terrorists and make them betray their comrades. The DOP is doing good work. I'm on their side. It's worth bending the law to catch out the bombers, the ambushers and the blackmailers. We don't write about the DOP—the government forbids it. I understand the need for secrecy—I applaud it—but this is not just a matter of crushing the balls or knocking out the teeth of some terrorist. The German should have talked to me. The kidnapping of one of the angels of Dien Bien Phu is news."

"Where can I find the DOP?" Harry asked.

Sabatini wrote the address on a piece of copy paper. "It's a big, white villa above the harbor. You'll have to go by yourself. They told me to stay away. When the DOP threatens, I obey."

"From the way you talk, I guess you don't have any personal contacts in the FLN," Harry said.

"Why do you say that? Of course I have acquaintances who are fellagha. I told you I grew up in Bab-el-Oued. I'd have to be blind, deaf and dumb to live in Bab-el-Oued and not know any FLN."

"But why don't you turn them in to the DOP?" Harry said.

Curly Sabatini chewed angrily on his cigar and pulled shreds of tobacco out of his teeth.

"I am not a snitch," he said. "What kind of man would turn in his neighbors to the cops? When I call the Arabs rats and swine, I mean the terrorists. The fellagha are not all terrorists. Many Arabs are pretty good boys. They're like the Negroes in your southern United States—they're not all bad by any means. It's a few that cause trouble for the many. What if a few hundred started blowing up cafés and machine-gunning Negroes and white people alike?"

"You're outnumbered ten to one," Harry said.

"The FLN's fight is against the rich *colons,* " Curly said. "If I was a slave in the vineyards or fruit orchards and the *colon* paid me in beatings and forced me to grovel in the dirt and eat worms and roots, you bet I would make him swallow a hand grenade up his asshole. But the Arabs must beware of the fury of us *pieds noirs.* This is our country by birth. We are innocent of exploiting Arabs. We are working class. Beware of our rage."

"I want to you put me in touch with somebody high up in the FLN."

"Maybe I can."

"I'll make a bargain with you," Harry said. "You put me with leaders of the FLN and I'll fix it so you get the exclusive story on solving the kidnapping. Your byline."

"For *The Paris Dispatch?*"

"For *The Paris Dispatch, The New York Dispatch* and the *Dispatch* Syndicate."

"You'll double-cross me. I know your reputation. You would wade through your mother's blood to get a scoop."

Harry grabbed Curly Sabatini by the shirtfront with both hands and jerked him out of his chair.

"This is my wife and kid I'm looking for, not a story," Harry said.

Curly tried to pull Harry's wrists away, but Harry was too strong for him. "All right, all right, let me go." Harry released him, and Curly looked ruefully at a button that dangled from a thread on his shirt. "I'm not scared of you, but I am a human being, after all. I respect your anxiety over your wife and baby. I'll do what I can to help you."

Harry walked to the Hôtel Aletti. A lorry of paratroopers rumbled past and stopped at the Place du Gouvernement. The soldiers climbed down and began erecting barbed-wire barricades to make traffic checkpoints. Gulls swooped among the masts of the fishing boats. The villas on the cliffs reminded Harry of Cannes or Nice. He wondered which of the villas he could see from the Hôtel Aletti was DOP headquarters. Harry knew that the customs agent and the desk clerk had informed the army and the police that he was in Algiers. He felt his gut tighten as he thought about the German. If the DOP was as good as the Gestapo, Max von Eschel would know which room Harry was in by now.

Outside his door Harry paused and sniffed the air. It smelled as if the Cardinals had changed uniforms in there. Harry unlocked the door and pushed it open with his foot.

From the hall, he snapped: "Pelwa! I know you're in my room. Is von Eschel with you?"

"Hey, Mister Chicago, gangster man, don't shoot me, please," squealed Pelwa. "I'm a poor errand boy. If you want to get rough, take it out on my chief. He sent me to bring you."

In his memory, Harry saw Pelwa wearing the black SS cap on his round head, his beard scraggly, a brown cigarette clamped between broken yellow teeth, a filthy bandage on his left hand, his stout torso draped with cartridge belts and hand grenades, his thick hairy legs disappearing into heavy jungle boots.

The man who stepped into view in Harry's hotel room wore a rumpled corduroy suit, a Babe Ruth–style suede cap and brown suede shoes with gum soles. A clean-shaven face revealed Pelwa to be ten years younger than Harry had thought. The corporal could have passed as a businessman doing trade around the harbor—a businessman of sorts. Above the knuckles, where three fingers were blown off at Dien Bien Phu, was the tattoo in bold blue letters that said BORN TO DIE. His odor was unmistakable, and the brown cheroot danced in his lips. He grinned at Harry and squinted through the smoke stinging his eyes.

"You never thought you'd see me again, hey, Mister Chicago?"

"Would you like a drink?" Harry said, nodding toward the bottle of The Famous Grouse that Pelwa tucked in an armpit. The bottle had been in Harry's canvas bag.

"Sure, sure, a drink is the way to say hello again to your old friend Pelwa. I'll share your whiskey with you."

The contents of the bag had been tossed on the bed. The Skywriter sat on the table by the window. Pelwa had opened the bottle and lowered it by two inches. The corporal handed the bottle to Harry.

"What's the matter, you didn't bring your golf club?" Pelwa asked. "They've got golf courses in this town. This is not like the Shit Pot."

"How did you get out?" Harry said. "I saw Lola blown into a crater filled with muddy water. You are dead."

Pelwa crushed his cheroot on the carpet and tore the cellophane on a package of Harry's Chesterfields that came out of Pelwa's shirt pocket.

"On the last day we could hear the Reds chinking and clanking and hammering a few meters beneath our feet. We knew the end was there. The chief rounded up the Headhunters who were alive on Lola—seventeen of us. Only old comrades crowded into the wine cellar. Anybody who wasn't one of us, a Headhunter, out they stayed on the hill to deal with the Reds."

Harry was starting to understand.

"The wine cellar was made out of cast concrete," Harry said. "Stronger than being inside a tank hull. Frontenac built a very safe cellar to keep his wines in. Not a monsoon, not an earthquake, not a bomb would destroy a bottle of that man's vintage wine."

"When the Red miners blew up Lola . . ."

". . . Your wine cellar stayed in one piece like a big box."

"The hill caved in on us. It rained hard in the night and we dug out through the Reds' tunnel. We slipped across the Nam Yum in the monsoon and headed west into the jungle instead of east toward Hanoi. We crept through the jungle for months, and we didn't leave witnesses. Fifteen of us made it to Chiang Mai in Thailand."

Harry offered the bottle to Pelwa again.

"Chiang Mai is where Claudette and I got out of the country," Harry said.

"Oh, we didn't get out of the country right away. The chief is cunning, always thinking how to take care of his boys. We rested awhile in a hidden camp and then we went back in the jungle."

"To get revenge on the Reds?"

"No, you fool, to get rich. We harassed the opium trails from Thailand to Burma to Cambodia. Powerful plunder there, comrade, to be taken by those that dare to do it. Nobody's a more formidable opponent in the jungle than us Headhunters."

"Your chief scorned the opium trade."

"We discovered we could ambush one mule train and get a million in cash plus another million in raw opium that we sold in Chiang Mai. It was child's play for us against the Opium Mafia. Their mercenaries didn't have a chance in the jungle against Headhunters. We slaughtered them. The Mafia offered to pay us for protection. We took their money but robbed their mule trains anyway." Pelwa laughed. "The chief deposited our money in a bank in Switzerland. You are looking at a wealthy Bavarian here, Mister Chicago."

"You're crazy," Harry said.

"Hey! Hey!" Pelwa roared, punching himself on the chest with five fingertips and two thumbs. "I'm wealthy in the export trade, mister. Don't you talk to me like I'm a common soldier."

"If you're rich, why are you here with the Legion?"

"The Opium Mafias went crying to Paris. One day the 11th Shock Battalion showed up in our face."

The 11th Shock Battalion was a French dirty-tricks commando force that had begun operating in Indochina during the last year of the war.

"The 11th Shock was coming out of the jungle, on their way to Algeria, and they had orders to bring us with them. The 11th is a proud outfit. To fight them or escape them would have been useless. They learned their stuff from us."

"Why didn't you face a court-martial for desertion?" Harry said.

"That was their intention. But the chief made a bargain for us. The chief would have been a great lawyer. We can keep our money in Switzerland and will be free to spend it."

"What's the catch?"

"We swore to serve in Algeria until we put down this uprising.

The French need us to round up terrorist suspects for the DOP that the law is too chicken-shit to touch. We operate under 'Headhunter law.' When the FLN is dead, the Headhunters will be honorably discharged from the Legion. We'll be free to go spend our money anywhere but in France."

Pelwa lit another Chesterfield, his small eyes shifting around the room on continual alert for an ambush. He was growing impatient.

"Okay, let's go see your chief," Harry said.

Waiting for them at the service entrance of the Hôtel Aletti was a black 1946 Ford V-8 with a taxi flag on the driver's side. The auto windows were covered with wire mesh to deflect fire bombs or grenades. Behind the wheel was a man wearing a burnoose with the hood up to hide his head, so that Harry could see only sunglasses, a broken nose and a blond mustache.

At the lower entrance to the Casbah, the European appearance of the city changed abruptly to Turkish. Now the houses had overhanging upper floors supported by wooden beams. The narrow streets and alleys of the ancient Turkish quarter twisted and turned in a labyrinth as they climbed among mosques and decaying Moorish mansions toward the ruined Fort of the Casbah on top of the hill. Muslim cries and scoldings and laughter and prayers rang through crooked lanes that smelled of spices and oil. The shops were full of sweet candy and honeycakes.

Four paratroopers in red berets and tiger stripes manned a checkpoint with machine guns, barbed wire and sandbags, watching everyone who entered or left the Casbah. They pulled Arabs aside to be searched. Three Arabs were thrown into the back of a two-and-a-half-ton truck.

"Hello, Pelwa," said a sergeant with a dimpled chin, bending to look into the backseat. "Who's this man?"

"A comrade-in-arms," Pelwa said. "A Legionnaire on special assignment."

"What's your name?" the sergeant asked.

"Justus Selchauhansen," Harry said.

A sneer rippled along the paratrooper's mouth. "You Kraut bastards," he said. "All right, Pelwa, drive through. But watch your ass. We killed a sniper behind the old palace an hour ago."

Honking the horn and screaming curses in German, French and Arabic, the driver slowly progressed, driving the Ford three blocks in ten minutes into the Casbah. He parked the vehicle in front of a café. The driver got out to sit on the fender with his MAT 49 across his knees. High-pitched bazaar music blared all around them, intense as a dental drill. Pelwa and Harry took a table on the sidewalk and ordered coffee from a waiter in tarboosh and slippers. They were waiting, Pelwa said, for a signal from the chief that it was clear for them to enter the house.

"You don't think the civilian clothes fool anybody, do you?" Harry said, sipping bitter, syrupy liquid in the tiny cup.

"It's the chief's idea." Pelwa shrugged. "No more uniforms, he says. We've worn uniforms fifteen years. Now we dress as we please."

"Your old buddy, Ali Saadi, ought to be useful. He must be having a picnic rounding up his former landlords to help them have their fingernails torn off by the DOP."

Pelwa coughed and spat on the sidewalk.

"Don't say his name," Pelwa said.

"Didn't he make it back from the jungle?"

"He's a traitor. He betrayed us."

"How?"

"He went over to the FLN." Pelwa's voice shook with bitterness. "I saved that boy from the Casbah cops. I pulled him through basic training in the Legion. I whipped the sadists off his back. I killed a Norwegian sergeant for him in Orléansville. I watched over him for six years in the jungles. I dragged him out of the cellar on Lola and carried him in my arms across the Nam Yum. I'll tell you as one human to another, Chicago, I loved that Arab boy. But now I hate him."

"What made him change?"

"At first he was happy at the idea of getting out of Chiang Mai with his pockets full of loot. But when we came here, I could see in his face, how he refused to look me in the eye. No matter how he tried to hide it, he was an Arab in the blood. Two weeks ago we caught his cousin, a fellagha named Yassef, who operates a bomb factory somewhere in the Casbah. We arrested Ali Saadi's relatives.

One of them was a girl. Saadi begged the chief to let her go, but he wouldn't do it. We must find that bomb factory. We took the girl up to the White House with the others and turned her over to the DOP. Those assholes drowned her in a bucket of mop water. I was sorry to hear it—so was the chief—but how could we help it? Ali Saadi wailed and wept and carried on like a typical Arab. First time I ever heard him making those ulu . . . ulu . . . how do you say it?"

"Ululations?"

"Saadi waited until Sergeant Kleiner took a shift bodyguarding for the chief. In the middle of the night he cut Kleiner's throat. Imagine, old Kleiner, his Legion brother through many battles. Ali Saadi sliced his throat like some sheep whose blood he was draining for an Arab feast. Almost cut Kleiner's head off. Here they call it the 'smile of Kabylia.' Saadi sneaked into the chief's room with Kleiner's blood dripping from his knife," Pelwa said. "But the chief is too smart for any Arab. He woke up and attacked Saadi. The Arab broke away and leaped out the window of the chief's bedroom and escaped into the Casbah. Now we have bars on our windows."

Pelwa's eyes ceased roaming for a moment and settled on Harry's face with a look of hurt and disappointment. Harry almost felt sorry for him.

"Two more questions," Harry said.

"Don't ask me about your wife, please. I don't know nothing. You'll have to ask the chief."

"All right. But why does your chief live in the Casbah?"

"We like to be close to our work," Pelwa said with an effort at a smile. "It makes good sense for us to live in the Casbah. The Casbah is our hunting ground. Living in the Casbah keeps us out of sight of prying eyes. Some journalist has written an article in *France Observateur* that says 'Is There a Gestapo in Algeria?' The chief got a laugh out of it. He taped the article to the toilet at our house."

A stout wooden door opened in a blue stucco wall beside the café. A tall Arab wearing a burnoose and veil stepped out and beckoned to Pelwa.

They stood up. Pelwa touched Harry's sleeve. "You're not going to try to hurt the chief, are you, Chicago?"

"Why would I want to hurt him?"

"I warned you nobody could take a woman away from the chief."

"She came here to see him?"

"Who could blame her? Well, come on, mister. The chief will tell you what you need to know."

They went through the wooden door in the wall and entered a courtyard that smelled of moonflowers and sweet jasmine. The courtyard was silent after the babble of the narrow street outside. White tile walkways stuck out like spokes from the fountain in the middle of the gardens. The fountain was a marble *djinn* with water gurgling from its mouth and pattering into a pond where goldfish swam. The house made up the other three walls of the garden. Balconies with wrought-iron grillwork and tall French doors gazed down on the courtyard from three sides. It reminded Harry of the French Quarter in New Orleans. The veiled Arab slammed shut the bolt in the door behind them. Looking up to the roof, Harry saw a stone chimney surrounded by sandbags. The barrel of a .30 caliber machine gun poked out of the sandbags and covered the courtyard.

Harry and Pelwa followed the veiled Arab into the house. A blond man in khakis with burn scars on his face nodded and grunted at Pelwa and then looked back at the Donald Duck comic book he was reading, propped against his MAT 49. The Arab led them up the stairs to the second floor and down a narrow hall with plaster peeling from the ceiling.

As they entered a large sitting room, Harry smelled the cloying, too-sweet licorice odor of opium. He saw a long ivory opium pipe on the sill in front of barred windows and a wooden block pillow on the floor at the head of a straw mat. A portable hi-fi record player on a bookshelf was playing an LP record that had scratches on it. Harry recognized the music as the "Academic Festival Overture" by Brahms.

Then he saw von Eschel. The lanky chief of the Headhunters lounged on heaps of pillows in one corner of the room, staring at his long bare toes, which he wriggled with pleasure. The hood of a white cotton burnoose was down around his wide shoulders. Harry saw that von Eschel had shaved his beard and cut his hair short. Without the hair von Eschel had a firm chin and muscles that moved in a long, lean jaw. Harry recalled that the first time he saw

the German he thought of a mad monk. There was still the attitude
of a wolfhound about the way he carried his body, but with the
removal of the facial hair and the warrior's uniform, von Eschel
looked like John the Baptist after marine boot camp. His eyes
glittered in his skull like the polished desert stones that in New
Mexico are called Apache tears.

"Where is she?" Harry said.

Von Eschel stared at him. The two men locked eyes for thirty
seconds in silence.

"I want her more than you do," said the German. "She is the
mother of my son."

Harry picked up the pipe and sniffed it. The smell of opium was
fresh and powerful. He dabbed a forefinger at the gummy residue.

"Why did you start smoking? You said it was a subhuman activity."

"You showed great relish killing me in the newspaper," von
Eschel said. "Not a bad job of writing, Sparrow. Fanciful in spots,
but about as true as will be told from Dien Bien Phu. You had to
write your story on the spot. You didn't have the luxury of reflecting on the facts to rearrange and reinvent them."

Harry said, "I'll find Claudette and your kid myself. But I want
to know about the note on her pillow. If Arabs stuffed her into a
taxicab on the waterfront, they wouldn't leave a note at the Saint-
Georges in the midst of the French High Command. What were
you doing in her room when the police spotted you?"

Von Eschel gathered his long legs beneath him and rose gradually to his full height.

"What would you expect me to tell the police? Should I have said
Claudette and I are lovers? I told the police I'd found a kidnap note,
but it was a DOP matter and not to be disclosed to them. On the
pad at her nightstand I found Claudette had written the name Ali
Saadi and an address on the waterfront."

"She wouldn't go to the waterfront to meet Ali Saadi."

"She knew him from Dien Bien Phu. She saw him here before
he betrayed us. Claudette was physically attracted to him. It's not
surprising she would go to meet a handsome Arab boy."

"With a baby in her arms?" Harry said.

"Claudette is not the chaste creature you imagine she became when you gave her the title of wife. When I went to Bangkok, I saw in a French magazine that you and Claudette had married at a church near where I was opening bank accounts for my Headhunters. I stayed in the Oriental Hotel in the same room you slept in with her. I slept in your wedding bed. I felt grateful to you, Sparrow, for taking care of her for me. I thought she'd have a good life with you in case I didn't survive the jungle. But she never loved you. She married you because she was pregnant."

"You're a liar. I'm going to find Ali Saadi and pay him whatever he wants and take Claudette and the kid home," Harry said.

"Maybe Saadi wants to sleep with the angel of Dien Bien Phu."

"He's had plenty of time to get that done by now. Anything else he wants, he can have that, too, so long as I get her back," Harry said.

"Why don't you offer to trade the two of them for me?"

"I don't trust you," Harry said.

Von Eschel lifted his robe and cinched a trench knife to the calf of his right leg. He pulled a pair of soft red slippers over his long, bony white feet.

"I wonder how anxious you'll be to take her home if they've given her an Arab beauty treatment?" von Eschel said, straightening up again.

"Dead or alive, I'm taking her."

The German gestured at the tall, veiled Arab.

"Lower your veil a moment, please."

Harry's jaw fell slack when the Arab removed the veil. His nose and lips had been sliced off with a clean stroke. The center of his face was a phlegm-draped hole.

"His crime against the FLN was owning the café where you and Pelwa just drank coffee. What do you think the terrorists might do to a notorious symbol of colonialism like an angel of Dien Bien Phu?"

Pelwa stuck his head in from the next room.

"Hey, chief, our boys have grabbed Ali Saadi's nephew. They're taking him to the White House."

"Well, Sparrow," said von Eschel. "Shall we go ask the Arab where your wife and my son are?"

18 The transmission of the black Ford V-8 growled with throaty power as the driver dropped to first gear for the climb up the corniche. The whitewashed pastel walls that guarded the villas glittered with broken glass and barbed wire. Slashes of paint on the plaster said FLN and ALGÉRIE FRANÇAISE and GUERRE À MORT and MORT AUX RATS. Pelwa sat beside the driver with a submachine gun in his lap. As the Ford made a sharp turn, Harry could see whitecaps down in the harbor where fishing boats rocked at anchor.

The air of tranquility von Eschel had sucked through the stem of his opium pipe lingered in his expression as he gazed at the slogans of rebellion on the walls. He lifted an open palm and slowly closed his long fingers as if crushing insects in his fist.

"In a few more weeks we will mash them," he said. "We will know all their money couriers and extortionists and bomb makers. We will kill them. Every courier, every organizer, every political cadre—we must kill each individual. Terrorists are individuals, remember, not an army. The only way to defeat terrorists is to hunt them down individually. The French Army thinks it can win here by destroying villages in the *bled*. If the army could get permission, they would bring tanks and artillery into the Casbah and blast the whole place to rubble to wipe out one bomb factory. But terrorists don't mass for battle. This French war machine is frustrated again. Their foolish action makes all Arabs the enemy. It could turn into a Holy War if the army keeps on shelling huts in the *bled*."

"Planting a bomb in a café and blowing up innocent people is murder. Murder is for the police, not the military," Harry said.

"Exactly what I'm saying," said von Eschel.

"Police—like an international force from the United Nations working for Interpol: They would arrest terrorists anywhere in the world and bring them to trial before the World Court. We would find out who the terrorists are. If they're Reds, we'll know it. If they're your boys, we'd know that, too."

"What if your police knew the guilt of a certain terrorist but couldn't reach him? Would you object if your police sniper put a bullet in his head?"

"No," Harry said.

"Then we are on the same side." Von Eschel unrolled a tinfoil and removed a ball of opium the size of a pea. "Want a bite of opium?" Harry shook his head. "It calms one's nerves. I was surprised how pleasant and easy it is to become a lover of opium."

"You've started losing your nerve?" Harry said.

"I believe for me opium is like the Church is for Claudette. It is a sacrament and a friend. It makes reality unreal."

"Suppose you murder the FLN leaders. Do you think the French would let you leave Algeria alive?" said Harry. "Allow an SS officer to have credit?"

"When terrorists with North African names begin exploding bombs in airports and banks and restaurants in the United States, you will remember me, Sparrow. I warn you, I am fighting on your side. You are too smug and conceited to believe it. You Americans never dream that one day in your own lifetime the Red butcher with bloody hands will be at your door, demanding your wealth and your lives."

"What did you come back for, von Eschel? I don't believe the

11th Shock Battalion scared you into finishing your obligation to the Legion. A superman like you, chief of the Headhunters, survivor of Lola, you could have evaded the 11th Shock if you had wanted to."

"I came back to get Claudette."

"You don't love her. You love chaos and murder," Harry said.

Von Eschel leaned his neck against the seat. The blue tarboosh crinkled on his forehead. The pink tassel dangled to touch the bridge of his long straight nose. He took off his aviator sunglasses and pinched his nostrils, shutting his eyes. Harry had seen the expression when they played chess.

"I know what you must mean by that," the German said. " 'The strong men, the masters, regain the pure conscience of a beast of prey, monsters filled with joy . . .' Is that what you think I am? One of Nietzsche's or Treitschke's monsters filled with joy? The SS taught me Himmler's favorite philosophers, but I have learned for myself the difference between right and wrong. No one is innocent of this question—call it religion or politics, but all will have to answer. Whether I could have eluded the 11th Shock Battalion is irrelevant, because I chose not to try. My place is here in Algeria. My goal is to wipe out the FLN. I undertake it with pleasure."

The Ford stopped outside a villa indistinguishable from others in an upper-middle-class European neighborhood that clung to the rim of a cliff. This was the White House. Sea birds rode wind drafts up the sheer granite face from the crashing surf. An eye peered from a slit in the iron gate in the wall. Harry climbed out with von Eschel and Pelwa. The Ford motored away with a deeply satisfying murmur. The 1946 Ford V-8 was one of the great motorcars, Harry believed.

"If it should cross your mind to write about what you see here, remember you would be betraying the Legion," von Eschel said. "You drank an oath to those who are in the sands. If you break your oath, you will die for it. The Legion will kill you."

There was no threatening tone to provoke a reaction from Harry. The captain said it as an unarguable fact.

The iron gate swung inward, and the three entered. Two Lizard Men wearing red berets eyed Harry with hostility. He noticed silver lightning badges on their berets. It was the emblem of the 11th Shock Battalion, a copy of the old double slash of the Waffen SS.

"What's your name?" the lieutenant said, staring at Harry as if his face was familiar. The lieutenant was in his early forties, a professional. A captaincy could be expected at forty-five in the colonial army. "I've seen you before, haven't I? Who are you?"

"I vouch for him," von Eschel said. "He's on assignment with me."

"Another SS bastard," the veteran 11th Shock lieutenant said. "Let them go past. It makes me sick to look at them. I remember when these turds were on the other side."

They walked on Persian tiles, inlaid in an arabesque, that crossed the lawn to a shaded veranda with a view across the bay to the main part of the city. Against the northern horizon, the smear of a squall line lay along the Mediterranean. The breeze was fresh and cool. Pigeons fluttered among the pines. There were eucalyptus and olive trees. A bicycle stood by the corner of the veranda with its kick-stand down. Suspended by chains from the roof, a wooden swing creaked softly. Bougainvillea and moonflowers covered the trellises. A little black rooster perched on a weather vane.

Two Aryans, wearing burnooses, came out of the garage escorting a small, slender young Arab. The young Arab's ankles were locked in leg-irons, with a chain that led up to his cuffed wrists. He had a bruise under his left eye. His hair was cut like Elvis Presley's. The young Arab looked at Harry and ventured a smile, trying any hope to survive the day. The Headhunters prodded the Arab forward, and he frog-hopped in his chains toward the front door of the house, smiling back at Harry in embarrassment.

"He knows where Claudette and the kid are, huh?" Harry said.

"Yes," said von Eschel. "He knows where they both are."

"Let me talk to him, then. He'll tell me where she is. I'll make a deal with him. I'll give him money, take him back to Paris, whatever he wants in trade."

"He also knows where Yassef's bomb factory is."

"Let me have him. You can find somebody else who knows where the bomb factory is."

"You are under the misimpression that I am in command here. I am not. This is a French military operation. I take orders from the French Army. I couldn't turn that Arab over to you if I wanted to. He is going to be tortured."

"Let me ask him. Tell the DOP it's a Legion matter from Dien Bien Phu. For God's sakes, let me have a crack at him before they start breaking his teeth."

"All right," von Eschel said. "It might work your way. Perhaps you can persuade him."

Harry and the Germans went up the staircase to the second story, where a half-dozen closed doors led off a large gallery. From behind the doors as they walked past, they could hear snuffling, groaning, wheezing sounds, like the laments of trapped and dying animals. They heard people weeping without hope of being heard. Harry wondered which *grand colon* had owned this house, which well-fed matron had demanded that her architect make the bedrooms and the upstairs gallery have views of the sea and the ice-blue mountains. How many lost souls had gazed from the DOP house with yearning at the water and the snow peaks?

They stopped at a door that had the number *3* scrawled on it with crayon. Von Eschel rapped on the door. They heard a dead-bolt click. A beefy, unshaven face peeked out, recognized the captain and opened the door. The man and his partner wore rubber waders, a rubber apron and rubber gloves that reached halfway to the elbows. A sawhorse stood in the center of the bare room. A portable generator sat on the floor in the corner beside a coiled garden hose, which was attached to a faucet in the bathroom. The young Arab was naked. On his hands and knees, with a bucket of water and a GI brush, he scrubbed blood off the pine floor. He looked around at Harry, and his eyes brightened with hope.

"Come to see the show?" asked the sleepy-looking torturer. "This Arab looks like a mew-mew. Mew-mew-mew, like a little pussy. Look at him tremble."

"Let me talk to him," Harry said.

"My Legion comrade wants to question the prisoner," said von Eschel.

"Stand up, little pussy," the torturer said.

The Arab rose and faced them.

"I apologize for being naked in front of you. I am ashamed," he said.

"Where are the European woman and the baby?" Harry asked.

"What woman?" said the Arab. "I don't know of a baby."

The sleepy-looking torturer backhanded the boy across the mouth and knocked him staggering against the wall.

"Don't hit him again," Harry said angrily. "I'm trying to talk to him."

The two torturers exchanged grins. "He's right," said the sleepy-looking one. "I think I bruised my hand. Let's stick that hose up this boy's ass and pump him full of hot, soapy water." He looked lazily at Harry. "Is that gentle enough to suit you, Your Highness?"

"But he'll shit on the floor and we'll have to spank him," said the second torturer.

"Where is Ali Saadi hiding the European woman he kidnapped?" Harry asked the boy.

"I don't know," the Arab said.

The sleepy-looking torturer grabbed the Arab by the shoulders and bent him backward across the sawhorse. The other torturer thumped the Arab's testicles with a middle finger as one would test a melon. Harry felt his own genitals draw up in empathy with the pain. The Arab groaned.

"You've got to tell me," Harry said. "I appeal to you as one human to another. She's my wife."

"I'm sorry, but I don't know," the Arab said.

"Your wife! Why didn't you say so?" said the sleepy-looking torturer. "We'll make this little pussy open up right away."

"If you tell me where she is, I'll get you out of here," Harry said to the Arab.

"Sure he will. You'll be as free as an eagle," said the second torturer. He slid the magneto across the floor and tossed a pair of electrodes to the young Arab. "Hold these buttons against your balls, you shit, while I plug in the machine—or maybe this fellow whose wife you kidnapped would rather crank the generator himself until you decide to talk. He might feel it's more satisfying that way."

"Could you get me out of here?" the Arab asked.

"Yes," said Harry.

"Please do it. Please get me out of here."

"Where's my wife?"

"I don't know. I swear I don't know. No matter how much they torture me, I still don't know."

"We get two kinds in here—those who know and those who don't know," said the sleepy-looking torturer. "We treat them both the same."

"Please, mister, I'll find your wife and baby if you'll get me out of here. You've got to believe me. I don't know where my uncle Ali Saadi is. I don't know anything about your wife. But I'll find out for you if you get me out of here."

The second torturer switched on the current. There was a sizzling zap, like the sound made by the device that hung from a tree limb to fry mosquitos in Harry's parents' backyard on Peach Street in St. Louis. The smell of scorched hair flooded the room, and the Arab shook and broke out in a heavy sweat. The Arab moaned piteously and bit his lips. He pissed on his legs and his body jerked with spasms.

Harry grabbed the cord and yanked it out of the wall.

"Stop this! Stop it! I won't allow it!" he yelled. To the Arab he said, "Come on, we're getting out of here."

The sleepy-looking torturer swung a baton at Harry's head. Harry ducked and heard it whistle past. Pelwa leaped between Harry and the two angry torturers in their rubber boots and aprons.

"You can't hit him. He's one of us," Pelwa growled.

"Come on! Hurry!" Harry said, reaching for the Arab.

The baton cracked across the Arab's knees like a rifle shot. He grunted and fell sideways to the floor. The Arab looked down with astonishment and horror at a white bone thrusting through the skin.

"You better take your crazy friend out of here, you Kraut swine," said the sleepy-looking torturer.

"We protect our own," von Eschel said. The menace in his voice made the two torturers step back.

The Germans grabbed Harry by each arm and wrestled him

toward the door. The Arab lay holding his gruesomely damaged limb. He caught Harry's eye with a last imploring look.

Then Harry was roughly and rapidly escorted down the stairs by the two Germans. Harry jerked his arms free. He straightened his jacket and firmly tilted his hat. He kept quiet until the three of them were let out the iron gate by the young Lizard Man. The veteran lieutenant made a show of pinching his nose in disgust.

"Germans shit in their pants," said the lieutenant.

When the bolt had rattled shut on the gate, Harry whirled on von Eschel in a fury.

"That monster-of-joy bullshit is another way of saying you're a homicidal psychopath. We're not on the same side. You must have lured Claudette to Algeria to show you your son, but I don't believe she could love you."

The black Ford V-8 crept up the corniche toward them.

"You're disturbed. Come back to the house," said von Eschel. "We'll argue the rights and wrongs over coffee and a pipe."

"I've had more than enough of you already," Harry said. "I'm going out to find Claudette my own way. I'll find your kid, too, von Eschel, but you won't get him back."

Harry started walking up the sidewalk, going higher up the hill.

"Come back here, Sparrow," said von Eschel.

Harry walked faster. He didn't like the way things were looking. Common sense told him not to get into the Ford. He heard heavy footsteps behind him and recognized Pelwa's raspy breathing.

"Leave me alone," Harry shouted, still walking. "I'm going on alone."

"It's too dangerous for you," called von Eschel. "You'll be safe with us."

"Never mind," Harry yelled.

"Sparrow, listen, you can't be allowed to roam around. You have to stay at our place in the Casbah," called von Eschel. "It's orders, Sparrow—orders from the Legion!"

Harry heard the hum of the black Ford as it threatened closer behind him. He could almost feel the heat of Pelwa's breath. Just ahead, the corniche took a hard right turn. A four-foot-high stone wall and a reflecting warning sign guarded the turn.

"Grab him, Pelwa!" shouted von Eschel.

Harry sprinted to the stone wall and leaped on top of it.

The cliff dropped straight down for sixty feet. At the bottom, the waves lashed against boulders that protected the entrance to a deep cove with water so clear Harry could see fish swimming at the bottom.

Harry glanced back at the running Pelwa, who shouted, "Don't be stupid, Chicago! You'll kill yourself!" Harry heard the black Ford's brakes screech, and the ratchet sound of the emergency brake, and the broken-nosed Aryan in the burnoose leaped out with his MAT 49. Pelwa flung up both arms and groped for Harry's ankles.

With a fleeting instant of regret at their loss, Harry kicked off his cordovan loafers and dived from the stone wall.

19 Harry made a powerful spring, high and far from the wall. He spread his arms and arched his back and nosed over into a dive. From his years of training as a platform diver, he knew that balance and poise were uppermost. The water foamed around the boulders and rushed up toward him. Sea birds were startled as he plummeted down through their wind drafts, his Borsalino spiraling upward and away like the birds.

At Catholic summer camp in the Missouri mountains, he used to go off the fifty-foot platform as an initiation every June. The high platforms at Forest Park and the University of Missouri were easy compared to that dive into the lake at camp. The tougher divers, like Harry, would do somersaults from the fifty-foot platform to show off in front of the girls.

He stretched his arms over his head. Ten feet above the water, the rocks were coming fast and close, but his spring from the wall had carried him far enough that he entered the water six feet from the rocks.

An icy electric shock struck him. Under the water, his natural planing motion curved him upward through the green world, but before he could reach the surface, another set of waves hurled him tumbling head over heels into an undertow.

Dragged deep into colder water, his lungs bursting, Harry saw the two-story white house on Peach Street in St. Louis, surrounded by mighty oaks on the hill above the river. He saw his father and mother wearing summer clothes entertaining guests at a picnic on the lawn. With blissful calm, Harry was pleased it was this easy to die.

But the water became warmer and light filtered into his vision. Harry realized the undertow had spun him free, and he was inside the cove, shooting toward the surface. His face broke the water. He gulped air, looking up toward the top of the cliff. He could see the stone wall, but there was no one.

Probably they had piled into the black Ford and were now racing to the bottom. There was no beach around the cove and no road— only a footpath that emerged from a tangle of gnarled cypress. Harry swam toward the opposite side of the cove, away from the path upon which at any moment he expected to see von Eschel and Pelwa. He noticed that what he had taken to be a mineral stain on the cliff wall at the waterline was in fact a grotto. Inside the grotto, hidden in shadow, was a boat with an outboard motor. Standing in the stern was a man wearing a cap, sweater and dungarees and smoking a pipe. The man put down a box he was loading into the boat and pointed a shotgun at Harry. "Keep away," the man hissed. "Don't come in here."

Harry swam toward him.

"Keep away, damn it! Do you want me to shoot?"

"Please," Harry said. "I've got to come inside that cave. Please."

The man peered at Harry. In his wool cap and coarse-knit sweater, the man looked like a fisherman. He appeared to be a Mediterranean European, middle-aged, his face cracked by the sun.

"You escaping from them that's on top?" the man said.

Harry weighed his answer carefully. This man did not seem to be a cop or a member of the DOP, but he did have a double-barreled, 12-gauge, sawed-off shotgun, popular with smugglers in Sicily and Corsica.

"I have five hundred dollars that belongs to you," Harry said.
"Get in the boat."

The man grasped Harry's collar with a meaty hand and hauled him over the side. Inside the grotto on a ledge, Harry saw a dozen crates of American cigarettes.

"Help me load the boat, and you can go down the coast with me," the man said.

"Five hundred says we go now."

"First the cigarettes, then your five hundred," the man said, hefting another box.

Harry scrambled to help load the boat. After two minutes of frantic work, the cigarettes were stowed. The outboard motor started with a roar, amplified by the water and the cave walls. "Hold on tight," the man said.

The motor revved up to high speed, and then the boat shot out of the grotto, cut a wake in the surface of the cove and threw a sheet of spray toward the rocky path down which Harry now saw three figures clambering. Harry recognized the outsized height of von Eschel and the bulky but agile Pelwa. The third figure, in a burnoose, raised his MAT 49 and fired at the boat, the bullets falling short in the foaming wake.

"They must want you real bad," the man with the shotgun said with a scowl. "To shoot at a European—that's not their style."

"Yeah," said Harry. He wondered what he had done to provoke the shooting. He could understand why von Eschel would want Harry in the Casbah under watchful eye, but why would they want him dead? Could he have seen too much by entering the White House? Maybe the third Headhunter had fired without von Eschel's approval. But Harry knew he must not go back to the Hôtel Aletti.

"I was tortured by the Gestapo myself," said the man in the boat. "I hate the FLN, but you found a brother in me if you are wanted dead by those torturers on top of the hill."

The speedboat headed north out of the bay, rounded the lighthouse point and turned west along the coastline. With the sun going down, the choppy waves were touched with gold. The clouds meant rain twenty-five miles north on the horizon. Harry shivered in the cold wind. The man with the shotgun dug an

American GI olive-drab blanket out of a compartment and tossed it to Harry. Wrapping himself in the blanket, Harry noticed the toe of a white tennis sneaker and the cuff of a khaki trouser in the compartment. Harry leaned forward and tapped the man on the shoulder.

"I could make it six hundred if we work out a swap of clothes," Harry shouted against the wind and the motor and the banging of the hull against the waves.

The man spat between tobacco-stained teeth.

"I have a better plan," the man said. "You can have the dry clothes, and I will take all your money."

The man was delighted to find Harry was carrying eleven hundred dollars. He returned Harry a handful of coins in a gesture of brotherhood against torturers. Dressed in the sneakers, khakis, wool sweater, denim shirt and wool knit cap of a fisherman, Harry looked like a *pied noir*. The smuggler landed him on a beach near an old Moorish palace that had been strung with electric lights and converted to a bathhouse and pavilion. The shape he could see on a hill across the coastal highway was Notre-Dame d'Afrique. Walking along the highway toward the distant towers of the city, Harry came to a checkpoint manned by paratroopers. Cars waited in line for a half-mile on either side of the barricade. As Harry walked past the cars, he saw the frightened faces of Arabs and the angry gestures of *pieds noirs*. The foot traffic around him was almost entirely Arabs, most barefoot and in rags, some herding sheep, others with flocks of goats the size of fox terriers, all of them, it seemed, with children.

Approaching the barricade, Harry felt his heart beating faster and sweat on his palms. His level of tension increased as night fell. Filing slowly forward to be inspected by a paratroop corporal, Harry found himself growing angry. Looking like a *pied noir* made the odds in his favor that the corporal would not demand to see identification or order him into the shed for strip-searching. But the idea that it could easily happen on the whim of the short, muscular boy in a red beret, made Harry entertain the notion of backing down the line and slipping into the confusion of the blocks of flats he could see farther inland. But would looking like a *pied noir* make him a target for a terrorist sniper or a grenade? He had to be as cautious of the Arabs as he was of the DOP.

Harry saw a street sign at the intersection by the barricades: RUE BAB-EL-OUED. Those blocks of flats in the western suburbs were Curly Sabatini country. Harry knew how to behave with the para-troop corporal.

"You boys turn your heads for a couple of days, and we'll take care of this sand-nigger problem," Harry said with a wink to the corporal.

"Keep your nose clean, dad. We'll handle it for you. Move along now," said the corporal.

Harry bit off his reply and turned on the Rue Bab-el-Oued.

He was walking in the working-class district where *pieds noirs* and Arabs, Catholics and Muslims lived side by side, often in the same building. Around the neighborhood, shutters were closing in the upstairs rooms, and iron grates were being locked across doors and windows downstairs. The cries and laughter of children, which one would have expected in a family quarter, were silenced by the nightfall. Adults on the street moved quickly and with purpose. No one sat on the steps and gossiped in the early evening. Harry could hear radios playing and smell olive oil frying in skillets. The wind became chill. Arabs and *pieds noirs* averted their eyes from Harry. In an area where every person was a potential assassin and any garbage can or baby carriage might contain a bomb, Harry was an outsider and doubly dangerous.

He came to a corner bistro with a sign that said CAFÉ NEGREB. Inside, the air was pungent with clouds of Algerian tobacco. Greasy cooking stained the walls. A bald man who looked like a wrestler sat behind the zinc-top bar and listened to Edith Piaf singing on the radio. In the rear of the room, the kitchen partition was open. Harry could see the cook smoking a cigar and reading a magazine. The six tables were empty. One man in cheap European clothing stood at the bar drinking a glass of tea. When Harry approached the bar, the man hurried out.

"Do you have a telephone?" Harry asked.

"Is it important?" said the bald man.

"Please," Harry said.

"Look in the coat closet."

Inside the closet was an aroma of sweat and wool from the half-dozen coats hanging on a pipe. It crossed Harry's mind that perhaps there was a dice game upstairs. With two of the coins the man in the boat had left him, Harry dialed the *Dispatch* Syndicate bureau. After a few seconds of clicking and buzzing and beeping, a voice came on the line.

"*Dispatch* Syndicate."

"Curly?"

"This is Rodolfo Sabatini. Who is this?"

"It's me. Harry."

"Sparrow?" Sabatini sounded agitated. "Where the hell are you? Gruber has phoned from Paris, Epps has phoned from New York. They want to know if you have been shot or knocked on the head. What can I tell them?"

"Anything new from the police?"

"Nothing. Three days and still no ransom demands, no threats. It sounds like the worst."

"No negative thinking, Curly. Did you contact those people?"

"I'm sorry about your wife and baby. But this is a news story to me, remember? Where have you been all day? Are you back at the hotel? Where are you?"

"At the Café Negreb."

Harry heard Sabatini draw in his breath in surprise.

"Do you know the place?" Harry said.

"Of course I know it. You stay right where you are. I'll be there in twenty minutes. The big fellow behind the bar is the owner. His name is Omar. Tell him you're a friend of mine. He'll protect you. I hope."

"Protect me from what?"

"Nothing. Never mind. Just stay at the bar till I get there. I have important news for you."

The phone went dead. Glancing at the collection of coats on the rack, Harry returned to the bar. His remaining coins rattled as he dumped them on the zinc. Omar looked annoyed. He leaned a crumpled ear closer to the radio. "Hold me close and hold me tight, the magic spell tonight . . ." sang Piaf. When the song ended, the big man sighed tenderly, living again the sweet pain of an old love. He ambled over to Harry and said, "What the devil do you want, you idiot? Couldn't you see I was occupied?"

"I'm a friend of Curly Sabatini's."

Omar eyed Harry as if this information was barely sufficient to keep him from throwing Harry into the street.

"What will you drink?"

"Scotch whiskey."

Omar searched beneath the counter and came up with a dusty bottle of malt liquor. He put the bottle in front of Harry, slid a flyspecked glass across the bar, picked up the coins and studied Harry for a moment with the curiosity a bear in the zoo might display toward one who had tossed him a peanut.

"I don't allow no trouble in here," Omar said.

Harry poured himself a glass of whiskey.

"Have a drink with me?" Harry said.

"I don't talk to Sabatini or any of his friends," said Omar.

He turned his enormous back to Harry and went to his stool beside the radio. Omar turned up the radio louder. Harry was glad it was Piaf and not a Sousa band concert. Omar's fat face took on a look of blessedness as he listened to the woman singing of spring and rain and broken hearts. Harry realized his shoulders were aching from the impact of his dive. He drank half his glass of whiskey and selected a black Algerian cheroot from the cedar box on the bar. He lit the cheroot on a candle that burned in a saucer. Omar watched him with a mind that was far away in misty gardens.

When Sabatini arrived, Omar scowled and poured him a vermouth cassis without speaking. The stringer seemed not to find Omar's behavior unusual, but Sabatini was nervous, anyhow. He tugged Harry's elbow and guided him to a table against the wall. The two sat down. Curly bent forward over the flickering candle to whisper.

"You should give this up, Sparrow. It's too dangerous. Leave it to the police."

"No," Harry said. "It has to be done right."

"Feelings are running very high right now," Sabatini said. "A couple of Arab boys killed a white boy in the neighborhood this

afternoon. They'd been friends since they were babies. Everyone
is anxious. There will be murders tonight. You're not safe here. Go
back to your hotel and lock yourself in."

"The FLN, Curly. How about it?"

"Personally, Sparrow, I think you're an arrogant shit and I don't
like you very much, but I don't want you to get hurt."

"Start talking," Harry said.

Sabatini sighed. "All right. I tried," he said. He pulled a dirty
handkerchief out of a coat pocket and patted his forehead. There
were ink stains around his frayed shirt pocket. "I spoke to a fellow.
He will take you to see people. Maybe he will take you to Ali Saadi
himself. I don't know. I'm only guessing. I have known this person
all my life. I halfway hope I'm wrong and he don't know Saadi, but
I'm not wrong."

Curly gave him directions to an electrician's shop a few blocks
away. Harry was to ring the bell at the shop, Curly said, and
identify himself to a man called Krim. "He's a Muslim but a good
man. Krim got an education in the law, but he chose to go into
business. Talk to Krim, and then we will see what we will see. I
will go back to the bureau and wait for word from you."

The scrape of the chair as Curly stood up brought a scowl of
irritation from Omar, hunkered beside his radio. Harry and Curly
picked their way along the narrow space between the tables and the
bar; Piaf was crying. Outside the cold wind blew. Curly's Dodge
sedan was parked at the curb. The street was empty, save for occasional figures that crossed quickly through patches of light and
vanished again.

"Is this guy Krim as good a friend of yours as Omar?" Harry
asked.

"What did Omar say about me?" Curly said, as if almost afraid
of the answer.

"Nothing."

"Nobody trusts me anymore in my own neighborhood—because
I'm a journalist. It used to be they all wanted their name in the
paper. A birthday, a wedding anniversary—call Rodolfo, he'll take
our picture and write it up and peddle it to the newspapers. But
now the trouble has started, they all treat me like I'm an informer."

"How about dropping me at Krim's shop in your car," Harry said, rubbing his palms together in the cold.

"If anybody sees my car at Krim's at night, it'll be the death of him, Sparrow. You're on your own."

Walking to Krim's shop, Harry had the feeling he was being followed. A garbage can fell over with a crash half a block behind him, and he turned expecting to see dogs or cats prowling in the refuse, but there was nothing except the lid wobbling into the gutter. Shutters rattled on the balconies above him. Harry stayed close to the wall, fearing a flowerpot would fall on his head, and not by accident.

Krim's shop was behind an iron grate that covered the door and windows. Harry pulled the bell cord, and the ringing sounded harsh in the silent streets. He heard a shutter opening above his head. A man's voice called softly, "Sparrow?"

"Right," said Harry.

"Are you alone?"

"Very."

"Go around the corner and down the alley to the rear of the shop. Wait for me."

The alley was in shadow and smelled like urine. Harry forced fear out of his mind. Now he felt a bit ridiculous. Why this skulking? He considered going back to the bureau and putting a full-page ad in the *Echo d'Alger* offering any amount of money for Claudette and the kid. A reward should mean more to the FLN than two more corpses.

A garage door clanked as it slid upward. A panel truck with the lights off moved into the alley and turned sharply in the narrow space. The garage door dropped shut. Harry saw signs painted on the truck in French and Arabic. The sign in French advertised fast, reliable electrical repair.

"Get in. Hurry," the driver said.

The truck emerged from the alley and entered the askew grids of the Bab-el-Oued streets. Krim wore white coveralls and a square white cap. He had a beak of a nose, prominent eyes and a pointed chin. The back of the truck was full of coils of wire and boxes of tools and equipment. It occurred to Harry that an electrical shop would be a good place to make bombs.

"Where are we going?" Harry said.

Krim shook his head.

"Is my wife still alive?"

"I know nothing about your wife, M. Sparrow."

"The baby?" Harry said.

"I say nothing."

"Who are you taking me to see?"

Krim shook his head again. "Better I say nothing."

Harry looked out the window as the truck headed westward out of the Bab-el-Oued, turning and doubling back until Krim was satisfied they were not being followed. A string of plastic worry-beads swung wildly from the rearview mirror above a copy of the Koran on the dash. They kept to obscure roads and avoided check-points. Harry caught glimpses of the Mediterranean off to his right, past the coastal highway. He saw again the shape of Notre-Dame d'Afrique high on its hill. They went through an area of villas and gardens with tall stone walls and veered toward the sea.

"Curly says you're a lawyer," Harry said.

"This country is no good for Arab lawyers. Better I drive and not talk."

Now there were fewer houses and electric lights. The moon shone on fields of ruins left by the Greeks, the Romans, the Mauritanians, the Christians, the Vandals, the Berbers—huge blocks of stone, Ionic columns, mausoleums, cemeteries. Harry thought of the Legion toast: "To those who are in the sands." For thousands of years the sands had swallowed all who came to this place.

"Someone is behind us, driving without lights," Krim said.

In the side mirror Harry saw the dim shape of an auto pulling up fast from back toward the city.

"Your boys?" Harry said.

"Not likely." Krim licked his lips and glanced down at the speedometer. "No way we can outrun them in this old truck."

"If it's the army, let me do the talking."

"The army would have put on their siren and spotlight by now," said Krim. "I hope it's a smuggler. He's coming quick enough, we'll soon know. Allah be with us, please. Let the car go on past and keep going."

But the car closed on them and then kept pace. As another mile clicked on the odometer, it was obvious the car was for them.

"How much farther to the rendezvous?" Harry said.

"We're close," said Krim.

"It's bound to be your boys. An escort," Harry said.

"No. They would signal."

"Maybe it's a smuggler letting us run in the lead in case there's a new checkpoint ahead."

"I fear it's a liquidation team," said Krim.

"Headhunters?"

"I don't know who they are—*pieds noirs,* the butcher, the baker, probably some police, maybe some soldiers." Krim's voice cracked with fear. He jammed his foot against the accelerator as if he could force the truck to go faster. "They're coming up, Sparrow. They're coming up on my side."

"Block 'em off," Harry said.

Krim moved his lips as if praying and his knuckles cracked as he squeezed the wheel, but he kept to his lane. Harry got a look at the front right fender of the car approaching Krim's window.

"Swerve!" Harry yelled. "Knock 'em off the road!"

Harry grabbed the wheel and twisted it, but Krim had a powerful grip. The barrel of a shotgun poked out of the car window. With a loud splatter, Krim's head blew apart like a cantaloupe dropped on the sidewalk. Harry heard the blast and simultaneously saw pepper spots of blood spray on the windshield. The panel truck careened out of control. He struggled to crawl over Krim and take the wheel, but suddenly Harry realized he was upside down and tumbling and there was a shrieking sound and he bounced hard on his neck and shoulders on the roof of the cab, and then the truck was rolling over and over.

He was aware he was lying in a field of stones. Harry sat up and plucked a rock from under his buttocks. He saw the panel truck upside down with both doors open and Krim's body lying half-outside the cab with no recognizable head. The car that attacked them had stopped at the side of the road. By its silhouette, Harry recognized a Citroën. He heard the car doors slam four times. The shapes of five men approached. The road was empty of lights or movement in either direction. Harry could hear the crunching of their feet. He noticed how bright and close the stars looked in the desert sky.

"Throw a match in that truck," said an oddly muffled voice.

In an instant, an orange fireball erupted and coughed into the air, and then the truck was burning with a roar.

"Where's the other one?" said another muffled voice.

In the light from the flaming truck, Harry saw that the men were wearing pillowcases over their heads. They had cut eyeholes and slashes for breathing; the muffled tones were caused by the hoods. As a boy in the thirties in St. Louis, Harry had seen the Ku Klux Klan marching by the light of a thousand torches, men made bold by pillowcases and sheets that hid their identity.

"Here he is. Over here."

The hooded men shined flashlights on Harry. He was caught in a circle of light. The beams came from five directions. Harry lowered his eyes to keep the diamonds of light out of his vision. He covered his eyes with a hand, shaking his head to fake dizziness, gathering his wits and his strength for whatever was about to happen. He was not going to cower on the ground and take anything they had in mind for him. If they were going to blow off his head with a shotgun, as they had done poor Krim, it was not a burden he would receive kneeling.

"He's hurt. Look, he's covered in blood."

"The Commie shit, kick his ribs in."

"We better not kill him, he's a white man."

"He was with that Commie."

"He's a Commie, too, I tell you. He's a Commie agent."

The men crunched closer, discussing Harry as if they were judging livestock. He managed to gather his feet beneath him in a crouch while he covered his face from the light.

"I think he's one of their couriers. Let's beat him up before we kill him."

Harry launched himself at the voice. He hit the big man in the pit of the stomach with a solid tackle. He felt his shoulder driving into flesh, rearranging interior organs. It was satisfying to hear the big man grunt in pain as Harry kept his legs churning and locked his wrists in the small of the man's back and lifted him off his feet and smashed him against a hunk of marble from an ancient monument.

They rolled off the stone and onto the ground with Harry on top. Harry grabbed the pillowcase with both hands and ripped it up the middle, exposing the face of Omar, the Piaf fan from the Café Negreb. Omar was sputtering and coughing and cursing.

Harry dug his thumbs into the hollow of Omar's throat. The struggling and hacking ceased. Harry could have killed him by crushing the carotid arteries. But when he had Omar's death in his hands, something prevailed that Harry would not have called humanity or the human impulse. It was more like a cerebral telex from the Old Man that said WRONG.

Harry leaped up with Omar's heavy military flashlight in his right hand and cracked the nearest Klansman across the pillowcase with such force that the lens cap flew off and the barrel bent. The cloth was blotching red as the man staggered and fell. Harry was expecting to hear a blast and feel buckshot tear into his body, but the other three hooded men backed away from him. The one with the shotgun kept the barrel aimed at Harry, but he was in a defensive posture, as if unsure whether to run away.

Armed with the bent flashlight, Harry stood panting in the circle of light as Omar slowly arose, massaging his throat, glaring at Harry.

"Who the devil are you?" said Omar.

Two of the hooded men knelt beside the one Harry had downed. They pulled off the bloody pillowcase. From the hang of the man's jaw, it was broken.

"I'm a journalist from Paris," Harry said.

"No mere journalist could knock me down. You've been trained in hand-to-hand combat. What're you from, the KGB?"

"I'm from the M.U.," Harry said.

"Jesus Christ, the M.U. No bleeding wonder." Omar rubbed his neck and poked fingers beneath his rib cage to probe his liver. He moaned with pain. "The damned M.U."

Harry nodded. "M.U." sounded threatening—University of Missouri would not have impressed them.

"Let's kill him and get out of here," said one of the hooded men.

"You want the whole M.U. to come looking for you, you idiot?" said Omar.

"Well, shit, look how deep we're in already. We've got no choice but to kill him."

"Find out where he was going with Krim. Maybe we'll root out a big nest of FLN."

Two of the hooded men helped their comrade with the broken jaw to his feet. With his arms around their shoulders for support, he sagged and gazed at Harry with eyes clouded by pain.

Omar said, "Let's just leave the bastard here. Robbers will take care of him for us."

"Fool! He's seen your face."

"Oh. Yes." Omar looked at Harry. "We'll have to kill you then."

Harry thought of the childish, simpleminded pucker of Omar's lips as they formed the words intended to be a death sentence. His anger flamed but inside a voice was telling him: *Observe these poor saps and try to understand them, for they are full of fear. They think they are doing the right thing, but nobody has ever given them a break, much less clued them in on the facts.*

The wind from the sea made him shudder involuntarily. He wanted the hooded men to know that he was not frightened. Why that should matter, he neither guessed nor cared, but it did matter. Standing in the frigid wash of moonlight and battery-powered glare with a broken flashlight in his fist, hearing the heavy breathing of Omar and his comrades in the otherwise silent night of the desert, Harry felt his inner voice calling not for pity and understanding but for a grin.

What a perverted twist of a glorious scheme his tale had become: That he should be murdered alone and uncelebrated amid stone relics of the ages at the hands of frightened men who were confused by politics—to die like some wild creature crushed on a highway that appeared from nowhere—this struck him as a joke only the Old Man could invent.

Harry turned to face the hood who aimed the shotgun. Though partially blinded by the flashlights, Harry caught a glimpse of wraithlike figures beyond the circle of light, darting soundlessly among the ancient stones like spirits.

Harry realized poor dead Krim had almost delivered him to the rendezvous.

"Omar, you boys may as well put down your guns," Harry said. "You're my prisoners now."

"What? Are you crazy?" One of the hooded men laughed. "Shoot him."

"Wait," said Omar. "I saw something move."

The wraiths were suddenly among them. Brown-skinned Arabs leaped from concealment behind the stones. Moonlight glinted on their blades.

"Drop your guns," Harry said to the fat man. "It's your only chance."

Harry saw a familiar figure strolling toward him, wearing a kepi with a winter drill cover, goggles strapped around the body of the cap like a tank commander and a sand-colored djellaba that brushed the toes of his parachute boots. There was no mistaking the handsome swagger or the smile that would have made a Beverly Hills orthodontist proud.

"Hallo, Meester Sparrow," said Ali Saadi. "Now you will put my name in the paper, huh? I will be famous too?"

"I'll pay you anything you want for Claudette and the kid," Harry said. "Name your price, man."

"First we must deal with these terrorists." Ali Saadi grinned.

The man with the shotgun let out a hoarse gasp, as if a fishbone had stuck in his throat. He lurched forward two ridiculous steps, his head wobbly as a baby's. Next, Omar's heavy chin was yanked up and back, and the "smile of Kabylia" appeared on his throat.

On the ground in front of Harry and Ali Saadi, the ragged band of maquis killed the *pieds noirs* with knives and began pulling the clothes off the corpses.

"I'll pay anything you want," Harry said.

"I want very much."

"You'll get it. Is she hurt?"

Arab women and children folded the clothing of the dead *pieds noirs* and collected their weapons. The knives flashed again, and the mutilation of the corpses began.

"I think she is not hurt. No," said Ali Saadi.

Harry saw a man shaking Omar's testicles toward the moon and howling like a wolf.

"What do you mean, you think she's not hurt? I'm talking about a big reward here, pal. You're on your way to Acapulco for a life of ease if you turn my wife and the kid over to me," Harry said.

"Krim said you'd pay plenty."

"Where are they?"

"Not far."

The corpses were being gutted. Harry heard sounds like footballs puncturing and smelled methane gas.

"Do they have to do that? Couldn't it wait?"

Ali Saadi ignored the carving up of the *pieds noirs*. "We've located your wife and the baby today, Meester Sparrow," he said.

"What do you mean, today? Did she escape from you?"

"We never had her in the first place," Ali Saadi said. "What would we want to kidnap your wife for? Now, I know the answer: to get plenty of money in ransom and make us famous in the news. But I wouldn't have thought of doing it. I don't want to hurt her. She helped many people at Dien Bien Phu. I don't hurt babies, either."

Harry began to feel sick.

"She wasn't kidnapped, was she?" he said.

"Not by us."

"Where is she, then?" Harry said.

"At a farmhouse close enough we saw the truck burning. Krim was bringing you to meet us in the woods by the house. She and the baby are in the house."

"Is your chief with them?"

"The German is not my chief," Ali Saadi said. "I have no chief but Allah. But we saw the German and Pelwa go into the house with your wife and the baby."

"Show me the house," Harry said.

"Oh no. First you must agree when we find her and the baby we are going to kidnap them, and then you can buy them back."

"Agreed. Let's get going," Harry said.

"Also, you will have to buy yourself back. We've kidnapped you too now, you see? You should be worth a fortune in ransom money, hey?"

Harry was already walking away from the things that were going on with the corpses of the *pieds noirs*. He had come to find Claudette and the child, and he wanted to take them home.

20 Groves of olive trees threw shadows in the moonlight across a farmhouse built in a shallow bowl of land. It was a sturdy house of mud-brick and pine. Smoke poured from the chimney, but light escaped only through slits in wooden shudders fastened over the windows. The black 1946 Ford was parked in the barn. Enclosing the grounds around the house was a fence of pine rails. Beside the dirt road that led to the gate lay the granite and marble ruins of a Roman necropolis, rocks gleaming white as though knocked over last week rather than in the time of Christ.

Harry lay flat on the pine needles of the forest above the exposed site the settler had chosen for his house. Like the planners who built a fort in the valley of Dien Bien Phu, this settler had ignored the principles that one must occupy the high ground and never gather forces on a plain at the foot of a mountain. The villages in the mountains of Kabylia were not found in the valleys but on the ridges. The survivors knew that valleys attract invaders. The farmer had not prepared for a life that included being under attack. Harry was surprised that von Eschel would have chosen an exposed house for a hideout. The German's new fondness for the opium pipe might explain it—or perhaps the house was bait.

Harry saw the glow of a cigarette in the backseat of the Ford.

"There's three Headhunters outside the house," Ali Saadi whispered. His garlic breath made Harry wince. "We've got them located on the sniperscope." When Ali Saadi deserted, he had stolen a two-and-a-half-ton General Motors truck loaded with American-made arms and ammunition. Among the deadly toys in the truck was an infrared scope that could see in the night and was attached to a 30-06 sniper's rifle. This piece of equipment was complicated to operate and would have been useless to the fellagha had not Ali Saadi been drilled by the Legion until he was expert with every infantry weapon. "I can knock them off one, two, three—*mitte, mitte, mitte,* just like that. I am a very good *Abwehrschütze.* I could shoot off a Viet's nose at three hundred meters."

"You're sure nobody's inside the house but my wife, the baby, the captain and Pelwa?" whispered Harry.

"Yes."

"Then I'm going down there."

"The German will kill you. If you are dead, nobody will pay me a big reward for you—or maybe for your wife or the baby either. No, I am in command here," said Ali Saadi. "I use the silencer, like we did in Indochina. I pop off the three Headhunters in the yard. Then we creep to the house. I look for a gap in the shutters I can shoot through to kill the captain and Pelwa."

"What if you can't find a gap to shoot through?"

"We kick in the window, throw grenades, I climb through shooting and then I cut their throats."

Ali Saadi's eyeballs glinted white as he rolled them toward Harry. The young Arab had a classic profile. Wearing the kepi with the goggles on top, his breath blowing frost as he showed his white teeth, Ali Saadi could have had a smashing career as a gigolo were it not for the accident of birth. Harry knew what Ali Saadi was thinking: Why do you want back a woman who came here all the way from Paris to be with the German? Ali Saadi would never ask Harry such a question. As long as Harry thought Claudette and the baby were worth a big reward, that was the important thing to Ali Saadi.

Before the Arab could prevent him, Harry rose and stepped out
of the cover of the pine trees into the moonlight. Harry cupped his
hands to his mouth and shouted:

"*Legio! Legio patria nostra!*"

"Who is it?" shouted a German voice from the barn.

The cigarette winked out, and there was clicking of machine-gun
bolts. The Headhunters in the yard had him in their sights. Marching boldly down the slope toward the house, his feet slipping on the
loose stones, Harry began to sing in German:

Mein Regiment, mein Heimatland,
Ich bin allein auf dieser Welt . . .

"He's one of ours."

"It's a trick."

"Identify yourself!"

Harry reached the gate in the rail fence. He could smell pine
smoke coming from the chimney. The wood of the gate was smooth
to the touch. Harry opened the gate and walked the path toward
the front porch. He sensed the Headhunters crouched nearby. The
clank of a steel butt plate against a door told him one was in the
barn. The creaking of springs meant another was inside the Ford.
A movement at the corner of the house betrayed the third.

"Hands up! I say, hands up!"

"Look, it's him."

"It's the journalist from Dien Bien."

Harry hammered a fist against the front door of the house.

"I'm here, von Eschel!" he shouted.

Pelwa opened the door.

"Chicago!" Pelwa said.

On the far side of the room, kneeling in front of the fireplace, was
Claudette. With a motoring glove on one hand, she was retrieving
a kettle from a hook above the flames. A teapot, a strainer and
several cups sat on a rough table near the fireplace. At the end of
the table, his long legs crossed, a wolfhound grin spreading across
his face, was von Eschel. The German held baby Henri in his lap.

"I've come to take my wife and the kid home," Harry said.

"We were wondering how long it would take you to find us," said von Eschel.

Claudette dropped the kettle into the flames and rushed to throw herself against Harry. Her body trembled. He could feel her ribs, and he heard her spine make a snap as she hugged him tighter. It was as if she were rooting onto him, growing around him like ivy. They had always fit well, but her joy at his arrival sharpened his curiosity. If this farmhouse was a bizarre lovers' trysting place, the intruding husband should not be so enthusiastically greeted.

Harry grasped Claudette's upper arms and lifted her away from him. He looked at von Eschel. Little Henri's chubby hands grasped the German's long fingers.

"What are you going to do about it?" Harry said.

Von Eschel's gaze shifted to Claudette.

"Get the kettle out of the fire and make the tea," von Eschel said.

"Never mind the kettle, Claudette. We're leaving."

"Make the tea, Claudette."

"Harry, I must. I must make the tea. I mustn't make him angry."

Claudette ran to the fireplace and dug the kettle out of hot coals with an entrenching shovel. She poured boiling water from the kettle into the teapot. Pelwa stepped inside the room after a tour of the yard.

"The boys say he walked out of the forest singing a Legion song in German," Pelwa said.

"You're a very nervy fellow," von Eschel said to Harry. "It's fascinating to me. Deep in the jungles of Laos and Cambodia, after Dien Bien Phu, I would encounter people who had heard of our singing bayonet charge on Lola. One fellow read it in the *Sydney Sun*, another in *The Paris Dispatch*, another had seen it in a newspaper in New York. My notoriety goes straight back to you, Sparrow. Most of the men who took part in the charge are dead, and the survivors are silent, but you wrote about it and made me a target for everyone."

Claudette had filled the cups with tea. When she gave a cup to Harry, her eyes were wide with apprehension.

"What did you fake the kidnapping for?"

"It was no fake, Harry," she said. "Pelwa and two other Headhunters kidnapped the baby and me. I took Henri for a ride on a rental bike beside the harbor. They blocked my path in their black Ford and yanked us inside."

"But you did come to Algiers to see von Eschel?"

"I did," Claudette said. "I admit it. I am sorry. I was a fool to come. But I thought Max had a right to meet his son."

"She came because she loves me, Sparrow."

"Please, Harry. Max phoned me in Paris and said he had something important to tell me about my father. I was so surprised Max was alive, I was shocked, and I told him about little Henri. He begged me to let him see his son. You don't believe I came here because I want to be with him, do you?"

"Why ever you did it, that's over with," Harry said. "The important thing is to get out of here. All right, von Eschel? This incident will go to the sands with me. I'll make up a story about mysterious bandits who got cold feet and let them go. I could write a story that gives you credit for rescuing her—and the kid."

"You think you go everywhere in life on a round-trip ticket, don't you, Sparrow? You journalists, you golden boys, you go close to the fighting when you want to exploit our blood and pain for what you call the news, but you travel on a round-trip ticket. You can waltz into Dien Bien Phu and get an unholy dispensation from the Red devil himself. That is a good thing so far, because you brought my woman out for me. You brought Claudette and my son out of Dien Bien Phu, and I appreciate it. But your round-trip ticket has been punched this time: *voided—end of the line.*"

Von Eschel lifted the hem of his burnoose and removed the Kabar commando knife from the scabbard on his calf. He licked his thumb and felt the edge of the seven-inch blade.

"In Bangkok when I learned you two had gotten married, I decided if I ever got out of the jungle, I would come to London or Paris or wherever you were living, and I would break up your marriage," von Eschel said. He smiled, his lips widening slowly, his eyes intense. "But you beat me to it, Sparrow. By the time I got out of the jungle, you had already lost her."

"You've got to believe me, Harry. I had an Air France reservation to leave Algiers the night we were kidnapped. I was taking Henri home. We were flying back to Paris on the Clipper."

"The airlines were checked, Claudette," Harry said. "There was no reservation under your name."

"I used the name Mrs. Harriet Snow."

He looked at Claudette again. He believed her.

"That's why they kidnapped us, Harry—to keep us from leaving." She turned to von Eschel. "Tell him, Max. You claim you love me, so do me the honor of telling Harry the truth."

He stabbed the knife point into the rough oak table, and the blade quivered in the firelight.

Von Eschel said, "I'd smoked more pipes than usual before I went to the hotel to make love to her. She pushed me away and ran out. She said I'd smoked too much opium to make love. She said she was fed up with me and was going to take my son back to France. I phoned Pelwa to pick them up. I was using the phone when the hotel cops looked in. I had the inspiration of announcing a kidnap note."

Harry said, "But why blame it on the FLN? Unless you intended to kill her, you'd never make that story stick."

"I was in a fit of temper. You see, I do believe she had made a rendezvous with Ali Saadi. She's hot for him. She's had him before, Sparrow. While she was my lover at the Hôtel Saint-Georges, she was slipping out to meet my Arab corporal in the Casbah. How does that make you feel? Where do you think you rank in her heart?"

"Liar. You filthy liar. Nothing he says is true, Harry."

"She makes love to other men. You might as well face it," the German said.

"Claudette didn't slip off to make it with Ali Saadi with her baby in her arms," Harry said.

"She begs me to make love to her, Sparrow."

Harry looked hard at von Eschel.

"Are you going to try to stop me from taking my wife out of here?" Harry said. "I'll be good to your son. There's nothing good you can do for him."

"Claudette, suppose my war had ended in Indochina? Suppose I was a gentleman farmer in Saxony now, and we lived in a cottage, surrounded by green meadows full of cows, living the quiet, comfortable, middle-class life of a prosperous farmer? You and me and our son. Suppose that is us—and Sparrow here, well, he is only himself. If you had to choose between me and him under such circumstances, who would it be? Who would you choose? Who would be the best for Henri?"

Claudette took the baby in her arms and stepped back from the two men.

"I would choose Harry," she said.

Von Eschel pulled the knife out of the table.

"You are quite sure?"

"Yes. It would be Harry."

Von Eschel's eyes became cold and withdrawn.

"Congratulations, Sparrow. Your ticket is round-trip again," the German said.

"I'm going to take them out of here now," Harry said.

"Very well. Go."

Claudette was wary. "You promise, Max? We can go?"

"If Sparrow will keep his word, so will I. I owe him my life from Dien Bien Phu. Go. Unlock the door for them, Pelwa."

"In the likely event you're killed again soon, von Eschel, what would you like your kid to know about you?" Harry said.

Von Eschel said, "I want you to tell my son that I was not a monster. I was not insane. I understand the world as it is. Make my son learn the martial arts at a very young age. He will need to be a warrior to survive in the times that are coming."

"I don't want him to be a fighter, Max," she said. "I will tell him his father was a great warrior, but I won't raise him to be one."

"Tell him the whole truth. Tell him about his grandfather, his namesake," von Eschel said.

"What do you mean, the whole truth?" Claudette said.

Von Eschel pinched the red chin of little Henri.

"If you are going to raise my son to be another French business-man, you should know what you're doing."

"You've heard enough of his lies, Claudette. Let's go," Harry said.

Claudette said, "What do you want to tell me about my father, Max?"

"Pelwa killed him."

She looked at Pelwa, expecting him to deny it, but Pelwa nodded. "I'm sorry, miss, but your father could not be allowed to live."

"It was bad enough that Henri Frontenac was paying blackmail to the Vietminh," said von Eschel. "That was very bad, we thought, very unethical, to be paying money to the Marxists so that he could keep his part of the opium traffic flowing."

"My father was a minister in the Department of Finance."

"But bad as it was to pay blackmail, the rubber companies did it too, and the oil companies, and others. And your father was a friendly sort, couldn't do enough for us, got in all our good graces."

"Why did you kill him?" Claudette said.

"I discovered what he was," von Eschel said. "He was more evil than merely another corrupt bureaucrat in the drug trade. Henri Frontenac paid the Vietminh blackmail with mortars as well as money—U.S. mortars. That's the price the Reds demanded to allow his opium ponies on the trails. He paid them. With the mortars from your father, they wiped out two companies of the 13th Foreign Legion to the last man—an ambush. Your father was responsible for it. The Legion pronounced the death sentence. Pelwa carried it out."

"What right does the Legion have to judge my father?"

"Your father made a profit killing Legionnaires," von Eschel said.

"What a liar you are. First you lie to Harry about me and then to me about my father. My father was an honest government official and a patriot. My father was not in the opium trade. He hated drugs. He could never have done what you accuse him of."

Von Eschel shrugged.

"He doesn't matter anymore," von Eschel said. "Evil is winning. Everything is out of control. There are so many doing what your father did, so much greed and anger all up and down the scale, that there is little hope for any of us. In Laos and Cambodia I saw the death camps the Marxists are preparing—marked off with ribbons in the jungle, camps where the Communists will murder millions upon millions. So many millions the numbers will make the Jews' Holocaust sound like a small affair in the history books."

Von Eschel slammed a magazine into his submachine gun.

"I see Capitalism rushing to meet the totalitarian Left head-on at Armageddon, and all is totally out of control. Sparrow said I am a lunatic who is in love with murder. Well, I am in love with death, but not as a madman. I am in Algeria to kill Marxists. We all three live off the misery of others—Sparrow with his journalism, Claudette off the interest from a narcotics fortune paid for by dead Legionnaires. Whose misery will this child live off of?"

Claudette wrapped the baby in a blue blanket and started toward the door.

"Maybe I could have talked her into staying with me, Sparrow. I might have found a way to keep Claudette in Algeria with my son until I'm through with my work here. But you showed up. I'll be glad to see the last of you." Von Eschel gestured for Pelwa to open the door. "You are free to go. Give my regards to Ali Saadi—both of you."

"You know he's out there, don't you?" Harry said.

"How else could you have found this farmhouse?" von Eschel said. "Only Saadi could have brought you here. Arabs died in the torture rooms and wouldn't reveal where Ali Saadi was, but you found him in one day because some fool trusted you."

With an enormous blast, a vast rush of air and a roar, the rear wall of the house blew apart. The impact and flying debris knocked them off their feet. A second explosion followed almost at once. The rear of the house became a smoking gap, open to the night. Harry moved quickly toward Claudette and the baby.

"Bazooka," cried Pelwa.

The night crackled with small-arms fire. Harry saw flashes near the house and from the forest. Either Ali Saadi was not able to shoot the Headhunters before he pulled his surprise attack, or there were more Legionnaires than Saadi had thought.

Von Eschel and Pelwa crawled out of the mud-brick rubble and scrambled to the smoking hole in the wall.

"They're coming," von Eschel shouted with something that sounded to Harry's ringing ears like glee. The captain's MAT 49 began to sputter. Pelwa was shooting toward moving shapes with a tommy gun.

Von Eschel looked around and yelled, "Take the child and go! Get him away from here."

The concussion had knocked the front door open and left it hanging crookedly. Claudette clutched the baby to her breast as she and Harry crawled out from the shelter of the oak table and scuttled toward the open door. Most of the firing seemed to be behind them. Harry glanced back and saw von Eschel watch them scrambling out the door. It seemed for an instant as if he tensed to follow them.

They crawled into the shadows of the barn. A dead Headhunter lay beside the black Ford. The car was punctured with bullet holes, and they smelled leaking gasoline.

"Are you hurt?" Harry said.

"No. But your face is bleeding."

"See that mausoleum halfway between here and the forest?"

"That big pile of marble?"

"Yeah. Give me Henri. Don't stop running until we get there."

It was two hundred yards, but they covered the distance at a dash, ducking between rails of the fence and bounding among stones that littered the open field, Harry carrying Henri like a football. The shooting behind them was louder and more frequent, as if additional forces had arrived, and they heard the thumping of a .30 caliber machine gun.

"Now what? To the woods?" said Claudette, breathing hard.

"In one rush," Harry gasped. "Follow me."

But when he showed himself in the moonlight a bullet knocked a chink of marble out of the mausoleum beside Harry's head. There were dots of light, like striking matches, at the edge of the forest, and bullets cracked and whined off the marble. Harry and Claudette ducked behind the tumbled slabs.

"Somebody has us on a sniperscope," Harry said.

Claudette took the baby. She pulled a spiderweb off his blanket. The boy hadn't cried once, Harry realized. Henri appeared to be enjoying himself. Henri, Harry—they sounded alike. Harry could detect scratching sounds in the ruin of the mausoleum as scorpions and centipedes were awakening.

With a roar the roof of the farmhouse thundered into blaze. Orange flame belched into the desert sky, washing the bowl of land around the house with a copper hue. The flashes and shooting grew heavier on the opposite side of the house from the mausoleum. Harry thought he heard the motors of trucks on the dirt road beyond the house. Machine guns were firing steadily, and, with a *whump*, another bazooka rocket tore into the farmhouse. From the volume of fire, coming and going in all directions, Harry's guess was that more Legionnaires had arrived in trucks, and more fellagha had come in through the forest. Harry wondered if von Eschel had ambushed the Arabs or if it would be the other way around.

Claudette yanked on his sleeve and said, "It's him. Look. He's running toward us."

The unmistakable, long-legged figure had shed his burnoose for khaki shorts, but the feet were still wrapped in Arab slippers. Von Eschel hurdled the rail fence and ran zigzagging toward the mausoleum. His bony, wide-shouldered torso was bare. He ran with the MAT 49 in one hand like a pistol. His cropped hair and high skull made him look like a desert wildman.

Von Eschel called as he ran, but they couldn't make out his words.

The rattling of rifle fire came from the edge of the forest when von Eschel was a hundred strides short of the mausoleum. The captain staggered and fell. He got up and stumbled a few more steps, was hit again, and lurched headlong into the stones of the desert.

"He's still moving!" shouted Claudette.

"I'll go get him," Harry said.

But when Harry began to edge around the corner of the mausoleum, sniper bullets hammered the marble by his head. They had this spot well sighted in the sniperscope.

"Don't try it, Harry."

"We're pinned. There's nothing we can do."

Then they heard a shrill scream above the crashing of the flaming roof and the popping of the rifles and machine guns. It was Pelwa. He was screaming in a frenzy. Pelwa had rushed out of the barn and ran toward von Eschel, who writhed in the dirt, groaning and cursing.

"Chief," they heard Pelwa crying, "I'm coming for you, chief!"

The marksmen from the tree line opened up with a barrage of hundreds of shots. The big corporal was hit a dozen times before he fell to his knees. More slugs tore into his body. Pelwa slid limply to one side and tumbled on his face. He lay twenty yards short of where von Eschel rolled in agony.

From the extent and location of the firing, the Headhunters and their reinforcements appeared to be holding the remains of the farmhouse. The fellagha were shooting at two sides of the house from the tree line past the mausoleum. Neither the Headhunters nor the Arabs could improve their positions, but neither gave way. Caught in the open between the two forces was the wounded von Eschel. Four Arabs made a dash toward him from the trees. They were shot down by the Headhunters at the house. The steady firing continued, and the flames of the farmhouse began to diminish as another wall fell over, showering sparks and smoke. In the changing light from the fire, new shadows appeared in the field between the house and the mausoleum—shapes of rocks and of ancient tombstones, now all intermingled with the lumpen shadow of Pelwa and his chief.

During a lull in the firing, they heard von Eschel shout:

"He's coming! He's coming closer! Help me!"

In reply to his voice, the two sides took up shooting again. Harry kept peering at von Eschel, who tried to rise on his elbows, but flopped back.

"He's here! God help me, he's here!" von Eschel shouted.

His cry was drowned out by shooting. Harry felt Claudette's shoulder as she crept onto the slab beside him. They stared, searching the shadows around von Eschel. The only movements were the desert wind in the olive trees and the leaping of the flames.

From what Harry guessed to be eighty paces away, they could see nothing around von Eschel. They heard no more cries. The erman lay still. The wind blew sand across him.

Before dawn they heard the clanking of armored cars coming along the road. The sporadic shooting from the tree line and from beyond the house dropped away. With the approach of daylight, the fellagha were gone, blending into the mountains or among the crowds in the ice cream shops. Several figures slowly stepped away from the smoldering house and the barn. They were Headhunters who had survived another fight. In the yard around the house lay bodies of Legionnaires and Arabs.

Harry and Claudette walked toward von Eschel as the first armored car crushed a path through the rail fence and growled across the Roman gravestones. A young lieutenant rode with his red beret and parachute blouse proudly out of the turret, field glasses bouncing against his chest.

The lieutenant hopped down from the armored car as the rear doors opened and a dozen paratroopers fanned out with submachine guns, sweeping the area in search of targets. The few surviving Headhunters sat wearily in the ruins and lit cigarettes and stared into the distance.

"What do we have here? A little roughhousing?" the young lieutenant said jauntily. His tiger-striped fatigues were faded from hard wear and repeated washing—the badge of a paratrooper who had served in Indochina.

He reached von Eschel first. The soldier turned away from the corpse. "You better not look, lady. It's disgusting what these gooks think of."

Claudette crossed herself. She put the baby into Harry's arms. She looked at von Eschel's body for a long moment. The young lieutenant was surprised at her toughness. Then she turned away and pressed her face into Harry's chest. Harry put his arms around her. He hugged her tightly, feeling her tears. She tugged at his neck and he realized she had found and was holding in her fist the lucky jade *Korat* he had put on again before he left London. He let her take little Henri and stepped closer to von Eschel.

The German had not been delirious. He must have seen his assassin slithering toward him in the shadows from the moon and the flames, flat against the stones of the cemetery as the bullets sang above. He must have been able to see the face of the person who reached for him.

Von Eschel's eyes were torn out. His Achilles tendons were slashed. His penis was cut off and stuffed in his mouth. The murderer had wanted the German to suffer a humiliating death.

Taking von Eschel's MAT 49, the killer had crawled to Pelwa and repeated the mutilation. Probably Pelwa was dead before it happened. His tommy gun was missing. Harry preferred to think it was Ali Saadi who killed von Eschel. Unless they found the Arab's body on the field this morning, that's how it would be if Harry ever wrote the story.

Harry poured a double slosh of The Famous Grouse on two ice cubes as the DÉFENSE DE FUMER sign went off and the Air France Clipper out of Algiers leveled off and headed across the Mediterranean toward Paris via Marseilles. He put his Smith-Corona Skywriter on the folding tray at his seat, glanced out the window at the red lights flashing on the wing tips, rolled two sheets of yellow paper with a sheet of carbon into the little typewriter that had been more faithful than any lover. He began to ponder the opening paragraph of his new series of columns—columns that should be read whether they made the front page of *The Paris Dispatch* or not. He should have won the Pulitzer Prize last year with his front-page stuff. If he couldn't win it by writing what he believed was important, old Joseph Pulitzer wouldn't have wanted him to have it.

"Who is Rodolfo Sabatini?" Claudette said, looking up from the *Dispatch* that she was reading in the seat beside him.

"Our man in Algiers."

"But he's got most of it wrong. He says the baby and I were kidnapped by bandits who blamed it on the FLN. He says we were rescued by a patrol of Legionnaires who were killed in the effort. He says the paratroopers arrived in the nick of time. He doesn't mention you were there. He doesn't mention von Eschel."

Harry grinned. He had fed Rodolfo something other than the correct facts, but *The Paris Dispatch*—and the *Dispatch* Syndicate—had put across a whopping scoop on PHIBBS: OUR MAN IN ALGIERS and the rest of the reporters in the bar at the Saint-Georges.

"He says you are little Henri's father," she said.

"No harm done, is there?" Harry said. He had decided not to straighten out Rodolfo on the matter of Henri's parentage. Harry glanced at the baby, wrapped in the blue blanket and sleeping peacefully in Claudette's lap. Harry thought little Henri was better off if the world didn't know the truth. "I can live with it if he can. Can you?"

"It's nobody's business but ours, Harry."

The stewardess brought Harry more ice cubes and handed Claudette a glass of white wine. The stewardess smiled at Harry. "If there is anything at all you need, Mr. Sparrow, push my button," the stewardess said.

"Do you know this man?" Claudette asked.

"Mr. Sparrow? I never miss his column in *The Paris Dispatch*. I wake up with Mr. Sparrow and don't get out of bed until he's finished."

Claudette watched the stewardess's buttocks as she went back up the aisle.

"Are there many like her?" Claudette said.

"What? Like who? I'm sorry, I wasn't listening. I've got a column to write."

"You don't believe what Max said about my father being involved in narcotics, do you?"

"No."

"Are you sure?"

"What if he was? It's all over now."

"If he was," Claudette said, "I'd give the money away to a Catholic charity."

"Your father was innocent, believe me. Now leave me alone a few minutes, please? I need to think."

Harry lit a Chesterfield and blew smoke at his reflection in the window. Beside him in the aisle seat, Claudette raised the *Dispatch* to finish reading the rewrite desk's version of Sabatini's version of what Harry had told him at metropolitan police headquarters. The police wanted to put the angel of Dien Bien Phu problem behind them, the sooner the better. Exit papers for Harry and Claudette and the infant were stamped at the office of the governor-general. They were driven to the Air France gate in a police car. The Clipper from Paris brought the usual thirty-six copies of *The Paris Dispatch*. The circulation department blew it as usual, Harry thought. They could have sold a hundred thousand papers in Algiers that day.

He became aware that Claudette was speaking to him again.

"What?" he said.

"How much longer do you have the option on the house at Royal Bowling Brook?" she said.

Harry looked at her with full attention.

"Why?"

"I want to give life with you another try," she said. "I need you, Harry. I'll try to understand why you love your crazy job. I also know you'll never get better about it, not altogether. There will be times when you want the story more than you want me or Henri. But I'll make some compromises and you'll make some . . . at home."

Harry realized he had won a prize that wouldn't fit on the mantel.

"But Harry—I won't ever like golf. Or The Famous Grouse. I am 'The Famous Frog' and I will have my own life, too."

"I wish we had a chessboard," he said.

"But I always travel with a small chessboard. I didn't know you play chess. Why did you never tell me? Are you very good?"

Claudette removed a shiny hardwood case from her Air France flight bag. She opened the case on her seat tray above the sleeping baby in her lap and began to set up the pieces.

Harry glanced at the chessboard, looked at the yellow paper in the Skywriter and consulted his watch. A game of chess would be the thing to start the left side of his brain functioning. Harry placed the Skywriter with its blank page on the floor.

"I'll play white," he said. The German had warned him that she was too strong for him at chess.

"Why, Harry," she cried, delighted, "I'm happy you play chess. There's hope for us yet."

He had plenty of time to do the column before they arrived in Paris. He had decided to write a series: TERRORISM—THE WAR OF THE FUTURE.

Epps would say it wouldn't play in Peoria. Maybe nobody cares in South Bend or Gotham, but Gruber would run the series in full somewhere in the *Dispatch*.

And, who knows, maybe the Pulitzer jury would decide it was his turn this time. No matter what, this was a story he had to write.

He could knock out the first installment in an hour.

ABOUT THE AUTHOR

Edwin "Bud" Shrake was born September 6, 1931, in Fort Worth, Texas. He began his writing career as a sportswriter, first in Dallas and later for *Sports Illustrated.* For many years a foreign correspondent and a columnist for the Dallas *Morning Herald,* he is also the author of several screenplays, including *Tom Horn, Nightwing,* and (with Kris Kristofferson) *Songwriter.* His previous novels include *Limo* (with Dan Jenkins) and two titles recently reissued in the Texas Monthly Press Contemporary Fiction Series, *Strange Peaches* and *Blessed McGill.* Mr. Shrake lives in Austin, Texas.

MAZER, NORMA FOX, 1931

OUT OF CONTROL /

1993.
37565009125435   CENT

Out of Control

ALSO BY
NORMA FOX MAZER

I, Trissy
A Figure of Speech
Saturday, the Twelfth of October
Dear Bill, Remember Me?
and Other Stories
Up in Seth's Room
Mrs. Fish, Ape, and Me, the Dump Queen
When We First Met
Summer Girls, Love Boys
and Other Stories
Someone to Love
Taking Terri Mueller
Downtown
A. My Name Is Amy
Three Sisters
B. My Name Is Bunny
After the Rain
Silver
Babyface
C. My Name Is Cal
D. My Name Is Danita
E. My Name is Emily

WITH HARRY MAZER

The Solid Gold Kid
Heartbeat
Bright Days, Stupid Nights

EDITED WITH MARGORIE LEWIS

Waltzing on Water

Norma Fox Mazer

Out of Control

MORROW JUNIOR BOOKS

New York

Copyright © 1993 by Norma Fox Mazer

All rights reserved. No part of this book may be reproduced or
utilized in any form or by any means, electronic or mechanical,
including photocopying, recording or by any information storage
and retrieval system, without permission in writing from the
Publisher. Inquiries should be addressed to William Morrow and
Company, Inc., 1350 Avenue of the Americas, New York, N.Y. 10019.
Printed in the United States of America.

1 2 3 4 5 6 7 8 9 10
Library of Congress Cataloging-in-Publication Data
Mazer, Norma Fox.
Out of control / Norma Fox Mazer.
p. cm.
Summary: After joining his two best friends in a spontaneous
attack on a girl at their school, sixteen-year-old Rollo finds that
his life is changed forever.
ISBN 0–688–10208–5
[1. Sexual harassment—Fiction. 2. Friendship—Fiction.]
I. Title.
PZ7.M47398Ou 1993
[Fic]—dc20 92-32516 CIP AC

Once again, for Harry,
dear friend and companion of my life.

Hello, this is Rollo Wingate speaking on a cassette recorder—

How am I going to do this?

Just start talking, I guess. Okay, here's the thing. What happened that day in school is sort of on my mind. I mean it *is* on my mind—

Wait. I feel nervous talking about this. I'm going to close the door.

Okay.

Start again. Uh, hello, this is Rollo Wingate speaking on his cassette recorder. It's Christmas vacation, and I'm lying on the floor of my bedroom with my eyes closed and I'm sort of nervous. I'm going to try to tell what . . . what, uh, happened that day.

I don't know what to call it. It wasn't what my father said. It wasn't an assault. We didn't beat her up or rape her or anything. It wasn't like that. It was just . . . it was something we did and, like Candy said, it got a little out of hand.

That's one good thing about Candy, he can take a situation and say something about it so you feel reassured. Like that time a few years ago when we were thirteen and wanted to go swimming in the quarry. We hid our bikes in the underbrush on Tower Road and climbed over the gate United Gravel had put up. Candy was pissed about the gate. He's lived in Highbridge all his life and nobody ever kept him out of the quarry before. It was a hot day. We went across the field toward the quarry. The guardhouse they'd put up was empty. We pried a window open in back and climbed in.

It was just one little room with a cot and a stove and a desk. It was so hot the flies were dying against the windows. "We could bring girls here," Candy said, and we laughed like a couple of maniacs.

All of a sudden, we heard men's voices. It sounded like they were right outside. I almost pissed my pants.

We scrambled and hid under the cot until they went past. "What if they'd caught us?" I said.

"If they left the stupid place unlocked, nobody would have to break in," Candy said.

And I thought, Yeah! That's right!

It was exactly the way I felt when Candy said that things got out of hand with her. I thought, Yeah, right! And I felt relieved.

I wish I could forget it, though.

I called Brig the first day of vacation before he left for Florida with his family. He said, "Rollo, baby! What's up?"

"Not much. How about you?"

"Everything's okay."

"Brig, are you thinking about it?"

"Thinking about what?"

"You know. Her."

"I don't have any hers on my mind, Rollo."

"I mean, what happened—"

"Nothing happened, Rollo."

"Brig—"

"You hear me, Rollo? You listening? I'm telling you, just like I told Mr. Principal, just like I told my father, nothing happened. She's a bigmouth and a liar."

* * *

Okay, time out. I'm going down for something to eat.

Here I am again. Maybe I should tell something about myself. Maybe someone is going to hear this tape someday and they'll want to know, Who is this guy? What kind of person is he?

That's what my father said. "What kind of person are you? Are you my son?"

Shit.

Okay, okay, I don't want to think about that now. Describe myself. Right. I'm a big guy. I've been big ever since, well, ever since I can remember. Bigger than everyone from kindergarten on. I'm built wide, broad in the beam. I've got big arms, big legs, big bones, big hands, big feet. Everything's big except my mouth. I've got a little mouth, like a girl's. I don't like that. I don't like saying it.

In grade school, everyone always wanted me on their team, and the team that didn't get me, the guys would run into me and hit me as hard as they could. Every guy wanted to be the one to knock me over. They'd say, "You love it, don't you, Rollo?" And I'd say, "Yeah!" But it scared me. It scared me when guys screamed and got this look on their face, excited, sort of like dogs, grinning the way dogs grin.

I remember when I met Brig and Candy. It was the summer after my mother died, and we had just moved to Highbridge. The bell rang, I went to the door, and I saw a little guy and a taller, freckled guy. "He's a monster," the little guy said, staring at me. The tall one with the flat, freckled face grinned. "Don't listen to anything Brig says."

The two of them started punching each other. Then we went out and played football on the lawn. Brig kept trying to get past me. He was the same then as he is now, like steam spouting out of a kettle, always moving, always going for it, always pushing. And Candy—just like now, he had a way of blowing off Brig, sometimes laughing at him, sometimes calming him down. It had always been him and Brig, but they let me in, and we did everything together from then on.

My father told me Candy's father was State Senator Candrella. "A big shot," I said, sort of impressed. Candy didn't act like a big shot, though, unless it was the way almost nothing seemed to bother him. He was the one who gave us a name. The Major Three. In seventh grade we changed it to the Lethal Threesome. In ninth grade we all agreed, Let it drop, we're too old for that crap.

But a few months ago, when the high school paper

did a Stars of the Junior Class feature, they posed us together in the gym and printed the picture with LETHAL THREESOME underneath. In parentheses under Candy, they wrote MR. PREZ OF STUDENT SENATE; and under me, MR. STOMP OF FOOTBALL TEAM; and under Brig, MR. STAR PITCHER AND MR. PREZ OF HONOR SOCIETY.

The two Mr. Prezes and me.

"What a bunch of bullcrap," Brig said, but he loved it. We all did.

We get along great, only sometimes Brig will say something to get under Candy's skin, like joking about Candy's parents being the Beautiful People in public but killing each other in private. We all know Candy's parents fight, but we don't talk about it. Sometimes Candy blows it off, but once he went for Brig like he wanted to kill him. I thought I was going to have to mop up the blood. I pried them apart. I wouldn't take sides. I never do. Sometimes I say, "You're right, Candy," but another time I'll say, "Brig's got it." Mostly, though, I just lean back and say, "Whatever."

I love that word. You can just . . . say it. Drawl it out. And the moment you do, you can relax. You don't have to choose: Candy or Brig. You don't have to decide if you want cheese pizza or pizza with sausage, if you want to go swimming or play racquet-ball, if you want to see a movie or rent a video. You don't have to think about anything. You don't have to think about . . . her. You don't have to figure out if what you did was right or wrong. You can just sort of blank your mind and go . . . *whatever*.

– 1 –

Rollo is sitting outside school with his friends, finishing his lunch. It's one of those early December days that are cold, but sunny enough so you can sit on the stone steps and not freeze your ass. The sun on Rollo's face is great. He ignores the off-and-on throbbing in his elbow. He's getting really relaxed. No pressure, no tension, just letting go, getting really, really relaxed.

He takes a bite of his sandwich. It's so perfect sitting with his friends like this. He sees them in his mind like a picture. THREE FRIENDS TOGETHER. The big wide one in the middle, loose-limbed smooth old Candy on one side, and Brig, all wires and springs, on the other side. Sometimes, the best times, like now,

Rollo has this pure, certain feeling that the three of them *belong* together and that they'll always be together.

He leans back on his elbows, then jerks upward. He can't put pressure on his right elbow. Feels like little knives cutting up a steak. From September until Thanksgiving, when football ends, and even after for a while, he always aches and throbs someplace in his body. His ribs are still sore from Brady, that ox from Boonville, butting him. The last game, and Brady sure wanted to smash him, but Brady was the one who went down, with Rollo on top of him and Scipio slipping through with the ball.

Last week, Coach gave them his end-of-the-season speech. "I want you men to stay in shape the rest of the year. We had a decent season, not a great season, but nothing to be ashamed of. We did our best, we gave it our all, that's what counts." He made them hold hands and yell, "We did our best, we gave it our all!"

Then he went around grabbing each player by the shoulder and telling him all his excellent points and how he should work out through the winter and spring and have strong mental thoughts about playing next year. He gave each one a hug and a big slap on the back.

When he came to Rollo, he gave him the slap on the back, but not the hug. "Wingate, you disturb me," Coach said. "You should be better than you are." His face was puckered up: he looked like his teeth hurt. "Something's missing, Wingate. What is it?" Coach tapped Rollo's chest. "A four-letter word, begins with *T,* and a six-letter word, begins with *S.* I'll give you a hint. The four-letter word is *team.*" Coach's face was right up against Rollo's.

Rollo stood straight, his shoulders back, his neck rigid, like a marine in one of those movies where the sergeant is yelling at the recruit, and the recruit is not supposed to show any feelings, only yell out, "Yes, SIR! . . . No, SIR!" Rollo wished he could just tell Coach the truth.

"The six-letter word ends with *T,*" Coach went on. "I'll give you some of the other letters, because this is a tough question. *S. P.* Blank. *R.* Blank. *T.*"

Everyone was listening. A lot of the guys were laughing. Coach waited, and Rollo had to say it, feeling like a damn fool. "Team spirit."

"Right! And I don't think you have it."

"Uh, I do," Rollo lied. "I do. Really." He said it to make Coach feel better. It wasn't Coach's fault the way Rollo was. Coach had done everything a coach should do. He'd screamed at Rollo, he'd pushed him, he'd called him names, he'd whacked him across the side of the head, he'd even appealed to him.

But Rollo still lacks team spirit, still doesn't like football. He doesn't know why. He doesn't understand why he's this way, when other kids would give anything to be on the team, in his shoes. Maybe it's the same way he doesn't like clams or listening to his father's music. Matter of taste.

"Let Rollo decide," Candy is saying. "Yes or no, Rollo?"

What's he supposed to decide? He hasn't been listening. "Whatever," he says and shifts on the cement steps, sucking in the fresh cold air. God, he feels happy. Football is over. He is free as a bird. Nobody telling him to do anything. Nobody on his case. Nothing to think about.

"Hey, Rollo," a kid says, coming up the steps. He gives Rollo a big, hero-worshipping smile. "Rollo, man!"

"Yeah, hi," Rollo says. There are always kids around like that, looking at you like you're something special because you're on the team. The kid gives Rollo a kick in the ribs as he passes, like he thinks Rollo is made of stone.

Candy and Brig laugh. "Rollo, man!" Brig says. "That kid's in love with you. You return the feeling?"

"Shut your nasty mouth, Briggers."

"Get off your oversize ass, Wingate, and make me."

They slap hands.

"When do you guys think my brother did it the first time?" Brig says.

"Knowing your big brother, when he was in diapers," Candy says.

"Close. He was thirteen."

"Says who?" Candy sounds cool, but Rollo notices that his freckles get bright. Whatever Candy does, playing basketball or leading an assembly, he makes it look easy, but sometimes those freckles give him away.

"What about you and Arica?" Candy says to Brig.

"What about us? Eat your heart out."

Rollo wonders if it's true, or . . . Probably it is. Brig and Arica. Sure. By now . . . He watches Denise Dixon crossing the bare, half-frozen lawn. Now, there is something perfect. She's wearing a green sweater, down vest, and black pants. Blond hair, pink cheeks, tiny waist. You just want to put your hands around that waist and squeeze.

Rollo is sure Denise Dixon is the kind of girl you could talk to, and she would listen and make it easy for you to say things. She sits behind him in Mr.

Maddox's class. Sometimes Rollo feels Denise
Dixon's breath on the back of his neck and senses her
pretty legs behind him, and then everything fades
away—Mr. Maddox's voice becomes a faint drone,
the classroom is gone, everything is gone, Rollo is
gone. . . .

They have never talked. She's one of the smart
girls, one of the beautiful, perfect girls you can just
look at and think about in private. Sometimes a girl
will glance at him in the hall and say, "Hiii, Rollo.
How are *yooou*?" But not Denise Dixon. That's okay,
because if she did talk to him, what would he say?

"I might go out with her," Candy says, pointing
with his chin.

"Who?" Brig asks.

"Denise Dixon."

"You're going out with Denise Dixon?" Brig whistles. "When?"

Candy rubs his chin. "When? When I decide to."

Brig sits back. "You putz."

"Got you that time, Briggers." Candy slaps hands
with Rollo.

"You need help, Candrella," Brig says, "serious
help. I'm going to have to fix you up."

"The hell you will," Candy says, but he leans forward.

"Yeah, I'm going to do it. I'll ask Arica to recommend someone for a desperate guy. No, wait." Brig's head swivels. "I have a better idea. You should go out with *her*."

They all watch a tall girl crossing the street. She's wearing a long coat, men's work boots, and a gray fedora with a big droopy feather in the brim.

"I'll go out with her if I can keep my eyes closed," Candy says.

They laugh and Brig punches Rollo lazily. "Candy's an amusing cuss," he says.

Valerie Michon clumps up the wide cement walk toward them. They are sprawled out over the steps like it's home and they aren't inviting anyone to enter. They have left a narrow aisle at one end, but as Valerie approaches, Brig shifts and spreads out, so he takes up that space, too.

She stops at the bottom of the steps. "Are you going to move?"

"Why?" Brig spreads out a little bit more.

Rollo and Candy look at each other, smiling.

"I want to go in the building," she says.

"So go."

She walks up the steps, straight up, as if Brig doesn't exist, not trying to get around him or by him, and she steps on his hand, which is in her way, steps right on it with her big, work-booted foot. Brig swears and, quick as lightning, smacks her on the leg.

She jumps like a chicken. She squawks and snatches off her hat as if she's going to beat him up with it. Brig cowers in mock fear, her face goes red, and the three of them are laughing and laughing as she goes into the building.

− 2 −

At the first rumble of thunder, Kara, who's been in the kitchen baking cookies, is out of there and into the front hall closet. "I'm scared I'm scared," she cries. "Rollo, Rollo!"

"It's okay, I'm here," he says, coming in from the living room. "I'm right here, you can come out. Are you coming out?"

"Noooo."

He sits down on the floor near the closet. This is going to take a while. It always does. "Kara . . . are you listening to me?"

There's an acknowledging sob from inside the closet.

"Kara, I have a joke for you."

The windows light up. Thunder rattles every pane in the house, and Rollo's belly jumps. Close strike.

"Are you scared?" Kara cries. "Rollo! Are you very scared?"

"Of course not," he lies.

He looks up at the round stained-glass window over the front door, daisies entwined with lilies. There is something soothing about it, something about it that always makes him think of his mother. She would have liked that window, she would have liked this house.

The first time his father brought them here, Kara had shouted, "Nice house! I love it! Nice house, Daddy!" But Rollo, looking into each empty echoing room, had realized with a pang that moving to Highbridge from the city meant leaving behind the place where his mother had lived with them. Everything about Highbridge had seemed strange and lonely until he met Brig and Candy.

"Kara," he says, "are you listening? Here's the joke. Do you know how to catch a special rabbit?"

"What is a special rabbit?"

"Kara, you're supposed to say, *How?*"

"How?"

"Unique up on it."

"Whaaat?"

"Unique means 'special.'" He waits. "And it sounds like 'you sneak.'"

"What?"

"Let's try the second part of the joke. Do you know how to catch a tame rabbit? Now you have to say—"

"How?" she cries triumphantly.

"Tame way. Unique up on it."

There is silence from the closet, then Kara says, "Is that a funny joke, Rollo?"

"Not very," he admits. The rumbling in the sky seems to have swung away to the north.

"Rollo. Tell me the story when you were hit by lightning." She pronounces it like three separate words. Light. En. Ing.

"Kara, you always cry when I tell you that. We don't have to talk about it. I'm safe and sound, I'm right here, and I can never be hit again."

"I know, I know! Because lightning doesn't strike two times," she says. "When is the thunder going away?"

"Now. I can hardly hear it anymore. It's raining, that's all. Come on out now." He doesn't want their father to come home from work and find her in the closet. "Come on, honey," he coaxes. "Come out."

The door opens a crack, and Kara appears,

scrunched down, arms wrapped around legs. She duck-walks to him.

"Why are you doing that?" he says.

"I'm being super-safe. Closer to the ground is safer." She sits down and leans her head against his arm. "Tell me about being hit by lightning."

"I've told you so many times, Kara."

"How many times?"

"I don't know. Ten. Twenty. A million."

"A million! That's funny!" She laughs and thumps her head against his shoulder. "That's funnier than rabbit jokes! A million times! I love you, my funny brother, and I love Daddy. And I love your friends, and I love my friends."

"I know, you love everybody."

"Yes," she says with satisfaction.

"Aren't you hungry? I'm starved. Let's go get something to eat. Those cookies smell great."

"I never eat when it's thunder and light. En. Ing. It's a rule. It's a good rule I made up."

"For once, you could break your rule."

"Tell me the story first," she says cannily.

Rollo gives in. "Mom and I were on the porch," he begins.

"You were little."

"Right. I was sitting in her lap—"

"No. You have to say you were little first."

"I was little first."

"No, Rollo! Say it right. Say the story right."

"Is that the phone I hear?" He puts his hand to his ear. She loves answering the phone.

"No, stupid, it's not even ringing."

"Are you sure? I think Maureen said she wants to eat supper with us. Maybe she's calling."

"Maureen! Oh, no! Now I have to fix up the dining room," Kara moans.

The only time they eat in the dining room is when Maureen, their father's girlfriend, comes for supper, which is practically never, since she thinks they are a bunch of slobs. They aren't *that* bad. It's just that she once caught the three of them eating spaghetti from a common pot, and she's never forgotten it.

"Oh, what a day." Kara clutches her head. "First lightning and now Maureen. I have so many things to think about."

Rollo takes pity on her. "I'm wrong, Kara, I got mixed up. Maureen's not coming today."

"Anyway, you can't answer phones in storms," Kara says, "it's a rule. Don't sit by windows, it's a rule. Don't put on TVs, it's a rule. Outside, stay—"

"All right, enough rules. I got it."

"—low to the ground, it's a rule. Don't sit on—"

"I'm telling you the lightning story," Rollo says. "Do you want me to tell it or not?" Anything is better than listening to Kara going on about her rules. "I was little and there was a storm with thunder and lightning. Mom and I were watching from—"

"You shouldn't have been outside," Kara interrupts. "It's dangerous."

"Mom thought we were safe on the porch."

"We had a big porch then. I remember."

"Right. It was the house Dad and Mom rented for the summer on the lake. You were sleeping, taking a nap. Mom and I were on the porch, sitting in a metal chair—"

"You were just a little teeny three years old."

He nods. "So the lightning hit the ground near us and surged to the porch."

"Surged to the porch!" she moans.

"Kara, it just means it traveled."

"It traveled on its lightning feet! It ran to the porch and it got my little brother and my mommy!" Her face fills.

"Come on, it's only a story. It's all over, it was a long time ago. I'm not going to tell you if you cry."

"I won't! But I can't help it too much. My poor

little Rollie. What did you feel like?" she begs him.

"Poor little Rollie felt like you do when your hands are wet and you touch something electric."

"Zzzzz," she says, grinding her teeth. "Zzzzzzz!"

"Only I felt it all through my body. Zzzzz zzzzz everywhere."

"Ugh!" she cries. "And what about Mommy? You didn't tell me that part again."

"Mom got knocked unconscious for a few minutes. It was worse for her than me, because she was in direct contact with the metal. I was in her lap, so I was mostly protected."

"Yes," Kara says, "it was worse for her. Then what?"

"Well, then she came to, and Dad came home and she told him about it, and he said, 'Oh, my goodness, I'm so upset, I feel so bad, where's my Kara, is she all right?' "

This is the part of the story Kara really likes. "He was worried about me. He was so worried about me."

"But you were safe, taking a nap." Rollo tries to wind up the story quickly. "And it never happened again, and we all got smart and we don't ever sit in metal chairs on porches when there are storms. Let's go fix something for supper."

Suddenly Kara farts. "Oops," she says.

"Kara, that was gross. Remember what Dad told you?"

"I know, I know! I'm supposed to go out of the room, but it just jumped out and surprised me." She giggles. "Excuse me, that was rude. Are you mad? Don't be mad at me."

"I'm not mad at you," he says, holding his nose.

She giggles again and hugs his arm. The storm has really passed by now, and in a few minutes they go into the kitchen and start working on supper together. "I'm a good worker," Kara says, slicing a tomato carefully. "Mrs. Rosten said, 'Kara, you are a good worker. You clean the tables so good. Kara, it's a pleasure to see you, you always have a smile on your face.' " She smiles to show him. "Mrs. Rosten is my social worker. Did you remember that, Rollo?"

"Yes."

"Can I make some tea with sugar?"

"I guess so."

"Oh, good! Thanks!" She puts on the kettle, then stands staring out the rain-smeared window, her thumb in her mouth, her finger absently rubbing her nose. His sister. His big sister, born ten years before him. He had passed her when he was six years old. Ever since, he's been getting older, but Kara has stayed pretty much the same age.

– 3 –

Rollo stares at Sara Hendley—fluffy blond hair, big big blue eyes. She is one of the girls who sometimes says hello to him in the hall.

"She's gonna get all red," Brig predicts.

Candy disagrees. "I've seen her in class, she's cool."

They are in the cafeteria, sitting at their table, the one they staked out for themselves at the beginning of the semester. They are leaning back, sipping sodas, and looking at girls. Behind them, the high windows are streaked with a cold gray rain.

"Red face, big time," Brig says firmly. "Rollo?"

"Uh, maybe she'll twirl her hair," he suggests.

Candy laughs and says he'll go with that. But then Sara Hendley looks up, sees them staring at her, and turns bright red. So Brig wins that round.

It's a game. They choose a girl, then guess what she'll do when she becomes aware of their staring. Sometimes the girl drops something—her napkin, her purse, her fork. Sometimes she gets very animated and starts talking really fast to her friends. Sometimes she tries to pretend she doesn't know they are staring, but they can always tell—she knows. They always get some reaction.

They take turns picking the girl. After Sara Hendley, it's Rollo's turn to pick one. He rubs his elbow where it's sore and glances around the cafeteria. His gaze lingers for a moment on Denise Dixon. No. He squirms a little on his seat. He would never suggest her for the game.

"Well, who?" Brig elbows him. "Don't fall asleep on us."

"Let the big guy think," Candy says.

"Big guy doesn't think," Brig says. "Big guy just goes ugga ugga. He's not that interested in girls, anyway, are you, Rollo?"

"I am," Rollo protests.

"You never get stirred up about anything. If Sara Hendley flashed in front of you, you wouldn't even blink. You'd rub your head and say to yourself, Is it getting hot in here or something?"

They all laugh. Rollo laughs the loudest.

"So who is it?" Candy asks.

"Her." Rollo makes a quick choice, lifting his chin to indicate a tall, rangy girl sitting two tables away from them.

"That dog. That's the best you can do?" Brig complains. He punches Rollo. "We're supposed to pick pretty ones."

They all stare at Valerie Michon.

"She's going to drop her book," Rollo says.

"No, she'll pretend she doesn't notice and talk to that guy sitting next to her," Candy says.

"She's not going to talk to him, she's going to dump her milk on his head," Brig says.

"She's going to start yapping," Candy says. He likes to be right. "She looks like a yapper."

"She was in my AP class last year," Brig says. "I hate girls like her. She argues about every goddamn little thing."

They stare at Valerie Michon, waiting to see which one of them is right. It's a game, just a game, just something to do on a boring, rainy day in December.

Gradually, she becomes aware of them; she looks their way, frowning, sees them staring at her, sees that all three of them are looking at her, just her, pinning her with their eyes. It's always funny watching this happen. Sometimes the girl's head comes up abruptly and she glances at them, then away, then back again, as if she can't quite believe. . . . Sometimes it's just a little side glance that tells her, *Yes, right, someone, no, three someones are staring at you.* . . . And then the red rises in her face or the fork falls or she giggles wildly or . . . whatever.

When Valerie Michon realizes they are staring at her, though, she stares back, just stares right back at them. The game's no fun with her. They should have known. "Remember the way she went up the steps?" Candy says. They all groan. She had come down on Brig's hand as if she was out to break every bone in it, the bitch.

Rollo leans back, thinking about Denise Dixon again. From here, he can see the long straight line of her back, the thick honey-blond braid tied with different-colored yarns. *Lovely thing.* . . . Sometimes he thinks things like that, they just pop into his mind—things he would never say to anyone. *Lovely lovely thing.* . . .

He has completely forgotten Valerie Michon, and then there she is, standing at their table, looking at them, and saying in a voice of utter contempt, "Morons."

4

"Valerie." Someone touches her on the back, and without thinking she jerks away, reacting as if it were one of those boys.

"Valerie," Mr. Maddox says again, hovering, tall and slightly stooped, over her, "how're you doing? I miss you in class." He pushes up the sleeves of his white sweater with pale, soft hands. Does he know that kids say he's gay? "I don't have anybody to keep me on my toes this year," he says.

"You mean nobody to argue with you!"

She's been told she talks too loud and too much. That just really means she says what's on her mind. Sorry, but if all you can do is utter polite lies, you might as well not live. Just go jump off a cliff and get it over with.

"What are you up to these days, Valerie?" Mr. Maddox says. "Are you working on your art?"

She frowns. "I don't want to talk about that." She doesn't have anything going right now. For some reason, she hasn't been inspired lately.

"What about college—where are you going to apply?"

"I might not go to college."

"Valerie, I don't know if I like that. I don't want to see you throw your talent and ability away."

"Maybe I'll just go to New York City . . . and live and be an artist." How does she get the nerve to call herself an artist? She's an amateur, a beginner, a novice. She wants to take back the words and, at the same time, she wants to shout them out. "Do you really think I have talent?" she can't help asking.

"First prize in the Art Open!"

"School stuff, Paul. I'm not impressed." Is he going to take offense that she used his first name? "I hope, I believe I have talent and—"

"You do, Valerie." He's looking at her with warm eyes.

"That's why I have to . . . I have to *do* something

with it! The whole thing with my hands is so mysterious." The same thing she said to her father last night. Did he understand? He gave her one of his vague, sweet smiles. "When my hands get on the clay, they do things I don't even know are in me. It's as if God gave me something, I mean if you believe in God, which I don't, actually. I do believe in something, a higher power. There has to be something regulating the universe, it can't just be chaos."

She's talking too fast, but he's listening, and she rushes on. "I feel I'm part of whatever this is, something bigger than me—a great universal spirit—and I can't just go off to college and waste my father's money and not do what I'm supposed to do, whatever that is. College, art, talent—it's all tied in together," she finishes. She waves her hands, her heart is pumping, she doesn't know if she said anything that made sense.

"You think if you go to college, you won't be serving your talent?" Mr. Maddox says.

She loves that he puts it all into one simple sentence. She loves that he uses the word *serve*. That he understands. She feels like hugging him, but of course she can't. Her eyes light on his sweater with its intricate knit pattern around the collar and cuffs.

"Fabulous sweater." She knows that will please him. His wife knits all his sweaters.

"My wife made it," he says eagerly. "Talk about talent, Valerie! I want Sandy to go into business. Already one whole room in our apartment is filled just with her patterns and wools. She has so much dedication—"

"Mmm, mmm." Now Valerie remembers that when Mr. Maddox talks about his wife, he is as close to boring as he ever gets. Thank goodness, the bell rings, and she can head upstairs for the art room. It's empty and all hers. She breathes in the quiet, the sharp smell of paints, and the damp acrid smell of clay.

She gets the clay out of the covered tray, sits down on a stool, and starts warming the lump in her hands. Maybe, if something starts happening with it, she'll skip sixth period. Catching a glimpse of herself in the mirror, she straightens her back. Does she look like an artist, someone free and unconventional? She's tall and thin, with pale skin and dark hair. A description that could fit a million people!

She begins working the clay, watching her hands. Are they really an artist's hands? Does she have talent or only cleverness? Her father says everybody has latent talent. She'll never know, though, until she gets out into the real world. Her fingers dig into the clay, and she dreams about living in a little apartment somewhere in Brooklyn. That's where all the artists are now. That's where she can really be herself.

In Highbridge, everyone lives in the same kind of house, drives the same kind of car, goes to the same school, wears the same clothes, and has the same interchangeable parents. Well, actually, there is one exception. As Janice, longtime next-door neighbor and mostly good friend, has said more than once, "Val, your father is *different.*"

For starters, he's fat and doesn't have a job. Every other father Valerie knows is trim and in shape, they all jog and do strenuous things at the Racquet Club, and they're all doctors and lawyers and professors at the university in the city. Her father has a workshop in the basement where he spends his days inventing things, like a padded helmet for a baby, so that if the kid climbs out of her crib and falls on her head, she won't get brain-dead.

Once, years ago, a big national company bought one of her father's inventions, something to do with making a little part in a big machine more efficient and cheaper. The company paid her father enough money for them to live on, carefully, for a long time.

Ever since, he has been hoping to come up with something else that will make their fortune.

Last spring, the two of them went to New York City to check out Inventors Expo. Thousands of people in the Javits Center, hundreds of booths and inventions like electric underpants or an electronic hairbrush with a display that told you when you'd brushed your hair enough for maximum health. There'd been at least a dozen versions of steel wool holders and maybe a hundred spaghetti and noodle dippers. And what about the Inter Visuometer or the Polyphase Variable Frequency Inverter? Not even the inventors, standing proudly by their inventions, could make clear what they were for.

Her father had fretted about the noise and the crowds, but Valerie had loved it. "It's incredible, Dad! It's incredible," she kept saying. The people in the street dazzled her—their colors, their shapes, their clothes, their *differentness*. Just walking down Fifth Avenue, she heard at least half a dozen languages. If only she'd had her paints with her—acrylics in bright primary colors were what she wanted to catch the clashing, energetic spirit of the city. It's everything that Highbridge isn't.

She looks at what she's done with the clay. Her hands have worked of their own accord, shaping a head. Prominent eyes, full lips. Mark. "Head of a grut," she says and feels like smacking herself across the mouth. *Grut* is like *spick* or *Polack,* an insult. Even to think it makes her as absurd as everybody else.

She probably is.

An image she doesn't want creeps into her mind: those guys in the lunch room staring at her like she's a . . . thing. A wave of depression hits her. What makes her think she's special? She's no better than anyone else. She's just a small-town girl from a small-town high school. Her head sinks down. She's probably not even that talented. She's probably just a mess, an ordinary mess.

5

"Rollo!" Arica calls, as he comes out of school.

"Hi." He puts up his hand.

"Come on over!" She and Brig are standing at the top of the steps. Brig is leaning against one of the stone pillars, arms crossed. Arica, facing resolutely away from him, has her books mashed against her chest.

Rollo doesn't want to get too close to whatever is going on there, but Arica reaches for him, almost spilling her books. "We're going to get something to eat," she says. "Come with us."

They start down the hill into town. It's a nearly silent walk. Rollo can never think of small talk, and right now, with Brig so silent, anything he thinks of doesn't seem worth saying. But walking between Arica and Brig, he imagines that he's their guardian . . . guardian angel, maybe. Taking care of them. Maybe he'll get them to make up. They've quarreled before, and it always makes Brig miserable.

A few snowflakes fall. "Maybe we'll get enough for powder," he ventures.

"That would be great!" Arica's enthusiasm is nice. Every now and then she sways against Rollo, as if blown by a little wind. Really, she's so pretty he can hardly look at her.

"Do you cross-country or downhill, Rollo?" she asks.

"Downhill."

"Me too. I love it. Isn't it awful, the middle of December, and we still haven't had a good snowfall?"

He nods. With just a tiny movement of his hand, he could touch her. With a tiny movement of his other hand, he could touch Brig. He's so much bigger than both of them that he could gather them up in his arms . . . and crush them . . . or kiss them. The wind blows. His face feels rough and burning. Stupid thoughts. He's always having stupid thoughts.

They pass the YOU ARE ENTERING THE TOWN OF HIGHBRIDGE, POP. 13,560 sign and go the length of

Seneca Street, past the bank, travel agency, book-
store, restaurant. The old Stoddard Hotel always flies
the American flag from the balcony. Here's the tiny
movie house that Kara loves, there's the copy shop,
and now they're passing his father's office, which is
upstairs above the antique store.

"She's talking about breaking up," Brig says suddenly. He jerks his thumb across Rollo at Arica. "She
doesn't like me anymore. What do you think of that,
Rollo?"

"It's not true," Arica says. "I do, too, like you."

"Doesn't like me," Brig says. "Doesn't like me."

"Stop!" Arica puts her hands over her ears.

"Sorry," Rollo says.

"What are you apologizing for, Rollo?" Arica says.

He doesn't know. He just wishes everyone would
be more friendly.

Suddenly Brig pushes Rollo aside and gets next to
Arica. He pulls her toward him. "Stay with me,
babe," he says in a kind of rough, movie-gangster
voice, "or I'll rub ya out."

"That's not funny, Brig."

"Rollo thinks it's funny, don't you, Rollo?"

Rollo grins responsively, feeling stupid again.

Arica pulls free. "Brig, I'm going to say this again,

in front of Rollo, like a witness. All I said to you was that my mother doesn't want me getting too serious. She says—"

"I know what your mother says."

"—I'm too young to be tied to anyone, and you and I—"

"I heard it! Don't tell me that again!"

Arica bites her lip and is silent. They walk across the McDonald's parking lot and into the restaurant. Rollo takes off his jacket and rolls up the sleeves of his shirt. It's hot here; the baskets of plants hanging from the ceiling seem to give off a steamy warmth.

"We can still go out, Brig, we can still be friends," Arica says as they stand in the food line. "I just can't go out with you so much. I can't be exclusive, is all."

"You want to go out with other guys," Brig says. "That's what this is all about. Why don't you admit it? Maybe you want Rollo here. Maybe that's who you want."

"Order me a shake," Arica says and walks away.

"Where're you going?" Brig calls.

She stops briefly. "To wash my hands! I hope, when I come back, Brig, you can be in a better mood."

Rollo and Brig get the food in silence and sit down. "So what do you think?" Rollo says.

Brig is biting the inside of his cheek. "What do I think about what?"

"Will Arica change her mind?"

"How do I know? How do I know anything that goes on in a girl's mind?"

Rollo pours ketchup on his hamburger and looks around for Kara. He spots her swabbing the floor in another aisle. He sees her mouth moving, and he knows exactly what she's saying as she swabs past each booth. "Watch your feet. Watch your feet." She'll say it even if the booth is empty. Sometimes she'll vary it. "Express train coming! Watch your feet!"

When Arica comes back, she hesitates, then sits down next to Brig. She unwraps her straw and puts it into the shake.

"Nice clean hands?" Brig inquires.

Arica smiles tightly.

Nobody says anything for a while. Rollo catches Arica staring at his bare arms. What is she thinking? His arms are hairy, and they seem to him, looking down at them, like enormous, dark sausages. Is she revolted? He checks on Kara again. She's talking to a man sitting alone. Rollo recognizes the sparkling, excited look on her face and hears her voice above all the other voices. He can see only the back of the man's head, but he imagines his startled, annoyed face and half stands. "Kara," he calls.

She looks up. "My brother!" She drops her mop and comes running over. "Rollo!" she says joyously, as if she hasn't seen him for years. She kisses him on the cheek, a loud wet smack. "My darling brother is here! And Mister Brig! This must be my lucky day!" She eyes their food. "You're having a snack. That's great! What's your name?" she says to Arica. "You're pretty!"

Her cap has gotten knocked sideways in the excitement. Rollo pushes it straight. "This is Arica," he says. "Arica, this is my sister. I just wanted to say hello," he says to Kara. "Maybe you better go back to work now."

"Arica, I love you!" Kara bends over and kisses Arica on the cheek and the neck. "Lovely lady Arica!"

Brig laughs. "You're something else, Kara." He likes her.

Arica is looking a little startled. "Did you leave your stuff in the middle of the floor, Kara? Someone might trip over it and hurt themselves."

"Oh, my goodness." Kara looks horrified. She rushes away.

"She's Down's syndrome," Rollo says to Arica.

"I thought it was something like that. Is she always that goofy?"

Rollo dips fries in ketchup. Kara's motor does get sort of revved, but she's not goofy. That's not an accurate way to talk about her. He's disappointed in Arica. If he had a girlfriend and she said something dumb about his sister, what would he do? Dump her or try to improve her attitude?

"Look who's here," Brig says. He's looking over Rollo's shoulder, toward the food line.

Rollo turns. Valerie Michon is in line with a guy he recognizes from around school—Mark Saddler, a senior, one of the kids who comes from Union. A grut.

"That's the girl I told you about who stepped on my hand," Brig says to Arica. He's still staring at Valerie Michon.

"Is that her boyfriend?" Arica asks.

"She's too ugly to have a boyfriend."

"I don't think she's that ugly."

"You wouldn't."

"What does that mean?"

"You girls stick together. You don't even know her."

"I was just giving my opinion, Brig, but I can see you're not interested."

"Oh, I'm interested. I'm always interested in your opinion. And I'm interested in your plan. What is your plan, Arica? First you break up with me, and then you get yourself someone else?"

"I told you, we can still be friends and go out sometimes."

"And I told you, I don't want to be your damn friend."

Rollo tries once more to ease the tension. "You guys ever hear about the grut who picked his nose because he thought he could make it through school by being snotty?"

Arica laughs like she's never heard a grut joke before, but Brig still looks really furious.

– 6 –

They see Valerie Michon in the hall near the art room a day or so later. They are all together. "Look who's here again," Rollo says. Suddenly Brig veers toward her, and Rollo and Candy veer with him. She doesn't see them coming at first; when she does, her face gets this sort of puffy, twitchy look. Funny as hell. They go straight for her, rushing, like a mini-phalanx, like war.

At the last moment, Brig puts out his hands as if he's going to grab her tits. And then, at the last last moment, he veers off, and they sweep by her. Definitely amusing. Rollo and Candy can't stop looking at each other and laughing, but Brig just shrugs. Since the fight with Arica, Brig has not been pleased with anything.

After school, Rollo goes home with Brig. He's complaining about his father, who, he says, has got a new bug in his ear. "He's after me to go to vet school. He says it's not too soon to make up my mind. He says he built up his business and he wants his son to take it over."

"What do you think?" Rollo says.

"No way. No way am I following in Dr. Briggers's tiny footsteps. Not this son."

"Maybe your brother will go to vet school."

Brig coughs dryly. "Forget that. Justin makes my father nervous. You know what my mother told me once? 'Nature didn't favor your brother with as quick a mind as yours, Julian, so your father and I have to give him incentives.' Bribes, she meant. That's how Justin got the Ford, for passing his junior year. And then the Honda, for getting into college."

Rollo nods. It seems like a good deal to him. Brig has been the owner of the Ford since September; in two months, he'll take his road test, and they're all looking forward to it. Rollo and Candy both have licenses, but no cars—Rollo, because his father says he can't afford it, and Candy, because his father says he doesn't want him driving until he's older. What

Candy's father really doesn't want, they've all agreed, is Candy getting into trouble that could make bigger trouble for Senator Candrella.

At Brig's house, they head for the kitchen, and Rollo mixes a power shake, dumping in raw eggs, vanilla, ice cream, and peanut butter. While he mans the blender, Brig hangs from the doorframe: he's trying to lengthen himself, stretch himself taller. An ongoing project.

"Hello, son." Brig's father comes in from the clinic next door. He's wearing a white smock with a stethoscope dangling from the breast pocket. He goes to one of the refrigerators and takes out a brown bag. "Julian," he says.

"What?" Brig says, dropping to the floor.

"I said hello to you. I didn't hear a response. When I speak to you, I expect a response."

Rollo gets a couple of glasses from the cupboard and wishes he could just leave right now. He knows what's coming.

"When I say, 'Hello, son,' the response I expect is 'Hello, Dad.' "

"Okay," Brig says.

Dr. Briggers pours beans into the coffee grinder. " 'Okay, *Dad*,' is the proper mode of response."

"Okay, Dad," Brig says tightly.

"Thank you." Dr. Briggers washes the coffeepot. "What happened in school today?"

"Nothing."

"I believe you had a test in history?"

"Yes."

"What kind of test was it? True, false? Fill in the blanks? Essay?"

"Essay."

"Ahhh. Essay. What was the subject?"

"World War Two."

"Julian. Look at me, please. This is something you'll want to do in the world—look people straight in the eye. What aspect of World War Two did you write about in your essay?"

Brig pours the shake into the glasses. "Paris."

"Why Paris?"

"Mrs. Bardino said we should write about some aspect of the European Theater in World War Two."

"Ahhh. What was your background expertise for writing about Paris?"

"I read a book about the liberation of Paris in 1945. *Paris Is Burning.* You want to know who wrote it? Two guys with French names." Brig is talking fast now. "Was it interesting? Yes. Did I like it? Yes. It was pretty exciting for history. Rollo and I are going into the family room now." He motions to Rollo and they start out of the kitchen.

"One moment, son. You didn't say good-bye."

"Good-bye."

"Good-bye, what?"

"Good-bye, Dad."

Dr. Briggers now looks at Rollo.

One of these days, Rollo is going to say something to Brig about his father, something truthful like, *Your father is a crazed psychotic maniac.* "Good-bye, Dr. Briggers," he says politely. He follows Brig into the family room, takes the chair by the window, and drinks his milk shake in one long, relieved gulp.

Brig paces, punching his fist into his hand. "My father has been taking care of dogs and cats for too long. He thinks the whole world is pets and masters." He flings himself on the floor and begins doing push-ups. ". . . five . . . six . . . seven . . ." Up and down he goes, up and down like a machine.

Rollo lets the thought of doing push-ups drift through his mind. Drift in, drift out. He did enough of that stuff under Coach's prodding. He sinks deeper into the chair, sliding down on his spine. What a good thing it is that nobody can see into his mind. *You are weird, Rollo, let me count the ways.*

There. That's just what he means. Bad enough he sort of likes poetry, but now he's mixing the stuff into his regular thoughts. *How do I love thee? Let me count the ways.* That's from a poem Mr. Maddox read them, which is from a whole bunch of poems called something like *The Portuguese Sonnets.* Elizabeth Barrett Browning was the poet. That name just cracks Rollo up, he doesn't know why. Elizabeth Barrett Browning, who wrote all these love poems for her husband.

"First he was her lover," Mr. Maddox had told them. "Yes, you all find that interesting? Robert Browning was a poet, too, a great poet. Men do write poetry. Does that shock you people? It's one of the grown-up things men do, whether you believe it or not."

Brig says Maddox is a homo. Rollo wonders how that can be if he's married, but Brig says he knows one when he sees one. Rollo likes Mr. Maddox. He's fair. Sometimes he's funny. And sometimes he's a pain in the ass, especially when he gets going on how kids don't appreciate anything except videos and football. "Open your minds. It's not a crime to allow a little real passion and feeling to come through. Release your minds from the grip of the ordinary. Be open, receptive. Receive. Expand!" He always has spit on the corners of his mouth. The poor guys up front have to duck not to get sprayed.

". . . seventy-nine . . . eighty . . ." Brig counts, pumping up and down. He keeps going. He passes one hundred.

"You want your shake?" Rollo says. He could drink another one, easy.

"Hands off. . . . Hundred twenty-five . . . hundred twenty-six . . ." Brig gets to 130 and falls flat. Then he jumps up and stands tall in front of Rollo. "What do you think?"

Rollo looks him over. Is Brig taller than the last time he asked? Rollo doesn't see any difference. "Could be," he says judicially.

"Better be! I hang from that goddamn bar fifteen minutes every morning." Brig takes a long drink of his shake. "I'll tell you something, Rollo, I'm not going through life this size. This is not acceptable. Shorter than Candy, shorter than you, shorter than my father, shorter than my goddamn brother. I might as well go into a circus and be a freak." He drinks and paces. "I'm doing something new called visualizing."

"Visual what?"

"Visualizing. Candy gave me the article about it. He found it in one of his mother's magazines. You think about what you want, you visualize it, you put it in your mind, you concentrate on it, and it happens. The idea is for mind and body to work together. Mind visualizes me getting taller, and body does the work. Crackpot idea, isn't it?"

"It could happen," Rollo says. "You're probably still growing."

"What do you mean, probably?"

"I mean, you are."

"Why don't you say what you mean the first time?"

Rollo shrugs and licks out the inside of his glass. Does Brig realize he can be just like his father sometimes?

The phone rings. Brig punches the SPEAKER button. "Briggers residence."

"I want to speak to Julian Briggers," a girl's voice says.

"This is Julian Briggers. Who's calling?"

"Valerie Michon." Her voice is loud in the room. "I have something to say to you."

Brig puts his index finger to the receiver. Bang! Bang! he mouths to Rollo.

"Keep away from me. Keep your hands away from me. Just stay away."

"Hey!" Brig says. "What do you mean, calling up and yelling at me?"

"I am not yelling."

"No? You're going to bust my eardrum like you busted my hand when you stepped on it."

"You refused to move. What was I supposed to do? You know, you're not just rude, you're *crude*. The way you came at me in the hall—"

"I feel sorry for you, if you can't even take a joke."

There is a moment's silence. Then she says, "I understand you go out with Arica Hamilton. That's who I feel sorry for. I pity her."

"Save your pity for yourself, bitch." Brig punches the button and cuts her off. "Do you believe the nerve, to bring Arica in?" He's pacing again. "I talked to her last night. Did I tell you? We talked for an hour, but it was all the same thing, anyway. Her mother says this, her mother says that." He goes to the window and pulls aside the curtain. "I hate that girl," he says with quiet vehemence.

"Arica?" Rollo says, startled.

Brig turns and looks at him. "No, you idiot. Valerie Michon."

– 7 –

When Valerie enters the empty cafeteria, Mark doesn't look up. He is sitting on one of the benches at the back of the room, hands clasped behind his head, eyes fixed on the ceiling. She sits down next to him and waits. "Hi," she says after a moment.

He pushes his glasses up on his nose. "Oh, hi." As if he's just noticed she's there. He is wearing his usual combo of good-fitting jeans, shirt out, and motorcycle boots. He looks at his watch, which he keeps on a long key chain. "You're late."

"Big five minutes," she says, wishing he were less cute. She wants to be businesslike about this tutoring, but she's really attracted to him. When she and Janice were talking on the phone last night, Janice commented that Mark looked like a younger version of Indiana Jones. Now, Valerie sees that it's true—the same wire-rimmed glasses, the same sort of lean, homely-sexy face.

"If I'm five minutes late for my job," he says, "I get docked a quarter of an hour."

"That's not fair!"

"Who said it was?" His expression makes her feel naïve and inexperienced. "Who said anything is fair?" Behind his glasses, his eyes look wet and tired. He's a part-time security guard at a warehouse four nights a week and holds down another job over the weekend. Valerie thinks it's probably illegal for him to work so many hours while he's still in high school.

"Did you work last night?" she asks after a moment.

"Sure did. What'd you do?"

She frowns. What can she say? *Sketched for an hour. Made a phone call to a nasty boy. Had a headache afterward. Made supper for me and Dad, listened to Janice complain about her clothing allowance, got into the spirit and complained about mine. . . .*

Boo-hoo! What a hard life! What if she told him there are times she wishes that she lived in Union, wishes she were a grut? Not that she wants to be poor, no; it's just that it's so ordinary to be her,

Valerie Michon of 50 Academy Street, Highbridge. At least people in Union have *real* problems.

"Anything special you want to work on today?" she asks.

He opens his notebook and takes out a sheet of paper. "A comp I wrote for Mrs. Parryman. I thought you could go over it for me."

"With you," she corrects. She bends over the paper, but she is aware of his watching her. With the eyes of a student? Or a friend . . . or a male? It seems as if their relationship is a confusing mixture of all three.

Sometimes he is almost humbly grateful for her help, and that is nice, and embarrassing, too. She always wants to say, No no, tutoring is something *I* need to do, to contribute. Then sometimes he takes off his glasses and looks at her with those deep brown eyes, and she gets distracted and starts wondering about things that have *nothing* to do with learning. And other times, they get in a certain mood and just joke around, like friends, and that is really nice.

And sometimes he annoys her. He'll do petty things, like he did today, catching her out for being five minutes late. That's when she wonders if he resents her, resents that she lives in Highbridge, that she knows things he doesn't. But what does she really know, except stuff anyone can learn in school—spelling, grammar, things that have nothing to do with life. He's the one who has the real knowledge: he's worked since he was eleven years old.

"Done yet?" He smooths his small bristly mustache, smiling a little, as if he knows she hasn't gone beyond the first sentence.

"In a moment," she says briskly. It's a short composition, not elaborated, not on a very sophisticated level. A lot of errors, too. Disappointing. She's been tutoring him since the beginning of October. It's already mid-December. In more than two months, you'd think—

Stop, she tells herself. What do you want from him, Harvard-quality work? Yes, probably. He's smart and he's tough, and she has got herself involved in wanting him to succeed. She sits for a minute, collecting her thoughts. "What was the assignment, exactly?" she asks.

He produces a small spiral notebook from his shirt pocket and reads, "Two-page essay about life and family." He always has the notebook and two pens neatly lined up in that pocket, as if he's already an engineer.

She glances at the paper again. "Aside from spelling and stuff, which we'll go over, this is basically okay. It's pretty interesting, but it could be better. I have some suggestions."

He takes a pen and waits.

There is something about the way he does this that gets to her—something so patient and hopeful in his face that she almost wants to cry. Instead, she makes her voice as dry as possible. "I think what you intended, Mark, was to contrast the towns of Union and Highbridge. You began doing it, but you didn't carry through. You didn't give any details to substantiate your point of view."

"What details? Everybody knows the difference between Union and Highbridge. All you Highbridge folks have three-car garages, giant fireplaces, and at least two Mercedes-Benzes."

"Saddler, that's ridiculous."

"Looks that way from where I sit."

"Okay, we won't argue about it. Those are your details about Highbridge. What about Union?"

"There's nothing to say about Union."

"Of course there is."

"Do you know Union, Valerie?"

"I've driven through it with my father on the way to the interstate."

"There you go. That's it. Everyone drives through Union on the way to the interstate. That says it all."

"There's got to be something else."

He leans back again, hands clasped behind his head. "Sure there is. Dumpy houses. Biggest store in town is the Salvation Army Thrift Shop. The most action is at Bob's Off-Brand Gas Station. Best restaurant, Pete's Pig-out Pizza. Come on, Valerie, you know Union, it's nothing, the people who live there are nothing, and it's nothing anyone wants to read about."

"I can't believe the things you say. They're totally absurd! You're more prejudiced than anyone in Highbridge."

"You think so?" he says mildly, but there's a flash in his eye.

"Look, the point is, you've got to put the details in the essay. All that stuff will make an excellent contrast to your observations about Highbridge."

"Ahh, yes, the fine details of Union, an excellent contrast to my profound observations . . ."

Okay, so she had sounded stuffy. "Write it down," she orders. "You know you can do better than this. Some of your vocabulary is so lazy, like using 'bummed-out.' And you've got run-on sentences, plus spelling errors."

He sucks on the end of his pen. "Is this stuff going to help me get into college?"

"It's going to help, yes. I wouldn't be doing this, spending all this time, if I didn't think so."

"All this time," he repeats. "Your valuable time."

A little heat comes up into her neck. Why is there always this barrier she can't get past with him? Why does he put this wall up between them? All she wants is to be his friend. Doesn't he get it! What sort of person is he behind those flip remarks—is he genuine? You can't tell about some people. Faces can be so deceptive, and maybe guys' faces, especially, because she's always distracted by how their hair grows a certain way or their eyes have a particular light.

The thought of those three jerks swims into her mind. Perfect examples of the adorable face–cruddy attitude syndrome. Briggers has a great body and fantastic hair. Candrella is sort of an All-American type. He could step into an ad and model shirts or jeans. And the other one, the football one—she's forgotten his name, but the one who's fat and dumb—even he isn't so bad to look at. With his round eyes and round mouth and fair hair cut straight across his forehead, he looks like a cute boy doll.

She glances at Mark again, at his eyes, hidden

now behind his wire rims, and wishes, not for the first time, that she knew what really went on in his mind.

"What are you looking so serious about?" he says.

"Just thinking about your sentence structure."

– 8 –

The day it finally snows in earnest, Kara is so excited she can hardly sit still at supper. "I'm going sledding," she says, bouncing in her chair. "It's snowing and blowing and the cat has snow on his whiskers. Rollo, will you go sledding with me?"

"Maybe," he says, reaching for another slice of pizza.

"Rollo, 'maybe' means 'yes.' Did you know that? The cat has snow on his whiskers, that's the joke." She has her face tipped to the side, her eyes opened wide. "I want to go sledding in the cat-whisker snow. Daddy, did you hear me?"

"I heard you, honey. Quiet down now. Let's finish up. Maureen's coming over later."

Rollo glances across the table at his father. It still comes as a surprise to him that his father has a girlfriend. To be brutally truthful, his father is overweight, has a pot belly and round shoulders. His teeth are yellow, too. Do he and Maureen . . . ?

"Maureen's coming over?" Kara says. "Uh oh, this is a mess!" And when Rollo laughs, she repeats it, rolling her eyes, making a nutty face. She knows she's being cute. Just then the phone rings. "It's Maureen," Kara screeches, hoping for another laugh. "Get it, Rollie."

It's not Maureen, it's Brig, who says he has to talk to Rollo and he's coming right over. He doesn't even say good-bye, just hangs up. What's that all about? Arica, probably. Which means Brig won't want to talk in the house, because Kara doesn't know the meaning of the word *privacy*.

"I'm going outside to wait for Brig," he tells his father. "We're probably going for a walk or something."

"Okay," his father says, and, ever the efficient accountant, he adds, "You might as well start shoveling the walk while you wait."

The wet, heavy snow packs into cubes with each shovelful, and the wind blows into Rollo's face. He heats up and tears off his jacket. He has shoveled out to the street and is doing the sidewalk when Brig pulls up. The top of his car is covered with a fat pancake of snow. He rolls down the window and waves Rollo over.

"How come you're driving?" Rollo says, leaving the shovel in a snowbank.

"Because I feel like it."

"What'd your father say?"

"He's at a convention in Texas. Come on, get in!"

"What about your mother? She know you got the car?" Rollo slides into the front seat.

"She's out with friends tonight. Any more questions?"

"You want me to drive?"

"No! Guess what Arica told me—she's going to break up with me."

"I know that. She said that already."

"No, you don't know that!" Brig hits the steering wheel. "She'd changed her mind. I got her to change her mind. Yesterday I talked her out of it." He pulls away from the curb, and the tires spin in the snow. "Then she calls me back tonight and says never mind what she said before."

"Maybe she'll change her mind again."

The car lurches ahead. "If I just didn't have to see her every day in school."

"Winter vacation is coming," Rollo says, trying to be helpful. "A few more days, then you won't have to see her for a long time."

"You don't understand anything." Brig groans and steps on the gas. The headlights barely penetrate the falling curtain of snow.

They drive up the hill, past the school, past the cluster of houses on Birch Hill, and out of Highbridge. Brig is talking about Arica again, his voice choked, saying all the things he's said before: how he feels like crap and how it's Arica's fault he feels this way.

Rollo shifts around. He wants to tell Brig something, maybe to take it easy, maybe just what he'd thought that day in the restaurant when Arica made her dumb remark about Kara. *She's pretty, Brig, but don't get all wiped out over her. There are plenty of other girls around. . . .*

"Where are we going?" he asks, after a while.

"I don't know. . . . How does grut hunting sound?"

It sounds tough and funny, like something someone would say in a movie.

They take the back road over by Union Falls, a winding road of sudden curves that pitches steeply down into the valley. Brig is a good driver; probably they won't be stopped by a cop, but Rollo wipes the side window dry and keeps an eye out, anyway. Banks of snow line the shoulders. The roadbed is covered by a thick blanket of wet snow, and the back of the car is torquing all over the place.

"Want me to slow down," Brig says, not slowing down.

"Go," Rollo says. He loves the speed, loves the way Brig lets the car hurtle down into the valley on the snow-clogged road.

Suddenly there's a gleam of green-gold in midair, and a deer leaps toward them, leaps through the falling snow like a dream. Brig jerks the wheel, and the car slides sideways across the road into a snow-bank. They sit for a moment, looking at each other. The deer is gone, swallowed by snow and trees. "He could have totaled the car," Brig says. "He could have killed us."

"Killed us!" Rollo says. He starts laughing with relief and excitement.

They're both laughing as they push the car out of the snowbank. They talk about the deer—how big it was, how much it weighed. "A hundred fifty pounds," Brig says solemnly, "maybe two hundred."

Two hundred pounds of hooves and bones and forward energy that could have smashed them to bits.

"But here we are!" Rollo says triumphantly. They're still laughing as they roll into Union. The main street is nearly deserted. Wreaths are strung around the light poles, and almost every house has blinking candles in the window and a Santa Claus with elves or deer on the roof. Brig drives up one street, down another. The plows haven't been through some of the streets yet.

"How many people do you think live in this town?" Brig says.

"Not many."

"Right, and they're all related, which is why they're all morons. Do we know anybody that lives here?"

Rollo laughs. "You kidding?"

"That guy we saw Valerie Michon with."

"We don't know him."

"He looked grutty!"

"True."

"We could go over to his house and pay him a visit."

"Why?"

"Because I feel like doing something." Brig's voice is tense again. "I just freaking feel like doing something. What's his name?"

"Who?"

"The grut! The one that was with Michon."

"Saddler or something."

"Right, that's it. Mark Saddler. I wonder where he lives."

"We could check the phone book," Rollo says.

Brig jams on the brakes. Across the street is a gas station with an outside phone booth. They get out of the car. The door of the booth is half off, and someone has tried to rip the phone book off its metal chain. Brig thumbs through what's left of the book. "Got it," he says after a minute or two. "There's a Saddler on Elm Street."

They drive around looking for Elm Street. After they go by School Street for the third time, Brig rolls down the window and calls to a girl coming out of a pizza place, "Where's Elm Street?"

She stares into the car. She's holding a stack of white pizza boxes, her chin resting on top. "Over that way." Her lips are outlined in bright pink.

"You going to eat all those pizzas yourself?" Rollo suddenly says. He's getting hungry again. Besides, he likes the way she has those bright neon-pink lips, and he wants to say something to her.

She gives him a nice little smile. "Don't worry about it, sweetie. I've got friends as big as you to help me out. Take your first right," she says to Brig, "go down two blocks, hang a left at the light. Nice car. Whose is it?"

"Mine."

"Honest to God?"

"Two more better than this at home."

"Liar," she says.

"I swear."

"Where's home?"

"Highbridge."

"Oh, that follows."

Her directions are good. The house on Elm Street is painted green, with a square front porch. Santa Claus and three reindeer outlined in red lights are running across the roof.

"What do you think?" Brig says, parking behind another car at the curb.

"Looks okay to me," Rollo says.

"What do you mean it looks okay? You think we're buying the place?"

"I don't know what we're doing."

Brig laughs. "Me either. Let's find out."

"Find out what?"

"If he lives here."

"Then what?"

"I don't know. Didn't you ever hear of improvisation?"

They sit in the car, looking at the house. There are lights on everywhere and they can faintly hear music. Rollo feels a little nervous and clears his throat a few times. "What if it's the wrong house?"

"What are you whispering for?"

Rollo digs his hands into his pockets. "We don't even know this guy, Brig. It's crazy."

"That's the way I feel, crazy."

The front door of the house opens, and a man wearing a green jacket and carrying a gym bag comes down the walk. As he gets closer, they see it's Mark Saddler, and Brig rolls down his window. "Mark," he calls.

Mark Saddler pushes up the nosepiece of his wire-rimmed glasses and bends down to look into the car. "What's up?"

"Where's your girlfriend?"

"What are you talking about?"

"You want to watch out for her," Brig says. "Valerie Michon. She's unnatural."

"What?"

"You know the type, she's like a guy in disguise."

"What do you want? I'm on my way to work, I don't have time for this bullshit." He looks at them. He doesn't say anything else. He just looks, and there is something menacing in the way he does that, in the way he half crouches outside the car, his eyes directly on them, not saying anything, just looking at them as if he's permanently fixing a picture of them in his mind.

Rollo, sitting next to Brig, is not quite breathing. Not holding his breath, either. It's more like his breath is suspended, or maybe it's like being in a dream. No, more like watching the dream. The same as watching a movie. You're waiting for something to happen. You're in suspense. You're interested, absorbed. You're noticing things. You're noticing how Brig's fingers do a little drumbeat on the steering wheel. How, under his bulky jacket, Mark Saddler is in great shape. How your feet on the car floor are pointing in two different directions.

You notice things and you hear things, and you're there . . . but you're not quite there. You're not scared and you're not nervous and you're not belligerent, you're just . . . waiting. You're just there, watching the movie and waiting for the next thing to happen. And it's all interesting and a little thrilling.

"Why don't you just get out of here, Highbridge boys?" Mark Saddler says. "Get the fuck out. You don't belong here."

"Hey!" Brig says. "This is a free country."

Saddler straightens, walks to the car ahead of

them, and reaches into the front seat. Rollo leans forward, his forehead touching the cold windshield. Is Saddler going to come out with a gun in his hand? The slam of Saddler's car door is like a pistol shot.

Saddler starts cleaning the snow off his windshield with a plastic ice breaker. He cleans the window thoroughly, then does the side windows. He goes around to the back of the car and cleans off that window. He doesn't look at them. When he's done, he gets in the car and starts the motor. A cloud of exhaust puffs into the snowy air.

Brig starts his car, too, and turns on the headlights, but neither car pulls away from the curb.

"What are we doing?" Rollo says.

Brig shrugs. "Let him go first."

They sit there for maybe ten minutes, until Brig gets tired of it. "Oh, screw it." He pulls away, skidding his car close to Saddler's as he passes.

Rollo sees Mark's startled face. "You see that," he says to Brig, and then they're both laughing again, and it's just like those moments after the deer almost hit them. They start laughing and they can hardly stop.

– 9 –

"You know what she did now?" Brig says, meeting Rollo near the gym between classes.

"Who, Arica?"

"She walked by me without even saying hello."

"Maybe she didn't see you," Rollo suggests.

"She saw me! That's it, I'm through with her." But that night he phones Rollo and asks him to call Arica and talk to her. "Tell her to come back with me—"

"Brig—"

"She likes you, she thinks you have a nice way of talking. She'll listen to you."

"I won't know what to say."

"I just told you. First you start by saying something

good about me, then you get across to her that she's making me feel lousy."

"Brig—"

"I'm going to hang up. Call her right now," Brig says.

Rollo sits in the hall on the steps for a while before he punches Arica's number. As he listens to the phone ringing in her house, he remembers her calling Kara goofy, and he thinks, since he's actually calling a girl, why her? Why not Denise Dixon? The phone rings again. Does Arica remember what Brig said that day they were all together? *You want Rollo? Is that who you want?*

What if she's been thinking about him? What if she really wants to break up with Brig so she can have *him*? Suppose she gets all excited when she hears his voice. *Rollo, I'm coming over.* He wouldn't have to do anything. He wouldn't have to say anything. He could just wait, and she would come over, and they would go up to his room and lie down on the bed together and—

"Hello?" a high voice says. It's a kid who can't pronounce his *l*'s. "Hewwo?"

"I want to talk to Arica," Rollo says.

"This is Brian. Arica's not here."

"Who is this?" Rollo says.

"Brian. I towd you already. Who is this?"

"Rollo."

"Oh. Arica's at, she's with her girwfriend. Do you want Mommy?"

"No." He hangs up.

Almost instantly the phone rings. "Rollo," Brig says, "how come you didn't call me back?"

"I just hung up."

"So what did she say?"

"I didn't talk to her."

"What do you mean, you didn't talk to her?"

"She was out. Her brother, I guess it was her brother, answered the phone."

"Brian? You talked to Brian? He's the one who told you Arica was out? What'd he say, that she was at her girlfriend's house?"

"Something like that."

"He always says that. You should have said, *Brian, go get Arica!* She was probably right there, watching TV or something. I bet you anything she was in the house. Call her again."

"Again?" Rollo says.

"Yeah. Call her and then call me."

"Okay."

"You're going to do it?"

"Yeah."

"When?"

"Pretty soon."

"You won't forget?"

"I won't," Rollo says. But he does.

– 10 –

Saturday morning, Rollo labors around the track at the Racquet Club. Candy, high-stepping, passes him and taunts, "Puff, puff, puff." Rollo runs twenty laps and cuts out. He could have gone around another dozen laps, but it's too boring. He finds Brig in the weight room. Candy joins them after a while, and the three of them sit around until their racquetball court is open. Then they play cutthroat, two-on-one, switching partners after each game. They play hard for a couple of hours.

Afterward, standing in the showers, Brig analyzes their games and instructs Rollo about his mistakes. "There's such a thing as hitting too hard. You can't hit the ball and not think about the next shot."

Rollo turns off the shower. Okay, he powers the ball, but that's what he has going for him—power and muscle. He loves to let go and smash the ball. He loves the sound of the ball smacking against the racket. He isn't swift and showy like Brig, who likes to run up the walls and kill every ball, and he isn't a precision player like Candy.

"This is a game of strategy, not strength."

"I got strategy," Rollo says.

"Where, in your ass? You see the ball and your muscles start popping and, *pow,* you send it to kingdom come. That's why we lost that third game to Candy." Brig punctuates his words with snaps of the towel. "All you did was set Candy up. You kept sending the ball right back to him."

"Hey, that was my superior playing that won that game," Candy says. He's in front of the mirror, towel knotted at his waist, blow-drying his hair.

Brig zips up his pants. "Why didn't you call me back last night, Rollo? I was waiting."

"Last night?" Rollo dives into his locker for his shirt. "I didn't talk to her," he mumbles.

"Who?" Candy says.

"You didn't talk to Arica?" Brig says.

Rollo shakes his head. "I'll do it, I'll call her today, you can count on it. Just remind me—"

"I'm not reminding you of anything!" Brig's face twitches, and he walks away toward the washroom.

Rollo looks at Candy. "He wanted me to call Arica for him."

"He's really cut up over her. He got too involved. I feel sorry for him. Don't say anything to him now, but I'm going out with Vera Mullin next week."

"Who?"

"Vera Mullin. Don't you know her? Black hair, blue eyes, she's in eighth grade."

"Eighth grade." Rollo rolls his eyes. "You asked her?"

Candy grins. "She asked me."

A group of men walk in and noisily get their gym bags out of their lockers and walk out again.

"You know how I started going with Arica?" Brig says, coming back from the washroom. "She was hanging around my locker. She was giving me the eye. She was saying cute things." He drops down on a bench. "What am I talking about her for? I don't want to talk about her. It's all over." He punches his leg, and he's crying.

Rollo has never seen Brig cry. It's terrible. Brig is making these hoarse, choking sounds, and Rollo can hardly stand it. He pats his friend's shoulder over and over. "I'm sorry, Brig. I'm really sorry. I should have called her. Brig, I'll do it."

"Forget it, I said. I don't care."

"That's the way," Candy says, hovering over Brig, too. "Just forget her. What do you care about her?"

"I don't. I don't care about her."

"Good. You can get another girl."

"Right," Rollo says. "There's lots of other girls,"

"They're like fish in the ocean," Candy says. "Brig just has to drop in his line."

Brig slaps at Candy halfheartedly. "What do you know about it, Candrella? You ever have a girl-friend?"

"Plenty."

"You did?" Rollo says. "When was that?"

"When was that?" Candy mocks, sitting down next to Brig. "You think you know everything about me?"

Rollo lets his mouth drop open and shakes his head like a rube. He's playing dumb, doing it for Brig, to cheer him up. And it seems to be working. Brig is almost smiling.

They sit on the benches facing each other, their knees banged in together, and talk about how many years they've been friends and all the things they've done together. They talk about the other night, how crazy it was the way Brig and Rollo drove down into Union, and the way they faced off with Mark Saddler.

Candy brings up the time he and Rollo broke into the guardhouse near the quarry. And after that they go over the famous night when they all sneaked out of their houses at midnight. "We stayed out until two in the morning," Rollo says.

"No, it was three o'clock," Brig says.

"That was great, that was really great," Rollo says.

"Don't laugh, you guys," Candy says, "I know what I'm going to say is corny, but you know what I'm thinking sitting here listening to all this?" He looks from one to the other of them. "I'm thinking how our friendship is more important than any girl."

Rollo's eyes get damp. He gets his arms around Brig and Candy and sort of hugs them. Then they're all hugging, and their faces are close. Close enough to kiss, Rollo thinks. A weird thought, but maybe Candy has the same weird thought, because suddenly he pounds Rollo on the leg, really pounds him hard, and says, "Hey, cream puff! Hey, you big cream puff!" And they all laugh and break apart.

"Morning," Rollo says. Kara's at the table already, and his father is standing at the counter, looking at the newspaper and drinking coffee. "Oversleep?" his father asks.

"Yeah." Rollo sits down, yawning, and pulls over the corn flakes box. Kara has overfilled her cereal bowl, and milk slops over the sides.

"Slurp it up," Rollo says.

"Not good manners!" She's wearing her pj's and a yellow-striped wool hat.

"You going to work that way? Is that the new uniform?"

"Oh, you joker brother."

Rollo studies the corn flakes box. He has them

every morning. "Do we have any waffles?" No one answers. He pours corn flakes into his bowl.

"What time is it?" his father says, handing Rollo the paper. "Kara?"

She pulls up her pajama sleeve and checks her watch. "Seven-ten. You go to work at seven-fifteen." She stares at the digital dial. "Now it's seven-eleven."

Mr. Wingate bends down and kisses her. "You two have a good day. I'm off now."

" 'Bye," Rollo mumbles, looking at the sports page.

"Daddy, don't go yet," Kara calls, studying her watch. "It's only seven-thirteen."

"Don't worry about it, scout," Rollo says, "it's going to be seven-fifteen any minute now."

It's an ordinary morning, and as usual he meets Candy and Brig on the corner of Locust Street, and they walk through town and up the hill to school together, talking and throwing snowballs at every STOP sign.

It's still an ordinary day when Rollo enters his homeroom. Mrs. Schwartz takes attendance; the principal is on the P.A.

"Good morning, Highbridge-Union students. In three days, our winter vacation starts. I know a lot of you have big plans and are eager to get them under way, but I want to emphasize that these days are still regular working school days. I also want to emphasize that this morning's assembly is for the entire school. Mr. Asquith and the Drama Club have worked hard for many months on this modern interpretation of Charles Dickens's famous play *A Christmas Carol*. Let's reward them with complete attention. Assembly will proceed through fourth period. Those of you who have fourth lunch will just have to go hungry today. No, no, no, only joking, you'll be allowed five minutes extra to buy your lunch and bring it to your next class. . . ."

Later, Brig, Candy, and Rollo each come to the assembly with his own class, but they find one another and go to the back of the auditorium. Coach notices them. "You guys. Do you belong here?"

"Sitting down right now, Coach," Rollo says quickly. Coach nods and turns to some other kids.

Teachers are pacing up and down the aisles. The orchestra is tuning up. Kids are calling to each other. Still an ordinary day. Then Brig sees Arica sitting down front with some other girls, and he motions to Rollo. "Look at her." Up to this moment, he hasn't even mentioned her once. Now his face seems to heat up, his lips thin. He leans forward tensely.

"Brig . . ." Candy says. He looks at Rollo, who digs

in his pocket and finds half a candy bar. He breaks it into pieces and shares it out. Maybe food will make Brig feel better.

The orchestra finally gets going and plays a medley of Christmas carols. Brig is still sitting forward in that tense way, staring toward Arica. The lights go off, the curtain rises, and the play starts.

Candy whispers to Rollo, "Tiny Tim, Scrooge, the Ghost of Christmas Past, blah blah blah."

"You said it." Rollo yawns. At least Denise Dixon is in the play, and the modern clothes make it a little different. Still, his attention wanders, and he's at least half-asleep when Brig elbows him and nods toward one of the EXIT doors, where a girl is leaving the auditorium.

"Michon," Brig says, almost to himself.

He slides out of his seat.

– 12 –

The hall is empty. The three of them stand still for a moment, then Brig walks quickly toward the stairs. Rollo and Candy follow. When they turn the corner, they hear footsteps on the stairs.

"Let's get her," Brig says, and they run up the stairs. They run up the stairs quickly and quietly.

Or maybe Brig doesn't say anything. Maybe Rollo only thinks he hears Brig say that. Maybe it goes like this: They hear footsteps on the stairs, and no one says anything, but they run up the stairs, anyway. They run up the stairs after her. They are fast, they are quiet. They are taking the stairs two at a time. They are running up the stairs quickly and quietly.

On the second-floor landing, they listen, and they

hear the footsteps still going up. Going up to the third floor. They follow. They go up after the footsteps. After Valerie Michon's footsteps. They don't talk about it, they just do it.

It's a game. Fun. They glance at each other, and they take the stairs swiftly, grinning. It's a game, and then, too, it's like a dream. Rollo feels something dreamlike in the way he is running up the stairs, running after Brig so smoothly, so swiftly, and the way Candy is running after him, and the way they are all running up the stairs after the footsteps.

Maybe there is nobody there, Rollo thinks. Just for a moment he thinks that—nobody there, no body, no person, no Valerie Michon. Nobody, just the footsteps leading them on.

Then they are on the third floor and they see her.

Her back is turned to them. She is at the end of the corridor in front of the window that looks out over the woods behind the school.

She doesn't seem aware of them. She's leaning forward, her hands on the windowsill, looking out.

She's like a shadow against the window, like cardboard, a dark cutout against the wintry white light flooding in from outside.

They trot toward her. They are not so quiet now.

She turns and looks at them. She says, "What do

you want?" Her eyes flicker one way, then the other.

She starts to move around them and Brig grabs her. And then they all grab her. They just do it, all together. It happens fast, so fast. It's like reading each other's minds. *Let's get her.* Did Brig say it? They don't say anything now, they just grab her, and you can't tell who does what, whose hands are where.

"Stop! Quit! Oh, damn, no . . . oh . . . oh . . . stop. . . ."

Rollo hears panting. Maybe it's himself. He hears grunts, and he's aware of his hot breath. His face and hands are burning, and his hands are on Valerie: he has some part of her in his hand, some soft flesh, some thrilling part of her.

She's twisting around, trying to get away, trying to get free, but they have her.

Rollo's sweating and grinning. He can feel the grin stretched across his face, and he remembers slipping and sliding down the winding road into Union, the car skidding through the snow . . . dangerous, thrilling. . . . You know you should stop but you keep going, you don't want to stop, you just want that thrill . . . that thrill. . . .

Valerie is flailing and yelling. She wrenches free, her arms swing wildly, and she stumbles and crashes to her knees. Then Brig is trying to straddle her, trying to get on her back, and she's jerking around frantically.

A bell rings and it shrills into Rollo's brain.

He blinks and stumbles back, breathing hard.

Candy pulls at Brig.

Valerie is up on one knee. Her hair is down around her face.

They leave. They walk down the hall, tucking in their shirts.

The auditorium is still dark. The play is still going on. The same characters that were onstage when they left are still onstage, sitting around the laden table: Tiny Tim, Scrooge, the "baby" in the high chair. . . .

Rollo moves quietly toward his seat. He tiptoes, lifting one foot at a time, the way you do when you're entering a room full of people, and you're trying not to disturb anyone. You pick up each foot carefully, put down each foot carefully, and carefully lower yourself into your seat, hoping the floor won't squeak, the seat won't creak.

He sits and looks up at the stage. Denise Dixon is there, her head tilted to one side. Any moment now Tiny Tim will say, God bless us all. . . . Rollo stares at Denise Dixon, and for a moment everything blurs. Nothing is distinct. The stage and everyone on it, the auditorium and everyone in it, collapse into a smear of sound and light. He looks at his friends. Brig is leaning back, legs out, arms crossed over his chest. He catches Rollo's eye and nods soberly. Candy seems absorbed in the play, bent forward, chin in hand.

Rollo's heart slows down, his breath is quiet. He watches the stage.

From the corner of his eye, he sees a door open on the other side of the room. A bar of light appears. Someone leans into the auditorium, someone else rises. All the way across the dark room, Rollo senses whispers, ripples of movement. The door closes again.

"God bless us all!" Tiny Tim cries.

A moment later, a hand taps Rollo on the shoulder. Mr. Maddox's tall and slightly bent form is standing over him. "Come with me," he whispers. He taps Brig on the shoulder, then Candy. The audience is clapping. The three of them follow Mr. Maddox into the hall and down the corridor.

"Where are we going?" Rollo says.

Mr. Maddox glances at him. "Principal's office."

It's not much of a walk, just over the bridge into

the addition, down three steps, and around the corner, but it seems long, because no one says anything
after that. Brig whistles quietly. The only other sound
is the muted thump of their feet on the wooden floor.

In the outer office, the secretaries look up when
they enter. A printer is spitting out paper. A phone
rings. One of the secretaries answers, and another
phone rings. Each time, Rollo's stomach lurches a
little.

Mrs. Andresson, the one with gold hair and two
chins, nods to Mr. Maddox and says, "I'll say you're
here." She raps on the door beyond the counter that
says S. FERRANTO, PRINCIPAL, opens it, and goes in.
When she comes out a moment later, she tells the
boys to sit down. "Thank you, Mr. Maddox," she
adds.

Mr. Maddox bends over Rollo and looks into his
face. Like Coach at the end of the season, he goes to
each of them and bends close, but, unlike Coach, he
makes no speeches. He only stares, as if he's trying to
understand something incomprehensible.

He leaves. The door shuts quietly behind him.

Candy, who's sitting between Rollo and Brig, says,
"What do you think?"

"Michon must have told," Rollo says.

"Right." Candy glances at the women working

behind the counter. "What do you think she said?" he asks quietly.

"A bunch of lies," Brig says.

Rollo can't get comfortable on the wooden bench. He crosses and uncrosses his legs. He's hungry again. He watches the women working behind the counter. He wishes Mrs. Andresson would smile at him. He likes her. She never raises a fuss when he needs a pass or forgets his locker key.

They sit there for a long time. People look at them, but nobody talks to them.

– 14 –

Mr. Ferranto blows his nose, then points to the three chairs lined up in front of his desk. They sit down. He puts a cough drop in his mouth, sucks on it for a moment, then slowly reads their names from a piece of paper on his desk. "Julian Briggers. Kevin Candrella. Roland Wingate."

Rollo hates hearing his full first name, especially the way Mr. Ferranto says it, lingering on each syllable. Ro-land. Row land. Probably Mr. Ferranto thinks it's a stupid name, too.

"Mr. Briggers. Mr. Candrella. Mr. Wingate. I have had a very disturbing report about you three." He clasps his hands in front of him on the desk. He has a thick gold ring on one hand, a thick silver ring

on the other. "Another student says that this morning, on the third floor, you three assaulted her."

Rollo looks down at the carpet, remembering that
when he was a little kid he loved doing somersaults
on the carpet in his parents' bedroom. It's a family
story that he couldn't say the word and called them
"somertallts."

Why is he thinking about that now?

"I'd like to hear what any of you have to say about
this," Mr. Ferranto says.

Rollo looks steadily down at the floor. If he doesn't
look at Mr. Ferranto, maybe he won't have to answer
any questions. But sitting that way makes him feel
guilty, and he lifts his head and glances over at Brig.

"Who says we did this?" Brig asks finally.

"I think you know who it is."

"What did she say we did?"

"Mr. Wingate," Mr. Ferranto says. "What do you
know about this incident?"

Rollo shakes his head back and forth. His mouth
is dry.

"I see. Mr. Candrella, what about you?"

Candy doesn't say anything.

"And you, Mr. Briggers?"

Again, silence.

"I'm warning you, stonewalling me is going to be

counterproductive. I want to know exactly what happened this morning. Who's going to tell me?"

"Nothing happened," Brig says.

In the outer office, Rollo hears voices and the phones ringing. He studies a framed picture on the wall behind the desk. There's Mr. Ferranto sitting on a couch, looking pleasant, with his wife next to him, and their two kids smiling behind them.

Mr. Ferranto coughs heavily. "Maybe I haven't impressed this on you sufficiently, but this is a serious situation. I take it very seriously, and I think you would do well to do the same. Let's start with a simple question: Did you leave the assembly this morning?" He looks at Rollo.

Under Mr. Ferranto's gaze, he can't help nodding.

"You did?"

"I . . . guess so."

"Thank you, Mr. Wingate. All right, you left. And so did you, Mr. Candrella? And you, Mr. Briggers? Why did you all leave?"

"I didn't say I left," Brig said.

"But you did. You were all on the third floor, weren't you?"

"Yes." It's the first thing Candy's said. "We got tired of the play."

"You all got tired of the play at the same moment?"

"You see it every year, the same play," Rollo says.

"So you went up to the third floor, and there you met the other student and assaulted her."

Brig exclaims, "She's a liar! Valerie Michon is a liar and a troublemaker. We did have a slight encounter with her this morning, but it was no big deal."

A slight encounter . . . Rollo almost wants to laugh. Brig says that so precisely and pompously, as if he's the principal. Maybe twenty years from now he *will* be the principal, sitting behind his big shiny desk, his arms folded, giving some kid a hard time. Maybe it'll be Rollo's kid, and Rollo will have to phone his old friend, Principal Briggers. *Brig, give him a break. He's just a kid. . . .*

Brig sits forward on his chair and starts recounting for Mr. Ferranto the things Valerie has done to them over the past few weeks: the harassing phone call, calling them names, and even deliberately stepping on Brig's hand. "She could have broken every bone in my hand," he says.

Mr. Ferranto scribbles on a yellow pad. "This is quite a shopping list of complaints. Am I to infer that, after all this harassment, you decided to teach her a lesson?"

"No." Brig sits back, folding his arms across his chest.

"But you did go to the third floor this morning, and you went after she was there."

"She could have left if she didn't want to be there when we were."

"But she didn't leave, and you were all on the third floor at the same time. And what happened?"

"Nothing," Brig says. "We weren't even there five minutes."

"No, no, no," Mr. Ferranto says, holding a tissue to his nose. "I don't want to hear *'nothing'* again!" He sneezes several times rapidly. "I know something happened." He wipes his streaming eyes. "And you know something happened. Now just tell me what it was. Mr. Candrella!"

"We . . . saw her there," Candy says.

"And? Did you speak to her?"

"No," Brig says. "No, we didn't speak to her."

"You didn't say hello? You didn't ask if she was bored with the play, too? Weren't you interested in talking to her about anything?"

"I'm never interested in talking to her."

"But you approached her. Why did you approach her?"

"No special reason."

"Mr. Candrella, how about you? Do you remember why you approached Miss Michon?"

"Not really," Candy says softly.

"Try to remember, Mr. Candrella. It shouldn't be too hard for a bright young man like you to remember something that happened only a little over an hour ago. . . . What about you, Mr. Wingate? Do you remember?"

Rollo looks up. "Nothing," he says.

"What does that mean?"

His head is hot. "I, uh, don't remember why we, why we approached her."

"Did you speak to her?"

"No." He swallows.

"You just went up to her, grabbed her, and roughed her up, got your hands all over—"

"Is that what she said?" Brig interrupts. "I told you she's a liar."

"Mr. Briggers, I'm telling *you* that I know you three were involved in something unpleasantly close to a sexual assault.

"What!" Brig says. "No way!"

Mr. Ferranto holds up his hand. "Listen to me, all of you. If you know what's best for you, you'll tell me exactly what took place on the third floor this morning. You are not going to get out of this by playing games with me. I expect you to be straight with me. Now . . . Mr. Briggers?"

"Maybe we shook her up a little," Brig says at last.

"Can you be more precise about that?"

"I don't think so."

"Why did you shake her up?"

"She was mouthing off at us. She told us to get the hell out of there, and then she shoved me. And you know, she's no little delicate girl, and that was no little delicate shove."

"So then you took her by the shoulders and shook her?"

"No. I never did that."

"I thought you said you shook her."

"Mr. Ferranto, I said, 'shook her up.' I meant we got her worked up, okay?"

"Well, did you shove her back?"

"We might have."

"Did you pull and tear her clothes?"

"Were her clothes torn?" Rollo blurts in surprise. He doesn't remember that. He doesn't remember the things Brig is saying about Valerie shoving him, either. Is that the way it happened? He doesn't remember exactly how it happened, not the way Mr. Ferranto wants to hear it. *She did this, we did that.* . . .

"If her clothes were torn, she tore them herself," Brig says. "I wouldn't put it past her. That's the kind of person she is."

"You didn't touch her clothes?"

"I wouldn't say that. How do you shove a person without touching their clothes? But she touched mine, too. How come she's not here being cross-examined?"

Mr. Ferranto taps a pencil on the desk. "Miss Michon says you got your hands under her clothing, on her body."

"We didn't do anything like that," Brig says evenly.

"Mr. Candrella, what did you do exactly during this time, while this shoving or pushing and touching of clothes was going on?"

Candy moves around on the chair. "You know . . . I'm not really sure. . . ."

"How about pushing her down to her hands and knees and then trying to—"

Brig looks straight at Mr. Ferranto and shakes his head disbelievingly. "Nothing like that. She's got an imagination!"

"Mr. Briggers. Mr. Wingate. Mr. Candrella." Mr. Ferranto leans forward, speaking slowly and hoarsely. "I hope that you understand how serious this is. Do you understand that you have brought harm to a young woman? That you terrorized her? That you sexually harassed her? That this is a crime? Do you understand that you can be expelled from this school? Do you understand that this can go on your school record and that every college you apply to next year will see that on your record? Do you understand that your whole life might be changed by your mean and thoughtless actions?"

There is silence.

"You know," Brig says at last, "whatever happened, I mean the shoving and stuff, Mr. Ferranto, it was just like a minute or something, that's all."

Mr. Ferranto takes another tissue and wipes his eyes. "I don't see that the time element has much to do with anything, Mr. Briggers." He glances at his watch. "I want you all to go home now. I want you back in school tomorrow, and until that time I don't want you talking about this to *anyone*. Have you got that?"

"Got it," Brig says, already half on his feet.

"Sit down, Mr. Briggers! I didn't dismiss you yet." He looks from one to the other. "Don't misunderstand me, any of you. I'm not through with you people."

15

TO: DR. SAMUEL WILLIAMS,
  SUPERINTENDENT OF SCHOOLS
FROM: STEPHEN FERRANTO, PRINCIPAL,
  HIGHBRIDGE-UNION HIGH
CONFIDENTIAL

December 21

Dear Sam,

Today, while our student body was in the auditorium for the annual pre-Christmas-vacation assembly, an event took place which I feel I need to inform you about.

During the assembly, four students left without permission. One, a female, who had left first and alone, subsequently complained that she was attacked by the three male students on the third floor of the old building. In addition, she said, they have been harassing her for some time, and this attack was seen by her as a culmination of previous small incidents, one of them clearly sexually tainted.

I have talked to all four students, as well as to one of our secretaries, Patricia Andresson, and to Paul Maddox, head of the English department. The girl initially told her story to Mrs. Andresson, appearing in the front office in some disarray and quite evident distress. Mrs. Andresson urged her to go to the nurse, then to come to me, but the girl insisted that she wanted to talk to Mr. Maddox first. He was called for and spoke to her for a time, which seemed to calm her somewhat. I then spoke to her and received her story. After this, I sent her home. At this time, Mr. Maddox was asked to bring the three boys to my office.

I want to make clear that at the time of the incident, none of these students had permission to be anywhere else. I also want to make clear that my teachers are an outstanding group, but with the best will in the world, it is still not possible to account for every one of our 1,400 students at every moment.

As I see it, we face two problems. (1) To ascertain the truth from the conflicting stories of the three boys and the girl. (2) Damage control.

To be blunt, Sam, the second problem is the one that concerns me most, and frankly, I am torn in two directions.

Background: the girl is one of our gifted and talented students. She does volunteer tutoring work (one on one). She took first place in the county-wide Art Open for the past two years. However, she does have some problems: she's an underachiever (given her IQ scores) and twice this year has been sent to me for inappropriate disagreements with teachers.

The boys are also outstanding: one is on the football team, one president of the student senate, one on the baseball team and president of the honor society. They have never been in trouble before.

After interviewing all of them, the question remains: Was this nothing more than a shoving match brought on by her verbal aggression, or was it an unprovoked sexual attack?

It's clear to me that something did indeed happen. The girl was distraught. Her clothes were in disarray. There is no reason to believe she would fabricate this. The boys admit they were on the third floor. They admit, at the very least, to shoving her around. However, her appearance and general distressed emotional state speak of much more than shoving.

I'm aware of what might be called "the political nature" of this incident. Sexual harassment is very much a topic of the day and I would not like to be accused of taking it lightly. Yet I believe my duties as a principal come first, and I am concerned not to draw unwanted and unpleasant publicity onto our school and our excellent, hardworking faculty. I think it would be *most unfair* if the anxiety of parents was aroused by knowledge of this incident and, as a result, our teachers were accused of lack of concern with student safety. As you know, this very thing happened in another school in our district only two years ago.

I believe that if this situation is not handled carefully, if it's not kept within "the family," so to speak, it could develop into all kinds of unpleasantness. This is the kind of incident the media love to play up for sensational value. In these times of budget cuts and delicate relations with our admittedly hard-pressed parent population, I see publicity about this resulting in *no good* at all.

I want to resolve this incident quickly and quietly, before we close down for vacation day after tomorrow. I do not want to be unfair to anyone in this situation. The fact is, I have no hard evidence. It is the girl's word against the boys. I have mulled long and hard over this situation for the past hours, and here is what I propose: (1) a two-week suspension for the three boys, beginning immediately after winter vacation; (2) that the boys' parents be informed of the incident and asked to take appropriate measures; (3) that the boys be informed in the severest terms that should anything of this nature ever again transpire, the legal authorities will immediately be called in.

I believe this will be fair to all involved and at the same time protect our school and faculty.

Yours sincerely,
Stephen

Candy and Rollo are walking over to Brig's house together. "Brig wants to talk about tomorrow," Candy says.

Rollo nods. They pass a couple of girls waiting for a bus inside a Plexiglas shelter. It's snowing again, a thin gray snow that melts as it hits the sidewalk. One of the girls glances at Rollo, then away quickly, as if she knows him. As if she knows what happened. That's when he remembers the girls he saw when he left Mr. Ferranto's office. Two of them, holding each other and sobbing. Maybe they were crying because they messed up their nail polish. Or forgot their homework. Or failed a test. He doesn't know what they were crying about, he doesn't know them, he doesn't even know their names, but what he thought when he saw them—what he felt convinced of—was that they were crying about Valerie, and that they hated him.

At Brig's house, they get sodas and go out to the garage, where they sit in the car with the motor on and the windows open. Candy's up front with Brig, twirling the dials on the radio. In the back seat, Rollo yawns, his eyes half-closed. If he shuts them, he sees those girls, hugging each other and crying.

"Did Ferranto call your father?" Brig says.

Rollo shakes his head.

"Candy?"

"Mr. Briggers," Candy says, and he's got Mr. Ferranto's voice down exactly, "this is serious indeed. Don't you think I would have conveyed something so important to you?"

Brig laughs and pours soda on Candy's head. Brig's in an excited state, gesturing and talking a lot, talking fast, taking charge. "Ferranto should have told us what Michon said. It's a legal point. We're being accused but not told what we're accused of. Not the details. Right, it's a bunch of lies, but if he hits my father with it—"

"I have a feeling that's in the cards," Candy says.

"Well, damn, don't be so calm about it! You know

what Dr. Briggers will do to me? How can you just sit there and say that?"

"Hey, this isn't calm you're seeing. This is me trying to think about it. What do you think my father's going to do, celebrate?"

"That bitch Michon. Why'd she have to run to Ferranto? Why didn't she just comb her hair and keep her mouth shut? And I'll tell you something else, she had it coming to her. What did we do that was so terrible? We didn't rape her, we aren't a bunch of crazed ax murderers. So we pushed her a little, maybe grabbed some skin. Rollo! Are you grabbed twenty-five times a minute on the football field?"

Rollo nods.

"And what about the locker room? People are always putting their hands on you, right? You're always getting patted on the ass or hit on the side of the head or slapped on the back. Has it ever hurt you?"

Rollo shakes his head.

"Girls act like they're made of glass. What'd she have to get her knickers in such a big twist over? Girls take everything seriously, everything's a major deal to them."

He backs out the car and they drive around for a

while. The streets are dark, the few people out are huddled over, hurrying.

They park in the McDonald's lot and stand outside, scuffing around in the snow. "Do you think we should go to school tomorrow?" Rollo says.

"Yeah, we should go to school tomorrow." In the sickly yellow light of the parking lot, Brig's face looks like wax. "Why wouldn't we?"

"Because . . . you know. Because of what happened."

"Nothing happened. How many times do I have to tell you? Want me to say it again?" Brig leans into Rollo's face. "Nothing. Happened. Candy, back me up, am I right?"

"Sure."

"Tell Rollo."

"He can hear you."

Rollo scratches his name in the snow on the back of Brig's car, *R O L L O*, then wipes it out with his sleeve. "So what are we going to say if somebody asks about it?"

"You? As little as possible. Just keep your mouth shut. We just have to get through this." Brig throws a snowball across the McDonald's parking lot. It smacks into a tree. "Okay, you want to know what to say? We were on the third floor. Michon was on the third floor. There was a little pushing and shoving. That's it."

Rollo leans against the car. He knows he's going to school tomorrow. It's just that he'd much rather stay home and lie around doing nothing, maybe watching some TV, maybe leafing through some old comic books. Whatever.

"You guys talked too much today," Brig says.

"What did I say?" Rollo protests. "I don't think I said anything. Candy, did I say anything?"

Candy smiles, shrugs. His smile is more like a twitch.

Rollo's head feels thick and stiff on his neck. Today was bad in Mr. Ferranto's office, but it would have been worse without Candy and Brig. What if Mr. Ferranto grabs him alone tomorrow? "I have this feeling Ferranto is going to try something," he says. "You know, like divide and conquer. What if he does that? He said he wasn't through with us. What do you think that means?" He grabs Brig's arm.

Brig jerks away. "Rollo, you're getting worked up. You've got to be cool, man."

"Right." His stomach pounds. Is he hungry? When he got home after school that afternoon, he'd been starved. He'd raided the cupboards, shoved chips and sugar cubes in his mouth, a foul combination, but he couldn't stop. Then he devoured two salami sandwiches, washing them down with milk. And he still couldn't stop. He ate noodles, ice cream, cookies. Then he ate supper, because he didn't want to tell his father why he wasn't too hungry.

"So what happened?" he says suddenly. "I mean, what happened up there on the third floor?"

Brig stares at him, as if he can't believe what he's hearing. "Candy, did you hear what this guy just said?"

"Things got a little out of hand," Candy says in his soothing voice. "Just a little out of hand."

"Yeah, right." Rollo lets that information flow into him, says it to himself. *Things got out of hand. . . .* He punches Candy gratefully. Maybe, tomorrow, if he sees those girls who were crying, he'll go over and talk to them. *Look, whatever you heard, I didn't mean anything. Things just got a little out of hand. . . .*

"What are you talking about, Candrella?" Brig says. "Nothing got out of hand, because *nothing happened*. You know, sometimes you talk too much."

Candy laughs with an edge. "I don't think that was me doing all the talking in Mr. Ferranto's office."

"Well, you guys screwed me up. First Rollo, *Yeah, I left assembly.* Then you, *Yeah, we saw her, we saw her in the hall.*"

"I didn't say that."

"You said it. You just about admitted everything. I'm doing a job for all of us, I'm saying, No, nothing happened, and you two are screwing me up. You're saying, Yeah, we were there. And now you, Candy, with your *things getting out of hand* crap. Is that what you're going to tell Ferranto tomorrow? Things got out of hand?" Brig throws several snowballs fast and hard. "Why don't you just tell him we beat Michon up and threw her out the window and have it done with?"

"I like that," Rollo says.

"What, throwing Michon out the window? Me too."

"Candy saying things got out of hand."

"You like that? There's no accounting for taste, is there? I find it stupid." Brig sits down on the back of the car. "I find this whole discussion stupid. Leave it up to you guys and we'd just roll over, go belly up."

Candy's freckles are standing out all over his face. "Bull."

They're barking at each other. All of them are sour and grumbling—scared, Rollo thinks. He is, anyway.

"Ferranto saying we assaulted her," Brig says. "What a bunch of crap! You get assaulted more just walking down the corridor when you're trying to leave school at the end of the day. You can get black and blue walking from homeroom to the front door. We have to get that across to Ferranto. Because if he tells my father these lies, Dr. Briggers'll be down my throat. He'll be down so far, he'll be dancing on my toes."

Rollo bursts out laughing. It's a relief to laugh. Brig grins, finally, and Candy throws an arm over his shoulder. And then they're all laughing, and that fine closeness of friendship is around them, wrapping them up like a big warm blanket, holding them to-gether again. They're going to be all right, Rollo thinks. Everything's going to be all right. Like Brig said, they just have to get through the next day.

17

Valerie presses herself against a dark wall as they march toward her: a row of huge fish glittering a sinister gold-green and walking malevolently on their tails. Their bodies are separated into three defined sections, and each section on each fish clinks and bends as they come closer. Their smell is unbearable.

She comes awake with a gasp.

She sits up in bed, then falls back against the pillow and looks around her room—tells herself that it *is* her room, that she is here, she is safe. And, resolutely, no matter that it's not light yet and her eyes ache, she tells herself she will get out of bed, take a shower, get dressed, and make coffee for her father.

She will do things. She will not let herself sink.

But she doesn't move.

Little drafts of cool air sweep over her. Her father always sets the thermostat down at night. He says it's wasteful to heat a house full of sleeping and warmly covered human beings. He is concerned about saving energy. He says, If we squander everything now, what will the next generations have?

Up until this very day, she believed—because *he* did—that the world was good, that all she had to do was be herself and never hurt anybody, and everything would be, if not perfect, if not wonderful at all moments, at least very, very good.

If she's not going to get up, she should try to sleep. She should stop thinking. Last night she lay awake for hours, her brain flashing image after image, like a crazed TV. At moments she couldn't breathe. Her throat closed, she sucked in shivery, desperate gulps of air.

And now it happens to her again.

Is this a panic attack?

STOP! The word appears like a red sign in her mind. She wraps her arms tightly around herself, hugs herself into a semblance of composure.

She hasn't yet told her father what happened. Will she? She wants to, but what good would it do? What difference would it make? Isn't she strong enough to hold this inside herself? Why must he be disillusioned and full of sorrow, because something ugly happened to her?

He probably wouldn't even understand. He would say, "Well, why did they do it?" He thinks there is a reason for everything. He believes that the world is a bright and special place. He believes people are good. When she thinks of that now, it is extraordinary. All the years he has lived and not found out how wrong he is! It's amazing. It's enough to make you cry.

She presses her hands against her eyes. *No tears.* She will not allow it. She doesn't dare. If she lets herself go, she's afraid that everything she is keeping so tightly bound inside will burst forth, a torrent that will wash her away and drown her father.

No, she is not going to tell him what happened.

Let him go on sleeping his peaceful, absurd sleep.

– 18 –

"Hey, big Rollo! Big Rollo, big boy." Pete Murando,
a kid who's always hanging around, grabs Rollo as he
opens his locker. "Rollo! Rollo! Big boy! I heard
you're in trouble, big boy, I heard! Take it easy!
Don't let them, don't let them—you know, you
know!" He punches his fist into his cupped palm.

Pete Murando is a fool. Rollo shrugs him off, but
as the morning goes on, it's clear that everyone in
school knows what happened yesterday, or at least
everyone knows something happened. Guys trail
after him. Some of them are winking and grinning,
saying his name, hitting him on the back. It's the kind
of commotion people make after a game. Like he's a
hero.

When he sees Denise Dixon, though, fourth period in Mr. Maddox's class, that's something else. There's a ripple of noise at his entry, and Wendell Smith drawls, "Waaatch out, it's Rooollover Rollo." Some kids snicker, but Denise, sitting in the seat behind his, gives Rollo a long, direct, hard look, the same look she might give a rabid dog in the street. A look that says, *Don't you dare come near me.*

Why that look? He didn't do anything to her. He thinks of saying it. *I wouldn't do anything to you! I wouldn't ever do anything to you.* He sits down and opens his notebook, but what he sees is not his scrawled notes but that cone of white wintry light on the third floor and Valerie standing silhouetted in it. The memory passes through his mind like a dream, with the same vagueness, the same unreality, the same insistence.

"I know vacation is on top of us, but we're going to continue reviewing the novelists and poets we've read this term," Mr. Maddox says, rapping on his desk for attention. He looks at Rollo, frowning as he holds up the literature textbook. "Who remembers what the initials *H.D.* stand for?"

"Hot dog," Wendell Smith whispers. "Right, Rollo baby?"

Mr. Maddox continues talking, but in a few moments he interrupts himself to say, "Mr. Wingate, I want to talk to you. Everyone else turn to page 55 and read the first three paragraphs."

Rollo follows Mr. Maddox out into the hall. "I want you to leave my class." Mr. Maddox says. "I don't think I can teach with you here today."

"Why?" Rollo asks.

"I find it too disturbing to see you sitting here in front of me, and I think you know what I mean. I can't discuss it with you. I think you know that, too. Go down to the office."

Rollo's stomach feels hollow. He doesn't want to be run out of the class. He doesn't want Denise Dixon to see this. He thinks he should smile to show he doesn't care. "What am I supposed to do there?"

Mr. Maddox is scribbling on a piece of paper. "Take this to Mrs. Andresson. She'll give you an answer to bring back to me at the end of the period. Do whatever you want. Just stay there until your next class."

"That's lunch."

"Fine."

"You know, I didn't . . ." Rollo starts.

"What?"

"Nothing." Mr. Maddox has his hands on his hips. His lips are pursed. He isn't going to believe anything Rollo says. "Are you kicking me out forever?" he asks.

Mr. Maddox doesn't answer.

Rollo spends the rest of the period in the office, sitting on the same wooden bench that he sat on yesterday.

"Rollo?" Arica says. "I want to ask you something."

The way she says it, he knows it's about Valerie. He's sitting in a carrel in the library, copying out some stuff for a report for Mr. Maddox that he's supposed to write over vacation.

"Are you busy?" she asks.

"No, that's okay."

Arica leans over the top of the carrel, staring at him. "Rollo."

"Yeah?"

"Is it true?"

"What?"

"What I heard about you and Valerie Michon. Is it true that you raped her?"

"Where'd you hear that? No, it's not true."

"It's all over school. You and Brig and Candy, the three of you."

"No."

"You didn't do that?"

"No."

"You swear to me you didn't? Rollo, tell me the truth."

"I'm telling you, nothing like that."

"You didn't do that?"

"No."

"She's not in school today."

"I don't know anything about that."

"What about Brig? I mean, maybe you didn't, but—"

"No."

She looks at him. "You're telling me the truth?"

"Yes."

"I know you wouldn't lie to me."

"I wouldn't."

"Everybody's saying you raped her."

"No. No way."

"If you say it, I'm going to believe you."

"I'm saying it."

"It's not true?"

"No way, Arica. Nothing like that! Nothing!"

She bites her lip. "Okay, I'm going to believe you."

"You can!"

"Okay." She puts out her hand as if she's going to touch him, then she pulls it back and walks away.

– 19 –

Mr. Ferranto leans across the desk and offers Valerie a mint from a glass jar. "How are you today, Valerie?" he says. "Are you feeling any better?"

She doesn't say yes. She doesn't say no. She doesn't take a mint.

"I know this is hard for you," he says. "For your sake, I want to settle this situation. I want you to put this behind you and go ahead with your life, Valerie. Sometimes bad things happen to people, and it's a shock, but you just have to pick yourself up and get on with it. I know you agree with me."

She doesn't reply.

Mr. Ferranto sighs. "We all need a resolution to

this situation. This is very unpleasant for you, and for me, too. It's good that you're calm," he adds.

Is that what she is, or is it numb? She picks at her thumbnail. This morning she told her father that she had a cold, and she went back to bed, but then Mr. Ferranto had phoned and asked her to come to school. "I need you here," he had said.

"I've given this a great deal of thought," he says now. "I've heard both sides of the story, and I want to be fair to everyone. Have you told me everything, Valerie? Is there anything you want to add or change? Now's the time. Do you want to tell me anything else about what happened and why you think it happened? Do you want to go over it with me again?"

Valerie rips the nail and tears a piece of skin with it. Yesterday she told Mrs. Andresson what they did to her. Then Mr. Maddox. And then Mr. Ferranto, the whole thing again, every sordid little detail. She told him once, and she doesn't want to tell him again. The thought of it makes her sick.

"Well . . . all right, let's go on. My wife, Hela"—he points to the picture behind his desk—"is a psychologist, and I consulted with her about this situation. I started the discussion by a frank relay of the incident.

I hope you don't mind that I spoke to her about it," he adds.

And if she does? Hela Ferranto may be a psychologist, but to Valerie she's just a stranger and, now, one more person who knows what happened to her. She concentrates on her nails, ripping each one carefully with her front teeth, straight across. That's the hard part, to do it straight, not ragged.

"I tried to give my wife a full picture. I explained where I stand. My stand is, I'm concerned about you, but I'm also, of necessity, concerned about the boys. It's my job to look after everyone in this school."

Spurts of heat race through Valerie's head. Phrases of Mr. Ferranto's bounce around in her mind. . . . *my stand is . . . started with a frank relay of . . . concerned about the boys . . .*

"My wife—Hela—pointed something out to me that I'd missed. She pointed out that these boys need to apologize to you."

When Valerie gets through with the nails on her right hand, she starts on the left.

"They need to do it for themselves, and they need to do it for you. You need to hear them apologize. This is what Hela explained to me. They have to be made aware that they've done something terribly wrong, and you need to hear them acknowledging that. Now, Valerie, if I bring them in here to do this, will you accept their apologies?"

She concentrates on her breathing. She read somewhere that if you take in deep breaths, breathe deeply, not shallowly, breathe right down into your belly and let the breath out with a nice regularity, it will slow your heartbeat and give you all sorts of great mental and physical benefits.

"Valerie, sometimes bad things happen, but we can't brood over them. We have to put them in perspective and go on with our lives. Can we agree that we'd like to put this thing behind us and go ahead?"

Should she tell Mr. Ferranto he's repeating himself? She breathes in. She breathes out.

"Valerie, my wife said, and I agree with her, that this is a healing thing to do." He reaches across his desk and presses a button on the intercom. "Mrs. Andresson, I'm ready for them," he says. And before Valerie comprehends what's happening, the door opens and the three boys swagger in.

Valerie leaps out of her chair.

Mr. Ferranto comes swiftly around his desk to stand by her side. She grips the back of the chair. She doesn't look at the boys. It takes every bit of her strength just to stand straight, not to bolt out of the room. Why did Mr. Ferranto do this? Why is he forcing her to be in the same room with them?

"Mr. Briggers," Mr. Ferranto says. "Mr. Wingate. Mr. Candrella. You know that a serious accusation has been made against you three. My investigation leads me to believe that your behavior yesterday, on the third floor, was totally out of line. And whatever happened between you and Miss Michon before that is no excuse!"

Valerie holds tightly to the back of the chair and concentrates on her breathing.

"Now, here is what I am going to do. I am going to inform each of your parents of the situation and they will take whatever action they see fit. Further, the three of you are suspended from school for the first two weeks of the new term."

"Mr. Ferranto, you can't do that!" That's Briggers.

"Be quiet, Mr. Briggers. This is my school, and I won't have such behavior go unpunished. I have one more thing to say to you. If ever there is a similar incident, if ever I hear of any of you being involved in harassing a girl again, I won't hesitate to call in the police." He pauses. "Do you have anything to say? . . . If not, I want each of you to apologize to Miss Michon. Mr. Briggers, you start."

"I can't be sorry if I didn't do anything," he says.

"Mr. Briggers! I won't put up with that arrogance. I'm telling you right now, you're going to do this."

There is another moment's silence, then Briggers says, "Sorry."

"Look at her and say it."

"Sorry!" he raps out.

"All right. You, Mr. Wingate."

"Sorry," comes the mumble.

And before Mr. Ferranto asks him, the third one, Candrella, says quickly, "I sincerely apologize."

"Thank you, Mr. Candrella. That's what I hoped to hear. Valerie, do you accept their apologies?"

They are looking at her, waiting for her to speak, all of them looking at her, all except the fat dumb one, who's looking down at the floor.

"Valerie," Mr. Ferranto says again, "do you accept the apologies of these boys?"

Finally she speaks. "Fuck you all," she says and walks out.

– 20 –

The first day of vacation, Rollo holes up in his room and sleeps. His room is dim, clothes are everywhere. He rolls up in his quilt and sleeps away the hours. He's on his way to sleeping through supper, until Kara appears at his door. "Daddy says come down, Rollo."

"Okay," he mumbles.

"Rollo, wake up! Daddy says it's time to eat. Daddy says put on some clothes and wash your face."

"Okay. . . ."

She pulls the quilt off him. "Daddy says now."

He rolls out of bed and sits numbly for a while. All those hours of sleep have made him groggy. Does he really have to get up? He doesn't want to face his father. He heard him on the phone late last night with Mr. Ferranto. Crap. What now, humble pie? *I'm sorry, I'll never do it again. . . .* But how can you promise a thing like that? How can you be sure what you will or won't do in some future time? Especially · when you obviously don't even know what you're going to do right now.

Rollo pulls on his jeans. The whole thing is so unbelievable. Did it really happen? A minute of craziness, stupidity, foolishness—maybe not even a minute, maybe thirty seconds, and everyone is leaping out of their skin, shrieking and screaming, shaking their fingers, stamping their feet, raising their voices. "Adult tantrums," he decides, looking with disgust at his face in the mirror. His eyes are like two little puffy slits.

"Rollo!" His father is calling now, and there's nothing for it but to go downstairs. All through supper he waits for the ax to fall, but it isn't until he's putting his plate in the dishwasher that his father says, "Rollo, come into my study. I want to talk to you."

He doesn't turn around. He doesn't follow his father to the study, either, but instead goes upstairs, closes himself in the bathroom, and brushes his teeth for a long time. After that, he shaves carefully, and all the time he's wondering if it's possible that his father might actually *not* know what happened in school. What if the call last night wasn't from Mr. Ferranto? What if it was from someone else, about something entirely different? And what if his father wants to talk to him because . . . because he's worried about a business problem! *Son, I don't want to alarm you, but times are getting hard, and—*

Dad, don't say another word. I'll go out tomorrow morning and find a job.

Rollo! You're a fine son. A truly good person.

Dad, I'm only doing what anyone would do for his family.

Music rises from downstairs. Kara is probably dancing around the kitchen, waving a dish towel and imagining she's a rock star.

Rollo smooths his finger over his upper lip. His eyes stare back at him from the mirror. Brown eyes, like his father's. Can you see the soul in the eyes, like they say? He looks into those brown eyes and doesn't see anything.

All of a sudden, like a smack in the head, like a hit of electricity, pain travels down the side of his face, rides through his cheekbone into his jaw. Then he seems to hear Coach screaming, *Wingate, you fat, overstuffed fart.* And after that, Mr. Ferranto's voice, *What you did was bad!*

He escapes the bathroom, goes across the hall to his father's room, and dials Brig. "Hello, you've reached the Briggers," Brig's mother says. "At the beep, leave your message for Marcia, Dr. Calvin Briggers, or Julian. If you want the clinic, call—"

He hangs up and tries Candy's number. "Hello!" the senator's deep voice says. "You have reached the residence of Senator Daniel Candrella. No one is home right now. . . ."

Rollo knows that. He knows the Candrellas are in Vail, maybe coming off the slopes this moment. They left early this morning. The Briggerses are gone, too. They took a plane for Orlando, for an unscheduled winter vacation. *They're* probably in the hotel dining room right now, eating a big fancy supper.

After Mr. Ferranto called them, they all decided to clear out of town. The senator was afraid something would leak into the papers. He wanted, Candy said, to be out of the line of fire. As for Brig's father, "He went crazy," Brig said. "He didn't know who he was madder at, me for getting suspended or Ferranto for suspending me."

Rollo finally goes downstairs, but at the closed

door to his father's study he hesitates again. Does he have to go in there? He closes his eyes, wishing he was eleven again, instead of sixteen. And he remembers when he *was* eleven and saw the house and this room for the first time. Then it had been an enclosed side porch, a long narrow room, its windows brushed by the branches of the pines growing outside. He had loved it and wanted it for his own. And suddenly he thinks that if this room had been given to him instead of being turned into his father's study, everything would be different right now. He knows it's an absurd thought, but he can't shake it off.

The door opens. "What are you doing standing out there?" his father says. He points to the ladder-back chair near his desk. "Sit down."

Rollo sits on the floor. He never sits in that particular chair. It used to be his mother's.

His father sits down and stares at him. "Your principal called me, and he told me something I'm having a lot of trouble with. He said there was an incident in school, that you and your friends . . ." His father pauses. "I find this so hard to believe I can hardly say it. . . . Mr. Ferranto said you three . . . attacked a girl."

Attacked . . . He hates that word.

"Is this true?" his father says.

"I guess so," Rollo says, low.

"You guess so? What does that mean, son? Did you do those things to that girl or didn't you?"

Dad, I prefer not to talk about the subject. . . . Rollo looks out the dark window. The pines brush against the glass, like spirits asking to be let in. He shakes his head, then nods.

"Which one, yes or no? You did or you didn't?" his father says.

Rollo wets his lips. "Did." He barely moves his mouth.

"Did," his father repeats. He's tearing a piece of paper into long slivers. "Did," he says again. "You attacked a girl."

"No. We didn't attack her."

"You didn't do it?"

"We didn't *attack* her. It wasn't like that."

"What was it like? It wasn't an attack?"

"No. We just sort of, we sort of shoved, we . . ." Rollo looks down at his hands. Hates his pudgy fingers. "It was no big deal, I don't know what everybody's getting their knickers in such a twist about," he says, repeating Brig's words.

"What?" his father shouts. "What did you just say?"

"Nothing!" His heart is jumping.

"Nothing? No big deal? Three of you and one girl? Where did you learn that? You never saw me doing anything to a woman."

"No," Rollo says.

"I've never laid violent hands on a woman."

"No."

"Why did you do it? Why?"

How can he answer? How can he tell his father what he doesn't know himself? *It's just the way things happen. . . . They happen. . . .* He rolls his head around. He's leaning against the edge of the bookcase and something is jabbing him in the back of the neck. The pain feels good.

His father takes off his glasses, rubs his eyes. "I don't know what to say," he says.

Is his father done? He's just sitting there, rubbing his eyes. Rollo starts to rise, but his father is talking again.

"Do you realize your principal could have called in the police on this? The child welfare people? Do you realize that you could have ended up in the courts, with a record? They could have taken you away."

Rollo shakes his head.

"You didn't know that?"

"No."

"You didn't think about that?"

"No."

"Did you think about the girl? Do you think about anything? Rollo, look at me! This is the way life passes, Rollo. Like *this.*" He snaps his fingers. "It seems long to you now, but it's not. It goes fast. And you only get one chance at it, that's why you've got to *think.* You've got to *think* about what you're doing, and you've got to live right."

Rollo nods. He's remembering running up the stairs after her . . . seeing the black silhouette of her in front of the window . . . like a cutout . . . and then what they did, all that crazy thrilling stuff. . . .

"Right now you think life is forever. You think time is endless. You don't have a sense of urgency. You think you can do anything and it doesn't matter. That's not true. *Everything matters.* It matters to you. It matters to the other person. Do you understand what I'm saying?"

Rollo nods again.

"Do you have anything to say? Anything at all?"

Sure he does. If his father wasn't yelling at him and going crazy with lecturing, Rollo could tell him things . . . about being with his friends and how good it feels and how you never want that good feeling to stop and how that's why you do things sometimes that maybe aren't so smart.

But his father wouldn't understand, anyway.

His father doesn't know about things like crapping around and making jokes and all the dumb stuff he and Candy and Brig do that's just . . . *good*. Just part of being friends.

"What you did was thoughtless, stupid, vicious. The least you could be is sorry."

"Okay." Why does his father have to call him names?

"Okay? Is that all you can say? Don't you feel anything for that girl, for what you did to her? Rollo! What kind of person are you? I don't see anything on your face, no feeling, nothing."

Rollo stares at the floor and thinks about his friends, about always knowing you have somebody in your corner, and how your friends never let you down, and how they never make you feel like shit. Like he feels now.

"I never thought I'd say this, but I'm glad your mother's not here now." His father's voice thickens. "I'm glad she's not here to know that her son would do such a thing."

Rollo scrambles to his feet, his face burning. He hates his father for saying that.

"I'm not finished," his father says as Rollo reaches

for the doorknob. "I'm not finished with you or this subject!"

Rollo waits, standing by the door, but he doesn't hear anything else his father says, and he doesn't look at him. There's only one thing he wants now. He doesn't want to break down and cry in front of his father.

Dear Great Listener . . . dear Someone . . . whoever you are . . . are you there? Are you listening? Great Spirit! Big Ear! Listener! Whatever you are, please . . . give me a sign. Do you hear me? Can you hear me? Will you hear me?

Valerie pauses and draws in a breath. She's in the room behind the kitchen, which her father calls his office. Maybe it was a pantry once. No windows. Just a tiny room with a desk and floor-to-ceiling shelves overflowing with books and paper. She's sitting in front of the computer, writing something, maybe a letter. They're words, anyway, a spill of words like water pouring over a dam.

Dear Big Ear, did it ever occur to you that there are

things missing in this world? Things absent. Things not in place. Things gone. Things like justice and sanity and kindness and care. People should be kind to each other, but instead they're cruel and hurtful. Okay, I know, I'm indicting the whole world because of three boys. Sorry, but it's the way I feel.

I want to know why it happened. I was standing at the window, looking out at the woods. I was going to go in the art room and work, and then they were there, and they did things to me nobody has a right to do to another person, and nothing has been done to them in return. Two-week suspension? Baby stuff. I don't call that anything.

SOMETHING WICKED THIS WAY COMES.

She stares at the screen. All on their own, her fingers have typed those words. SOMETHING WICKED THIS WAY COMES. Where did that come from? Something Mr. Maddox once read them? She types again. *SOMETHING EVIL THIS WAY CAME.*

She breathes, calming herself, remembering the day she ran on to Mr. Maddox about the Great Universal Spirit. Is there really Something out there, a transcendent, overarching spirit? She has always believed it. She has to go on believing it. Otherwise, everything is too meaningless, too absurd.

In the kitchen, she hears her father moving around. In a few minutes he will call her to supper. Later he'll come in here and use the computer himself. They've always shared it, always respected each other's privacy. He would never look at anything in her files without her permission. But what does it matter if she's private or not? He knows what happened. Sort of. Mr. Ferranto called and told him.

She didn't want that to happen, but it did, and then he came to her, her dear unworldly father, and he said, "Val . . . sweetheart . . . your principal called." His face was pale. He took her hands. "What happened? What did they do to you?"

How to tell him? She'd always protected him, looked after him as much as he looked after her. Was it a bargain they made a long time ago or something she had decided on?

She paced . . . and she told him, but she didn't tell him the way it really had been. She used words like *grab* and *push,* as if that were all of it. She said, "Yes, three boys . . ." and shrugged, as if they were no more than three cutups, three clowns who got a little wild and out of control. She made less of what happened, much less.

He wanted to know about the boys, and what did Mr. Ferranto say? Were they being punished? When she told him, "Suspended for two weeks," he nodded approvingly. Then he looked at her again, and held her hands, and said, "Are you really all right?"

She nodded. Oh, yes, yes. But there was something about the way he asked her that, and the way he looked so sorrowfully and carefully into her face, that almost brought her to tears. She wouldn't cry, though. She wouldn't let herself. Not in front of him. "I'm fine," she said. "I was shaken up, but now I'm fine, I'm really fine."

She wants to believe that.

She starts typing again.

I know they say it's good to talk . . . shouldn't keep things locked up inside yourself . . . but who do I talk to? Not my father.

Janice? She's too flakey.

I've thought about Mark, but that's crazy. I don't know him that well. What makes me think he'd even understand? And what if he said, Did you yell, Valerie? Did you order them to stop? Did you defend yourself? Did you hit them? What were you doing up there, anyway? I don't want to hear those questions!

Big Ear, better listen while you have the chance, because I can wipe these words out in one split second. Too bad I can't put my feelings up on the screen and wipe them out just as fast. I hate the way I feel. I keep wanting to cry, don't want to get out of bed in the morning, think about being an artist and know it'll never happen. . . .

When am I going to feel good again?

When am I going to stop thinking about it?

Big Ear, are you listening? There's something else I need to get off my chest. Before this happened, I never wanted to even think about things like this. I wouldn't read the stories in the paper or watch them on TV. I said to myself, Nothing to do with you, Valerie. . . . I thought it was a different class of person things like this happened to. Someone who wasn't so smart or did something wrong or lived in a bad place. . . .

What I think now is that you don't have to be dumb or live anyplace special or do anything wrong to have it happen to you. You can be minding your own business, just looking out a window, and it happens. Just standing there, and it happens.

It happens. And nobody knows what it feels like until it happens to them.

– 22 –

Rollo is watching TV; at least, he's staring at the screen. He's hardly moved for the past hour, except to push the button on the remote. He keeps looking at the clock, waiting for Kara to come in from work. For two days now, she's the only person who's acknowledged his existence.

His father acts as if Rollo has ceased to be someone real. He doesn't seem to see Rollo. He definitely doesn't talk to him. He walks around him as if he's not there. He doesn't even notice him when Rollo sits across from him at the table. It's not that his father's distracted or busy or thinking about other things. He doesn't have any difficulty with Kara. He notices her reading a new Nancy Drew, he asks her what chapter she's on, discusses the plot enthusiastically with her, and then goes off with her for a walk. Only Rollo gets the silent *you are not my son you might as well be dead* treatment.

Rollo's thoughts, addressed to his father, go like this. *You don't understand, Dad, but I'll try to tell you how it can happen that you do something not so great . . . okay, something rotten. Right, I agree. Let's call it rotten and vicious. The thing is, you're not thinking, even if on one level you know what you're doing isn't right. The thing is, there's something in you that's saying, Don't think about it . . . so you don't, and that's easy, because you don't want to think about it, anyway, you don't want to say something and be a jerk, you just want to do what your friends are doing. So you do it. You do what they're doing, you grab the girl and . . . you do all those things. . . . Okay, maybe later your stomach sort of turns and you feel sort of amazed and ashamed and sort of sick of yourself, but you're not, suddenly, somebody a person can't see or talk to, you're not suddenly a monster. . . .*

The phone rings then, and as Rollo is trying to decide if he'll answer it or not, Kara walks in the door. "I'll get it," she yells. "Nobody else! Hello!" he hears her say. "This is Kara! Who is this?"

It's probably a sales pitch for aluminum siding.

"Hang up, Kara," he calls. "You know what to tell them."

He hears her say, "No, we don't buy anything over the phone. Good-bye!" She comes in, sits down next to him, and gives him a kiss on the neck.

She looks cute as hell. She's wearing black tights, a skirt printed with gold butterflies, a black T-shirt, and a big yellow bow in her hair. "How was work today?" he asks.

"Good and bad. A man hit his little boy. I said, 'Don't hit him!' Then he was mad, he said, 'Mind your own business,' then Carl said, 'What is the problem? Is everything all right? Go back to work, Kara.'" She hugs Rollo's arm. "You wouldn't hit a boy or a little teeny fly, even."

"Kara, I kill flies all the time."

Kara ignores the interruption. "I was sad because the man was mean to his little boy. I tried to make my head forget, but it wouldn't. See!" She wipes her eyes. "I'm sad right now, and then I have to cry and my life is ruined."

He wishes she would stop talking. He wishes he was someplace else. He wishes the thing in school had never happened and that Valerie Michon lived a thousand miles away and that he had never even heard her name.

"Rollo?" Kara takes him by the chin and holds his face tenderly. "Rollo, are you sad, too?"

For a moment, for a fraction of a second, he wants to tell her . . . *everything.* He wants to let the words roll out, he wants to say it all. Let Kara hear, because no matter what he says to her, no matter what he tells her, to her he will still be her perfect brother.

Her face is right near his. She is looking at him with her truthful eyes. His lips go dry. He's wrong. Wrong again. How could he think, even for an instant, of telling Kara? To tell her would be just one more disastrous thing. She is retarded, but she isn't stupid.

"I swing," Keefer yells from the couch, "Valerie, I swing, too. Me. My turn."

Valerie gives Keefer's older brother one last twirl, then picks up the little girl by the hands and swings her out and around in a wide circle. Keefer screams wildly.

"They're a couple of hellions," their mother said when she asked Valerie to baby-sit them over winter vacation. "Do you think you can stand them for whole days at a time?"

Mrs. Brunet manages a kids' clothing store. She pays Valerie really well. The money is great, but the money isn't what counts now. Valerie would take care of Wick and Keefer for free—she'd pay Mrs.

Brunet for the privilege—because when she's with the kids they keep her so busy it's almost impossible to think about anything else.

She doesn't want to think about a lot of things.

Like Mark Saddler and that awkward phone call last night. "Hey, Val," he said, "how's the girl?" He's never called her at home before. They carried on for a strained few minutes before she hung up. Does he know? It's possible. *Possible?* Sure he knows. Everyone in school knew in two seconds flat. Maybe, in his way, Mark was being considerate, letting her know he was on her side. Or maybe he just wanted some titillating details.

The numb sweatiness starts again. Her hands prickle—the back of her hands and the tips of her fingers. Don't think about it. . . . Forget it. . . . Then the questions begin. Why weren't there any words? She can't remember any words. What's the meaning of that? What's the meaning of anything that happened? Why did they do it? Why did they do it to her?

She keeps thinking, if only she understood she would be able to stop having crazy emotions. Last night, after Mark called, she had gone into the backyard and smashed plates against a tree, then picked up the broken pieces and smashed them again until there was nothing left.

The kids are running in circles, screaming and giggling, running around a chair, chasing each other. Keefer, who, at three, adores her brother, screams his name, "Wick Wick Wick Wick," in a shrill, unrelenting cacophony of love, her plump hands out to catch him. He runs from her, giggling, impish. "Can't catch me! Can't catch me!"

"Wick Wick Wick!"

"Can't catch me! Can't catch me!"

He flings himself at Valerie. "Save me from the Keefer monster!"

Valerie touches his sheaf of dark silky hair. His warm little paw is on her leg. Will he still be so sweet when he grows up? Is it possible those other three had been little boys once, sweet-smelling little boys with big brown eyes?

She tells them they're going outside and they all start picking up toys and throwing them into the yellow plastic toy baskets. "We don't want your mom to go crazy when she comes home and sees the living room a big mess," Valerie encourages them.

"Yeah! Mom go crazy," Keefer agrees happily.

They crawl around the floor, picking up toys. Suddenly, Wick jumps on Valerie's back.

"I'm a cowboy and you're my horse." He kicks her in the sides with his sharp little heels. And now all the effort Valerie has put into *not thinking about it* is for nothing. It's happening again, like a fast forward on the VCR, the images blurring, but everything there.

Her mind spares her nothing. The three of them marching toward her . . . crowding her . . . the sudden rush of hands, the hands, hands everywhere . . . and then she's down and one of them is trying to get on her.

"Get off me!" she screams. She shakes Wick off and stands up, stands over him. "Don't you dare do that!"

There is silence. The little boy stares at her. The little girl sucks on her fingers.

Valerie is trembling. Abruptly she remembers something that happened yesterday. She was walking past the corner of Seneca and Saratoga streets when a man sitting in the bus shelter greeted her. "Happy New Year, darlin'!" He wore a black cap, had a scarf wrapped around his neck. Maybe he was drinking. Maybe he was just being friendly.

What she remembers is her shock, her fear. How she hurried on, her shoulders pinched, her stomach throbbing. What she thinks is that *before* she would have shrugged or smiled. She would have felt safe. She would have said, "Happy New Year to you, too, you're a few days early."

The attack has changed her. They did it and they left, and they left something behind, and not just her picking herself up from the floor. They left her changed. Before, she always felt brave and alert and interesting—all kinds of positive things. Oh, sure, the negatives were there sometimes, the bad feelings, but they came and went. They didn't stay. Now something stays with her, something gray and ugly that was never there before. It's like something hard and stony. It's lodged itself inside her. It's got claws and teeth and it chews on her. It makes her feel scared and mean.

She looks at Wick and holds out her arms. The little boy slowly comes to her. He lets her hold him.

"Valerie, me too," Keefer says. "Me, a hug, too."

"You too," Valerie says and draws both children close.

− 24 −

Walking home after delivering some stuff of his father's to the cleaners, Rollo turns onto Mount Pleasant Avenue, a hilly street of large old Greek revival
houses. Snow is mounded along the roads and melting off the roofs in the sun. A cold clear day. Good
skiing weather, but Rollo doesn't have anyone to ski
with. He hasn't done a thing this vacation but sit
around and stare at the TV. All in all, it hasn't been
the greatest vacation, and it doesn't help that his
father is still mad at him, still not talking to him.

"I'm not finished with you," his father had said
ominously, the night he called Rollo into his study.
Since then Rollo has gotten the silent treatment. Is
that his punishment, or is there something else his

father is going to do? How long does he need to make up his mind? That blank face his father shows him is worse than any punishment. If he has something else in store for Rollo, why doesn't he do it and get it over with! Then Rollo can start living like a normal human being in a normal family again.

That's what he's fuming about as he turns onto Mount Pleasant Avenue and notices a girl coming down the hill toward him. It takes him a moment to realize it's Valerie.

He stops.

It's unmistakably her—a tall, gawky figure in a long coat. She's got two little kids with her, and she's lifting one of them over a snowbank.

Seeing her is a shock to Rollo. She's big, solid, her face is full of color. Sunlight glints off her glasses. And yet there's something unreal about her. No, what's unreal is seeing her here, outside, in the world, moving, striding down the hill. He hasn't thought about her since school, hasn't let himself think about her. And now here she is, coming straight toward him. Maybe that's why he stumbles, loses his footing, and falls. He goes down on the sidewalk like a kid.

He hops up, brushes himself off.

She sees him.

She stops dead and stares. Then she turns

abruptly, pushes the kids up the steps of a white
house, herds them inside, and slams the door.

This is the beginning of something Rollo can't
explain.

When he gets home he looks up Valerie's address—only one Michon in Highbridge—and discov-
ers it's Academy Street, not Mount Pleasant Avenue.
Maybe she's baby-sitting the two kids. Maybe they're
relatives. He locates Academy Street on the town
map his father has tacked up in the garage, and the
next morning he goes out to find it.

Her house is on one of the older streets near the
canal. A street of little houses with peaked roofs and
tiny windows. He doesn't stop or anything. He just
looks at the house and goes by. Then he walks over
to Mount Pleasant Avenue, and he doesn't stop
there, either. Just walks up the hill.

But later he calls Valerie's number, then hangs up
at the first ring. He does that a few times. Dials and
hangs up on the first ring, before anyone answers.
The next day he walks past her house again. In fact,
he walks past her house and the house on Mount
Pleasant Avenue two or three times that day.

What is he doing?

He's not sure, but he thinks if he sees her, he'll talk

to her. Maybe *she'll* want to talk. He'll listen. He's a good listener, probably a better listener than talker. He's definitely not a great talker, though he can usually find something to say. Anyway, they'll have a conversation. It doesn't have to be long. Maybe that's the first thing he'll tell her. *We can just talk for a few minutes.* They'll talk about ordinary stuff like the weather or Mr. Maddox or football, whatever she wants to talk about.

The next time he dials her number, he doesn't hang up, and she answers. "Hello . . . ?" He puts the phone down quietly. *Hello . . . ?* He goes on hearing her voice long after he's hung up.

Then he knows why he called her. He wanted to hear her voice. He wanted to hear her say something normal and nice.

Later he goes out again, walks the mile or so to Academy Street. It's dark, and when he comes to her house, instead of passing by, he slips along the side of the garage, through deep snow, past a tangle of frosted bushes and around into the backyard. He stands in the darkness and looks into a lighted window. He sees a table, a stove, a calendar on the wall. A bald man appears in the square of yellow light. He's fat and dressed in a mechanic's gray jumpsuit.

Valerie enters the room. Rollo moves closer to the

house, and as he does, something lands on his head. His heart kicks against his ribs, but it's only a lump of snow that slid off the roof. In the house, the man hands Valerie a plate of food. She sits down and begins to eat. Suddenly she looks out the window, seems to look straight at him. Again his heart kicks hard, and he leaps aside into the darkness. Did she see him? What if she comes rushing out of the house at him—what will he say? What excuse will he have? He can't explain why he's there. He doesn't know himself.

The next time he sees her, it's around six o'clock and he's on his way to meet Kara at work. As he opens the door to the restaurant, Valerie and the same two kids come out. He almost bumps into her.

She stares. Her face floods with color, and she pushes past him.

He goes after her. "Valerie," he calls.

She turns, swinging around so violently her glasses fall off. The little kids are gaping at him. She kneels and fumbles around in the snow. He hurries forward and picks up her glasses. "Here," he says. "I've got them."

"Why are you following me?" she says.

"No . . . I'm not."

"I know you are!" She raises her arm, and for a moment he thinks she's going to hit him.

She snatches the glasses from him, takes the kids by the hands, and rushes away. She's almost running, lifting the kids off the sidewalk. They're wearing red jackets and look like two low-flying balloons.

- 25 -

"Hello, Valerie?" she hears.

"Yes?"

"This is Rollo Wingate."

She hangs up.

"Hello, Valerie, I don't want to bother you, I just want to talk to you for a—"

She hangs up.

"Hello, please don't hang up."

"We have nothing to talk about." And she hangs up.

* * *

He calls again. He says, "I don't want you to hate me." She looks at the phone in her hand and considers this amazing statement. It would be no less amazing if he'd said, *I want you to be my best friend.* She hangs up.

The next time he calls, he says, "Hello, guess what—"

"What do you want?"

"—this is Rollo Wingate again," he finishes lamely.

"What do you want?"

"I just want to talk to you. I don't want you to hate me," he says again.

"I don't hate anybody."

"Thank you!"

Her eye throbs. His jubilation is unbearable. "You're the one who hates," she says quietly.

"No, no, I'm like you, I don't hate any—"

Her reserve breaks. "How dare you say that? You are not like me! I've never hurt another person in my life. Not the way you and your friends—" She stops herself and hangs up.

Valerie skates slowly alongside Wick and Keefer. It's a bright, sunny day, and the pond is packed with people. She takes Keefer by the hands and starts pulling her around on the ice. "Come on, slowpoke!" She skates backward, pulling the little girl across the pond. Then Wick has to have his turn. Finally she says, "Okay, guys, skate on your own for a while now."

She stands by the gate, watching them, ready to race out if either one needs rescuing.

"Hello," someone says behind her.

She turns pleasantly, not immediately recognizing the voice, but when she sees who it is, her chest becomes a knot of frozen breath. "Wick! Keefer!" she yells, moving out on the ice. "Come on! Off! We're going home!"

She sits them down on a bench to put on their boots.

He's leaning against the gate. Is he watching her? He's got ice skates on, but he's not going out on the ice.

"Keefer, let me help you." Valerie bends over the child, who's tugging at her sock. "We have to hurry."

"No," Keefer says. "Me I self do it."

"Hi, again." The bench creaks as he sits down on the other end.

Although the whole width of the bench is between them, he's too near. A chill presses against her back, as if she's feverish. If he tries to touch her, she'll kill him.

"Listen, what we were talking about the last time—" He just starts talking, as if she were waiting for him.

"We weren't talking about anything," she says, not looking at him. "Go away. Stop bothering me."

"Who's that guy?" Wick asks.

"I just want to say one thing," he pleads. "Okay?"

She doesn't answer.

"I never would have done—I mean, if I'd known you, I never would have—"

"If you'd known me," she repeats. "You're saying that a girl you know is safe. But a girl you don't know . . . you and your friends can come along and do anything you want to her."

"No! I didn't mean that! I was only trying to explain that it was different then. I mean, now I've talked to you, and I can see you're different than I thought, and if I'd known you then—"

She can't stand this. She can't stand what he's saying, his stumbling excuses, his blindness. His dumbness. His density. If he'd known her—what a horrible, terrible, crass, frightening thing to say.

"Valerie . . ." He's almost whispering. "I'm not a bad person. Honest. People tell me I'm a nice guy."

He's stupid, she decides, pulling Keefer's boot on. Wick has ambled away to watch the skaters.

"I didn't know it would be like that. It was just—it was my friends, and—I didn't have anything against you."

She wants this dopey, moronic guy to shut up, *now*.

"Remember when I said I was sorry? I meant it. Are you listening? Could you say something to me?"

"Okay, I'll say something. There was this guy, not too smart, who hit another guy over the head with a baseball bat," she says rapidly. "Why? Because he felt like it. He woke up one morning and he wanted to hit somebody over the head, so he did."

"I wouldn't," he says quickly.

"After he hits the other guy over the head, he goes back to him and says, 'Gee, fella, won't you talk to me?' He can't understand why the guy who's got the lump on his head doesn't want to talk to him, or see him, *or even know he exists*."

"No," he says, "it wasn't like that. It wasn't. I mean—no weapons."

"No," she says. "Just hands."

− 26 −

Now that he's talked to Valerie, there's only one thing he feels certain of in all the tangle of his thoughts, one idea he keeps coming back to: if only it hadn't happened.

If only he hadn't followed Brig.

If only he had stopped on the stairs.

If only he had said something. *What're we doing.* . . . *Why are we doing this.* . . . *Hey, guys.* . . .

If only he had looked at his hands and known that what those hands did was what he did, that they were attached to him, they were *him.*

If only life was like a movie you put on the VCR, and you could roll back time, make what happened unhappen. Flip REVERSE and watch all the parts you didn't like jumping back in a blur.

The three of them walking backward down the corridor . . . prancing backward down the stairs . . . falling into their seats in the auditorium . . .

Then he'd take the tape and snip off that bit, so they could never go forward the old way again. Instead, they would sit in the auditorium and watch the play straight through. They would be there as the curtain fell, they would applaud the actors, and when the lights went on, they would stand up and stretch and complain about how many times they had already seen this play.

They would be unaware of Valerie on the third floor, looking out the window.

And none of them would ever notice the difference in the tape. All that would be missing would be those few minutes.

– 27 –

Valerie's in her bedroom, writing in her journal.
"Something has been taken from me. Something has
been *stolen*. My sense of safety in the world, my
bravery. They belonged to me. And somebody's stolen them. Three thieves—"

The phone rings. She stiffens. She doesn't know
how she knows, but she knows it's *him,* one of the
thieves. She stares at the white phone on her desk.
She'd let the phone ring forever, but her father takes
it downstairs, and in a moment he calls up, "Val, for
you."

She picks up the phone.

Over the wire comes his nasal, uneasy breathing.
"I was thinking about what you said at the pond.

About the guy who hits the other guy? I thought, uh, we could talk about it."

She glances up, catches herself in the mirror, eyes narrowed, shoulders hunched venomously into the phone. Consciously, she leans back and assumes a softer posture. She doesn't want to become that person she sees in the mirror. It would only be one more thing they have done to her.

"You don't want to talk about it?" he says into her silence. "That's cool. We can talk about other stuff. My father says life is short, and even if I don't feel it now, I have to remember that. He said I have to have a sense of urgency."

For a moment she wouldn't mind talking about that. The idea of urgency is interesting. Is it really true that life is short? To her, it seems as if life is endless and time is forever. A week reaches to the horizon, a month stretches so far she can't even see the end of it. Take this vacation—it's been going on so long! And she's still feeling so bad. When will all this end? Will it ever end? What's short about this?

She drops the phone. She doesn't want to talk about life or time or *anything* with Rollo Wingate. Why did she let him babble on? He's done it again, tramped into her life without being asked. All she wants is to forget what happened, forget him and everything about him and his friends, and he's making it impossible.

"Valerie . . . ?" She hears his voice from the dangling phone and bangs the receiver into the cradle.

Her father comes up the stairs. "Who was that on the phone? Look." He fondly holds up his latest invention, a combination alarm clock–thermometer. The idea is that when you wake up, you know instantly what the weather is. "I think I've got some of the bugs worked out. This could change a person's whole outlook on life."

She nods and he passes by. Then she can't sit still. That abstracted look of her father's . . . his not-real interest in who called . . . he didn't even wait to hear her answer. She circles the room restlessly. All at once she wants to run after him, sees herself doing it— running, yelling. *Wipe that smile off your face!*

She looks out onto the dark street, trying to compose herself, not succeeding. Does he ever hear anything she says? Does he see anything but his workshop? How has he lived with her these past days and not even noticed how unhappy she is? He knows what happened to her! What does he think, one little discussion, and everything is peachy-keen?

"Dad!" she shouts suddenly. "Dad!"

"What is it?" He comes to her door, looking alarmed.

She's all set to blast him, all set to wipe that anxious smile off his face, to tell him some hard home truths. And then she stops. She can't do it. It's unfair; she was the one who protected him. Her choice. What had she said to him after Mr. Ferranto called? *It was nothing, Dad, really, just a prank, some shoving. . . . Three jerky boys . . . No, I'm fine. . . .*

"What is it?" he says again.

She raises her shoulders. "One of those boys keeps calling, trying to talk to me. What should I do? I think he wants me to forgive him."

"And do you want to?" he says.

It's such a nice sensible question—and she seems to know the answer. No, she doesn't want to forgive him! Why should she forgive, why should she forget? Why make it easier for him? Why take away his pain—will that take away hers?

In the morning, waking is like climbing out of a pit. A nightmare of the clanking fish pursues her out of sleep.

She stares at the ceiling. *Do you want to forgive him? No! No! No!* But the answer doesn't satisfy her this morning. The *No* isn't good enough. It doesn't release her. She wants what happened in school—the attack, the assault—to be done with, and it isn't. It doesn't go away. It doesn't end.

She gets up, takes a shower, gets dressed. She tells herself she's not thinking about it, she's not thinking about Rollo Wingate, the thief. But all the time a voice in her mind is whispering, *To err is human, to forgive divine.* "I won't!" Valerie cries. Forgiveness is fine for angels, but she's not in the angel league. It isn't that her wings are clipped—she doesn't *have* any wings. If she did, she would fly herself out of this pain. She would end it. Isn't there something she can do? "Please," she whispers.

He calls again that morning. She's eating breakfast. No place to go, as Mrs. Brunet has closed the shop until after the New Year and is home with the kids herself.

"Hello, Valerie, this is Rollo. Before you hang up," he says hastily, "I just want to ask you one thing."

She takes a bite of toast, spits it out, bangs down the phone.

He calls again immediately. "I was hit by lightning once. It was a long time ago at a lake where my parents rented a cottage. I was three years old, sitting in my mother's lap, watching a storm coming in, and then, zap!"

This is so bizarre, she waits.

"My mother took the main hit, because she was in contact with the metal chair. She was knocked right off the chair, me with her. Remember I said I had a question?" He starts talking fast. "Well, I'm going to ask, even if you say no. Would you meet me and talk to me? I just want to say something to you. I know you're going to say no, but could you just think about it? Okay?"

She doesn't say no. She doesn't say yes. She doesn't respond in any way—she can't—she couldn't even if she wanted to. Something is happening to her. Although she's still sitting in the same place at the kitchen table, with the phone in her hand, all that's around her has become vague, and all that she sees is an image in her mind. A mother and a child in a chair. Then the child in the chair alone. The image takes her over . . . takes her away . . . seizes her.

She's nearly trembling. The phone drops from her hand. A nervous quivering grips her, a joyful nervous twanging of her senses, the complete and true opposite of the grayness that has oppressed her for so many days now. She leans back, raising her arms.

She will make a sculpture. She sees it complete . . . and completed. It will be in two sections, two separate scenes joined by a single base: a mother and a child on one side in a rocking chair; on the other side, the chair again . . . the child alone.

She starts sketching on a napkin. The base will be more than its physical self, more than clay, it will stand for the meaning of the whole sculpture: how everything is linked, how nothing stands alone, how "before" and "after" are all part of a single entity, a single experience, an ongoing thing that is Life.

Her chair comes down with a bang. Oh, God, is she being pretentious? Maybe, but she doesn't really care. Her fingers are tingling. Already she can feel the damp, heavy texture of the clay. Already she's mulling over problems of proportion. Already she knows this will be different from anything she's ever done, more complicated and yet more focused, more challenging, more satisfying, more *everything*.

Then, in another startling moment, staring at the napkin, she understands that the sculpture will be a metaphor for what happened to her. Before that morning on the third floor, she had been like a child safe in its mother's arms, in the arms of the world, which promised her only good things. Then lightning struck: sudden, unexpected, destructive—and she was left alone, bereft.

He's still talking. She can hear his voice coming out of the receiver. She picks it up. "I don't think my

mother suffered any aftereffects from the lightning,"
he's saying. "She died when I was ten, but that was
something else. Car accident, the other driver was
drunk. . . . I miss my mother. I love her. She was, you
know, special."

For a moment she lets in sympathy for him, like
light under a drawn shade. She misses her mother,
too, but differently: she doesn't remember her
mother—how could she? What she probably misses
is *a* mother. She works on the idea of the chair. The
pencil sinks into the soft paper, and she looks for
something else to sketch on.

"What about your mother?" he asks.

She starts drawing on a brown bag. "What about
her? She's dead." She makes another sketch of the
chair, very simple, almost a single line. She should
end this conversation, but she doesn't, because something quick and glad is flowing through her. She is
full of light: everything is light inside her. Even Rollo
can exist in this light.

"Did she die in an accident, too?" he asks.

"Childbirth."

"I didn't think things like that still happened. Was
she very young?"

"Twenty."

"Neither of us have mothers," he says, as though

it's an amazing coincidence. But the only amazing thing here is that the raw material for what she already knows is going to be the best sculpture she's ever done was given to her by him. And for that, she can't help feeling grateful. Maybe that's why, when he asks her again to meet him, she hears herself saying yes.

– 28 –

Rollo looks across the table at Valerie. "You want anything else?" She's barely touched the cup of hot chocolate she ordered.

"What am I doing here?" she says.

He doesn't really know. He didn't think this through too well. His only thought had been that if they could meet, if she would sit and talk to him in a sort of normal and ordinary way, it would make a difference. He's not a monster—that's all he wants her to see.

"You could have a piece of pie," he says, and digs into the hot peach pie in front of him. A gob of vanilla ice cream slides across the top. He forks pie into his mouth, then a lump of ice cream. It's good, and he doesn't stop until his plate is just a smear of sticky crumbs.

Valerie is staring at him. She's sitting on the edge of the seat, one leg out in the aisle, her coat around her shoulders, as if she's ready for a speedy takeoff. "I thought you wanted to tell me something. What's the point of this meeting?"

"No point." He laughs nervously. "I just wanted you to see that I'm a nice guy."

Her cheek twitches. "Right. A nice guy who gets his kicks out of attacking girls."

"I don't," he says morosely. He already said he was sorry, but maybe he should say it again. He *is* sorry. He's gotten more and more sorry with each day. He could just say, in a dignified way, *I apologize, Valerie. I truly and sincerely* . . . What if she did something solemn, like putting her hand on his head? *Go in peace, Rollo Wingate. I forgive you.* Maybe he should say that. *I hope you forgive me. . . . I deeply regret and sincerely hope* . . . "You want to hear how it happened, you want to hear my story?" he blurts.

"Your *story?*" She pushes aside her cup, and cocoa sloshes into the saucer. "You think what you did is a *story,* your version or mine? You tell me yours and I'll tell you mine? Maybe you think I'll like your story better than mine. This is not equal time," she goes on, her voice thickening. "Something happened to me. You know what it was, and I know what it was. There is no *story*."

Her nose is red at the corners. Is she going to cry? He shoves his napkin across the table to her. This is not working out right. His idea was so simple, just two people sitting around talking, maybe even having a good time.

She's biting her lip, swallowing. She doesn't touch the napkin. "You trapped me, you held me, you didn't let me move," she says. "You got your dirty hands all over me—" Her voice breaks. "No, I'm not crying," she says, wiping her face with her sleeve. "Don't you worry, I'm not crying."

Why did he start this? Why did he ask her to meet him? What was on his mind? He can't remember now. He's sweating, and the pie in his stomach is like a block of cement.

She sits straight against the booth. "Now that you got me here, you tell me something. Why did you do it?"

He looks down at the table. "You know how these things are," he says, and he hears himself, and he knows that's wrong and that it makes him sound stupid, dull, unthinking. And if he didn't know it, her face would tell him.

"Why?" she says again.

"Because—" He can't say what he's thinking. Not to her face. Can he say they did it because they thought she was a bitch? Can he say that he followed Brig without thinking . . . and that he loved following him? Can he say that she was nothing to him but a pain-in-the-ass girl who was getting on their nerves?

They stare at each other. She's fingering the buttons on her coat. "Okay," she says. "I want to ask you something else. What if it happened to you? What if guys attacked you?"

"What?" He almost wants to laugh. What does this mean? Attacked him, like it happened to her? It wouldn't. It couldn't. "I'd fight them off."

"What if there were too many of them?"

"I don't know. . . . I'd get out of it."

"How? What if they were doing stuff to you and there was nothing you could do about it?"

"I'm too big. They don't mess with me." What does she want him to say?

"There're bigger guys than you," she says. "There's always someone bigger. Come on, Rollo, what if three big guys came up to you—what would you do, how would you feel?"

"You mean if they were fooling around, sort of

crowding me a little, sort of pushing in? I'd be looking for a way out, swinging at them—"

"I mean if they held you. Did what they wanted to
you, anything they wanted to do." She's tearing a
napkin into shreds. "What if they were doing that,
and there was nothing you could do about it?"

He knows what she's after, he's not exactly dumb,
no matter what she thinks. She's trying to make him
step in her shoes, trying to make him think about
guys on him, and him helpless, not able to do anything. "It couldn't happen," he says.

"But *if it did*? What then?"

He doesn't want to answer. He doesn't want to
think about being helpless, but she's forcing him to
think about it. Forcing him to think how humiliated
he'd be, how his cheeks would burn and his heart
pound a mile a minute.

"I'd crack them in the mouth, I wouldn't let them
do it, I'd kill them, I'd say, *Get the hell out of my way!*
I'd make them suffer, too." His hands clench. What
is he doing? Why is he saying all this?

"This is stupid," he bursts out. He doesn't want to
think about this. He doesn't want to talk about it. It
puts a weak, watery feeling in his stomach. He stands
up. He's not going to say another word to her. *Go to
hell,* he thinks. He doesn't care if he ever sees her again.

– 29 –

"I want to go to my party in the library alone," Kara says.

"Your brother's going to take you," Rollo's father croaks from the bed. He's been lying there for the past two days with flu.

The New Year's party, an annual affair thrown by the town, is not something Rollo ever looks forward to, and this year he's especially uninterested. Aside from the fact that it's always massively boring—the decor is balloons, the menu is punch—there's something else Rollo doesn't like. A lot of teachers show up for the party. Why face them any sooner than necessary?

"I don't want Rollo to watch me," Kara says. "I

watch myself. I can be mature." She's wearing a pink dress with a swingy skirt, a pink ribbon in her hair, red satin, high-heeled shoes. "You can't watch me, Rollo. That's final. That's my final final. Mrs. Rosten says I'm mature, and I can say something final."

"Kara, can it. I don't want to hear you yakking all night long."

"Daddy! Did you hear that? Did you hear what my brother said?" She grabs her coat and walks out. "I'm going to my party by myself! That's final!" She pounds down the stairs.

"Go after her," his father says.

Outside, it's a clear cold night, and the moon is coming up in the sky. He catches up to Kara. "Here I am."

She pouts for a moment, then asks, "Do you think I look pretty?"

"Gorgeous. And very mature," he adds.

The party is taking place in a big meeting hall in the Highbridge Community Center. The library is lit up and there are people everywhere. Almost no kids his age, except some boys, clumped together in a corner, who are looking around, sneering. Probably the kids from the Cedars, the county juvenile home.

Rollo wanders around, eating cookies and occasionally checking on Kara. It's easy to spot her in the pink dress. She's okay, rushing around hugging and kissing people. He doesn't care as long as she stays away from the Cedars kids.

Suddenly he sees Mr. Maddox talking to Mr. Ferranto. Of all the people he would least like to meet, his principal and his English teacher are on the top of the list.

He crosses to the other side of the room looking for Kara. They can go home early. He finds her by the front windows, and she's with Valerie Michon. He hesitates for a moment, then he calls Kara. She and Valerie both glance up.

"That's my brother!" Kara's voice can be heard across the room. "Rollo!" She hugs his arm. "I have a new friend!"

"This is your brother?" Valerie says.

"Yes! I told you I had a brother. This is my brother, Rollo."

"What are you doing here?" he says to Valerie.

"What are *you* doing here?"

"Valerie is here with a friend," Kara says importantly. "She says a friend baby-sitter asked her to come."

"No, Kara, she's not a baby-sitter," Valerie says. "She's the lady I baby-sit *for*."

"I know, I know! Oh, this is such a good party. Everybody good is here."

Kara is all keyed up. Her cheeks are flushed, and she's talking at high speed. "It's the best party! Are you having a good time, Rollo?" She pauses for a second to plant a kiss on Valerie's neck. "This is my friend, Rollo, this is Valerie. Do you like her gorgeous blouse?" She touches the embroidery on the collar of the linen blouse Valerie is wearing. "I'll give you a kiss in a minute, Rollo. I know I'm excited. Do you want some punch?"

"Kara, slow down," he says. "We're going home now."

"No, I'm not going home yet! I want to talk some more to my new friend, Valerie. I have to dance, and I have to have some more punch. I'm going to bring you a glass of punch, isn't that nice of me?"

"Kara," he begins, but she runs off, and he and Valerie are left staring at each other. Then, abruptly, she walks away, too, leaving him feeling, well, the way you feel when somebody walks away from you, even if she's the person *you* walked away from the last time you saw her.

He wanders down the hall and looks into the darkened movie room for a while. Some figures with white ruffs and swords are on the screen. "Begone!" somebody cries. Or is it "Begin!"? He can't make sense out of what he's seeing. He keeps remembering the way Valerie looked at him a few minutes ago. Why does he care? He doesn't . . . but he does. It's confusing and stupid. He can't get straight about her. He would like to never, ever, think about her again. He would like to wipe her and what happened out of his mind.

But when he goes back into the meeting hall again, the first person he sees is Valerie, talking to a tall woman in a green knit suit. He steers wide and clear of her. He circles the room, looking for Kara. "Did you see my sister?" he asks a woman refilling the punch bowl.

"Do I know her?"

"She's Kara. If you know her, you know her."

The woman shakes her head. "I don't know her."

He walks around, but doesn't see Kara anywhere. He goes out into the hall again. Maybe she's in the bathroom. He knocks on the door. "Kara?"

Valerie is coming down the hall. Right. It must be his fate. "Are you going in there?" he asks, and then quickly, before she can take it the wrong way, "Would you check if Kara's in there?"

She goes in and then comes out again immediately. "No."

"She's not in there?"

"No."

"You sure?"

"You want to go in yourself and see?"

"Okay, I just wanted to be sure." He stares around the hall, frowning.

"What's the problem?" she says.

"I don't know where Kara is."

"Maybe she went outside."

"Why would she do that?" But it's a thought, and he's already on his way to the door.

The moon is behind clouds, the parking lot is dark. His eyes search among the shadowy lumps that are cars. "Kara?" he calls. Then he hears something, a sound, a wail . . . maybe a car radio. Maybe Kara. He thinks of the boys from the Cedars and moves fast between the angled cars. He's aware of Valerie behind him. He hears that noise again, a sound he can't identify. Is Kara crying? He races, his heart jostling in his chest, and he imagines . . . everything.

Clouds scud across the sky, the moon comes out and lights the edge of the lot, and there is Kara, dancing in the cold air, swaying and singing, holding out the corners of her dress.

"Rollo!" she says. "Look at me dance in the snow!"

"What are you doing out here?" he shouts. The relief is terrible, it makes him furious with her.

"I told you, dancing in the snow," she shouts back. Her cheeks are glowing. Her mouth is turned up in a joyful smile.

"You were supposed to stay inside!" Conscious of Valerie behind him, he tries to lower his voice. "I was worried, Kara. You shouldn't have done this without telling me."

"I always dance in the snow. Every New Year, I dance in the snow with Daddy. Don't you know that, Rollo, you dummy!" She twirls around. "Come and dance with me."

He takes a step backward. All he needs is to make a fool of himself in front of Valerie. "Kara, you've danced enough."

Behind him, he hears Valerie draw in her breath. "Danced *enough*?" she says, almost under her breath, almost as if she's talking to him. "How can anyone dance *enough*? Even for you, that's stupid."

"Kara!" he barks. "Come on."

"Valerie, Valerie," Kara sings, ignoring him, "you come dance with me."

"Oh, Kara, I'm not a very good dancer."

"Just one little dance," Kara pleads, dipping and swaying. "Please, please," she sings, holding out her hands. She doesn't stop moving for a moment.

Valerie steps into the circle of packed snow Kara has made with her stamping feet. She raises her arms, and begins awkwardly dancing, turning, throwing back her head.

Rollo stares at his sister and Valerie—one tall gangly girl, one short and round—two dark shapes shifting and moving in the half-light. Valerie is laughing and holding hands with Kara as they jump around.

When someone laughs, you want to laugh, too. And when someone dances, you want to dance with them. But Rollo can't do that. Well, he could—he could leap into the circle, he could spin and throw himself around, too . . . but he wouldn't. He wouldn't get out there and jump around. He might think of it, but it's not something he would do, not something a boy would do.

Now the two girls are going round and round, faster and faster, and they're humming, and their voices sound like the wind or water, something strange and half-wild.

And watching them, watching Valerie spin Kara

around, Rollo remembers that figure against the window. And in a series of flashes, like bursts of light, he sees himself moving toward her, he sees the three of them looming, moving in, he sees them like a wall rising, a wall darkening the light.

When Valerie returns to school after vacation, she tries not to think about what happened on the third floor. Just as she tries not to notice that, often, a silence falls as she walks into a room, or that people watch her a lot, or that remarks trail her down the halls. She goes about her business, takes notes in classes, does her homework, and talks to Janice, who usually has something frivolous to say. And that's good, because Valerie doesn't have anything to say. There's a silence in her.

The second day she runs into Mark near the lab. She's unprepared for how shaken she feels by the sight of him. By his presence. "Valerie!" he greets her, making her name into three words—Val Er

Eee!—like a little cheer. He pushes up his wire rims and leans in toward her as if he wants to hug her. She shrinks back, yet, curiously, what she wants to do, what her arms are nearly trembling to do, is to hug him. But . . . no.

"Are you going to tutor me this term?" he asks, nodding his head as if to say, *Sure you are!*

"No." she says.

"No?"

"No."

A little smile flickers over his mouth, is there, then gone. "Why not?"

He sounds angry, and that makes it easier. "I'm not tutoring anyone." She walks away, then back for an instant to say, "Sorry." And saying it, she is almost bitterly sorry, but so what? She doesn't trust him anymore. When you get down to it, what makes Mark Saddler different from any other boy? What does she even know about him, except that he has a great smile? Well, so does Rollo Wingate.

That day, she goes up to the third floor, because there's no other way to get into the art room. She takes the long way around. She avoids even looking toward the window at the end of the hall. She thinks she may take the long way around forever. The important thing is to get into the art room and begin working on her sculpture. But once inside, she doesn't do anything, just doodles aimlessly and stares at the clay.

The next day and the day after, it's the same thing. What's the matter with her? This was supposed to be her big breakthrough, the work that would be the best thing she'd ever done, that would be unique and wonderful, energetic, profound, and important. *What pretentious bullshit.* She sits on a high stool and makes little clay beads just in order to keep her hands busy. *I'm not ready yet to start it. . . . There's a right time to begin working. . . . You have to wait for the moment. . . . More bullshit and self-delusion.* Truth is that she's under a pall of anxiety and self-doubt unlike anything she's ever felt. In fact, not to be fancy about it, she's simply afraid.

Afraid she can't carry it off, that all her enthusiasm and inventiveness was poured out that morning when she doodled on a napkin and "saw" the sculpture as vividly as if it already existed. Afraid she's all wrong about the idea, that it's banal, that it won't be good, that people will laugh. . . . A thousand afraids, but no matter what words she puts to it, what it gets down to is that she's not doing it. She's not doing much of anything.

She feels tired a lot of the time. Her father notices

and asks if she has a cold. Instead of thanking him for his concern, she snaps at him, "Leave me alone!"

She feels more miserable than ever and lies on her bed, mentally tallying up her life. On a scale of one to ten . . . would she even give herself a four? She thinks of the whispers and looks. She thinks how in one more week the three boys will be back in school. She thinks about being mean to her father. She thinks about her sculpture—her non-sculpture—and that she's blown off Mark. No, not even a four. A three, maybe a two. She rolls herself in a blanket and allows herself to cry. Why not? She doesn't indulge very often in self-pity. And can't too long either, because Janice calls.

"Val, I feel like talking, and I don't have anyone else to call." A typical Janice remark.

"I'm not feeling too great right now, Janice."

"Me either," Janice says enthusiastically. "My nail polish won't go on right. It is so frustrating. Of course, you intellectual types don't think this is a significant matter in the universe. You could be right, but I happen to like smooth nail polish. It makes my life just that much nicer. I wonder if this has anything to do with my horoscope for the day? It said I should put fear behind and do what is right. Do you think that means I should buy some new nail polish?"

When Valerie hangs up, she sees that she's doodled Janice's horoscope in block letters. PUT FEAR BEHIND, DO WHAT IS RIGHT.

In the cafeteria, Denise Dixon pauses by Valerie's table. "Hi. Okay if I sit here?" Denise puts her tray down and slides into the seat across from Valerie. She unwraps a sandwich with long, red-tipped fingers, a precise and almost delicate operation in which the wrapping isn't crumpled but carefully folded. Valerie eyes her, wondering what's coming. She and Denise definitely don't run with the same pack. Not that Valerie actually runs with any pack, but if she did, it wouldn't be Denise's popular-girl-active-student-every-teacher's-darling pack.

All at once, Valerie remembers the last time she really noticed Denise—onstage, the day of the Christmas play. Denise had been good—what Valerie had seen of her. She cuts off this train of thought and concentrates on her egg salad sandwich. Her father baked the bread. It's sort of dry, and little pieces crumble onto the table.

"So," Denise says. "Um . . ." She leans across the table. "I heard what happened," she says, finally.

Valerie doesn't say anything.

A slow flush creeps up Denise's perfect skin. "I want to—I want to say how sorry—"

Valerie nods and bites into her sandwich. A rain of crumbs falls. She's going to have to talk to her father about making the bread moister.

"It's so horrible," Denise says. "Have you talked to anyone about it?"

What does she want, gossip?

"Have you thought about a therapist?"

Valerie can't resist. "I can always go to Mr. Ferranto's wife," she deadpans.

"Oh, no," Denise says. "You should get someone not involved in the situation."

The beautiful Denise hasn't got much of a sense of humor, Valerie realizes. The bell rings then, and Valerie gathers up her books and her crumbs and her soda can, but Denise is still sitting there, staring at her earnestly, as if she wants to say something and is searching hard for the words. Valerie stands up. "Well, see you," she says.

Denise gets up, too. "Val . . ." She takes Valerie by the arm. "I wanted to say . . . I want to tell you . . . the same thing happened to me," she blurts.

Valerie stares. Denise? Why her? She's not the type to go around stepping on guys' hands or egos.

"Last year," Denise says.

"Those boys?"

"No, not them, another one. He was grabbing me, he just kept grabbing my butt."

They walk out of the cafeteria together. Now Valerie is the one who wants to say something, but whatever she thinks of to say is inadequate. *How awful. . . . I know how you feel. . . . I'm sorry. . . .*

"I kept trying to avoid him, but I couldn't. I tried to talk to him and tell him to stop. He said it was just a joke. He pinned me one day in the hall. Nobody was around, and he—you know—"

Words are only words, and words can't carry the weight of what Valerie feels listening to Denise: such a tangle of emotions that it's days before she recognizes that mixed in with the by now familiar pain and humiliation is equally deep anger.

− 31 −

Rollo's father says, "You need to do something for someone besides yourself. You have to start thinking more of other people. What kind of community service do you want to do?"

"Community service?" This is something he's never thought about in his life.

"Who do you want to work with? Think!"

Rollo says the first thing that comes to mind, which of course is not thinking. "Old people?"

And that's why, every day for the next two weeks, he goes to the Senior Center and does whatever they find for him to do, which might be mopping a floor, washing dishes, or bundling newspapers for recycling.

During his two-week suspension from school, he also studies at home two hours every day, then goes to the library and sits there and studies for another hour. These are the rules his father laid down for him.

Most days, too, he meets Kara and walks home from work with her. And most days, now that they've returned, he sees Brig and Candy.

"You're white as a worm," Brig says the first time they get together. He and Candy are both tanned from having been in the sun. They have stories to tell Rollo, and the three of them talk a lot the first few days.

Rollo thinks at first that he'll tell his own stories about Valerie, but, faced with Brig and Candy, they seem too bizarre, too weird, too whimpy. He can imagine what they'll say if they hear how he pursued her and phoned her, how he nearly begged her to meet him. *You said you were sorry to her? Sorry for what? We didn't do anything, so how can you be sorry?* So, of all the things they talk about, there's one subject they avoid. They never talk about Valerie. They never talk about the third floor and what happened there that morning.

* * *

Rollo is trying to explain a strange experience he's had several times lately: he's awake, but feels almost as if he's asleep. Not awake, not asleep, just awake enough to know that he's waiting for something to wake him up from the sleep he's not sleeping.

Brig just laughs, but Candy's interested. "This happens in the morning when you wake up?"

"No, anytime. Walking down the street the other day. It's sort of a not-here feeling, like something is incomplete, like I'm waiting for something to be filled in."

"This boy needs a cold shower and a cup of coffee," Brig says.

Maybe he's right. Maybe a hit of caffeine or a surge of adrenaline will clear his head of the junk in it. A big clean wind to sweep out his brain, so he can start fresh again and make some sense out of everything that's been happening . . . and have some peace, too.

His father has some serious talks with Rollo, and that's pretty good. Well, it's not *good*; it's uncomfortable. He actually hates it every time his father says they should talk, but afterward he always feels better, somehow. And sometimes, after these talks, he has thoughts. He's never had actual *thoughts* before, ideas that come to him in well-phrased sentences, not that he can remember.

One thought he has is that he was a go-along. A follower. Someone who didn't ask questions or think for himself. It's kind of scary to have that thought; the only good part about it is that he has another thought: I'll never be a go-along again.

Nobody knows about these thoughts. Brig and Candy think he's the same old Rollo, just as Brig is the same old Brig, right down to hanging from his bar every morning for fifteen minutes. Maybe Candy's a bit quieter, but he's still Brig's best pal and the oil on Brig's troubled waters. So everything is more or less the same. Almost the same, Rollo thinks, almost like it was, yet he feels that something has shifted. It might be their friendship—he's not quite sure; it might be his life.

One afternoon, when they go over to the Racquet Club to work out, a new guy is behind the counter. The sleeves of his T-shirt are cut off to show his muscles, and he's wearing wire rims, like the ones he was wearing the night Brig and Rollo were at his house.

Rollo recognizes Mark Saddler right away. It takes

Brig a moment longer, just long enough for Saddler to say, "What are you doing here?"

"What I'm doing here is waiting for you to wait on me." Brig shoves his ID across the counter.

"Are these the other two clowns?" Saddler says, looking at Rollo and Candy.

Brig slams his gym bag against the counter. "Towel, boy!" he orders.

"Go to hell," Mark Saddler says.

Rollo puts his hand on Brig's shoulder. "Let's go down to the locker room."

"Let him give me my towel and tell me to have a nice day," Brig snaps.

"I wait on *people* here. You're nothing but a pimple on a flea's ass."

"I'll get you fired!"

Saddler grabs the counter like he's going to jump over it and strangle Brig. Candy and Rollo pull Brig away. When they leave the clubhouse later, someone else is at the desk.

– 32 –

Valerie has known all along that the three of them were coming back to school: it was only a two-week suspension. But she knew it the way you know things with your head, not your guts. You know that it would be rotten to have a car accident, but you don't feel anything about it until you personally get smashed up. You know you'd hate to have three boys molest you, but you don't have a real idea what that means until they do. And you don't know *at all* what it's like to see those same three boys back in your life . . . until they're there.

She sees the short one first, coming out of the gym. The ringleader. Briggers. She gets such a shock she almost backs herself into the wall. A bunch of boys are with him. Are they talking about the third floor? Her stomach lurches. She turns to avoid even passing near them.

She sees the blond, freckled one next. He wings past her in the hall without a glance. He either doesn't see her or doesn't want to, which leads her to wonder which is worse—to be visible to Briggers or invisible to Candrella. In either case, it's like an erasure, isn't it?

At lunch, when she tells Denise this, though, the other girl says, "Oh, no, Valerie, we can't let them make us feel erased! We just can't. We can't allow ourselves to feel erased." Helen Moore, a girl who's always clowning around, rolls her eyes. "Better to be the eraser!" She bends over, making exaggerated erasing motions on the table. After a moment, Denise's face lifts in a little smile. She gets it.

Helen Moore is just one of the six or seven girls who have gradually joined Valerie and Denise at lunch every day. They've gotten a regular lunch club going, and not always, but sometimes, one or the other of them will lean in and start talking about what Marcella Thompson calls third-floor things.

"Named in your honor, Valerie," Helen Moore says, making a pious steeple of her fingers.

"I don't think that's funny," Denise says, until someone pokes her and says, "Denise. Joke."

When they talk about third-floor things, mostly their voices are dry, they make wry remarks, but sometimes someone cries a little, telling about something she was afraid or ashamed to talk about before this. Something she wasn't completely sure was wrong, but which made her feel terrible and wonder what she had done to make it happen. Like finding out that her name was written with dirty graffiti all over the boys' bathroom, or being asked who she was going to bang this weekend, or having her blouse flipped up, or her bra strap snapped, or her skirt unzipped, or her legs commented on, or—but the *ors* seem endless.

"As many *ors*," says Helen Moore, "as there are boys in school."

"No, there are some good guys," Marcella says. She's tiny, blond, and fiercely fair. She looks at Valerie. "Don't you think so?"

Valerie shrugs. "Probably right." But she isn't convinced. She leaves the lunchroom warily, her eyes scanning ahead for Candrella or Briggers.

It's the end of the day before she sees the other one, Rollo, the one who can't leave her alone. He's hanging around the art room and gives her a smile, that sort of humble smile he's so good at. She doesn't stop, but she notices that compared to her hatred of the other two, she feels, well, almost an edge of friendliness toward Rollo. But that wears off fast.

"The thieves are back," she writes later in her journal, "free as birds. It scares me. I don't feel safe with them around. I keep remembering Janice's horoscope. Put fear behind and do what's right. I want to put fear behind. What do I have to do? Why can't I just forget them?"

But she knows why. There's no escaping them. They're right there in school. They're *there*, in her face. All the rest of the term, they'll be walking the halls, sitting on the steps, playing on the teams, talking to the teachers, opening and closing their lockers, going in and out of classrooms. They're going to be in her face, no matter what she does.

She sits back, her hands over her eyes. There *is* one thing she can do anyway, one thing that's right, even if it isn't about them. She lifts the phone and dials.

"Hello?"

"Hi . . . Mark?" She draws in a breath. "This is Valerie."

"Valerie," he says carefully. "What's up?"

"Oh . . . I've been thinking about a lot of things, Mark, funny things like erasers and horoscopes. . . . I might tell you about it sometime, but what I called for—I've decided to tutor you, after all."

"Why?"

No whoops, brays, or hoots of joy. Just a flat *Why?* Did she say it wrong? This isn't the response she expected. "Because I want to."

"Well, thanks, but it's not necessary. I'm getting someone else. We're starting next week."

She walks around her room, phone in hand.

"There are quite a few other people tutoring," he says.

"Right." She drops into a chair and nibbles frantically on her thumbnail.

"Of course," he says after a moment. "I don't know if anybody will do as good a job as you. . . . I learned a lot from you."

She sits up straighter. "I thought we were a great team."

"My sentence structure will never be the same again," he acknowledges.

"We could start tomorrow."

"Okay," he says.

"Does that mean yes?"

"Guess so." He allows a bit of enthusiasm to creep into his voice. "Anyway, I probably couldn't find anyone else as smart as you to help me."

"Just so long as you know it," she says.

– 33 –

"Valerie, how are you doing?" Mr. Ferranto says, as if she's just come out of the hospital.

"I'm okay." She sits down. He's called her out of her AP math class. She searches her mind to see if she's run afoul of any of her teachers lately.

Mr. Ferranto leans forward over his desk and looks at her searchingly. "Valerie. How are you doing?" he says again.

"Okay," she repeats. What is this all about?

"Valerie, I've been thinking about you. I'm aware of the gossip in school, I'm aware that you are in a sensitive position. You remember that I told you my wife is a psychologist. She's been helpful in alerting me to the issues here. She suggested to me that coming back to school might be trying for you."

"I'm doing okay." The warmth of Mr. Ferranto's gaze is confusing. Since that day when he expressed his "concern" for the three boys and then sprang them on her, she has felt a kind of suppressed loathing for him, as if he were part of what happened to her. Is it possible she misjudged him?

He sits back with his fingers steepled. "I have several suggestions to help you get past this difficult time with as little strain as possible. My first thought was that you might be a prime candidate for self-study. We could certainly arrange it. A lot of creative people are autodidacts, and that method of learning has great satisfactions, I'm told. You've scored brilliantly in all the national tests, you're in the top percentiles, but your marks have never been consistent, which suggests—"

"You mean stay home and study by myself?"

"Exactly!"

"But—"

He holds up his hand. "I know, that's extreme. However, another more realistic possibility has opened up." He shuffles some papers. "I've looked into the details of your transferring to Hoover High.

It's an excellent school with an outstanding record, and they would be delighted to have you."

"Go to another school?" she says, and she thinks what it would mean: first and best, leaving behind everything that reminds her of that day. Never having to see them again. Wiping the slate clean and starting over where no one knows what happened to her.

Then she thinks about being a stranger in a new school, the new-girl-on-the-block thing, not knowing anyone, not seeing Mr. Maddox again, not having Denise to sit with at lunch, or the other girls.

"Do you realize Hoover High has a nationally recognized art department? I've talked to the art people there and here, and we all have great hopes for you. This other school could be an opening, a real door to the future for you. I want you to think about it seriously."

He walks her to the door and says, "Valerie, we'll talk again. I want you to think about it."

When she reports this conversation to Janice, the other girl, not half as dumb as she pretends, says, "He wants to get rid of you. He's worried that something might leak out about the third floor."

"That's ridiculous. Everyone knows about it."

"They do and they don't," Janice says. "It's more gossip than anything. People aren't sure of what really happened. He'd like to get you out of the way, so everybody could forget about it."

"What's he afraid of?"

"Valerie! Dummy! He doesn't want bad publicity for the school."

"Oh."

"Oh! Right! The light dawns, huh?"

"You mean if I said something in public . . ."

"Right. You're a little time bomb, Val."

Hardly noticing that it's happening, Valerie begins working with the clay. She's not thinking about the sculpture but about what it would be like to be home, studying by herself. An autodidact. Flattering word. It is kind of tempting. Or is it? Does she want to retreat into her own little workshop, like her father? After a while she looks down and sees that she has made the first tentative movements into the scene of the mother and child in the rocking chair. Maybe that's when she knows for sure she's not leaving this school, she's not taking any of Mr. Ferranto's suggestions. It's her school—hers, not theirs—hers, as well as theirs.

When she comes out of the art room, Rollo is there

and thrusts a paper into her hand. "I said I'd give it to you," he mumbles and lopes off. She smooths out the paper. DEAR VALEREE, I LOVE YOU. WILL YOU COME SEE ME AT WORK I HOPE SO. YOUR NEW FREND, KARA WINGATE.

At home, she tacks Kara's letter on her bulletin board to remind her that nothing in life is simple. She puts it up next to the operative words from Janice's horoscope, which are pinned above a scrap of paper on which she has written in black Magic Marker, REFUSE TO BE ERASED. Slogans, admonitions, but they're helpful: they remind her of things, they tell her what she needs to remember.

"You know," Helen Moore says to Valerie the next day at lunch, "I've been thinking. You were really brave to tell as many people as you did what happened to you. I didn't want anyone to know."

Valerie laughs. "I was not brave. I was mad!" Then her nose feels hot and her forehead burns, and she realizes that since it happened, since the first moments of anguish and anger, she has not allowed herself to be that mad again. She has hated and feared and shuddered and shivered, but she has not been plain out-and-out burning mad. Mad that this could happen to her. Mad that the boys went after her as if she were game in a field and they were

hunting dogs. Mad that everybody knows and nobody raised a fuss. Mad that Mr. Ferranto wants her
out of the school. *Mad, mad, mad.* Mad enough to do
something.

That weekend she writes a letter. She isn't sure
who's going to receive it. Maybe the newspaper.
Maybe the local TV station. She means to write the
letter without undue emotion, to simply make clear
what happened to her that day, and what has and has
not happened since then.

Dear Editor,

I want to tell you about something that happened to me last December. So far, nobody
has talked about it openly, in public. Whatever has been said about it has been said
behind closed doors or in small private
groups.

Here are the facts. I was on the third floor
of my school. I was alone. I was looking out
the window. And I was attacked by three
boys.

We all know these things happen, but

somehow we think they're happening somewhere else to someone else. We read about
things in the papers, see them on TV. Not
here, we think. Not us. Not me. That's what
I thought. Well, I was wrong. It was me. And
since this happened to me, I've found out
from other girls that it's happened to them,
too.

How much is going on that we never know
about? This is just one medium-sized school
in one medium-sized community.

I want to forget this, but if nobody is saying
anything, it's almost as if nothing happened. I
admit, for a while I didn't want to talk about
it, either. I thought I could put it away from
me, not think about it, make it disappear from
my mind. But that doesn't work. You don't
forget. You don't stop feeling. It doesn't disappear.

If those boys had trashed the school and
wrecked equipment, everybody would know
about it. There wouldn't be any hush-hush.
And it's pretty sure that they would have been
punished with more than a two-week suspension. Some people would even call what they
did a crime.

Why is what happened to me different? Am I less valuable than a room or a piece of equipment?

Why can't a girl be safe in her own school? Why can boys do what they did to me and get away with it? What are other boys thinking? Will the boys who attacked me do it again to some other girl? Will other boys get the idea that they can do this, too? Am I wrong to be worried for other girls? How do we stop those things from happening?

I hope you and your readers have some ideas.

Something bad happened that shouldn't have happened. Something that should never happen again. What should we do so that it never does?

Shouldn't a girl be able to stand in front of a window in her own school and be safe?

Yours truly,
Valerie Michon

Rollo's in the mall with Brig, killing time, waiting for Candy. "I'm telling you, I'm going to get it on the first try," Brig says. He's taking his road test tomorrow. "My brother had to take it three times. I'll save the family honor."

"Great." Restlessly, Rollo glances around. That's when he sees Valerie sitting at a table on the other side of the arcade. He begins to wave, then glances at Brig and drops his hand.

He's seen Valerie around school, of course, and once he saw her right here in the mall. But they don't speak, they've hardly exchanged a word since the New Year's party. He doesn't count the night she called to talk to Kara. He picked up the phone, she asked for Kara, that was it. It wasn't what you would call a conversation.

Brig goes off to get a soda, and Rollo, not giving himself a chance to think about it too much, walks over to Valerie. "Hi, it's me. Kara says to say hello."

"Oh, hi. Hello to Kara, too."

He shuffles his feet. "I'll tell her."

She's staring at him.

He clears his throat. "Well . . ."

"I was just thinking about you."

He drops into a chair. "Did you see me over there?"

She frowns. "I'm going public."

It sounds like something his father would say about stocks or an investment, but it's not what she means. He knows that right away.

"I'm sending a letter to the newspaper."

"Why?" His heart is thudding.

"Because people should know," she says, looking at him levelly. "Because I'm mad. Because you guys did what you wanted to me and you're home free. Because I don't see why I should go along with keeping it all under the table. I probably have about ten more reasons, but that's enough for now."

A letter . . . Will his name be in it? Even if it's not, a lot of people are going to know who she means. The thing will come out in a way it hasn't before. His father will be reminded. Kara will know. He thought it was over with, and now people will look at him and see a creep. They'll remember him as part of the gang who attacked her.

He looks down at his hands lying on the table. He remembers those hands on her, and for a moment it's very weird, like looking at two objects he doesn't recognize. He seems to hear Brig's voice. *That girl had it coming to her.* He must have said it himself.

"I wanted you to know before I sent the letter," she says. "Maybe it's foolish of me, but I think you're a little different."

"It'll just bring it all up again, won't it?"

"You mean for you? Yes. But for me, too."

His heart begins that peculiar thudding again, frightened, but in some way relieved.

"So it's all coming out?"

"Yes."

He nods. "It's coming out," he repeats. He stands up. "Okay," he says, and after that there doesn't seem to be anything else to say.

"Where were you?" Brig says, when he comes back.

"Talking to Valerie Michon."

"Michon!" Brig looks across the room, then at Rollo. "What the hell for?"

Rollo thinks of saying she's a friend, but that's not true. He shrugs and doesn't even try to explain. "I've got to get going," he says.

"What's the matter with you? We're waiting for Candy."

"No, I'm going."

"What's happening here, Rollo?" He looks across the room again. "It's got something to do with her, doesn't it?"

Rollo stands there. "It's complicated," he says. He fiddles with the strap of his knapsack, then slings it over one shoulder. "Brig." He holds out his hand. "Good-bye." After a moment, Brig slaps palms with him. "Good-bye," Rollo says again.

It really is good-bye, but he doesn't say that. Not now. He will soon. He walks away.